Jane Heller

CRYSTAL C·L·E·A·R

KENSINGTON BOOKS
Kensington Publishing Corp.
http://www.kensingtonbooks.com

KENSINGTON BOOKS are published by

Kensington Publishing Corp.
850 Third Avenue
New York, NY 10022

First Kensington Hardcover Printing: March, 1998
First Kensington Paperback Printing: February, 1999
10 9 8 7 6 5 4 3 2 1

Printed in the United States of America

WHATEVER YOU WANT TO CALL IT . . .

Terry reached into the bag he had set on the ground and pulled out what looked like a pair of wire coat hangers that had been bent out of their normal shape. "Come, Crystal," he said, motioning for me to stand next to him. "We're going to conduct a little experiment. Take one of these in each hand," he said, curving my fingers around the pieces of metal.

"What are they?" I asked.

"Old-fashioned divining rods," he replied. "When you're holding the rods parallel to each other and they suddenly start to crisscross, you're in an energy field, a power spot, a vortex, whatever you want to call it."

Terry positioned himself behind me, his arms encircling me as he helped me grip the wire rods so they would remain parallel to each other. His nearness turned my *body* into an energy field. It was uncanny how the man was, for all intents and purposes, a stranger to me now, and yet all he had to do was smile at me or give me a look or, God forbid, touch me and it was as if no time had passed, as if we were kids again.

"I think I'm fine on my own," I said, pulling away.

"You always were," said Terry, the comment taking me by surprise. I dismissed it and tried to focus on the divining rods, on keeping them straight.

Moments later, the rods crossed and I had stepped inside the energy field. I took stock of the way my body was reacting. According to my friend Rona, when you "intersected" with a vortex, you were supposed to feel an intense, almost overwhelming kind of electricity, a bolt of energy that imbued you with a sense of power and possibilty, a wave of connectedness with your surroundings.

Was *that* what was going on inside me? I wondered. Was *that* what the heightened nerve endings and tingling fingers and toes and throbbing heart were all about? The vortex?

Maybe. Or maybe it was something else. Someone else.

"Time to move on," Terry called out. "We've got lots to see and do today."

"Time to move on," I agreed, making a conscious decision to do just that.

BOOK YOUR PLACE ON OUR WEBSITE AND MAKE THE READING CONNECTION!

We've created a customized website just for our very special readers, where you can get the inside scoop on everything that's going on with Zebra, Pinnacle and Kensington books.

When you come online, you'll have the exciting opportunity to:

- View covers of upcoming books
- Read sample chapters
- Learn about our future publishing schedule (listed by publication month *and author*)
- Find out when your favorite authors will be visiting a city near you
- Search for and order backlist books from our online catalog
- Check out author bios and background information
- Send e-mail to your favorite authors
- Meet the Kensington staff online
- Join us in weekly chats with authors, readers and other guests
- Get writing guidelines
- AND MUCH MORE!

**Visit our website at
http://www.kensingtonbooks.com**

For Peggy Van Vlack,
the Queen of Sedona

ACKNOWLEDGMENTS

♥

Many thanks to the following people, without whom CRYS-TAL CLEAR would still be a germ of an idea: Barnes & Noble's Judy Martin, who said, "So maybe your next heroine goes to an ashram?"; the ingenious Ruth Harris, who came up with the book's title; my friend Jeanne Mayell, who sparked my creativity when I really needed it; my agent, Ellen Levine, who was supportive beyond the call of duty; and my editor, Ann La Farge, who worked her usual magic on my words.

Special thanks to my husband, Michael Forester, for allowing his aura to be cleansed, his energies to be palpated, and all the rest.

PART
O•N•E

CHAPTER ONE

♥

It all started when my secretary, Rona Wishnick, told me I needed my aura cleansed.

"My *what* cleaned?" I asked, then glanced down at my navy blue suit and inspected it for stains. It was 7:30 on a Friday night and Rona had come into my office to say she was going home. Or so I'd thought.

"I didn't say cleaned. I said *cleansed,*" she explained as she stood beside my desk, fingering the angel pendant wedged between her "heat-seeking missiles," as one of the more sophomoric men in the office had nicknamed her large breasts. "And I was referring to your aura, not your outfit."

I didn't have a clue what she was talking about. I was a CPA, for God's sake—a down-to-earth, practical-to-a-fault, nose-to-the-grindstone accountant. I was a whiz at preparing income tax returns but totally out of my element when it came to making sense of New Age-speak, Rona's second language. By telling me that my aura needed cleansing, was she suggesting that I should switch perfumes? Underarm deodorants? What?

"I've been wanting to talk to you about the problem for a while," she said as I popped two Bufferin, a NoDoz, and a Pepcid AC into my mouth and washed them all down with an Ensure Plus. My dinner.

"Oh, I get it now," I said, nodding. "You want a raise. Or is it more vacation time?"

She shook her head, marveling at my obtuseness. "*You're* the one who needs more vacation time."

"A trip on the astral plane, right?" I laughed.

"Go ahead. Make jokes. But I'm worried about you, about the pressure you put on yourself. Sure, there's a lot of work to be done around here, but it's Friday night and, once I'm out the door, you'll be the only one left in this office. Even the housekeeping people went home hours ago. The point I'm trying to make is that you're in complete denial of your ..." She stopped, grasping for the right word, then gave up after several seconds when she wasn't able to seize on it. Rona and I are both in our mid-forties—that age when grasping for the right word and not being able to seize on it starts to become embarrassingly routine. "Look, you're *this* close to total burnout, okay?" Rona said finally, holding her thumb and index finger about an eighth of an inch apart.

"You're sweet to care, Rona, but I think you're exaggerating," I said, polishing off the rest of the Ensure.

"Oh, really?" she said, tapping her foot on the white Berber carpet that had recently been installed in all the partners' offices. "Then why the canned milkshakes instead of a nice, home-cooked meal?"

"I like the taste of them," I said. "The chocolate one's terrific."

"I'll bet," she said. "What about the headaches, the

heartburn, the insomnia? You're telling me you're not stressed out?"

"Of course I'm stressed out. Who isn't?"

"Who isn't? People who have found their center, that's who. People who have achieved balance in their life. People who have *evolved.*"

Rona was, hands down, the most evolved person I knew. She meditated in the office every morning in one of the stalls in the ladies room, was a heavy user of the Psychic Friends Network and quoted frequently and liberally from *The Celestine Prophecy.* Recently, she announced that she was considering changing her first name to Raven because it sounded Native American and, therefore, more "spiritual." I didn't tell Rona this, of course, but there was nothing remotely ravenlike about her; she was a platinum blonde with a body that more closely resembled a bison than a bird.

"What I'm saying," Rona went on, "and I'm saying it with love in my heart, okay?—is that this place has become your entire universe, Crystal, and it's sad."

By "this place," Rona meant the Manhattan accounting firm where we worked, Duboff Spector. By "Crystal," she meant me, Crystal Goldstein. Rona liked to think my name was linked in some paranormal way to the chunk of rock she kept on her desk to ward off negative vibrations, but it was simply the name my parents had given me in memory of my maternal grandmother, Crystal Schwartz.

"Look, hon," Rona said tenderly. "You and I have been together for seven years and in all that time I've seen you successful but I've never seen you happy. Really happy."

"Rona," I sighed, patting her massive arm. She was so much more than an employee to me; she was the closest thing I had to a best friend. "You've been reading too many of those magazine articles about baby boomers who have all the trappings of success but are still searching for

Meaning in their lives. Well, *I* don't have time to search for Meaning or anything else. There aren't enough hours in the day. Besides, I hate people who sit around whining about whether or not they're happy. I'm happy enough."

"Oh, sure," she said skeptically. "You work like a dog, and when you do take ten seconds off, you either shlep up to Larchmont to see your father, who's too busy watching that big-screen TV you bought him to notice you're even in the room, or you grab a few hours with Steven, the man you say you're going to marry but never do. That's not my idea of bliss, Crystal."

I smiled. Rona's idea of bliss involved bathing in aromatherapeutic essences with her husband, Arthur, a manufacturer of doorbells.

"I appreciate your concern, Rona, and I promise I'll think about everything you've said. But right now the IRS is breathing down Jeff Jacobson's neck, and I'm the one he hired to straighten out his books. In other words, instead of searching for Meaning tonight, I'm gonna be searching for a way to keep this guy from an audit. Now, am I excused?"

She nodded grudgingly, then blew me a kiss. "Have a good weekend."

"You, too. Say hi to Arthur."

Rona was about to exit my office when the phone rang, making both of us jump. Instinctively, she reached across my desk and picked it up.

"Crystal Goldstein's office," she said. "Oh, Steven. Yes, she's still here. I'll put—"

I tugged on her sleeve and mouthed the words: "Tell him I'm busy." I hadn't made a dent in Jeff Jacobson's tax problems. Steven would have to wait.

Rona did as she was instructed and hung up the phone. "He said he'll be in his office for another fifteen minutes or so if you want to call him back." She shook her head disapprovingly as she moved toward the door. "You and *Stevie,*" she snorted. "You communicate through secretaries, answering machines, and E-mail. Is that what you call true love, Crystal?"

Before I could answer, she was gone.

Alone at last, I sank back in my chair and fanned myself with a legal pad. It was an unseasonably warm September night in New York, and since the air conditioning in the building automatically shut off at six o'clock and the windows were hermetically sealed, my office was as fetid and airless as a sauna and I felt weak, light-headed. Still, there was work to be done. I pulled up Jeff Jacobson's file on the computer and tried to focus on the numbers on the screen. But for some reason, Rona's comments kept floating through my mind, haunting me, taunting me, and before I knew it I wasn't concentrating on Jeff Jacobson's tax problems at all; I was asking myself the sort of insipid, self-indulgent questions I swore I'd never ask.

Was I on my way to total burnout? Was all my hard work worth it? And what *was* an aura, anyway?

The latter question suddenly inspired me to reach inside the top drawer of my desk, pull out the little mirror I kept there, and scrutinize my reflection. I had expected to see a sort of dingy cloud hovering over my head—wasn't *that* what an aura that needed cleansing would look like? But what I actually saw was a woman with dark circles under her eyes and dark roots along her hairline.

I continued to study myself in the mirror, and the more I studied, the more startled I became. I was still pretty at forty-three—big brown eyes, a straight nose, a strong chin with a little cleft in it, full lips—but I was no longer a dish by any stretch of the imagination. A dish*rag* was more like it. My once-bouncy auburn hair hung limply at my shoulders, my skin had taken on a sickly pallor, and the full lips men had always found so sexy were cracked and peeling where I'd been gnawing on them, another unfortunate habit I'd picked up during the last tax season, along with nail biting. I seemed to myself to have a sort of parched, dried-up look. The look of a woman who needed her aura cleansed.

I shoved the mirror back in the drawer and shuddered. Was *that* what Rona and everyone else saw when I walked into a room? The drabness? The brittleness? The pallor? Had my so-called "success" robbed me of all my juice?

My success, I scoffed. I wasn't exactly some big shot mogul. Please. I was just a professional woman who had put my career ahead of everything else in my life, mostly because there *was* nothing else in my life. Well, nothing except a boyfriend I rarely slept with, due to the fact that I was either too busy or too tired, and a father I rarely bonded with, due to the fact that I wasn't born a boy. My mother hadn't minded that I wasn't a boy, but she died when I was twelve, taking whatever warm and fuzzy feelings my father had with her. So I worked and worked and worked, making partner at Duboff Spector before I was thirty, buying a co-op on East End Avenue, tooling around in my BMW, squirreling away plenty of money for my Golden Years. I had "made it." I was in the right tax bracket. I felt good about myself.

Or did I? Was there Meaning in my life? Was I even in touch with my real feelings? Was I *happy*?

I gagged. Talk about self-indulgent. Talk about a cliché! I reminded myself of the "boomers" quoted in those nauseating magazine articles.

Maybe I'll give Steven a call back, I thought, hoping to snap out of my funk. I dialed his private line at the office and got his voice mail. Apparently, he had already left for the day.

He must be running off to have dinner with a client, I mused, or heading home with a briefcase full of paperwork.

An attorney, Steven was as consumed by his career as I was by mine, which was how we had managed to stay together for three years. Neither of us made demands on the other. Neither of us minded the other's long hours. Neither of us mentioned the word "marriage," although I was relatively certain we'd get to the altar eventually. Only Rona thought otherwise. She had done our charts and maintained that we were incompatible astrologically.

I leaned back in my chair and recalled my first date with Steven Roth—a blind date arranged by his mother, an extraordinarily pushy but well-meaning client of mine. I hadn't wanted to go on the date, figuring that if a guy has to depend on his mother for fix-ups there has to be something really wrong with him. But I hadn't been out with a man in months and decided it was probably a good idea to keep my hand in, so to speak.

"So, you're an accountant" was Steven's opening line at dinner that fateful night. He had chosen a Pakistani restaurant in an attempt, I assumed, to demonstrate how worldly and sophisticated he was. His mother had already filled me in on his extensive trips abroad. She had also warned me that he did not like it when people called him "Steve."

"Yes, Steven," I said. "I'm a partner at Duboff Spector." But then he already knew all that. Mommy Dearest had to have told him.

"Accounting. Of all the professions to go into," he said dismissively, as if I'd just told him I delivered pizzas for a living.

"What do you mean by that?" I asked, trying not to get my back up. I didn't care for his remark—or his tone.

"Just that it can't be very fulfilling," he said smugly.

"Actually, being an accountant is about as fulfilling as being a medical malpractice attorney," I said with a definite edge. According to Mrs. Roth, that's what her son was.

A forty-six-year-old "med mal" lawyer. A goddam ambulance chaser. And *I* was the one who was supposed to feel inferior?

"You sound a little defensive, Crystal," said Steven, who was patronizing but not bad looking. He had dark hair and green eyes—an attractive combination—and, for the most part, his features were quite pleasing. I say "for the most part" because his ears protruded from his head at ninety-degree angles. Okay, forty-five-degree angles. They weren't the stuff of Dumbo but they were *there* in a way that made me wonder why Steven hadn't had them "pinned back," as they used to call the procedure when I was a kid. On the other hand, maybe he did have them pinned back and the doctor screwed up the operation. Maybe *that* was why he'd gone into medical malpractice!

"You're right. I *am* being defensive," I said, "because you seem to be putting accountants down. We get enough of that during the day. We don't need it at night. On blind dates, for example."

Obviously, things weren't clicking right from the get-go. We were at that awful juncture in Blind Datedom when you're only minutes into the date yet you've already sized the guy up and decided that there is not now nor ever will be any chemistry between you.

"Look, I'm really sorry. I didn't mean to insult you," he said as he scanned the menu. Earlier, I had suggested that he order for both of us. I was not familiar with Pakistani food. I was a connoisseur of Ensure Plus. "I don't know why I said what I said about accountants."

"I do," I replied, sighing with resignation. "You said what you said because accountants are the Rodney Dangerfields of the business world—we never get any respect. Bean Counters, they call us. Number Crunchers. Anal Retentive Drudges. And do you know why they call us these things?"

Steven shook his head. I had his full attention now.

"Because we're like domestic help, hired to clean up people's messes," I continued. "Everyone thinks we're humorless nerds until presto—we save a client money. Then all of a sudden we're heroes and are spoken of in the same hushed tones usually reserved for doctors or, at the very least, dentists. And if we save the client *a lot* of money, we get invited to his kid's bar mitzvah. But most of the time, we're the butt of jokes. On national television, no less. The minute the accountants from Price Waterhouse walk onto that stage during the Academy Awards ceremony, it's one big 'Ha ha ha.'"

"I see your point," said Steven with a slight smile, his first of the evening, "since lawyers are the butt of jokes, too."

"Yes, but lawyer jokes hinge on the premise of lawyer-as-shark. Accountant jokes hinge on the premise of accountant-as-shlemiel."

He laughed. "I promise I'll never put accountants down again."

"My colleagues and I appreciate that," I said, feeling better after having vented my spleen.

"You mentioned the Academy Awards," Steven said, eager to change the subject, it seemed. "Are you a movie fan?"

"Yes, actually I am," I said after a deep breath. "Although I don't have much time to go to the movies anymore. I end up renting the video a year or two after the fact."

Steven nodded ruefully. "I understand," he said. "I still remember when I used to see a film the day it opened. But that was before I became a lawyer and essentially said goodbye to leisure time."

"Do you like being a medical malpractice lawyer?" I

asked, suddenly curious about the man sitting across from me. He was better looking when he wasn't scowling.

"I love it. Getting multimillion-dollar settlements for people who've been screwed by big companies gives me a pretty good feeling."

"You mean, it's *fulfilling,*" I teased.

"Exactly." He laughed in a self-deprecating way that made me think I had probably misjudged him. Perhaps he wasn't smug, just shy. "I feel *fulfilled* when the firm wins a 20-million-dollar award for an out-of-work electrician who had the wrong leg amputated by an intoxicated surgeon," he went on, then told me about some of his other recent cases before turning the focus of the conversation back onto me. "I gather that you like being an accountant," he said, smiling again.

"I don't know that I *like* being an accountant exactly," I said. "Part of me would rather be a backup singer for, say, The Artist Formerly Known As Prince, but I'm good at my job, so I must enjoy the work. According to my secretary, I enjoy it a little too much."

"Ah, the proverbial workaholic," said Steven. "I guess we've got that *and* movies in common." He chuckled, then gave the waiter our dinner order.

During the meal—don't ask me what we were eating; suffice it to say it was light brown—Steven spoke animatedly about his work, which apparently involved an incredible amount of research as well as travel. He was one busy guy. And smart, too. The more he talked, the more the memory of our bumpy beginning receded, and I found myself being drawn in by his anecdotes, excited by the very fact that I was out for dinner with a man for a change. By the time dessert and coffee rolled around, I had forgotten all about Steven's ears.

And we didn't just discuss business. No, we chatted about personal matters, too, discovering that we had several things in common. Steven was born in Manhattan and I was born in Manhattan. He was conflicted about his relationship with his widowed mother and I was conflicted about my relationship with my widowed father. And to top if all off, we were both allergic to mold spores, cat dander, *and* dust mites!

We were getting along so well that when Steven invited me up to his apartment for a nightcap, I surprised myself and said yes.

Steven, it turned out, lived on the penthouse floor of a gleaming, forty-story building on East Seventy-ninth Street. Unlike my place, which was sparsely furnished and looked as if no one lived there, his apartment was a Ralph Lauren showroom—a positive paean to paisley.

He poured us each a glass of cognac and we picked up where we'd left off in the restaurant, sharing little factoids about our lives. At one point, he confessed that he'd been married twice—to the same woman. Something his mother had neglected to mention.

"She's out of my life now," Steven pledged, referring to the ex-wife, his voice heavy with conviction. A little too heavy, if you ask me.

He didn't volunteer any further details but I could tell by how red his ears had gotten that the subject of this ex-wife was still a loaded one.

"How about you, Crystal?" he asked. "Have you ever taken the plunge?"

"Just once," I said. "Very briefly, when I was practically a kid." I'd been married right out of college, for only a year, and hadn't seen or heard from my ex in nearly two decades. Sometimes, when people asked me the "Have-you-ever-been-married" question, I actually said no, figuring the marriage hadn't lasted long enough to count.

Steven and I spent about an hour in his apartment that evening. A very chaste hour. At about ten-thirty—just after

I had tried unsuccessfully to stifle a yawn—he rose from
the paisley sofa on which we'd been sitting and said, "Well.
This has worked out better than I thought it would. I feel
very comfortable with you, Crystal. I'd like to see you again.
Would that be all right with you?"

I considered the question. Steven Roth hadn't exactly
lit the fires of passion within me, but he seemed like a
decent enough guy. Since I knew there was a terrible short-
age of decent enough guys, I thought: What the heck.

"Sure it would be all right with me, Steven," I said. "I'd
like to see you again, too."

"I'm glad," he said and walked over to his briefcase. He
pulled out his date book and studied it for a minute or
two. "I'll be out of town on business for a while," he said
finally. "What about two weeks from Sunday? We could
have lunch, then see a movie."

"Sunday is my father's birthday," I said. "I'll be spending the day with him." Why, I didn't know. I visited my
father every Sunday, and every Sunday the routine was the
same. *Hello, Dad,* I'd say. *How are you feeling today, Dad?
Would you like to hear about my busy week? You'd rather watch
television? That's fine, Dad. I'll just sit here for the next few hours
with my tongue hanging out in case you decide to acknowledge
my existence.* I assumed the Sunday of his birthday wouldn't
be a radical departure from this torture, except that I'd
probably bring a cake, cut him a piece, and then he'd tell
me he didn't want any. Rona said I was a glutton for
punishment when it came to my father and that I should
let the old geezer sit by himself on Sundays. But I was
determined to work as hard at getting his love as I did at
straightening out people's tax problems. "I should be back
in the city by six or so," I told Steven. "Maybe we could
do something that evening instead."

Steven shook his head as he ran his finger over the
entries in his date book. "I'm tied up that Sunday night

with a client and my weeknights are a disaster. What about the following Saturday night?"

"Are we talking about three weeks from tonight?" I didn't have my calendar with me.

"Yes. I can do a seven o'clock, seven-thirty, or eight. Do any of those times work for you?" said Steven, sounding like a doctor's receptionist.

"Off the top of my head, they're all fine," I replied. "If I have a scheduling conflict, I'll get back to you."

So. That's how it began with Steven and me—two people slotting each other in. And we'd been going along in that vein ever since, without so much as a harsh word between us. From my vantage point, the relationship was a good one—steady, dependable, like a Maytag washing machine. Who needed fireworks? I'd had those with my ex-husband and they'd blown up in my face.

Rona never let up about how wrong Steven was for me, as I've mentioned. But I kept telling myself that *I* knew better; that he and I met each other's needs perfectly; that, despite Rona's supposed higher state of consciousness, she didn't have all the answers. After all, she claimed that in a former life she was the wife of one of the kings of England, but she had no idea *which* wife or *which* king!

No, I don't need my aura cleansed, I smiled as I dismissed my friend's New Age mumbo-jumbo and refocused on Jeff Jacobson's tax problems. My life is fine and dandy.

CHAPTER TWO

♥

I tried to reach Steven over the weekend but kept getting his answering machine. It wasn't until the following Wednesday afternoon, while Rona was out of the office having her Tarot cards read and I was, therefore, stuck answering my own phone, that we finally made contact.

"Steven," I said. "You've been impossible to get hold of."

"Sorry," he said. "I've been crazed with work."

"Must be a big case," I said.

"It is."

"Are you working tonight?" I asked. It had been about ten days since I'd last seen him and Rona's all-work-and-no-play speech Friday night had left me wondering if I shouldn't try to spend more time with him. Quality time.

" 'Fraid so," he said. "But that's what's so great about you, Crystal. I never have to worry about telling you I have to work nights or weekends. You've been there. You *understand*."

"Of course I do," I said. "I just thought we could both use a break. Have dinner. See a movie, maybe."

"I could use a break, all right," he said, "but not tonight."

"Because of that big case you mentioned?"

"Exactly. I'll be home preparing for Littleton v. The Betty Ford Center."

"Somebody's suing the Betty Ford Center for medical malpractice?"

"Somebody's always suing somebody for medical malpractice. That's why I don't have a life anymore."

I nodded silently, knowingly, despondently. Nobody my age had a life anymore, what with the demands of job, marriage, kids, elderly parents, take your pick. No, nobody had a life anymore, except Rona, who, if you bought her adventures in regression therapy, had several. "Well, call me when you come up for air," I suggested to Steven. "I'll be going to see my father on Sunday, but I'll be around on Saturday night. We could—"

"Sorry. I've got another call," he interrupted, sounding rushed. "Talk to you later, Crystal." There was a dial tone.

Yes, later, I thought, an idea occurring to me. Steven had said he would be home all night working. What if I did something totally out of character for me—for him, too? What if I surprised him at his apartment with a shopping bag full of goodies from the gourmet takeout place near his building? He had to eat, didn't he? What if we ate together, sipped a little wine, relaxed, just for an hour or two? There might even be time for us to make love on his paisley sheets before he had to re-immerse himself in Littleton v. The Betty Ford Center.

I decided to leave the office early so I could hurry back to my apartment, shower and change, hit the gourmet shop, and head over to Steven's. Unfortunately, Otis Tool, one of the managing partners at Duboff Spector, telephoned just as I was almost out the door and asked me to stop by his office. He said he had something important he wanted to discuss with me.

"Sure, Otis," I said, dreading the meeting. Otis was a small man in every sense of the word. In his late sixties, he was as puny as he was petty—a mean-spirited gossip with a slash of a mouth, slitty eyes, and hands the size of a child's. What's more, he spoke so softly you had to stand extremely close to him in order to hear him. Either that or you had to read lips. One way or another, you always felt manipulated after even a few minutes in Otis Tool's company.

"Thank you for coming," he said as I sat in the visitor's chair opposite his desk. He was wearing a charcoal gray suit and a dour expression—everyone's idea of an accountant. Or an undertaker.

"What did you want to discuss with me?" I asked, glancing at my watch. I was eager to get going.

"It concerns your se . . ." he said in a voice that trailed off and was, finally, inaudible.

"My *what?*" I shouted. That was another thing about Otis: you found yourself yelling in his presence. To compensate, I guess.

"Your secretary," he said, as I leaned closer to him. "Mrs. Wishnick."

"What about her?" I said suspiciously. Otis lived for office politics, corporate intrigues, opportunities to spread nasty rumors about people. Trust me, he was a devious little gnome.

"The other managing partners and I were going over the payroll—we do have to keep our *own* house in order, don't we?—and we were startled to find that Mrs. Wishnick's salary is considerably higher than that of the other secretaries."

"Yes, because Rona has worked here longer than the

other secretaries," I said. "She's more experienced, too.
She knows as much about accounting as most of the CPAs
here." You included, asshole.

"But the job description calls for a secretary, not a CPA,"
Otis pointed out. "It doesn't call for a woman of her age
and experience."

"Of her *age* and experience?" What was the loathsome
creature getting at? I wondered. Rona and I were practically the same age.

"Yes," he said. "You know the trend in business these
days, Crystal. Everybody is cutting operating costs by replac-
ing the older, more experienced people—and their hefty
salaries—with more junior personnel, younger men and
women who may require a bit of training but don't drain
the bottom line, as it were. To be perfectly candid, we're
looking at this trend very carefully, reviewing *all* of our
people to see where we can do a little trimming."

I couldn't get over this. Was Otis suggesting that Duboff
Spector actually downsize Rona and replace her with some
eighteen-year-old? Or was there something else on his
mind? You never could tell with this guy.

And then a distant bell sounded. Yes, I was beginning
to get it now, get what this we're-reviewing-all-of-our-people
stuff was really about. It was entirely possible that, in his
typically oblique way, Otis was only using the issue of Rona
and her age, experience, and salary to tip me off that it
was *I* who should be sending out the résumés; that the
managing partners were considering *my* age, experience,
and equity in the company a drain on the bottom line;
that they were salivating at the thought of buying me out of
my contract and trading me in for a younger, less expensive
drudge, someone who'd literally just taken—and, theoreti-
cally, passed—the CPA exam.

Otis saw the mixture of bewilderment and betrayal on
my face and nodded.

"I knew you'd understand," he said, sensing that he had accomplished his mission. He knew he had told me without telling me that the other partners were looking to scale back by scaling *me* back; that a large firm like Duboff Spector could easily make do with one less partner; that even partners were disposable, whether they had a contract or not.

So that's how they do things now, I thought sourly. They don't fire you outright anymore when they want to cut costs. They "indicate" that you'll be canned somewhere down the line. The idea, I suppose, is to allow you sufficient time to find employment elsewhere. That way, you can quit instead of being canned. Which means that *you* can save face and *they* can avoid a lawsuit.

How humane, I mused, feeling as if I'd just been told that I'd been sentenced to death but that the actual date of the execution was still up in the air. How fucking nice of everybody.

"I think we're finished here," Otis said, rising from his chair. I rose from mine, too. "There's nothing for us to worry about today, of course. I just wanted to bring this matter to your attention and alert you that there may be a problem in the fu . . ." His voice was trailing off again.

"Would you mind speaking up?" I said. "I didn't catch the last word."

"Oh. Yes. Certainly," he said, surprised, as if I were the first person to notice his odd and thoroughly irritating speech pattern. "I said, I just wanted to alert you that there may be a problem in the *future*."

The future. I met Otis Tool's eyes, which were so narrow I wondered how he saw out of them. Did I even have a future at Duboff Spector? Had all those long hours I'd put in for the company, all those days and nights hunched over the computer, all those years of seemingly endless tax seasons, been for nothing? Absolutely nothing?

I felt shaky, off balance, about as stressed out as a person could be. I was dying for a Pepcid AC—my acid reflux was refluxing in a particularly distasteful way—but mostly I just wanted to tell Otis he could take his partnership and shove it.

Instead, I shook his moist little hand, wished him a pleasant evening, and left. I figured I would keep my mouth shut until I discussed the situation with Steven over dinner. He was a lawyer, after all. He would strategize with me, help me come up with a plan, tell me what my legal options were if Duboff Spector tried to squeeze me out. Yes, I thought as I fled the office. Steven is the ideal person to lay this on.

Not for the first time, I was grateful that the man in my life was not some superficial playboy who was forever juggling women behind my back but a conscientious attorney whose advice would be invaluable to me in my time of need.

When I finally arrived at Grace's Marketplace, the take-out food emporium on the corner of Third Avenue and Seventy-first Street, it was dinnertime. The place was jam-packed with harried-looking professionals, jockeying for position in front of the prepared foods counters, trolling for chicken this or pasta that or whatever looked microwavable, too exhausted to decide what to eat, let alone cook it.

I didn't have much of an appetite following my chat with Otis, but I assumed that Steven would be hungry so I bought food—lots of food—for the two of us. Appetizers. Bread. Salad. A main course. An assortment of side dishes. Even some pastries. And then I lugged the three shopping bags, along with my purse and briefcase, eight blocks to his building.

When I got there, arms aching, head throbbing, heart-burn off the charts, Jimmy, the silver-haired Irish doorman who usually worked nights, was absent from his post in the lobby. Figuring that he'd slipped off to the package room or men's room or wherever doormen go when they're not guarding the door, I didn't wait to be buzzed upstairs; I proceeded straight to the elevator. Once inside, I pressed "P" for penthouse, rested my bundles on the floor of the elevator, and rode the forty stories to Steven's apartment.

There, I got off the elevator, trudged down the hall with my bags, rang his doorbell, and waited.

When he didn't answer after several seconds, I rang again. He *had* said he'd be home working, hadn't he?

God, that would be a kick in the teeth, I muttered. I go and spend all this money on dinner, drag it uptown, and then Steven decides to work in the office, not in his apartment. Swell.

I rang his bell once again and was relieved when I finally heard him padding toward the door. So he's here after all, I thought, eager to see his face when he caught a glimpse—and the aroma—of my gourmet delights. I assumed he would be pleased to see me, too, of course.

"Crystal!" he said when he opened the door. He was dressed casually, in jeans and a polo shirt, as if he'd been home a while, long enough to change clothes, anyway.

"Hi," I said cheerfully. "I've got a special delivery for Mr. Steven Roth." I held up the shopping bags and smiled. A regular Avon lady.

"Uh, yes. You do," Steven said with a rather anemic expression. "Did we make plans to . . . I mean, you didn't tell me you were coming, did you?" His ears were bright red. I really *had* surprised him.

"Don't tell me you've eaten already," I said. I hoped he hadn't grabbed some Pakistani snack on his way home.

"I haven't eaten. Not a single bite," he said, shaking his

head back and forth repeatedly, as if it were stuck in the "no" position.

"Good," I said. "I've got dinner for two coming right up."

I bustled into his apartment, heading for the kitchen, but I never made it past the living room because there on the sofa, amidst all that paisley, was a blonde. A blonde with very big hair.

"Oh. Hello," I said, speaking of surprises.

"Hi. How're you doing?" said the blonde in a way that suggested she was completely unfazed by my presence.

We both glanced at Steven. Evidently not unfazed by my presence, his eyes were closed, his complexion was green, and his jaws were clamped shut. He appeared to be trying very hard not to be sick to his stomach.

"I'm Crystal Goldstein," I said, introducing myself to the blonde. I attempted to shake hands with her, but my hands were hopelessly entangled in the bags of food. I ended up sort of waving at her.

"Stephanie Roth," she said, rising from the sofa now, offering herself for my appraisal.

She looked like a hooker. I know that doesn't sound very sisterhoodish, but it was true. Between the big hair, the big makeup, and the microscopic dress, we were talking major slut here. And I'm not even going to dwell on the nails, which were the length of Manhattan and painted puce.

"Stephanie *Roth*?" I asked, trying to remember if Steven had ever mentioned a sister. A wayward sister.

"Stephanie is my ex-wife," Steven explained at last, putting me out of my misery. Or *into* it, depending. After our first date, he had never discussed his ex-wife with me, not even in passing. So her sudden appearance at his apartment was a stunning development, to say the least. "She dropped by unexpectedly, Crystal. Just the way you did."

"I see," I said, wondering if Stephanie, too, had brought Steven dinner from Grace's Marketplace and, if so, whether she and I had selected any of the same menu items. Actually, what I wondered most of all was what the hell she was doing back in his life when they were supposed to be history.

"Maybe I should go," Stephanie said, making eye contact with Steven. "So you can talk to her."

"Talk to *me*?" I said. Some irony. I had come to Steven's apartment hoping to talk to *him*. About a problem I was having at the office. Apparently, Otis Tool was just the tip of the iceberg.

"I think that would be best," Steven told the woman he had married and divorced twice. The woman his mother had neglected to tell me about.

Stephanie undulated past me, gave Steven a little bump with her rump, and made her exit.

"Here. Let me take those bags," said Steven in a burst of chivalry. I handed over dinner. "Why don't you have a seat while I put these things in the kitchen? I'll be back in a second."

I nodded and sat, forcing myself not to rush to judgment. Just because my career was suddenly in precarious shape didn't mean my relationship with Steven was, too, did it? Okay, so the fact that he had lied about spending the evening alone with Littleton v. The Betty Ford Center wasn't a particularly good omen. Neither was the fact that I had found him in the company of a scantily clad woman with whom he'd been intimate. But it was possible, just possible, that Stephanie *had* spontaneously stopped by. Maybe she was one of those ex-wives who was always trying to wheedle money out of her ex-hubby. Maybe she merely had cash flow problems and had dropped over, hoping to pick up a check. Yeah, right.

"Crystal," said Steven after returning to the living room and sitting down next to me. "It's not what you think."

I stared at him. Did he think I was a total doofus? When a man says, "It's not what you think," it *is* what you think. And worse.

"You've been seeing Stephanie again," I said.

"Yes," Steven admitted.

I laughed derisively. "I've got to warn you, Steven. I once read somewhere that if you marry the same person a third time, you don't have a prayer of getting any wedding presents."

"Crystal," he said, wringing his hands. "It's not what you think."

"You already said that," I pointed out. "I'm ready for a fresh line of bullshit."

"She and I aren't getting re-married," he said. "We're just seeing each other occasionally."

"How occasionally?"

"Every now and then."

"Was tonight a 'now' or a 'then?'"

"Look, Crystal, I'm confused. I acknowledge that. You and I have a nice thing going, but I'm not sure *where* it's going."

"Meaning?"

"Meaning that I don't feel that I know you. Really know you. Even after three years."

"But you know Stephanie, is that it?" What was not to know about Stephanie? I thought. She exposed her womanhood every time she crossed and uncrossed her legs.

He shrugged. "She and I have known each other since we were in law school together. We go way back."

"Stephanie is a *lawyer?*" I was dumbfounded. Talk about dressing for success.

"She *was* a lawyer," Steven explained. "Now she's a cabaret singer."

"A cabaret singer," I said, taking this all in.

"We're very different people, with very different interests."

"In other words, *you* have no intention of going from legal eagle to lounge lizard any time soon?"

"Of course not, Crystal. The point I was trying to make is that Stephanie and I aren't as compatible as you and I are. She and I can't go ten days without an argument."

"Ten days, huh? It's been about ten days since you and I last saw each other," I mused. "That's quite a coincidence."

Steven hung his head. "I don't know how to explain this to you," he mumbled. "I feel comfortable with you. I enjoy being with you. I care about you. But Stephanie has been in and out of my life for so long that I can't seem to get her out of my system completely."

"So let me get this straight, Steven. You feel comfortable with me. You enjoy being with me. You care about me. But you don't want to see me anymore. Is that it?"

"No, not at all. I want to see you. I just want to see Stephanie, too."

That did it. I started to get up from the sofa, but Steven stopped me.

"What?" I said, my heart thumping in my chest. "What do you expect me to say? To *do?*" I was not a yeller or a screamer. I did not throw ceramic vases at other human beings. I was, for the most part, someone who put up with the weaknesses in the people close to me, even when those weaknesses hurt me. I had a history of making excuses for them, looking the other way, denying the obvious. It was better to ignore than incite, I'd always reasoned.

"Tell the truth," Steven challenged. "In the three years since we've been together, haven't you ever thought about your ex-husband? Wondered how he's doing? Wanted to see him again?"

"No."

"Come on."

"Really." All right, so I wasn't being totally truthful. I did think about Terry Hollenbeck every once in a while. Like whenever I'd see some guy in the street who bore a slight resemblance to him. Or whenever anyone mentioned Colorado, the state where he was born and raised. Or whenever the Manhattan summer air took on its first crisp, cool hint of fall, since we'd exchanged our wedding vows on just such an afternoon. Sure, I thought about Terry, even though our marriage had been a lifetime ago, even though it had lasted only a year, even though it had ended badly. I admit I was mildly curious about where he lived, whether he was working, whether he was married, whether he was as attractive in his forties as he'd been in his twenties, whether he was still alive. But did I have the slightest interest in actually seeing him again? Yeah, about as much interest as I had in listening to any more of Steven's I-can-have-my-cake-and-eat-it-too crap.

I tried to get up from the sofa a second time. Steven stopped me.

"Give me a few days to sort this out," he pleaded. "I don't want to lose you, Crystal. I meant it when I said we have a good thing going."

"Maybe it wasn't so good after all. You also said you don't feel as if you really know me, remember? Well, I'm beginning to think *I* don't really know me. When I woke up this morning, I thought I knew how I felt about you, for instance. About my job, too. Now I'm not sure about any of it."

"Your job? Is there a problem at work?" Steven seemed concerned, which both touched and annoyed me.

"Yes, but I'll figure it out," I said, rising from the sofa, unimpeded. I left Steven in the living room, went into the kitchen to collect the bags of food I'd brought over, and returned to say goodbye.

"You don't mind if I take these home with me, do you?" I said, hoping none of the items had spoiled while they'd been sitting, unrefrigerated, on Steven's kitchen counter.

"Of course I don't mind," he said. "It was very considerate of you to—" His voice broke then and he began to sob. Quite loudly, in fact. "I don't want this to be the end of us," he blubbered, tears streaming down his face onto his polo shirt, a damp little blob forming on his collar. "Say you'll let me talk to Stephanie, to tell her that she and I are through once and for all. It'll be different this time, I swear it."

"I've heard that one before," I said wryly, walking toward the door.

"Not from me, you haven't."

"No, not from you," I acknowledged, knowing exactly where I'd heard it. Terry had said it. Whenever I had threatened to leave him. "It'll be different this time, I swear it," he'd promised over and over. Which was why, when Steven had asked if I had any interest in seeing my ex-husband again, I'd said no.

CHAPTER THREE

♥

I spent the rest of the week in a state of high anxiety, going through the motions at work, staying out of Otis's way, refusing to take Steven's phone calls. I also made a stab at deflecting Rona's questions but wasn't up to the challenge.

"My God, you look terrible, Crystal. Did something happen?" she asked when she walked into my office on Thursday morning.

"You always tell me I look terrible," I said. "That's what friends are for, right?"

"I'm serious," she insisted. "Remember when I said you needed your aura cleansed?"

"How could I forget?"

"Well, whatever was going on with you then has obviously gotten much worse. Now you need your chakras balanced, too."

Rona hailed from Brooklyn and had the accent to prove it. As a result, "chakra" came out "chawkrah." Was she trying to tell me that my skin was chalky? I wondered, placing my hands on my face, Macaulay Culkin-style.

"Your *chakras*," Rona said tolerantly, realizing I wasn't getting it. "They're the energy centers that run along your spinal column. There are seven of them, according to ancient Eastern healers, and they correspond to the seven emotional aspects of your personality—love, sexuality, creativity, etcetera. When you balance these chakras, you reduce your stress level."

Rona began moving her hands over her body in an effort to demonstrate the ancient art of chakra balancing, but what came to mind as I watched her was the ancient art of go-go dancing.

"Crystal," she sighed when the demonstration was over, "why don't you just tell me what's wrong?"

"I'm taking stock of things, that's all," I said.

She brightened. "You mean you're re-evaluating your life? Searching for Meaning?"

"I guess you could say that."

She squealed and enveloped me in a bear hug, nearly knocking the wind out of me, not to mention impaling me on the wings of her angel pendant. "This is exactly what I've been hoping for," she said. "You're finally tapping into how badly you need an emotional clearing. Now, what provoked this sudden self-exploration?"

"Okay," I said. "I might as well tell you. Otis Tool intimated yesterday that the company is on the verge of downsizing us."

"Us?"

"You and me, and it's all about saving money. We're expensive and, therefore, expendable."

Rona frowned. "You've practically killed yourself for this company."

"So have you," I reminded her.

"Yeah, but I have a life to fall back on if they fire me.

You don't." She had a point. "And I don't take this sort of thing as seriously as you do. I've learned that we can't control what we can't control, that we've got to let go."

"But they're gonna let *us* go, Rona. Don't you see?"

"What I see is that if they do fire us, then a better opportunity will be right around the corner," she said, suddenly serene. "Everything is in divine order. When one door closes, another opens."

God, I felt as if I'd stepped into a fortune cookie. "You're sure about this?" I asked. "If Duboff Spector gives us the heave-ho, we'll find other, better jobs?"

"Absolutely," Rona assured me. "As I just said, life is about letting go."

"Well then, speaking of letting go, Steven is having trouble letting go of his ex-wife," I said.

"You're kidding," said Rona. "I didn't think she was even in the picture anymore."

"Neither did I," I replied, "but I met her last night. She was right there in his apartment, acting as if she owned the place. Steven said she used to be a lawyer."

"And now I suppose she writes legal thrillers," Rona said, rolling her eyes.

"No," I said, "and she's probably the only former lawyer who doesn't. She sings in nightclubs."

"Nightclubs. Interesting."

"Steven said they've been seeing each other again." I shook my head disgustedly. "After marrying and divorcing twice, you'd think they would have given up by now."

"They sound pretty out of touch to me," Rona said. "I mean, when a man and a woman spend years breaking up and getting back together and breaking up and getting back together, it's like: Hello, people! Wake up and smell the codependency!"

"Steven claims he's prepared to break up with her once and for all," I said. "But my trust in him is shattered."

"I don't doubt it."

"On the other hand, I can sort of understand why he started seeing Stephanie again."

"You can?"

"Sure. You said it yourself—communicating through secretaries, answering machines, and E-mail. Steven and I are both guilty of putting our work before each other, but over the past few months I've been doing most of the neglecting. I haven't returned his phone calls. I haven't spent much time with him. And—here's the biggie—I haven't made love with him, not in ages. It's no wonder that he fell victim to Stephanie, who, as well as sharing his knowledge of the law, shows a great deal of cleavage."

"Now I see why you look so terrible," Rona said. "First, the job. Then, the boyfriend. There's nothing else, is there?"

"No, but bad things usually come in threes, don't they?"

"Yes," she said. "Yes, they do."

On Sunday I drove up to Larchmont for my weekly visit to my "male parental unit," as I often referred to the man who, through no fault of my own, happened to be my father. His name was Howard, he was eighty-two, and he lived in his BarcaLounger in the same modest house in which I'd grown up—the same house in which my mother had died of heart failure. He spent nearly every moment of every day in that BarcaLounger in front of the TV, pressing the buttons on the remote control. The man watched so much television I often wondered if his was a Nielsen household and he was actually getting paid for all that channel surfing.

A retired engineer, he was in pretty good health for an

eighty-two-year-old. He made his own bed, cooked his own meals, mowed his own lawn, that sort of thing. What he couldn't seem to do was relate to me. Ever. Granted, he wasn't much of a talker, even when I was a child; it was my mother who was definitely the chattier of the two. But while he at least made an effort to be cordial to others, he was impossibly unresponsive toward me, as if I were somehow a humiliation to him instead of a reasonably attractive career woman who had never been pregnant out of wedlock, never been forced to declare bankruptcy, never been in trouble with the law. I mean, if I were the Unabomber, I could understand his remoteness, but I had never done anything *really* wrong in my life. I was the type of child a father could be proud of, flaunt a photograph of, brag to his friends about. And yet, when I showed up at his door every Sunday afternoon, the guy treated me as if I'd come over to exterminate his carpenter ants.

Of course, the fact that I kept visiting him every Sunday was pretty masochistic—just another example of my tendency to stick my head in the sand when it came to my personal relationships. But old Howard was my only living parent, he was my only connection to my dearly departed mother, and he was alone. I felt a certain duty to visit him regularly. Or, to put it another way, I worried that if I didn't visit him regularly, I would burn in Daughter Hell.

On this particular Sunday, I was especially vulnerable, given what was going on in my life, and so when my father opened the door, permitted me to kiss him, and then went back to the BarcaLounger without so much as a "How are you, Crystal?" I began to cry.

At first, he just stared at me, his pale blue eyes full of dread, as if he feared he'd be forced into some hopelessly girlish psychodrama. And then, when it became clear to him that my crying wasn't going to let up any time soon, he turned away from me, flipped on the TV to the USA Network, and started watching a rerun of "Barnaby Jones."

The act so wounded me, so infuriated me, that instead of sitting there and sucking it up, as I usually did, I reached across the big gut my father had acquired in his old age, ripped the remote control out of his hands, and shut the TV off.

"We're going to have a talk," I said, barely able to contain my fury. "I'm not leaving here today until you tell me why you dislike me so much."

He looked away defiantly, a recalcitrant child.

"I want an answer," I said, trying not to lose my nerve. I had never spoken to my father in such a forthright manner. And I had never, ever dared to turn his television off. "I've been dragging myself up here every goddam weekend, just—"

"I won't put up with that kind of language in my house," he interrupted.

Fine. So he'd scolded me for cursing. At least he'd spoken to me.

"I've been driving up here every weekend, hoping you'll show me some fatherly affection, and yet you never do," I went on. "Why is that, Dad? I'd really like to know."

He was silent, his eyes cast down at his lap.

"Did I do something to make you angry?" I asked.

He said nothing.

"Did I do something to embarrass you?"

Still no response.

"Okay, I give up," I said, becoming so unglued I thrust my face in his. "What is it that I've done to displease you, Dad? *What the hell is it?*"

Howard seemed frightened of me. I was a little frightened of myself, of how out-of-control I felt. And his eventual answer to my question did nothing to calm me down.

"You're not Charlie. *That's* what the problem is," he said, his mouth contorting with emotion.

"I'm not who?" I said, bewildered.

"Charlie," he said.

"Charlie?" Who in the world was he talking about?

And then I realized that he must be referring to my mother, whose name was Charlotte. "Charlie" was probably his pet name for her.

I felt a stab of pity for the man suddenly. Sure, he had treated me badly, but now, at least, I understood why. He was admitting that he had never gotten over my mother's death, that he mourned her to such an extent that he blamed me for not *being* her, for not being able to take her place.

Yes, that has to be it, I decided. I must have underestimated the depth of my father's love for his wife.

I cried silently, missing my mother, too, wondering how different my relationship with my father would have been if she had lived, wondering how having an affectionate, demonstrative father would have affected my relationships with other men.

"I had no idea how you felt," I said softly, grateful that he had finally revealed a piece of himself to me, that he had been honest, for once, about the real reason for his antipathy toward me. "I can only guess how much you must miss her." I placed my hand on his shoulder and patted him.

"How much I must miss *her?*" He shook me off in a gesture of impatience and added with a puzzled look, "Miss *who,* Crystal?"

"Charlie," I said hesitantly. "You know."

Jesus, I thought. This is like some Abbott and Costello bit. "You said the problem between us is that I'm not Charlie, Dad. I assumed you were talking about my mother, that 'Charlie' was a nickname you—"

"Charlie," he said again, holding his head in his hands in utter frustration.

"Yes, but who's—"

"Your brother, all right?"

"My *what*?"

"Your brother," he said again, in a hoarse whisper.

"But I don't have a brother," I said, becoming dizzy, light-headed, sort of the way I'd felt in Otis's office and Steven's apartment, only worse.

"You did have a brother," my father said. "He died."

"Oh. Yeah. Sure, I had a brother," I said, humoring the old man. Perhaps the elevator didn't go all the way up to the top floor anymore, as they say. "Look, I know you really wanted a boy instead of a girl, Dad. Mom told me how you were into that whole 'I'm-going-outside-in-the-backyard-to-play-catch-with-my-son' thing. But you know, girls play catch, too. *I* would have played catch in the backyard with you. All you had to do was ask."

"Charlie was your brother," he insisted. "He died before you were born. When he was three."

"Dad, I—"

"Wait." My father got up from his chair, disappeared into his bedroom, and returned several minutes later with an album of baby pictures—pictures that weren't of me. "Charlie," he said, pointing to the cherubic toddler in each of the black-and-white photographs. "Charlie."

The little tyke was adorable, anyone could see that, and he was adored—anyone could see that, too. My mother must have been the photographer because she wasn't in any of the shots. It was my father who was front and center in each one—he and this boy, this Charlie, this brother I had no idea I had, this child I could never, no matter how hard I worked or how much money I made, replace in Howard Goldstein's heart.

So it's true, I thought, reeling from the news. My entire

life has been a lie, my relationship with my parents a sham, my belief that I was an only child a gross miscalculation.

An only child. That's how everyone in the family had always referred to me. And that's how I'd always thought of myself—as sibling-less Crystal Goldstein. But I wasn't sibling-less after all. There had been another product of my parents' union. An older brother I never got to know, never got to look up to, never got to feel protected by. An older brother I never got to love.

The tears returned then and I didn't bother to wipe them away. I was overcome by a mixture of sadness and resentment—sadness that Charlie wasn't around, resentment that I hadn't been told of his existence. A double loss.

Several minutes passed as I tried to adjust to the fact of Charlie's life and death. I was filled with questions about him, of course, and when I felt composed enough to speak, I fired them at my father, one after the other. He answered in a sort of monotone, for the most part.

"What did Charlie die of?"

"Pneumonia."

"Did he die in the hospital or here in the house?"

"The hospital."

"What year did he die?"

"Nineteen forty-eight."

"Okay. Now this is a tough one, Dad, so don't answer too quickly."

"Go on."

"Did you and Mom have any other children you forgot to mention?"

That one drew a nasty glare.

"Sorry," I said. "Let's try this one. Why *didn't* you and Mom tell me I had a brother? Why did I have to find out at age forty-three?"

"We didn't want to upset you."

I shook my head. "You mean, you didn't want to upset *you*. The irony is, you've been upset for as long as I've known you. I just never understood why."

"You have to realize that the subject was very painful for us," my father said. "Your mother and I never discussed it, even with each other."

"Never discussed it?" I asked, absolutely stunned. "You two lost a child and you swept the episode under the rug, made believe it never happened? Now that's what I call Family Values."

I was pacing around the room by this time, agitated as well as sad and resentful.

"We handled it the way we thought was right," said my father. "There's nothing I can do about it now."

"So I should just pipe down and let you get back to 'Barnaby Jones'? Is that what you mean, Dad?"

I stood there staring at my father for a few seconds, waiting for him to reply, but he did not. He closed the photo album, rested it tenderly on the coffee table, sank into the BarcaLounger, remote control in hand, and flipped the TV back on.

I didn't know exactly what to do then. The whole thing was just too weird, just too much, especially on top of the other bombshells I'd been hit with over the past few days. I felt as if my world had been turned upside down, as if my life had descended into chaos. And I wasn't the type of person who operated well in chaos. I liked order. That's why I'd gone into accounting.

I moved to go.

"You're leaving?" my father asked, not deigning to look up from the television set. "Usually you stay all afternoon."

"I think it's time I took a break from 'usually,' " I said.

He responded by changing the channel on the TV, this time to HBO.

"I don't know this movie," my father remarked as he studied the actors on the screen. "Have you ever heard of this one, Crystal?"

"Yeah, Dad," I said. "It's called *Reality Bites.*"

I walked out the door and closed it firmly behind me.

CHAPTER FOUR

♥

A cold front swept through the New York area on Sunday night, and by Monday morning the temperature in the city had plummeted thirty degrees. By the time I got to the office it was a damp, blustery forty-eight outside—the kind of raw, rainy weather that makes your joints ache and your mood grim. Rona took one look at me as I hung my trenchcoat on the back of my office door and furrowed her brow.

"Now what?" she asked, plopping herself down in the chair opposite my desk. "Something else went wrong, I know it."

"Your psychic told you?" I said.

"She's not a psychic," Rona said indignantly. "Illandra is my intuitive counselor."

"Your intuitive counselor," I repeated. "So this Illandra told you I ran into a new problem?"

"Yes," Rona confirmed. "Illandra is incredibly gifted."

"Really? Then did she tell you I had a brother who died

when he was three? A brother I didn't know existed until yesterday?"

"My God. You're not saying that you just found out—"

"Yes, I am. My father forgot to mention it to me."

"So *that's* the something else that went wrong," Rona said, nodding empathically. "You went up to see your father and, instead of ignoring you, he told you about this brother who crossed over?"

"Crossed over? The boy was three, Rona. I don't think you cross over or come out of the closet or whatever you want to call it until much later in life."

"Crossed over to *the other side*," Rona explained. "To the spirit world."

"Oh, I see what you're saying. Well, yes. That's what happened. I demanded to know why my father always treated me like paint spackle and he came out with the bombshell about the boy. Charlie, his name was. I'm still trying to make sense of the whole thing. Of so many things, in fact."

Rona sighed. "Look, I know I sound like a broken record, but you're burned out, Crystal. Everything that's happened in the last few days is a guidepost, telling you it's time to make changes in your life. Before it's too late."

"By 'changes,' I don't suppose you're suggesting I cut my hair," I said, fingering my shoulder-length locks.

Rona shook her head.

"Or start working out at a gym."

She shook her head again. She knew how I felt about women who spend every waking moment obsessing about their "abs."

"Okay. How about this," I said. "I'll take time off from work, get out of the city."

"A vacation? You?" she said, looking skeptical. "It's been so long since you've been anywhere, you probably think the airlines still give you hot meals."

"They don't?"

"No. Now they give you telephones. Speaking of which, Steven has already called twice this morning. He certainly seems to want you back."

"Sure he does, now that he's broken up with Stephanie and he's between women. How does the saying go? 'Abstinence makes the heart grow fonder?'"

"So when do you plan to take this vacation?" Rona asked.

"As soon as possible," I said. "My sanity's at stake. It's now or never."

"Wow. I'm so proud of you," Rona clucked. "Where do you think you'll go?"

"What about a spa?"

Rona waved her hand dismissively. "If you hate gyms, you'll really hate spas. Besides, your physical body isn't the problem. It's your inner self that craves attention. You need to spend ten days in a place that's *spiritual.*"

"You mean, I should check in at one of those ashrams?"

"Maybe."

"God, I bet their mattresses are as hard as a rock."

"That's the whole point of going to an ashram. Without creature comforts, you can focus totally on your inner growth."

"But aren't ashrams basically retreats where Hindus pray? I don't even speak Hindu, let alone pray in it."

"You don't pray in Hind*u,*" she corrected me. "You pray in Hind*i.*"

"I don't pray in either," I said.

"No, Crystal. What I mean is, Hindu is the religion. Hindi is the language."

I sighed. "Tomato, to-mah-to. Potato, po-tah-to. Let's call the whole thing off. I'll go to Las Vegas."

Rona laughed. "There *are* other options."

"Such as?"

"Sedona."

"As in Arizona?"

"Yes. Red Rock Country. About two hours north of Phoenix and two hours south of the Grand Canyon. Believe me, Crystal, Sedona is the most spiritual place there is."

"You've been there?"

"No, but I've always wanted to go. Unfortunately, it's about 4,500 feet above sea level, and you know Arthur and his fear of heights. He gets vertigo when he goes out on the terrace of our apartment to water the plants. And we're on the ground floor."

"You know, now that I think about it, I've never been out west except to L.A. and San Francisco on business. Oh, and I went to Denver many years ago. To meet my future in-laws when Terry and I were at B.U."

"That's right. Your long-lost ex was from Denver, wasn't he?"

"He was, and he couldn't wait to take me there. We spent the weekend with his parents the spring before we were married and I had a great time."

Rona pretended to faint.

"All right. What is it?" I said.

"I just heard you say you had a great time," she replied, recovering. "It's been a while since that happened."

"I did have a good time," I said, starting to recall the weekend more specifically. "Back then, Terry was the proverbial Big Man on Campus—starting pitcher on the varsity baseball team, social chairman of his fraternity, Mr. Charisma—and I was the lucky girl who snared him. He proposed in April of our senior year and I took all of six seconds to accept. The next day he had this spur-of-the-moment idea—Terry had lots of spur-of-the-moment ideas, I discovered—that we fly off to Denver so we could share the news with his folks. Mr. and Mrs. Hollenbeck—Peg and Ron—were terrific people, it turned out, real outdoorsy. They didn't own a TV, much less a BarcaLounger, thank God, so we spent most of the weekend sightseeing and skiing and telling stories by the fire. So, yeah, when I think back on that weekend in Denver, I have pleasant memories of it. Of course, I didn't have a clue what was coming next. I mean, Terry and I were twenty-one years old. Babies! We didn't know what marriage entailed, or even what real life entailed. How could we? When we fell in love we were still living on a college campus, talk about fantasyland. There were no meals to cook. No jobs to apply for. No bills to pay. We didn't have anything to fight over. Well, then came graduation and the move to Manhattan and the wedding at my father's and the first brushes with reality. Suddenly the bubble began to burst and we—"

"Crystal?"

"Yes?"

"That was a fun trip down memory lane, but we were talking about the vacation you're going to take, about how you want to put some distance between you and your *past*."

"Right. Sorry." I paused to collect myself. It wasn't like me to start foaming at the mouth about Terry. "Tell me more about Sedona."

"For starters, it's absolutely breathtaking. People say you can look up from anywhere and see these spectacular mountains and canyons and rock formations, each one over 350 million years old and each one a different shade of this incredibly rich, deep red. The Native American Indian tribes who first settled in Sedona believed they were inhabiting sacred land, and the tribe members who still live in the area consider it sacred, too."

"Probably because they've got all those casinos going up now."

"Not in Sedona they don't. Sedona is a very spiritual place, I'm telling you."

"Are there other reasons it's so spiritual? I mean, besides the Indians and the scenery?"

"Of course. There are vortexes in Sedona."

"Vortexes? That sounds like the brand name of something polyester."

"Well, it's not," she informed me. "It's a huge concentration of energy that's emitted from the earth. In other words, vortexes are power spots. They're about energy. And Sedona has more of these power spots or vortexes than almost anywhere in the world. That's why it's the hub of the New Age Movement right now, the mecca for those seeking the ultimate mystical experience. Oh, Crystal, if you would only go to Sedona, visit the vortexes, meditate at the sites, allow yourself to be drawn in by the love and light there, you would come back to New York a very different person."

"How different?" I said, picturing myself sitting cross-legged on the floor of my office, chanting in Apache.

"You would come back with the kind of positive energy we all need for solving our problems," Rona said soberly. "You would come back with the inner peace you're searching for."

I didn't say anything for several seconds. My mind was racing, a jumble of emotions. Part of me—the accountant—resisted being taken in by Rona's sales pitch. I mean, come on. Like I was really going to climb up on some rock, stand there with my eyes closed, and suddenly find the answers to Life? The notion was totally wacky, completely nuts. But the other part of me—Prince's backup singer—thought the whole thing sounded sort of cool, sort of sixties, sort of Why not? I believed that knocking on wood brought good luck, didn't I? Was it that big a stretch to believe that meditating at vortexes brought positive energy? That it put you in touch with yourself? That it helped you find inner peace?

And it wasn't as if I couldn't afford the trip; I had more than enough money for a ten-day vacation. Even if Duboff Spector did decide they wanted a leaner, meaner accounting firm, they'd *have* to give me a major parting gift. It was in my partnership contract.

So what was stopping me from going to Sedona? I asked myself. Not my job, which would either be there when I got back or it wouldn't. Not Steven, who would undoubtedly take right up with Stephanie the minute my plane left the ground. And not my father, who wouldn't even notice I was gone. No, there was nothing keeping me from heading west, checking out frontier territory, playing pioneer woman. The weather in Sedona would be dry and sunny. The shops would be filled with all that pretty turquoise and silver jewelry. The restaurants would be . . .

"Rona?" I asked, interrupting my musings. "Is the food in Sedona supposed to be any good?"

"Sure. Southwest cuisine is the hottest there is."

"That's what worries me," I said. "All I have to do is look at jalapeño peppers and the acid reflux kicks in."

"I didn't mean 'hot' as in spicy," said Rona. "I meant 'hot' as in trendy. But I'm sure you could ask them to leave out the jalapeño peppers."

"How about the hotels? Know of any good ones?"

"I've heard of a few, but it depends on what you're looking for," said Rona. "There are some that are more spiritually oriented than others."

"Why, because they have psychics on call instead of doctors?"

"No, because they're located near one of the vortexes."

"Vortexes. Shouldn't the plural be vortices?"

"Maybe, but all the spiritual people I know call them vortexes."

"I guess grammar isn't as important as inner peace."

"No, it isn't," said Rona. "Now, are you going to take this trip or not?"

I considered the question. "You're sure that after cleansing my aura and balancing my chakras and getting in tune with my power spots, I'll come back from Sedona with an entirely different outlook on life?"

"Let me ask you something," said Rona. "How is your outlook on life right this minute?"

"Bleak."

"Then you don't have much to lose, do you?"

I got on the phone to some clients who'd been to Sedona and asked for their recommendations of things to see and do in the area. Then I called a travel agent for more serious information. By noon, I had booked myself on a nonstop America West flight to Phoenix out of JFK Airport for the very next morning. No point in hanging around once I'd made the decision to go, I figured. I also reserved a compact-sized Avis rental car for the two-hour drive to Sedona, as well as ten days at a hotel with the highly improbable— or highly predictable, depending on your viewpoint— name of Tranquility.

"Are you sure it's not one of those retirement homes?" I asked the travel agent after she had suggested it.

"A retirement home?" she scoffed.

"Well, I just thought, you know, since Arizona has such a large population of senior citizens," I said.

"Tranquility is a five-star resort," she explained. "The name refers to the fact that the hotel is nestled right in Boynton Canyon, one of Sedona's most sacred places."

"Sacred? So this Boynton Canyon is a vortax?" I asked. I was so proud of myself for using one of Rona's woo-woo words. Then I realized that I'd said vor*tax* instead of vortex. An honest mistake, given my profession, don't you think?

"Yes, Ms. Goldstein," the travel agent replied. "Boynton Canyon is a magnificent spectacle of red rocks, Indian ruins, and hiking trails. It's a stop on every vortex tour."

"There are actually guided tours of these so-called power spots?" I still thought of power spots as places where Rupert Murdoch and people like that ate breakfast.

"Absolutely," she said. "In addition to its many amenities, including twelve tennis courts, four swimming pools, a fitness center, and a putting green, Tranquility is known for its famous Sacred Earth Jeep Tours, which take guests to the vortex sites as well as to other attractions in red rock country."

I thought about inquiring whether the hotel's VIP guests got Sacred Earth Mercedes Tours but decided against it.

"Should we reserve the Sacred Earth Jeep Tour now, at the same time that we're booking the hotel room?" I asked, fearing I might miss out on all those vortexes. I wouldn't be able to face Rona.

"That won't be necessary," the travel agent assured me. "It's September. Sedona's high season really doesn't start until October. You shouldn't have any trouble with Jeep tour availability at this time of year."

There certainly wasn't any trouble with availability when it came to securing me a room at Tranquility. There were several available—individual, adobe-style "casitas" with private porches, views of Boynton Canyon, and the requisite mini-bar.

"You're all set," said the travel agent when our transactions had been completed. "America West is a ticketless airline, so just give them your confirmation number when you check in at JFK tomorrow morning."

"I will. Thank you," I said.

"Thank *you*," said the travel agent, "and have a pleasant trip. I do hope it will be everything you're expecting."

"So do I," I said, wondering what, exactly, I was expecting.

That night, after I packed and before I went to sleep, I made three phone calls. First, I called Steven, to tell him I was leaving town. We hadn't spoken since the Stephanie incident and I thought I owed it to him after our three years together to at least inform him of my travel plans.

"Marry me," he said in response, instead of "Bon voyage" or something of that nature.

"Oh, Steven," I said. "There's no reason to make the Grand Gesture. I'm not leaving New York for good. I'm just taking a little trip."

"Then marry me when you get back," he insisted. "I mean it."

"What about Stephanie?" I asked.

"She's moving to L.A.," he said. "Some Hollywood producer came into the club where she was singing the other night and offered her a part in his next movie."

"How exciting for her," I said, tempted to ask if the movie was a porno flick.

"I want you to know that my marriage proposal has nothing to do with Stephanie's move," Steven maintained.

"No, of course not," I said, not buying it but wanting to.

"It's you I love, Crystal. I know that now. I realize that it was our being apart so much that made me vulnerable to Stephanie—the fact that we allowed our work to come between us."

"I've been thinking along those same lines," I said, "although it's possible that the reason we allowed our work to come between us was because we knew, deep down, that the relationship wasn't there."

"I don't accept that," Steven said firmly. "And I'm proving it by telling you I want to marry you. Won't you at least consider my proposal while you're away?''

"I don't know, Steven. I think we need time to—''

"We've had time,'' he interrupted. "Three whole years. We already know we're compatible. We already know we enjoy the same things. We already . . .''

It was 10:30 at this point and I found myself dozing off right in the middle of Steven's impassioned speech about our shared interests. I came to when he was waxing poetic about our mutual appreciation of moonbeams and sunsets and newly fallen snow, none of which we had ever discussed, let alone mutually appreciated.

"Steven,'' I said, rousing myself. "I'm sorry to cut this short but I've got an early flight in the morning.''

"Flight to where?'' he asked. "You never said.''

"I'm going to Sedona, Arizona,'' I replied.

"For a client meeting?'' he asked.

"No, for an emotional clearing,'' I said. "I'll call you when I get home.''

My father was next on the list. He answered the phone after numerous rings, explaining that he was in the middle of watching "Who's the Boss?''. Nevertheless, he grunted out a "How long will you be gone?''

"Ten days,'' I said. "You'll be all right while I'm in Arizona, won't you, Dad?''

"How many days will you be gone?'' he asked again.

"Ten,'' I repeated. I could tell he wasn't listening. I must have been talking over Tony Danza.

"I'll call you when I get home,'' I told him and dialed Rona's number.

"So you're really doing it,'' she said, marveling at my uncharacteristic impulsiveness.

"I'm really doing it,'' I echoed. "I'm not totally sure *why* I'm doing it, though. It almost feels as if I'm being led to Sedona.''

"Led! Oh, Crystal, honey! Listen to you! Sedona's positive vibrations are working their magic on you already!"

"But I haven't even left New York yet," I reminded her.

"Maybe your body hasn't but the rest of you has," she maintained.

"Does that mean I'm having an out-of-body experience?"

"No," she laughed. "It means you're overdue for a vacation. Way overdue."

"I'll call you when I get home," I promised, just as I had promised the others, never dreaming that the ten days to follow wouldn't be anyone's idea of a vacation.

CHAPTER FIVE

♥

It was still dark when the taxi picked me up at my apartment
building at six o'clock on Tuesday morning, but I was wide
awake and raring to go. I had been up for hours, organizing
the package I would be leaving with the doorman for
Rona—a week's worth of work that she was more than
capable of handling should my clients, or Otis, freak out
that I had taken off. And then there had been all that
unpacking and repacking. What on earth do you pack for
a vortex tour? An Indian headdress? Love beads? Spock
ears?

In the end, I packed nearly everything I owned and
figured I'd let the doorman and then the taxi driver and
then the curb-side check-in guy worry about lifting it all.

By 6:45, I had made it to the airport, an hour before
my flight was to depart, just as the travel agent had
instructed me. The cabdriver loaded my bags onto the
curb, where the nice fellow from America West took over.

I handed him the piece of paper on which I'd written my confirmation number and he, in turn, asked to see my driver's license. And then he said, "Has this luggage been out of your sight at any time?"

"Well, sure," I said, thinking it was an odd question.

He seemed concerned. "When was it out of your sight?"

"When it was in the trunk of the taxi," I said. "There was no way I could see it from the backseat of the cab."

He looked relieved, then asked, "Did you pack the luggage yourself?"

No, I had my wardrobe mistress do it for me, I thought, perplexed by this question, too. "Yes, I packed the luggage with my own two hands," I said.

"Has anybody approached you since you've been at the airport?" he asked.

"You mean, like a mugger or something?"

"Not exactly." He seemed frustrated. "You haven't flown in some time, have you, ma'am?"

"No," I said, slightly embarrassed. "Does it show?"

He smiled. "We're required to ask each passenger the questions I've just asked you. It's a security thing that's been in effect for quite a while now. We don't want anybody planting an explosive device on your airplane, do we?"

"No, we certainly don't." I had never been afraid of flying but I was, at that moment, rethinking my position.

Despite what the travel agent had said about September not being Arizona's high tourist season, the flight was heavily booked. Undetected explosive devices notwithstanding, I felt lucky to get a seat on such short notice. Of course, the seat I did get was 18E, a middle seat sandwiched between 18D and 18F, both of which were occupied for the entire five-hour flight by men so obese their flesh kept spilling over the armrests. These men were business associates traveling to a sales meeting in Scottsdale, it turned out—gruff, thoroughly charmless men who had booked the aisle and window seats well in advance in the hope that no one would be sitting between them. Over the course of the flight, they would glare at me with tremendous hostility, either because I had foiled their plan or because I continually made Larry, the one on the aisle, get up so I could go to the bathroom.

Aside from having to sit between Larry and his pal Dave, the trip to Phoenix was rather pleasant. For instance, as we waited for takeoff, the flight attendants, whose names were Sherry, Valerie, and Anastasia, handed out little shopping bags, each containing a buttered bagel. Never mind that this buttered bagel was the only morsel of food we were offered during the flight or that we weren't given anything to wash it down with. I was just glad there were no jalapeño peppers involved.

Then came the video. After the usual spiel about seat belts and oxygen masks and clearly marked exit doors, the monitors mounted along the ceiling of the plane showed us a short documentary called *Arizona: A Spiritual Journey.* It was, essentially, a montage of pretty scenery—mountains, waterfalls, cactus plants, sagebrush, the red rocks I'd been hearing so much about, lots of *National Geographic* stuff— all set to this really mellow instrumental music. New Age music. I could tell it was New Age music because of the extensive use of the flute, the harp, and, perhaps most telling, the triangle. There were also atmospheric moments of coyotes howling, rattlesnakes rattling, and a narrator announcing that we could purchase the video—or the soundtrack—from our flight attendants simply by illuminating the "Call" button above our seats. Hey, everybody, let's get spiritual!

The plane finally took off and we began our ascent toward what our captain promised would be a cruising altitude of 37,000 feet. I dozed on and off during the flight, but spent most of the five hours in that gauzy, daydream state where your thoughts move between fantasy and reality and you're not sure which is which. At one point, probably because I still associated the West with my ex-husband, I found myself recalling the first time I had an inkling that the marriage wasn't going to make it.

Terry and I had been married all of five and a half months when the sad realization dawned on me. We were living in a studio apartment on East Twenty-third Street— a very modest place that was fine for two kids starting out but was definitely not where I wanted to end up. I was working as a bookkeeper during the day and going to graduate school at night, the idea being that, by getting my M.B.A. and then passing the CPA exam, I'd be able to waltz into one of the big accounting firms and start earning some serious money. Terry, the former campus superman, didn't know what sort of a career he wanted now that he was out in the real world. He had majored in political science along with millions of others who'd attended college in the sixties and seventies, but he didn't have a clue about what he wanted to be when he grew up—something I had been too besotted with him to notice until it was time to pay the rent that first month.

With your people skills, honey, you'd be great at this and this and this, I'd say, listing the areas he should pursue in my opinion, trying to be the supportive little wife while we subsisted on love and tuna fish sandwiches. But despite my cheerleading, Terry seemed genuinely lost without the fraternity brothers, the baseball uniform, the warm glow of adulation that he'd enjoyed in college. Not that he let on, at first. He'd go on interview after interview, and when the job offers didn't pour in, he'd crack jokes, attempt to charm my worries away, make it seem as if all *I* had to do was lighten up and everything would be fine.

Eventually his father, who worked for a national pharmaceutical company, arranged for him to enter the company's management training program at the New York headquarters. He quit after three weeks.

"It was like boot camp—really rigid," he said. "I couldn't see myself going anywhere in that company, except maybe out a thirtieth-floor window. My father fits right into the corporate life, but it's just not for me."

What *is* for you? I wanted to ask but kept my mouth shut. That time.

Terry's next foray into the work world was a position in the sales and marketing department of an athletic shoe company—an organization he assumed would offer a more relaxed atmosphere. He stuck with that job for a whopping two weeks.

"I need an environment where I can have more freedom," he said. "A place where everybody isn't so uptight." To show me how uptight *he* wasn't, he pulled me to him and made love to me—a sure way to silence my doubts.

There were a few more jobs after that, none lasting more than a month. Again, Terry's complaints had to do with working in a restrictive environment and feeling stifled creatively. Having to wear a jacket and tie was also mentioned.

I was baffled that he was having so much trouble finding work, and I honestly think he was, too. In college, everything had come so easily to him. It wasn't just that he was good looking—he had an athletic, agile body that radiated self-confidence; shaggy, light brown hair that fell boyishly across his forehead; deeply set blue eyes that twinkled with mischief; a nose that had been broken when he was a kid and added a ruggedness to his otherwise too-handsome face. It was also that he was a smooth talker—a glib shortcutter who never had to go out and get what he wanted because it was already there for him. Had all his success as a college kid turned him into a lazy adult? I asked myself often as the marriage disintegrated. Had being the popular, center-of-attention guy made him weak? Irresponsible? Unambitious? Too ambitious?

Such questions ate at me because I had loved Terry so, had idolized him from the very moment I'd seen him. When our problems first surfaced, part of me resented him for not being willing or able to get and keep a job. The other part of me didn't care if he earned a dime, as long as he would let me remain in his orbit, inhale his magic. This was the seventies, don't forget—long before the term "enabler" became a 12-step buzz word.

And Terry did have magic. He was affectionate and spontaneous and never at a loss for ways we could entertain ourselves even on our tight budget—the perfect foil for my plodding, relentlessly pragmatic nature. It was he who whisked me off to Central Park for a Sunday picnic; he who dragged me out of the city when I was bleary-eyed from studying and took me to the beach; he who taught me how to kiss underwater as the waves crashed over us; he who showed me how exquisite lovemaking could be.

No, Terry wasn't a total washout as a husband, but when I rode the bus home from business school every night and allowed myself to really examine the relationship, I knew that I was in deep trouble, that I had married a man-child who would ultimately frustrate and disappoint me, that I was not about to pick up the tab while he spent the rest of his life adjusting to the cold, cruel world.

And so, five and a half months after we'd said "I do" in my father's depressing little living room, I admitted to Terry that I was thinking of leaving him. And that's when the promises began.

"It'll be different this time," he said on that occasion— and again and again and again as the months went by. "I love you. I don't know how I could have let you work your ass off to support both of us, but I'll hold up my end from now on, Crystal, I swear."

The first time he made the speech I was incredibly moved by what I perceived to be his remorse, his devotion to me, his intention to do anything to keep us together. But after a while, the apologies and the pledges and the it'll-be-different-this-times got old, very old. Still, I hung in. Our anniversary came. We went out to a nice restaurant for dinner. *I* paid. And then, a few weeks later, a job materialized.

Terry said he had an interview with the father of one of his fraternity brothers. The man was in the music business, he told me. An executive with one of the big recording companies in the city.

"They want me to scout the clubs for new, young talent," he said excitedly when he returned home after the interview to report that he'd been hired.

He quit after only ten days, claiming: "Life is too short to stay up all night listening to really bad garage bands. I'd rather be home in bed with you, Crystal."

People often think of "last straws" when they look back at marriages that fail, and I suppose if there was a last straw in my marriage to Terry it was his refusal to grab the opportunity his friend's father had handed him. But the truth is, there was no last straw. I just faced the fact that I had fallen in love with an image, not a flesh-and-blood person. I had fallen in love with the *idea* of the Terry Hollenbeck I'd known when I was a naive, impressionable student. I had allowed my worship of a college icon to blind me to a real man's faults.

When we broke up and went our separate ways, I simply carried on with my life, working, making money, paying the bills, just as I'd done when Terry was still around. Was I angry at him for not being the man I thought he'd be? No, I was devastated . . . the way children are when they discover that there isn't a Tooth Fairy . . . the way adults are when they discover that people aren't always what they seem . . . the way romantics are when they discover that love isn't always enough.

"The captain has turned on the 'Fasten Seat Belt' sign, indicating our initial descent into the Phoenix area," said Sherry or Valerie or Anastasia, I couldn't tell which, interrupting my descent into my old life. "Please make sure your seat belts are securely fastened and your seatbacks and tray tables are returned to their upright position. We should be arriving at the gate in twenty minutes."

Twenty minutes, I thought with a jolt, my stomach suddenly swarming with butterflies at the adventure of it all.

And speaking of stomachs, I peered over Dave's—no mean feat—so I could look out the window. It was only 9:30, Phoenix time, and there was a film of haze over the area which the captain had assured us would burn off by noon. He had also mentioned that the temperature in Phoenix was 98 and climbing. I was glad I would be heading north to Sedona, which, according to the travel agent, was always a good ten to fifteen degrees cooler than the desert.

"Have the two of you ever been to Sedona?" I asked Larry and Dave as the plane continued to descend. Neither of them had uttered more than a single sentence to me in five hours, but I was getting really keyed up about the trip at that point, and when I get keyed up, I get talkative.

"No," said Larry.

"Not me," said Dave.

"Well, I'm renting a car at the airport and driving up there today," I said, positively bursting with nervous energy. "I don't know what to expect, to be honest. I've heard Sedona is magnificent country, of course, but then there's the whole metaphysical thing, which isn't exactly *my* thing, but I'm convinced that once I'm in Sedona I'll be healed, spiritually and emotionally, because of all the vortexes, and if I actually meditate while I'm standing on them and surrender myself over to the natural beauty of Sedona's ancient and extremely sacred land, I'll return to New York not only with new meaning in my life but with the inner peace I've been severely lacking."

Larry looked at Dave and shrugged apologetically. "Next time *you* book the seats, okay?"

CHAPTER SIX

♥

I picked up my rental car, a burgundy something-or-other, loaded my bags into the trunk, and asked the friendly Avis lady for a map showing me how to get to Sedona. And then I set off on my journey.

Getting out of downtown Phoenix was a little tricky, but within twenty minutes or so I had passed through the blizzard of restaurants and hotels and retail stores in the center of town and found my way onto Interstate 17, where, with every passing exit, the terrain began to grow less and less populated and more and more like the sort of barren, sagebrush-and-cactus-covered desert you see in old Clint Eastwood westerns. As I continued to head north on I-17, moving further and further away from civilization, I started to come down with a case of the creeps—that out-of-kilter feeling you get if you've lived in a big city most of your life and are used to having people and buildings and at least one Korean produce market within eyeshot. Hoping for a little traveling music to keep me from flipping out altogether, I fiddled with the car radio in search of a decent station. All I got was static, and I ended up riding the rest of the way with the fan of the air conditioner as my only acoustical accompaniment.

I was about halfway to Sedona when it dawned on me that I was becoming perpendicular to the earth! Yes, I was no longer speeding along the flat-as-a-pancake desert, but driving almost straight upward into altitudes that were making my ears pop! Up and up and up chugged my car, its pathetic four-cylinder engine coughing and bucking and resisting all the hard work I was making it do. Higher and higher and higher I went, the two-lane highway curving and curling and threading its way between mountain ranges of increasing size and majesty. The word "awesome" became a casualty of the unfortunate Valley Girl period, but it really was the most apt description of the sights surrounding me that Tuesday morning in September. Especially when the road roller-coastered down into the so-called Verde Valley—a vast, low-lying expanse of pure greenery, smack in the middle of the stony gray mountains and dusty brown desert. The contrast was so startling that I had trouble concentrating on my driving. It was like watching *The Wizard of Oz* and having the movie suddenly switch from the black and white of Dorothy's life in Kansas to the dazzling emerald of Oz—right before your eyes. Where was I, anyway? I thought as I swallowed hard, trying to unclog my ears and my brain, opening the car windows to catch a whiff of the air, which was warm but no longer the furnace it had been back in Phoenix.

I turned off I-17 and continued northwest on Route 260, which, the Avis lady had assured me, would take me through the town of Cottonwood onto Highway 89A, Sedona's main drag, and would allow me to bypass the heavy midday traffic of what she had called "Greater Sedona." I laughed when I recalled the conversation. What kind of heavy midday traffic could they possibly have in Sedona? Bumper-to-bumper coyotes? I'd been driving for nearly two hours and had only seen a dozen other cars.

It was while I was passing through Cottonwood, the future site of Arizona's premier golf resort and conference center, if you believed the jazzy billboards, that I first saw the red rocks. They were still off in the distance but they were just as advertised: towering, timeless, individual—like finely chiseled pieces of sculpture, no two alike. Oh, and they were definitely red. The exact shade depended on the specific piece of rock and the exact time of day and the precise way the light was hitting it, but if I had to pick the predominant color out of a crayon box, I'd probably go for the burnt sienna.

Rona was right, I marveled, as I tried to keep my eyes on the road. If the outskirts of Sedona are this magical, what must the heart of town be like?

My curiosity grew with every mile as my rental car and I climbed 89A, which was presently winding uphill— steeply—taking me higher and higher, the air getting thinner and thinner. I sincerely hoped that being 4,500 feet above sea level for the first time in my life wouldn't cause me to lose consciousness. I had journeyed much too far to black out now.

When I reached the junction of 89A and Dry Creek Road—the Avis lady had told me to watch for a movie theatre on the corner with the too-precious name "Cinedona"—I turned left and followed the signs to Tranquility. The road led not only to the hotel that was to be my home away from home for the next ten days, but to Boynton Canyon, the famous red rock formation that was also a vortex site. Oh, boy.

The resort was as breathtaking as the canyon, I was

delighted to see after the guard at the hotel's entrance checked my name on the guest list and waved me through. Several dozen adobe-style buildings dotted the mountainside and were perfectly color coordinated with the surrounding red rocks. There was also a large building on the property that apparently housed the lobby, gift shop, and restaurants. It was in front of this building, in the fairly crowded lot intended for guests, that I parked.

I was about to get out of the car and stretch my legs when a man approached me—a young, blond man with a rather intense expression. He was wearing faded blue jeans, a turquoise-and-silver cross, and a T-shirt that read: "There's No Place Like Om."

"Yes?" I said as he poked his head through the open window of the car. "Is there something you want?"

"You're in a really bad space, you know?" he said.

"Oh, gosh. I'm sorry," I said sheepishly, thinking I must have parked in a space reserved for the handicapped. I peered out onto the pavement, searching for the ubiquitous blue lines and logo. There were none. I was confused.

"I'm talking about *here,*" said the man, placing his forefinger on his temple. "In your head. You're in a bad space. A really bad space."

Sure. Sure. I understand now, I thought. I'm in Sedona, and everyone I meet will speak in a language as incomprehensible as Rona's.

The man reached into the pocket of his jeans, and, before handing me his business card, said very proudly, "I know Reiki."

"You know Ricky?"

"No. Reiki."

"Reiki." I smiled politely, trying hard to follow him. Was this Reiki a Native American medicine man? I wondered. A psychic? A local drug merchant? Who?

"Yes, Reiki," he said. "I believe it can help you."

"It?"

"Reiki."

I shrugged, exasperated. "Look, I'm an accountant," I said. "This is all geek to me."

The man remained serious. "Then I will explain," he said. "I'm a healer and the method of healing I practice is the ancient art of Reiki." I felt a demonstration coming on and I was right. He rubbed his hands together rapidly for several seconds, then placed them on the top of my head.

"Hey, they're hot!" I said, referring to his hands, which felt surprisingly toasty on my scalp.

"Yes," he said. "And they have the power to pass along healing energy to the problem areas of the body."

I wasn't about to argue with him. I just wanted to check into the hotel, get something to eat, and take a nap.

"The material world is of no consequence to me," he added as I started to open the car door. "However, a love donation of $65.00 per one-hour session would be gratefully appreciated."

"I'll keep your card," I promised, stuffing it into my purse. "It was nice meeting you."

"You, too. Go with peace," he said and then tried his luck with the red convertible that had just cruised into the parking lot.

The hotel lobby was as attractively decorated as any I had ever seen. The colors were muted and soft, the furniture sophisticated but made of woods and fabrics indiginous to the area. Whoever was in charge of the place was obviously clever enough not to try to compete with the natural spectacle outside Tranquility—the truly magnificent Boynton Canyon—but to simply let the view make the statement.

I introduced myself to the fresh-faced young clerk at the

registration desk, who told me her name was Kara and
that she hoped I was having a beautiful day. I said I was
but that it was still early. She giggled, then began to search
her computer screen for my reservation.

"Did you book the spa vacation package, the tennis
vacation package, or the spiritual vacation package?" she
asked when she couldn't locate the reservation.

"I'm not sure I booked any of them," I said, feeling
increasingly like a stranger in a strange land. "I just came
to Sedona for a little R & R."

"A little R & R. So you *did* book the spiritual vacation
package," she said, nodding. "You're here for a little Reiki
and a little Rolfing."

I knew about Reiki, thanks to my pal in the parking lot.
Rolfing was another story. But one out of two wasn't bad,
I figured. Especially for someone as metaphysically chal-
lenged as I was.

"I kind of sensed that you'd booked the spiritual vacation package from the minute we started talking," Kara
said.

"And why is that? Because of my *bad space?*" I said,
wanting to fit in.

"Oh, no," she said. "Because of your name. I bet we
had ten or fifteen guests in the last month alone who
registered as Crystal. They were all booked for the spiritual
vacation package, too, of course."

"Of course," I said, suddenly wishing my parents had
named me Nancy.

Eventually, Kara found my reservation, gave me my room
key and a speech about Tranquility's amenities, and told
me that Todd, my bell person, would retrieve my luggage
from my car and take me to my "casita."

"Listen, before I forget," I said to Kara, "how do I book
the Sacred Earth Jeep Tour?"

"The concierge here arranges those," she explained,

then giggled again. "You'll never believe this but her name is Crystal, too."

I thanked her and told her to "Go with peace."

My casita was positioned along a particularly scenic section of Tranquility, which, if my first impression was accurate, was indeed tranquil. No drunken convention-goers. No rambunctious golfers. Not even a screaming kid. All I heard as Todd escorted me to my room were the sweet sounds of birds chirping and the occasional whoosh of a sudden mountain breeze. I was thrilled. The room itself was lovely, boasting the same muted tones and tasteful decor of the lobby. But, once again, the view stole the show. From my sliding glass doors and adjoining patio, I could look straight up at the enormous peaks of Boynton Canyon and feel an amazing connection with nature, an instant harmony with my surroundings, a genuine oneness with—

I know, I know. I was starting to sound like the rest of them, but the truth is, I really felt these things.

After I unpacked, I walked back to the main building and had a late lunch in the more casual of Tranquility's two restaurants, the Red Rock Grille. As I was taking the last bite of my Tranquility Turkey Club, my waiter came over and asked me if everything was all right.

"It was delicious," I said. "Especially the sage bread." Virtually everything on the menu had sage in it somewhere. Sage was the basil of Arizona, I guessed.

"No, I didn't mean the food," said the waiter.

I glanced up at him, wondering what else he could have meant. He was a waiter, after all. "I was asking if everything was all right with your energy centers," he explained. "When I took your order I tapped into some major problems there."

"Don't tell me. When you aren't working as a waiter, you're balancing people's chakras," I said.

"Not exactly," he said. "I do atunements."

"So you have a part-time job at a gas station?"

"No. No. You're probably thinking of tune-ups. Or maybe alignments."

"Probably." This was going to be more difficult than I thought.

"Atunements are healing sessions where I put your body in tune with its energy centers. They're $50.00 a session. Here's my card."

"Thanks," I said, slipping it into my purse next to the Reiki guy's. Then I looked down at my empty plate and told the waiter he could clear everything.

"That's terrific," he said. "I do clearings, too. Only $25.00 a session for those."

After lunch I met with Crystal, the concierge, and braced myself for a remark about my being in a bad space or needing a clearing or whatever. But she was all business as I asked her about the hotel's fabled Sacred Earth Jeep Tours.

"The tours are a marvelous experience," she said. "The drivers, many of whom are of Native American heritage, are extremely well versed in the ancient rites and customs practiced by the tribes that once occupied the land here. And the vehicles themselves are in tip-top condition. There hasn't been an accident or a breakdown or an incident of any kind since we started the program."

"That's reassuring," I said.

"Now, to the details. The tour is a five-day package—from nine in the morning until 4:30 in the afternoon each day—and bottled water and boxed lunches are included in the price."

"Which is?"

"Only $500.00, plus tax. And you can charge it to your room."

Five hundred bucks seemed like an awfully unspiritual price. "So it's a hundred dollars a day?" I asked, trying to convince myself that the tour was worth the money.

"Precisely," the concierge said.

"And you can visit all the vortexes in five days?"

"Oh, yes. The vortexes and much more. People come from all over the world to participate in these tours."

"Well, I guess I'm about to be one of them," I said. "Sign me up for the tour that shoves off tomorrow morning."

"Oh," said Crystal, looking dismayed suddenly. "I had no idea you wanted to take tomorrow's tour. It's completely full."

"You only have one Jeep going out each day?"

"No. Let me explain. Each Jeep seats six passengers. Those six passengers begin the tour on a specific day and end the tour five days later. In other words, you can't join a tour that's already in progress."

"And the tour that's beginning tomorrow has its six passengers?" I said.

"Yes, unfortunately. And the same is true with Thursday's tour, as well as Friday's and Saturday's."

"But my travel agent said I wouldn't have any trouble booking the tour. She said your busy season doesn't start until October."

"It doesn't. That's why we only schedule one new group per day now. During our high season, we book three or four groups at a time."

"Look," I said. "I'm not going to be in Sedona that long and I really have my heart set on taking your Sacred Earth Tour. Isn't there any way you could fit me into tomorrow's group? I'll skip the bottled water and boxed lunches if it'll make a difference."

Crystal smiled. "As I said, six passengers is the maximum number that most of the Jeeps can accommodate, but there are a couple of slightly larger vehicles that can seat seven, plus the driver, if it's absolutely necessary."

"It's absolutely necessary," I said. I hadn't come to Sedona to sit in my room.

"Then let me check with the head of the company that operates the tours for us," she said. "He'll be able to tell me which Jeep he's planning to use for tomorrow's group. If it's one of the larger ones, we might be able to squeeze you in."

"I'll keep my fingers crossed," I said.

"Give me your room number and after I've talked to him I'll leave you a message," she said. "Just keep in mind that if we can fit you in with tomorrow's group, there will be a tiny catch."

"How tiny?"

"You'll have to sit in the front seat of the Jeep, next to the driver."

"Well, that certainly won't kill me," I laughed, having every reason to believe it wouldn't.

CHAPTER SEVEN

♥

I took a long, slow stroll back to my room, and when I got there I noticed that the red message light on my telephone was blinking. I dialed the hotel operator, assuming that it was Crystal who had called about the Sacred Earth Jeep Tour. I was wrong.

"You had two phone calls from Rona Wishnick," said the operator, spelling out both the "Rona" and the "Wishnick" in a showy display of efficiency. "She said it was urgent that you call her back."

I called her back.

"Rona? What is it?" I asked anxiously when she picked up after the first ring. "Did that sneaky little Otis Tool fire you?"

"I haven't even seen Otis today," she said.

"Then what was so urgent?"

"Urgent? I just wanted to know how you like it out there."

"Is that all?" I breathed a sigh of relief. Rona was such

a drama queen. "I haven't done any real exploring yet, but from what I've seen of Sedona so far, it's everything you said it would be."

"I'm so glad. Is the hotel nice?"

"It's beautiful. First class."

"How about your room?"

"It's beautiful, too."

"Spacious?"

"Very."

"Private?"

"Absolutely."

"Great view?"

"Okay, Rona. What's really going on? You didn't leave two urgent messages so you could ask me about my accommodations."

She was silent for a minute. "All right, I'll tell you," she said finally, "but you aren't going to like it."

"It is Otis, isn't it?"

"No, it's Steven. That's why I was asking you about your accommodations. You could be sharing them."

"Sharing them? What on earth are you talking about?"

"Steven is making noises about flying out to Tranquility. To convince you to marry him."

"For God's sake, Rona. You told him where I am?" She was the only one to whom I had entrusted the name of the hotel, the point being that I didn't want anyone—including Steven—to come between me and my search for Meaning.

"What could I do?" she said defensively. "He started calling the office at nine o'clock this morning, begging me to give him your number."

"And you gave it to him."

"Look, Crystal, I haven't been a big champion of Steven's. You know that. But I didn't think it would be good karma for me to interfere in your relationship with him.

It's up to the two of you to decide if you want to get married. As Illandra always says, it's important to let people exercise their free will."

"So now he's coming to Sedona," I said. "I can't believe he'd actually take time away from his clients."

"Why not? You did."

She had a point. "What am I supposed to do when he gets here?"

"Do you want to marry him, Crystal?"

I pondered the question. "I used to think I did," I replied. "I assumed we'd get married and work hard at our careers and live happily ever after in his paisley apartment. But then came the whole business with Stephanie. And there's another issue: Maybe if I hadn't had such a rotten experience with my first marriage, I'd be more enthusiastic about taking the plunge a second time."

"Look, hon. The whole purpose of your trip was to go within yourself and figure out who you are and what you want out of life. True?"

"True."

"So why don't I call Steven and tell him you changed your mind about Sedona and went to Tahiti instead."

"What happened to letting people exercise their free will?"

"I'd be exercising *mine.*"

I laughed. "You don't have to tell him anything," I said. "I'm the one who has to handle the situation. Just not right this minute."

"That's the spirit. You go out and enjoy yourself. If Steven shows up, he shows up, and you'll sort it all out then."

I took Rona's advice. I left the room, hopped into my burgundy rental car, and went for a little drive into "Greater Sedona."

* * *

First, I stopped at a gas station on 89A. I pulled up to
the "full serve" pump and sat there for several minutes,
waiting for someone to fill up my tank. Finally, a man in
overalls and a red bandana asked me if I'd been helped.

"Not yet," I said.

"Then you might want to head over to The Clearing
House," he said. "They can help you, no question about
it."

"You're out of gas?" I asked.

"No, ma'am. You are," he replied in a way that suggested
that he wasn't talking about my car.

Here we go again. Another complete stranger taking my
cosmic temperature, telling me I need to balance my
energy centers. "Could we start this again?" I pleaded.

"Yup," he said cheerfully. "I asked you if you'd been
helped. You said no. I figured I should send you to The
Clearing House since that's where everybody around here
gets helped. They've got healers that come in all shapes
and sizes. Whatever ails ya, they've got a cure for it."

"That's good to know, but what if I just want $10.00
worth of unleaded gasoline?" I said.

"Oh, I can take care of that," he said. "But if I were
you, I'd make The Clearing House my next stop."

Sure, why not? I thought. If this Clearing House is where
the action is in town, I should definitely check it out.

I paid for the gas, thanked the man, and continued
along 89A, trying to keep my eyes off Sedona's spectacular
red rocks. They were so much more than just "scenery."
They were a constant source of wonderment, an exquisite
reminder of how young we are in comparison to the land—
or, to put it another way, of how ancient the land is in
comparison to us. I had never visited the great ruins of
Europe, never really concerned myself with how people

lived in previous civilizations—the occasional PBS special notwithstanding. But being virtually surrounded by these mountains, which were the epitome of timelessness, made me question what had come before me and what would come after me in a way that was entirely new for me. It also made me experience two conflicting feelings simultaneously: that I was insignificant, a speck, someone whose existence really didn't matter in the larger scheme of things, and that I was important, a bona fide life force, someone whose existence was an essential, pre-ordained part of The Big Picture.

Whoa, I thought. Would you listen to yourself, Crystal Goldstein? Contemplating your place in the cosmos instead of calculating your clients' capital gains taxes?

Maybe Sedona was beginning to work its magic on me. Sure, the place had more flakes than a piecrust, but it also had a certain "energy." And wasn't that the point?

I followed the gas station attendant's directions and after passing numerous shops selling merchandise that either promoted Native American Indians or exploited them— I actually spotted a hair salon called Scalpers—I came upon The Clearing House, a wood-frame building painted a deep red to match the omnipresent canyons. I drove into the parking lot, got out of the car, and ventured inside.

"Welcome to The Clearing House," said a woman wearing a flowing purple caftan. She told me her name was Zola, took hold of my elbow, and guided me into the store, which turned out to be a veritable Home Depot for New Agers. On the first floor were products—crystals, angel figurines, herbs, oils, candles, wind chimes, Tarot cards, books, tapes, videos, and, unfortunately for me, incense, to which I seemed to be highly allergic and which aggravated my sinuses to such an extent that I couldn't stop sneezing no matter how many times Zola chanted over me. There was also a booth where "aura photography" was performed. Zola explained that, for a mere $25.00, The Clearing House's enlightened photographer would snap a Polaroid of me in my aura field. I told her I'd take a pass, since I already knew that my aura needed cleansing and who wanted a Polaroid taken in a dirty aura?

"What's on the second floor?" I asked her.

"Our spiritualists," she said proudly. "The world's finest, all under one roof. They each rent rooms here at The Clearing House. Trust me, dear, if you have a problem, one of them will be able to fix it."

"By 'spiritualists,' you mean what, exactly?"

She smiled, indulging my ignorance. "Well," she said, "we have psychics and channelers, astrologers and numerologists, Reiki healers and Rolfing experts, hatha yoga instructors and harmonic wave theorists, angelic energy clinicians and past life regression therapists, I Ching practitioners and UFO believers, holotropic breathing facilitators and ear coning specialists, Feng Shui—"

"Excuse me," I interrupted, having become absolutely overwhelmed, the way you get when you're standing in the middle of a department store during an "Everything must go!" sale. "Would you mind explaining to me what, for example, ear coning is?" I had to start somewhere.

"Ear coning is a cleansing of the ear channels, eustacian tubes, and sinus cavities," said Zola. "Belinda, our ear coning specialist here at The Clearing House, inserts one end of a cone into the ear canal while the other end of the cone is burning. The vacuum created by the warm smoke clears out earwax, fungus, and other toxic debris. The process is excellent for people with allergies or sinus troubles."

I had both at that moment, but the notion of letting this Belinda insert anything into my body didn't appeal to me.

"What if I just wanted a simple atunement?" I asked,

remembering the waiter at Tranquility. "I ran into some-one who says he does atunements for $50.00 a session."

"Jazeem is our atunement specialist here at The Clearing House," said Zola. "Normally, her price is $60.00 per session, but if somebody else quoted you a lower price, we'll match it."

"Sort of like at a rug store," I joked.

Zola was not amused. "Would you like me to book you an hour with Jazeem?" she inquired. "I could see if she's free."

"Sure. Why not," I said.

Jazeem descended the stairs to the first floor to greet me. She was about my age, I guessed, and from the same Brooklyn neighborhood that Rona was from, judging by the accent. As she led me back up the stairs, to her private room, I asked her how she came to have such an exotic-sounding name.

"I had it changed legally about three years ago," she said. "My real name is Alice."

"I like Jazeem better," I replied, not knowing what else to say.

Jazeem was a very short woman and when she sat in her chair, her feet did not touch the ground. I tried to picture her driving a car and was sure she was one of those people you couldn't see over the steering wheel.

"Now," she said. "Get nice and comfortable. Okay, Crystal?"

I adjusted my position in the chair facing hers and told myself to relax.

"There," she said. "That's beautiful. I want you to close your eyes and take a really full, deep breath."

I shut my eyes and inhaled as fully and deeply as I knew how. Within seconds I was sneezing, just as I had been downstairs. Apparently, Jazeem had lit some incense after I'd closed my eyes, and my sinuses weren't handling it well.

"I'm sorry," I said between ka-choos.

"There is no 'sorry' in this room," she said, snuffing out the incense and sparing me further embarrassment. "Spirit has brought you to me and it is time to do his work."

"May I blow my nose first?" I asked.

"Of course," said Jazeem.

I grabbed a tissue from my purse and blew. "All set," I said.

"Good. Close your eyes again and together we will take a full, deep breath. *In* two-three-four, *out* two-three-four."

I inhaled and exhaled. Maybe an atunement is a little like a Lamaze class, I thought.

"Now, keeping your eyes closed, I'd like you to uncross your legs, put your hands together in the prayer position, and remain very quiet, while I come around to the back of your chair and begin the atunement."

I felt myself stiffen. Who knew what she was going to do to me? I mean, it wasn't as if my internist had referred her. The local gas station attendant had sent me.

"Just let go," she said as I felt her presence behind me. "Let it all go." Her voice was high-pitched but very soft and calming, like a little bell tinkling. I began to loosen up, to allow my limbs to turn to mush.

Jazeem placed her hands on the top of my head and left them there for a minute or two. I expected her to recite some sort of incantation at this point, but she simply inhaled slowly, then exhaled with a loud expulsion of air. Next, she came around to the front of my chair and flicked the tips of my outstretched fingers with her own. The sensation was odd but not unpleasant and it lasted for no more than a few seconds, after which she went back to her chair and sat down.

Is that it? I wondered, feeling a teensy weensy bit cheated.

"Don't move yet," Jazeem advised me. "We're not finished here." I nodded, keeping my eyes closed and my hands pressed together in the prayer position. "Now, I'm going to talk to you a little bit," she said, "and when I'm done you're going to feel better. Much better." Good, I thought. I'll be getting *something* for my fifty bucks. "We are all one, Crystal," she intoned, her voice suddenly lower by at least an octave. "We're one with each other, one with animals, one with the land, one with the sky, and, most of all, one with Spirit. Everything that happens to us happens for a reason. Whatever problems you've been experiencing in your life have happened for a reason— maybe to bring you here to Sedona, I don't know. What I do know is that when you leave this room today, you will understand that since everything happens to us for a reason, there's no reason to hang on to old behaviors, to try to control people and situations, to grumble about past hurts. Whatever's going to happen will happen with or without our resistance. So—we have a choice in our lives, Crystal. We can either live with negative energy, feeling sick and angry and sad, or we can live with positive energy, feeling strong and centered and happy. After today, you will choose the second option, Crystal. You will decide to live with joy. Now, I'd like you to repeat after me—I will decide to live with joy."

"I will decide to live with joy."

"Very good."

Jazeem didn't say anything after that. Not for a while, anyway. As for me, I stayed in my chair, eyes closed, hands together, silent. And I stayed that way for what seemed like an eternity but was really only twenty minutes, she informed me later. It was a trance-like twenty minutes, too; I didn't move a muscle or utter a word. I just sat there, thinking about what Jazeem had said, particularly in the context of my own life. When you got down to it, everything probably did happen for a reason. It certainly was reassuring to believe it did. And then there was Jazeem's remark about the choice between living in the pits or living with joy. I didn't want to choose the pits. Who would? But I'd never been an especially joyous person. It was possible that I'd need more than one atunement to get the job done.

I opened my eyes.

"Ah, you're back with us, Crystal," Jazeem observed, her voice returning to normal. "From the look on your face, I'd say the atunement went beautifully."

"Did it?"

"Well? How do you feel?"

"I feel . . . I feel a sneeze coming on." I sneezed.

"Bless you."

"Thanks."

Jazeem beamed. She motioned for me to stand, got up from her chair, and walked over to hug me. Since she was a couple of feet shorter than I am, it was like being hugged by a child.

"Go with peace," she said when we pulled apart.

"Same to you," I said, giving my nose another honk.

"Now," said Jazeem. "We take plastic or personal checks. Which do you prefer?"

I smiled and handed her my Visa. She had one of those credit card machines on her desk, right next to an extremely large crystal. She ran my card through it, I signed the receipt, and we said our goodbyes.

"Everything for a reason," she said, wagging a finger at me as I headed out the door. "Remember that. You were *led* to Sedona. Only time will tell you why."

I left The Clearing House feeling pretty upbeat and drove around town for a while. In addition to cruising past your basic bank, drugstore, and supermarket, I spotted dozens of metaphysical bookstores, several very upscale-looking art galleries, and a few restaurants that boasted something called "cowboy cuisine." This Sedona may be a small town, but it's definitely been yuppified, I thought as I swung back in the direction of Tranquility.

When I got to my hotel room, I saw that the message light on my phone was blinking again. It was Crystal, the concierge, calling to tell me that, yes indeedie, the bigger Jeep was being pressed into service in the morning, which meant that there would be a space for me after all.

Wow! My first-ever Sacred Earth Tour, I thought jubilantly, picturing myself hiking up those red rocks, arm in arm with my fellow vortex seekers, an authentic Native American Indian guiding us on our journey.

The very idea of the next day's adventure made me ravenously hungry, so I trundled off to Tranquility's fancy restaurant, Le Coyoté, ordered myself a fine rack of lamb and an even finer bottle of wine, and felt the memory of those Ensure dinners fade into oblivion.

Everything happens for a reason, I mumbled as I sank onto the extremely comfortable bed in my room and drifted off to my first untroubled sleep in months.

CHAPTER EIGHT

♥

I awoke to a sparkling, clear morning, the cloudless blue sky a stunning backdrop for the red rocks. After a hearty breakfast served on my patio, I chose my wardrobe for the first day of the Sacred Earth Jeep Tour: blue jeans, sneakers, and the Tranquility T-shirt I'd purchased in the hotel's gift shop the night before. I skipped the makeup, simply running a comb through my hair, applying a little sunscreen, and "letting it all go." I was feeling pretty laid back, for me—so laid back that I didn't jump when the phone rang, even though I knew it could be Steven, newly arrived in Sedona and ready and waiting to pop the question in person. As it turned out, the caller was someone from room service, asking if I had enjoyed my breakfast and whether he could come and retrieve my tray. After I had answered "yes" to both, he told me to have a beautiful day. I wished him the same.

Our tour group was supposed to assemble in the courtyard outside the lobby at nine o'clock sharp. I arrived at

8:30, a little over-eager, I guess. I sat down on one of the benches there, picked up the abandoned copy of the *Red Rock News*, Sedona's twice-weekly newspaper, and read while I waited for the others to show up.

The newspaper didn't provide much in the way of hard news—there wasn't a single article on the national or international scene—but there were a few columns devoted to life on Mars, as well as an editorial extolling the virtues of peyote. When I flipped to the back page, I noticed a sizable ad promoting the Sacred Earth Jeep Tour. I smiled proudly as I envisioned myself climbing canyons, forging streams, negotiating trails. A Jewish Sacajawea.

The other six people in our party finally appeared at about five minutes to nine, and when I saw who was in the group, the word "party" took on a whole new meaning. Don't get me wrong—I'm not a celebrity groupie or anything—but when I saw that Amanda Wells Reid, famous partygoer, famous socialite, famous rich person, would be going vortexing with me, I just couldn't believe it! To think that *I* would be riding in the same Jeep as the woman the tabloids referred to as "the millionaire heiress!"

I tried to act nonchalant as she stepped out onto the courtyard with her entourage, but I did stare at her, naturally. And as I did, I silently ticked off whatever tidbits of trivia I could remember about her.

She was born and raised in Texas, the debutante daughter of oil tycoon Chester "Chet" Wells. She was said to be in her fifties, although she would never divulge her age. She was married the first time to Pat Gandy, the organ transplant specialist who left medicine to become a race car driver. She was married the second time to Richard Lewiston, the British stage actor who sold out to Hollywood by starring in R-rated action films. And she was married the third time—and was still married, as far as I knew— to Harrison Reid, the legendary novelist who spent more time drinking and philandering than he did writing. As a result of these and other tawdry liaisons—and the fact that she was impossibly wealthy, of course—Amanda Reid was constantly being written up in the columns, photographed on the society pages, seated in the front row of fashion shows, invited to balls and galas of the type that were chronicled in *Town & Country*. She was also regularly joked about, parodied, and sniped at for speaking in that treacly southern accent; and for being ditsy as well as nasty and totally unaware that she was either. Mostly, though, when people gossiped about Amanda Reid, they gossiped about what a trendsetter she *wasn't*. Even with all that money, she was a trend *sheep*, someone who waited for her more daring friends to determine what was "in" and then followed along. If they wore it, she wore it; if they lunched there, she lunched there; if they donated money to it, she donated money to it. She was always a step behind the Blaine Trumps of the world, forever scrambling to play catch-up. She would latch onto the person who did their streaks long after they had already moved on to another colorist. She would rush to the plastic surgeon she thought was doing their face lifts, only to discover that they had already moved on to another flesh carver. You get the point.

"Poor woman," the media would titter. "She may have bigger bucks than most small countries, but she's so yesterday."

In a weird way, I felt I had something in common with Amanda Reid; I was pretty yesterday myself. After all, only twenty-four hours earlier, I had never even heard of ear coning.

"Is this the pickup location for the Jeep Tour, do you know?" Amanda asked me, the southern belle accent turning "tour" into "too-ah."

"Uh, yes. I think so," I said, momentarily taken aback that she had spoken to me.

"Well! You'd think they'd have some sort of a sign."

I studied her as she stood there with her hands on her hips, looking thinner and more brittle than she did in photographs. She was a beautiful woman—or had been once, before the skin on her face had been pulled and stretched and tucked behind her ears so tightly that her mouth had the wingspan of a 747. Cosmetic surgeries aside, she still had the luminous brown eyes, the patrician nose, the well-defined cheekbones, the Miss America posture. She was wearing her golden blond hair in a style that had, a year or two ago, gone out of style (surprise)—the layered "Rachel" cut, named for the character in the TV show "Friends."

She was heavier on the makeup than was currently fashionable (natch). And her outfit for the Sacred Earth Jeep Tour was something off an old Tammy Wynette album cover—slim-fitting jeans, a denim shirt with pearl buttons and fringes along the arms, and (get this) a cowboy hat and cowboy boots. I was sort of expecting her to belt out the chorus of "Stand By Your Man." Instead, she belted out commands to her five traveling companions. "Over here," she said, waving them toward the bench where I was sitting.

I rose then, and introduced myself. "I'm Crystal Goldstein," I said. "I'm signed up for the Jeep tour, too, so we'll be spending the next five days together."

"Oh?" She gave me the once-over, inspecting me from head to toe in a way that suggested she thought I might be crawling with lice. Deciding I wasn't, I guess, she deigned to shake the hand I'd extended to her—limply, with the grip of a raw salmon fillet.

Her cohorts ambled over to check out the interloper.

"Crystal Goldstein," I smiled. "I'll be on the Jeep with all of you."

"If it ever gets here," said Amanda, glancing at her watch and pouting.

"I'm Tina Barton," said a tall, thin, dour woman in her forties. She had shoulder-length, stick-straight dark hair, parted down the middle, and a sallow, sickly complexion. She was dressed entirely in black—black jeans, black shirt, black Nikes. Not exactly the color you want to wear if you're spending the day in the broiling Arizona sun, I thought. She smoked cigarettes, too—the skinny brown kind—and had a persistent, hacking, phlegmy cough. She clearly wasn't in the best of health, and I wondered why she would subject herself to the strenuous hiking we would be doing over the next five days. And then she told me that she was Amanda Reid's personal assistant and that accompanying Amanda on all of her trips was part of the job.

"My name's Billy Braddick," said a very muscular twenty-something with closely-cropped, reddish-brown hair and a matching goatee. He was wearing jeans, sneakers, and a turquoise tank top, his biceps crisping in tanning oil and bulging ostentatiously, like Popeye after a can of spinach. "How're ya doing?" he asked in that sort of swaggering, construction worker-ish way some men have when what they really mean is: "Want to fuck?" After I said I was just fine, thank you, he told me that he was Amanda Reid's personal trainer and that Mrs. Reid liked to have him around wherever she went. "In case she pulls a groin muscle or something," he winked.

"I am Marie Poussant," said a plump, disheveled French-woman in her fifties. She wore her short brown hair in a mess of tangled curls, her mascara was badly smudged, and her lipstick had been applied in such a haphazard manner that it only covered three-quarters of her mouth. As for her hiking attire, it consisted, not of Nikes and jeans,

but of Keds and a *shmatte*—a sleeveless print dress that
exposed her pale, heavy arms and made them look like
two loaves of unbaked bread. She told me that she was
Amanda Reid's personal chef and that, Mon Dieu, Madame
Reid would never travel without her. She would if she knew
you'd been hitting the cooking sherry, I thought, after
detecting a hint of the stuff on her breath.

"Jennifer Sibley! Great to meet you!" said an extremely
perky woman with a long, blond ponytail, a trim, athletic
figure, and the perfectly aligned white teeth of an
anchorwoman. I figured her for about thirty. She was wearing an outfit identical to mine, complete with the Tranquility T-shirt, and she had a cell phone protruding from one
pocket of her jeans and a beeper clipped onto the back
of another. "I'm Amanda Reid's personal publicist and
I'm always on hand when there's a media situation to
be dealt with," she explained, pumping my hand with
tremendous enthusiasm.

I was about to ask what possible "media situation" would
need to be dealt with in the middle of nowhere when
the final member of Amanda Reid's party-of-six stepped
forward.

"It's Crystal, right?" said a man of approximately my
age as he scribbled notes in a spiral-bound pad. He was
short, stocky, and balding, and he had a sort of world-
weary expression on his face, which was, unfortunately for
him, covered with childhood acne scars.

"Yes, it's Crystal," I said. "Crystal Goldstein."

"From?" he asked.

"From?"

"Where do you live?" he said, his pen poised to record
the answer in his notepad.

"New York. Why?"

"Oh. Sorry. I'm Michael Mandell, a contributing editor
of *Personal Life,*" he said. "I'm doing a piece on Amanda

Reid for the magazine, so I'm tagging along on this Jeep thing." He glanced first to his right, then to his left, and when he was sure that the others had moved away and were no longer within earshot, he whispered, "The story is really about Harrison Reid. He finally has a new book coming out after fifteen years. I'm covering 'the Mrs.' as sort of a sidebar. You know, a puff piece."

A puff piece. Still, I was thrilled. For all I knew, *my* name could land in *Personal Life,* which didn't quite have the cachet of *Vanity Fair* but so what?

"Harrison Reid has written a new novel?" I asked Michael. I'd spent most of my adult life reading tax returns, not fiction, but even I knew that Harrison Reid hadn't published a book since the mid-eighties and that he hadn't produced a real body of work since the seventies. Back then, his thousand-plus-page novels concerning such weighty themes as religion, race, and politics in America were widely acclaimed, staples of the bestseller lists, nominated for literary prizes, snapped up for television miniseries. But a long dry spell set in after the '84 novel and Reid was said to have descended into a life of debauchery—boozing and womanizing and appearing only occasionally with his wife, who attended most of her society soirées with a series of walkers.

"It's not a novel," said Michael. "It's a collection of humorous essays about death."

"Sounds like a scream," I said. "What's it called?"

"The Right Stiff," he smirked. "Ordinarily, the magazine wouldn't touch the book, but it's got Harrison Reid's name on it, he's agreed to let me interview him at length, and she"—he nodded at Amanda—"said she would be absolutely delighted to cooperate. Between you and me, I think she turned several shades of green when we did that valentine to Brooke Astor in the July issue. She's been dying

for us to shine the spotlight on her—and on her genius husband, of course.''

''Of course.''

I listened intently as Michael dished the dirt with me, dropped names, and bragged about his ability to take short-hand in an age when most celebrity interviewers relied on tape recorders.

''You know,'' he said, ''you're lucky there was room for you on this Jeep tour. Amanda's nutritionist, hairdresser, and masseuse were supposed to come, too, but I hear they all quit a week or so before the trip.''

''Quit? Why? Is Amanda Reid difficult to work for?'' I asked.

Michael rolled his eyes. ''Take a look at Tina, the one in black.''

''The assistant?''

He nodded. ''She's been with Amanda the longest of these folks. Does she strike you as a relaxed, happy person?''

I regarded Tina. She was dragging on her cigarette, then sucking on a strand of hair, then biting a fingernail, then tearing at a cuticle. She was a nervous wreck and she reminded me of myself, minus the cigarette, pre-Sedona. No wonder Rona was so worried about me, I thought with a shudder.

''The others don't seem to mind being here,'' I said, motioning toward Billy, Marie, and Jennifer.

'' 'Seem' is the operative word. I betcha they'll start show-ing a little wear and tear as this five-day tour gets going,'' he said.

''Tina! Didn't the hotel person say the Jeep was picking us up at nine o'clock?'' Amanda demanded of her assistant.

''It's only five after nine,'' Tina replied sullenly, tossing her cigarette onto the ground and mashing it with her sneaker. After what Michael had said, I had a feeling she was fantasizing that it was her boss's *head* she was mashing.

"You should go inside and see if there's a problem," Amanda directed Tina.

"Aw, come on, Mrs. Reid. The car will be here any minute now," Billy soothed as he moved closer to Amanda and began to administer a neck rub. She moaned with pleasure while Marie said "Mon Dieu" and Jennifer made a call from her cell phone.

"It is possible that the driver got lost, no?" Marie suggested.

"Of course not," Amanda answered sharply, as if her chef were a fool. "He comes here to pick up passengers every day of the week. Besides, he's probably an Indian, and Indians never get lost. That's why they were able to discover this land before we were, isn't that right, Billy?"

Billy shrugged and continued to knead Amanda's neck and shoulder muscles.

Michael was about to make a snide remark to me when we all saw a car speeding toward us—and I do mean speeding. It was a large red Jeep—an open-air, four-wheel-drive vehicle with an awning for a top and the words "Sacred Earth Jeep Tour" printed in navy blue along both sides. After doing a near spin-out, it came to an abrupt, screeching stop in front of the courtyard, kicking up dust and spraying us with it.

"Good Lord!" said Amanda, spitting microscopic pieces of sediment out of her mouth. "I'm not ready to put my life in the hands of this driver!"

I wasn't so sure about the guy myself: *I* was the one who was going to have to sit up front next to him for five whole days.

Amanda was still grumbling about the driver when he emerged from the Jeep.

The sun was nearly blinding me, so I shielded my eyes in order to get a better look at the man. I could make out that he was of medium height and on the lean, rangy side—broad shouldered but long limbed. He was wearing well-worn blue jeans, a blue-and-white-striped shirt with the sleeves rolled up to the elbows, red, earth-stained hiking boots, and a black, wide-brimmed hat that obscured most of his face but revealed a mane of brown hair that reached just below his shoulders and was tied back with an elastic band decorated with feathers.

"Well, I guess Tonto finally showed up," Michael muttered as the man drew closer to us.

I cringed at the reference and hoped that the driver hadn't heard it. If he had, he certainly didn't let on.

"Good morning, everybody," he said cheerfully. "I'm sorry I'm late, but . . . Well, I'll spare you the gory details about *why* I'm late. The important thing is, I'm going to be your guide today, so why don't we just get started, okay?"

Gee, the voice is vaguely familiar, I thought, wondering whose it reminded me of.

"What tribe are you from?" Amanda asked the driver. "I hear Indians practically own this state."

The driver laughed. "I wouldn't say that," he said. "But there are fourteen different tribes that call Arizona home—that's about 150,000 people living on twenty reservations. As for me, I'm not Apache or Navajo or any of them. I'm a White Anglo-Saxon Protestant boy who happens to like living here in Sedona." He turned to Michael Mandell then, directing his words to the journalist. "And, in case you were wondering, sir, my name's not Tonto. It's Terry. Terry Hollenbeck."

I heard myself gasp as he removed the black hat. He was twenty years older and ten pounds lighter, but the smile was the same and so was the attitude. I didn't know what I was going to do about it or even how I felt about it, but, sure enough, it was my former husband who was standing before me.

PART
T♥W♥O

CHAPTER NINE

♥

He didn't recognize me at first. He was too busy explaining to our little group how he had rushed out of the tour office in such a hurry that he had completely forgotten to grab the passenger list the hotel had faxed there the night before; how he hadn't had even a second to check our names; how the office would straighten everything out the next day. Blah blah blah.

I wasn't listening. Not really. I was focusing on the horrendous case of dry mouth I had suddenly developed, wondering how on earth I would be able to pry my lips apart when it came time to speak, trying frantically to rehearse the response I would deliver when Terry finally took a good look at me and realized with whom he'd be sharing his Jeep.

Why was I so undone at the sight of him if I had been so quick to dump him, you ask? For starters, it was a shock having him show up the way he did—a stunner, a heart-stopper, a coincidence of major proportions. Think about it: Would you expect to bump into your ex-husband after nearly twenty years of total estrangement? There ought to be some kind of statute of limitations on such things.

Then, there was the matter of Terry's appearance, which was a shock *and* a stick in the eye. He was still a handsome guy at forty-three. Entirely too handsome, it seemed to me. His shaggy brown hair had always been glossy, even when he'd worn it short, jock-style. But now that it was long, down his back, in a loose ponytail, it was positively gleaming—and not that moussed-up, Fabio-ish, stud-muffin type of hair, either. His face was new and improved, too, and I'm not talking about nips and tucks here and there. Just the opposite. His skin was lined—from spending so much time in the Arizona sun, I guessed—and while the lines did age him, they also gave him a cragginess, a character, a lived-in look, erasing his smooth, almost pudgy youthfulness and turning the boy I'd remembered into a man. At least, on the surface. As for his body, well, it hadn't gone to seed in the slightest, what with all that hiking and climbing and shlepping tourists from power spot to power spot. In fact, as I noted earlier, he was thinner than when I'd known him, leaner, harder, in better shape. Or so it appeared at first glance.

And then, there was the situation itself, which was bizarre at best. How are people who used to be married to each other *supposed* to behave when they're thrown together after nearly two decades? Particularly when they're thrown together, not for a college reunion, or a family funeral, or something equally run-of-the mill, but for a five-day vortex tour? I mean, this sort of stuff isn't covered in etiquette books or advice columns.

Of course, as Terry continued to yammer on about the places he would be taking us that day, I couldn't help thinking, just a little smugly, Okay, Crystal. You were right about him after all. You dumped him because you thought he would never get a real job, never behave like a responsible adult, never amount to anything, and, sure enough, here he is: a driver for Sacred Earth Jeep Tours, chauffering Tranquility's well-heeled guests around Sedona for whatever pittance he makes in tips. Not exactly a candidate for the cover of *Business Week*, I mused, reminded that the magazine had recently done a brief article about Steven. My Steven. The man who earned a very respectable living. The man who wanted to marry me.

I chuckled to myself, hoping that my feeling of superiority would mask the feeling of insecurity I was also experiencing. How would *he* react, I wondered, when it dawned on him that the woman who'd divorced him was standing within a few feet of him? Would he be pissed off that he was stuck squiring me around for almost a week, waiting on me hand and foot, serving me boxed lunches, having to take my money? Or would he act glad to see me again, still find me attractive after all these years, decide that I had held up well?

Yeah, sure, Crystal, I thought ruefully. You've held up so well that you flew all the way across the country so you could have your aura cleansed.

Wait a minute, I said to myself. Why should you care about this guy's opinion of you? He's a jerk, remember? That's why you booted him out of your life.

I snuck a quick peek at myself in the mirror of my compact while Terry was asking for everybody's name and suggesting that we form a little line next to the Jeep, sort of the way you're told to board an airplane.

"I'm Amanda Reid," said Amanda with a sugary, flirtatious smile as Terry took her hand and helped her into the backseat of the Jeep. "But then you probably knew that."

"Sorry, Amanda. I didn't," said Terry. "We've got our

share of psychics here in Sedona, but I'll tell you up front so you won't be disappointed—I'm not one of them."

"No, no, no. I didn't mean it that way," Amanda said, irritated that she had been misunderstood, the sugar turning to boric acid. "I assumed you had seen my photograph somewhere. That's all."

"On the wall at the post office maybe?" Terry teased, not the least bit intimidated by her high-and-mighty nonsense.

"Mrs. Reid is married to the novelist Harrison Reid," Tina said morosely, then took a long drag on her cigarette and flicked it onto the ground. "I'm Tina Barton, Mrs. Reid's assistant."

"Well, that explains it," he said with a touch of sarcasm. "Thanks for filling me in." Terry offered Tina a hand into the Jeep. "I'm a big fan of Mr. Reid's novels, so this is a real honor." A big fan of Harrison Reid's *novels?* I thought. How strange. When I'd been married to Terry, the only printed matter I'd ever seen him read were classified ads. "But there's something you need to know, Tina. I can call you Tina, right?" She nodded glumly. "Well, Tina, the name written on both sides of the Jeep you're sitting in is the 'Sacred Earth Jeep Tour.' That's *Sacred Earth,* get it? What I'm saying is that when you sign up for this tour, you don't toss your cigarette butts—lit or otherwise—anywhere but in an ashtray. Clear?"

"Sure," she shrugged, then began biting the nail on her right pinky.

"The name's Billy Braddick," said Amanda's personal trainer, brushing off Terry's attempt to help him into the vehicle. Billy was a manly man, apparently, and manly men never let other men help them do anything. Amanda shoved over, making room for him on the seat next to her so he could be right there in case she suffered a torn hamstring.

"Bonjour. I am Marie Poussant," Amanda's chef said

louder than was necessary. She waddled unsteadily over to Terry, who grabbed her fleshy arm just as she was about to hurl herself into the Jeep and land on her head.

"Hey. Hey. Easy does it now, Marie," he said, guiding her carefully up onto the seat across from Amanda, Billy, and Tina. The back of the Jeep consisted of two bench seats facing each other, with roll bars providing hand supports for the passengers, should the terrain get bumpy.

"Terry! Great to meet you!" Jennifer Sibley enthused after identifying herself as Amanda's "media architect." I caught Terry stifling a smirk.

"Great to meet you, too!" he said, an amazing mimic, matching Jennifer's perkiness perk for perk.

"It's incredible to be here, totally exciting!" she said, bouncing onto the backseat, jostling Marie. She smiled at Terry and gave him the thumbs-up sign. "All set, Mission Control!" She sounded like a goddam space shuttle astronaut.

"I'm Michael Mandell," the journalist told Terry as he climbed into the Jeep, occupying the last spot in the back of the car.

As Terry made small talk with Michael, who confided that he was chronicling Mrs. Reid's trek through the vortexes for *Personal Life* magazine, I inched forward, the only one left in line now, fighting the urge to flee—into the lobby of the hotel, into a hole in the ground, anywhere. Within seconds, I knew I would be forced to deal with what was sure to be an icky, embarrassing scene, in front of complete strangers. My mouth was so dry by this time that swallowing was a near impossibility.

Eventually, Terry finished his chat with Michael and turned casually in my direction.

I had wanted to be the one to speak first—to establish a certain dominance, I suppose—but I couldn't speak at all because my lips were sealed shut. I just stood there passively, waiting for Terry to recognize me, waiting to see if he *would* recognize me. If you've never found yourself in this predicament, you're lucky. It is not empowering.

I watched as the realization of who I was finally hit him. In stages. First, he removed his dark sunglasses. Then, he blinked. Then, he squinted. Then, he stroked his chin. And then, he broke out into a raucous belly laugh that I found really unnerving.

"Well, well," he said between chuckles. "Of all the gin joints in all the towns in all the world, she walks into mine."

It was the famous line from *Casablanca*, of course, and I immediately attached major significance to the fact that Terry had used it. Was he horribly in love with me after all these years, the way Bogie was with Ingrid? Did he think I was horribly in love with him after all these years, the way Ingrid was with Bogie? Would he and I have a torrid, rapturous affair, only to have me toddle off with Steven in the end, the way Ingrid toddled off with Paul Henreid? Was I nuts to even be *having* these thoughts, leaping to conclusions about a person I knew another lifetime ago?

"Crystal?" Terry said, shaking my elbow. "It *is* you, right?"

"Right," I said, managing to part the lips. "Your one and only ex-wife." I paused, aware that I had just made a ridiculous assumption. "Or have there been several ex-wives by now?" Probably as many ex-wives as there have been jobs, I thought.

Terry didn't answer. Instead, he smiled, shook his head and said, "Crystal Goldstein. Here in Sedona. I can't believe it. You look—"

"I look *what?*" I jumped in, in case he started in about my dirty aura.

"You look great," he said instead. "A little tired, maybe. But great. As great as I remember."

Before I could respond to the compliment, he grabbed

me around the waist and hugged me, twirling me around and around in circles in a move worthy of Torvill and Dean. The gesture was unexpected, obviously, and so I didn't hug Terry back at first; I let my arms dangle next to his body, giving them nothing to do and no place to go. But after a while, I got caught up in the spirit of things—Terry wasn't an ax murderer, after all—and allowed myself to hold him. Briefly.

He still smells the same, I thought as my face burrowed into the curve of his neck and I was instantly transported back in time. A person's smell can do that. Terry's wasn't a fragrance from a particular cologne or after-shave lotion, nor did it hint of a brand of soap. It was his own scent, a musky odor I had always found intoxicating and extremely difficult to resist.

I resisted, pulling away. I wasn't a dewy-eyed twenty-two-year-old anymore.

"Crystal Goldstein," he said again, appearing to marvel at the fact that he and I had landed in the same part of the world. "I can't get over it. What are you doing in Sedona?"

"You mean, other than taking this Sacred Earth Jeep Tour?"

"Yeah, that's exactly what I mean. Don't tell me you've abandoned New York—or given up accounting?"

"No. I'm a partner at Duboff Spector, working out of the firm's Manhattan headquarters." Unless Otis Tool had made other arrangements.

"I'm impressed. Duboff Spector is a big outfit."

"Huge."

"So you're on vacation?"

"In a sense." I wasn't about to tell him I was on a quest for Meaning.

"Alone?"

"I'm not sure."

"You're not sure?" He laughed again. "Crystal, you're being a little evasive. I'm not with the CIA if that's what's on your mind."

"Sorry. The truth is, my boyfriend—excuse me, my fiancé—is planning to fly out any day. He should have been here by now, but he's a *very* successful lawyer and his practice keeps him busy busy busy.

"How about you?" I asked Terry. "Are you just passing through Sedona? Working your way across the country? A job here, a job there?"

"I've lived in Sedona for eleven years," he said. "Long before you ever heard of the town."

"Eleven years?" I said, arching an eyebrow. The Terry Hollenbeck I knew couldn't stay in one place for eleven seconds.

"Yup," he nodded. "And I've owned the Jeep tour company for seven of those years, as well as a bunch of real estate in the area."

"You *own* the company?" I said, not even addressing the "bunch" of real estate.

Terry smiled wryly. "You can close your mouth now, Crystal. I know you never thought I'd own anything but my underwear, but the tour company does great business, especially during our high season. Sedona's the 'in' place these days and everybody and their sister wants to do the vortex thing. Like you, for example."

I wasn't buying it. "If you own the tour company, what are you doing here at the hotel? As our *driver*?"

"The driver who was supposed to take your group out today came down with the flu," Terry explained. "I'm the emergency backup. That's why I didn't have the list of passengers' names with me. The guy called in sick about ten minutes before he was scheduled to pick you all up."

It was possible that Terry was telling the truth. He may

have been a deadbeat when we were married but he was never a liar as far as I knew.

Everything happens for a reason. Wasn't that what Jazeem had said during my atunement? Had I been led to Sedona so I could be reunited with Terry? I wondered. And if so, who needed it? I was searching for inner peace, not my ex-husband.

I was about to ask him how he came to live in Sedona in the first place when somebody in the Jeep honked the horn. Insistently.

"What in the world are you two talking about out there?" Amanda whined. "You're keeping us waiting and it's very rude."

"She's right," I said. "She's not paying five hundred bucks for herself and her serfs to sit and listen to us take a trip down memory lane."

"So you're not part of her group?" Terry asked.

"Please. Amanda's the 'millionaire heiress,' in case you don't read the tabloids. I just met her and her pals this morning."

"Really. I would have thought that you and your fiancé moved in the same circles as someone like her. The New York monied set and all that."

I laughed. "The New York monied set? Steven and I—"

"Steven? That's the guy's name?"

"Yes. Steven Roth."

"Moth?"

"No, Terry. *Roth.* And you heard me the first time, didn't you?"

He nodded, grinning mischievously.

"Steven and I are much too busy for the sort of frivolous society galas that are Amanda Reid's whole life. She's in a different world. Steven and I make money by working hard. Amanda Reid makes money by breathing. She was born into money. She inherited money. She married money. Except in the case of her current marriage, that is. Everyone says Harrison Reid has squandered whatever he earned from his books."

"Lucky for him he's got a wife who brings home the bacon," said Terry, who, the instant he uttered the remark, realized he had just put his foot in his mouth. "I shouldn't have said that," he confessed after a few uncomfortable seconds. "I didn't mean to imply that when you and I were—"

"Forget it," I cut him off, as if the comment hadn't stung as much as it had.

"I'm sorry," he said.

"Don't give it another thought," I said.

Terry cleared his throat. "Well," he said, "I guess we'd better get the show on the road before Amanda runs us over. I left the keys in the ignition."

He walked me to the front of the Jeep, to the seat next to his.

"Besides," he said as he helped me inside, "you and I have plenty of time to catch up. This is day one of the tour. We've got four more to go."

"Only if you keep filling in for your flu-stricken driver," I pointed out. "The poor guy *could* make a miraculous recovery."

"He won't," said Terry. "I own the company, remember?"

CHAPTER TEN

♥

As he pulled out of Tranquility's long, winding driveway, Terry informed us that our first stop on the tour would be Airport Mesa, one of Sedona's most frequently visited vortexes.

"There's a vortex at an airport?" I asked. I had never thought of JFK or LaGuardia as especially sacred sites.

"Don't worry. You won't be ducking planes," he said. "There is a makeshift airport nearby, for the small craft that take tourists over the Grand Canyon, but Airport Mesa itself is a cliff on the edge of town. You climb up to the top and get treated to a sensational view of Sedona."

"Never mind the view. I can buy postcards for that," Amanda snapped. "I'm more interested in the energy fields. This Airport place is a vortex, you're sure?"

"I'm not sure of anything except death and taxes, Amanda," Terry said matter-of-factly, glancing at her through the rearview mirror, "but if there are such things as vortexes, Airport Mesa is one of them."

I looked over at my ex-husband, to try to determine from his expression if he was bullshitting us. Vortexes were big business now—*his* business now—and I wondered if he was a true believer or just a good salesman. But I couldn't read him. It had been too long. So I just sat there in the front seat next to him, my feet resting on top of the large Styrofoam ice chest on the floor of the Jeep— the container of our bottled water and boxed lunches, I guessed. I was still amazed that I was even in the same car as the man, still reeling from the unexpectedness of it all, still searching for my real feelings about running into him. It was impossible to relate to him without remembering what had gone before, impossible to place him in this new context. I had knowledge of him—of how much I had loved him, of how much he had disappointed me—and no matter how warm and friendly and, yes, appealing, he seemed to me now, there was no forgetting about all that. How could there be?

As we chugged along in the Jeep, en route to Airport Mesa, Terry gave us a little talk about the history of Sedona.

"Legend has it that millions of years ago this entire region was covered by water," he said, "which is ironic since the lack of water is what eventually drove settlers away. Anyhow, when these so-called 'seas' receded, what was left was the incredible chunk of geography you see now—the uniquely carved cliffs and mesas and spires, each with its own distinctive shape and personality. Numerous Indian tribes—the Sinagua, the Hopi, the Navajo, and even the Apache—called the area home at one time or another and designated the land as sacred. But it wasn't until 1902 that the town became a *town*, if you know what I mean."

"In other words, it was in 1902 that it got its first Block-buster Video," Michael joked.

"No, Blockbuster came in 1903," Terry joked back.

"Actually, it was in 1902 that Carl and Sedona Schnebly, a couple from the eastern U.S., settled here. Sedona Schnebly was quite the pioneer woman and loved the simpler, more rugged lifestyle she found out west. She and her husband became the unofficial Welcome Wagon in town, opening the first hotel here."

"Why on earth didn't you book us rooms at *that* hotel?" Amanda demanded of Tina. "Think of the historic implications, the local color, the opportunity to tell my friends that *I* stayed where it all began."

Before Tina could defend herself, Terry explained that the Schneblys' hotel no longer existed. It was currently the site of a large resort called Los Abrigados, whose Italian restaurant, Joey Bistro, served Sicilian dishes and was a favorite with tourists.

"The town finally got its name when Carl Schnebly became the local postmaster," Terry continued with his history lesson. "All his friends suggested he name the place after his wife, Sedona."

"A beautiful name," Marie commented. "It sounds Spanish, no?"

"Many people think so," said Terry. "But New Agers here attach a special significance to the word, because 'Sedona' spelled backwards is 'Anodes,' the conducting surfaces through which electrical current flows."

"Well! Now that's just the sort of thing that fascinates me. All that New Age-y information," Amanda said, sounding pleased.

"Mrs. Reid has become quite a student of the New Age Movement," Jennifer pointed out to Michael, prompting him to resume his note-taking. "She's thinking of asking Marianne Williamson to officiate when she and Mr. Reid renew their wedding vows next year."

"Is that right?" said Michael. I was facing front, so I

couldn't see him, but judging by his tone, I could tell that he was underwhelmed by the information.

"Yes, I've truly immersed myself in all things New Age," Amanda confirmed.

"When did you first become interested in the Movement?" Michael asked her.

"Let's see," she pondered. "I believe it was at a dinner party my husband and I gave in honor of the Duchess of York."

"Fergie?" said Michael.

"Who else?" Amanda sniffed.

"Ah, yes. I remember the dinner well," Marie said nostalgically. "I prepared a lovely Escalope de Veau, no?"

"No," Amanda said abruptly, angered that her chef had insinuated herself into the interview. "The veal was tough. The Duchess hardly touched hers. I remember *that* well."

Marie retreated.

"Getting back to your introduction to the New Age Movement," Michael went on, "you were saying—"

"I was saying that the Duchess took me into her confidence that evening, mentioning to me that she had been consulting a psychic," Amanda disclosed, "although she referred to the woman as her spiritual counselor. In any case, she spoke very highly of the woman, of how she had predicted this and that and how each and every prediction had come to pass. I was skeptical at first, of course, but then the Duchess smiled at me and said, 'Amanda, one must always keep an open mind because one really has no idea how the universe works, does one?' " Amanda paused, reflecting on the profundity of the Duchess's words. I looked over at Terry again. He was grinning. I had a feeling he heard wacky anecdotes like Amanda's all the time in his business, albeit not including quotes from members of the royal family. "By the time dessert was served—"

"Ah, yes. Beautiful little chocolate soufflés, no?" Marie volunteered.

"By the time dessert was served," Amanda continued, ignoring her cook completely, "I realized that the Duchess was absolutely right. We earthly beings don't know how or why things happen as they do. We can't say with complete certainty what fate has in store, for example, or whether angels actually exist, or even whether some people have a higher state of consciousness than others. I thought, I really should investigate all this. I really should become more *involved* in the subject."

"You felt this urge as a result of your conversation with the Duchess of York," Michael confirmed.

"Yes. And because the line of clothing I had hoped to market never got off the ground," said Amanda.

"I'm not following you," said Michael.

"I had planned to become a designer," said Amanda, "and, after that, to open a restaurant or host a talk show or launch my own Web site." She sighed. "Harrison said I should leave it to my friends to juggle all sorts of business ventures if they want to, but I plunged right in. Unfortunately, none of my projects went anywhere."

Poor thing, I thought. She really is a woman in search of an identity.

"And so I said to myself: 'Amanda, forget about all those worldly ambitions of yours and find out about this spirituality thing that everybody's talking about. Maybe there's money to be made there."

Terry and I both laughed out loud. It was impossible not to.

"When you say there may be money to be made, what do you mean, exactly?" Michael asked Amanda.

"Well, this is going to be quite a scoop for your magazine," she began, as if she didn't have a clue that the person Michael's magazine was really interested in was her husband. "I've decided that I don't care about the clothing line, the restaurant, or the talk show. What I care about now is becoming the high priestess of New Age. You know, the Martha Stewart of Metaphysics."

Before anyone could react, Jennifer, the media architect, jumped in, putting a spin on her client's announcement. "Mrs. Reid has a genuine thirst, not only for acquiring knowledge about the New Age Movement, but for communicating what she learns to the masses." She spoke in her usual enthusiastic way, but more slowly this time, so Michael could jot down every word. "She intends to deliver lectures, write books, produce audio and videotapes, star in infomercials, whatever it takes to reach people, to help people."

"And, of course, there *could* be a clothing line eventually," Amanda added. "A New Age clothing line." I tried to imagine who would buy such clothes, not to mention what they would look like, and then remembered Rona. "So you see, driver." She tapped Terry on the back. "I'm here to discover. I want to become as spiritual as a person can possibly become. In five days, that is."

"Okay, Amanda," said Terry as he swung the Jeep into a parking lot. "We're gonna start with Airport Mesa and work up to the more strenuous stuff. We find that it's easier on people if we save the heavy hiking for the last couple of days of the tour."

"The hiking's not a problem for Mrs. Reid," said Billy. "That's why I'm here. In case she pulls something."

Oh, she'll pull something, all right, I thought, having seen and heard how Amanda Reid operated. The question was: what?

Terry grabbed a package from underneath his seat, then led us up the cliff, which was a climb but not exactly Mt.

Everest. By the time we had all followed him to a relatively flat plateau, it was after ten o'clock and the place was swarming with tourists meditating, soaking up the sun, or sight-seeing. I spotted the intense-looking blond man who had approached me in Tranquility's parking lot the day before—the Reiki healer who had diagnosed my "bad space" and given me his card. He hadn't changed clothes; he was still wearing the blue jeans, the silver-and-turquoise cross, and the "There's No Place Like Om" T-shirt. And he hadn't changed his sales pitch—much; he was advising three topless sunbathers that they were in a bad space, and also telling them they were in a bad state. They probably thought he meant Arizona. I pointed him out to Terry and asked if he knew the man.

"Everybody knows him. Or, should I say, everybody has his business card." He laughed. "He's sort of a local character."

"I feel as if I've really arrived then," I said. "I have his business card, too."

Terry suggested we keep walking until we found a less crowded area where we could enjoy the breezes and the view in peace and quiet.

"We'll need quiet in order to tap into the vortex, is that correct?" asked Amanda.

"It's just a lot easier to connect with the land when everybody isn't on top of each other," said Terry. "That's one of the reasons people settled in the west all those years ago: so they could spread out."

"Speaking of spreading out—or, should I say, of being *unable* to spread out—my cowboy boots are a size too small for me, Tina," Amanda said testily. "I thought you ordered me a seven medium. These feel more like a six."

"Isn't the size printed somewhere on the boots?" Tina asked, apparently not as surprised by the non sequitur as the rest of us were.

"How do I know?" Amanda snarled. "I didn't turn them upside down. They're too tight, that's the point. In the heel, in the toe, everywhere."

"I'll take care of it when we get home," Tina said wearily. She was about to pull a cigarette out of the pack in her jeans pocket, then remembered Terry's admonition and decided against it.

I feel sorry for her, I thought, sorry for anyone who works for Amanda Reid. I suddenly wondered if being Amanda's husband was any easier than being her employee, and doubted it.

"Here. This ought to do it," Terry said when we got to an area that was free of other pilgrims. It was a craggy but level section of the red rocks we had just mounted—a sheltered spot where we could stand and observe not only the town of Sedona below, but the surrounding cliffs, mountains, valleys, and especially the sky, which felt close enough to touch.

Terry dropped the bag he'd been carrying, wiped the sweat that had accumulated on his brow, and extended his arms straight out into the open air. "Take a good look at this, folks. It won't last."

"What won't last?" I asked, marveling at the exquisite sight before me—a sight that blended colors and shapes and textures in a way that postcards could never capture.

"This view. This exact view," Terry explained, gesturing again toward the horizon. "When I came here over ten years ago, you looked out from Airport Mesa and saw nothing but nature's handiwork. Now you've got these trophy houses blitzing the landscape—big pink monstrosities built by yuppies from Phoenix as summer getaways. In five years, they'll be all over the place."

"Then now is probably the time to buy," said Amanda, not getting it. "Before the prices go through the roof."

Terry smiled at me and shrugged. In response, I smiled

at him and shrugged. Yet again, I felt transported back in time, this time to the English class we both took in our senior year of college. We'd sit next to each other and whenever the eccentric professor would say something particularly off the wall, we'd smile and shrug. Our secret code. The one we'd just used instinctively. As if twenty years hadn't intervened. The old days with Terry were coming back to me, whether I liked it or not.

"Frankly, I don't feel any different standing on this cliff than I did standing in the lobby of the hotel," Amanda remarked. "In terms of energy level, I mean. This *is* a vortex site, you say."

Terry reached into the bag he had set on the ground and pulled out what looked like a pair of wire coat hangers that had been bent out of their normal shape. "Come, Amanda," he said, motioning for her to stand next to him. "We're going to conduct a little experiment and you'll be our first guinea pig, okay?"

"Why not?" she said, approaching him. "I'm here to learn, as I've been telling Mr. Mandell, the journalist."

"Good. Take one of these in each hand," Terry instructed her, curving her fingers around the pieces of metal.

"What are they?" I asked as he was helping her grip them.

"Old-fashioned divining rods," he replied. "The Indians use them to divine the presence of water or valuable minerals. They also use them to divine the presence of energy fields. When you're holding the rods parallel to each other and they suddenly start to crisscross, you're in an energy field, a power spot, a vortex, whatever you want to call it."

"Sounds like a bunch of bull to me," Billy muttered.

"Hush, Billy," Amanda said. "*This* is why I came to Sedona. These divining rods must be very New Age. If they really work, I'll use them as centerpieces at my next dinner party. Blaine Trump will eat her heart out!"

"Okay, Amanda, now hold the rods steady," Terry coached. "Keep them straight out in front of you and start walking very slowly, toward Tina and the others."

Amanda began to take little baby steps across the cracked and dusty red earth, watching the rods carefully, waiting for the slightest change in their direction. "They're not crisscrossing," she whined after barely a second.

"Then you haven't hit the energy field yet," said Terry. "Keep walking."

As Amanda drew within a few feet of Tina and the rest of us, the divining rods began to cross, like swords on a coat of arms.

"Ooo! Look!" she squealed. "They worked! I'm in the energy field!"

"Are you sure you're not making them go like that on purpose?" Billy asked her, obviously threatened by his loss of control over his meal ticket.

"Of course not," she said. "I'm in a vortex right this very minute! I can feel my genitals hum!"

Terry lost it. "All right, Amanda," he managed when he'd stopped laughing. "Now turn around and walk back toward me. What we want to do is define exactly where the energy field begins and ends."

She did as she was told, humming genitals and all. As she came within a foot of Terry, the rods straightened again; she was outside the power spot.

"How marvelous!" she said. "Now what?"

"Now, we're going to let the others try it," Terry said. "Who wants to?"

Only Marie and I raised our hands. Michael was too busy taking notes, Jennifer was too busy making sure that Michael's notes were accurate—or, at least, distorted in a way that made her client look good. Billy was too busy rubbing Amanda down after her strenuous ordeal, and Tina was too busy sulking.

Marie went first. She, too, squealed when the divining rods began to move—but only because one of them nearly poked her in the eye.

When my turn came, Terry positioned himself behind me, his arms encircling me as he helped me grip the wire rods so they would remain parallel to each other. His nearness turned my *body* into an energy field. It was uncanny how the man was, for all intents and purposes, a stranger to me now, and yet all he had to do was smile at me or give me a look or, God forbid, touch me and it was as if no time had passed, as if we were kids again.

"I think I'm fine on my own," I said, pulling away.

"You always were," said Terry, the comment taking me by surprise.

I dismissed it and tried to focus on the divining rods, on keeping them straight as I walked toward Amanda and her group.

"You're getting closer," Marie called out, encouraging me, cheering me on. "Just a few more feet and you'll be in the power place!"

Moments after she'd spoken, the rods crossed and I had stepped inside the energy field—in exactly the same spot where the others had watched their rods cross. Gee, these wire things must be incredibly accurate, I thought. How else could we all have had the identical experience?

As I stood there shaking my head at the mystery of it all, I took stock of the way my body was reacting. According to Rona, when you "intersected" with a vortex, you were supposed to feel an intense, almost overwhelming kind of electricity, a bolt of energy that imbued you with a sense of power and possibility, a wave of connectedness with your surroundings.

Was *that* what was going on inside me? I wondered.

Was *that* what the heightened nerve endings and tingling fingers and toes and throbbing heart were all about? The vortex?

Maybe. Or maybe it was something else. Someone else.

"Time to move on," Terry called out, to me and the rest of our group. "We've got lots to see and do today."

I nodded, walked back to him, and handed him the divining rods.

"Time to move on," I agreed, making a conscious decision to do just that.

CHAPTER ELEVEN

♥

"What's next on our itinerary?" I asked Terry as we trudged down to the parking lot below Airport Mesa. It was nearly eleven o'clock. Almost lunchtime.

"Since there's only about an hour until we stop for lunch," he said, reading my mind—or hearing my stomach growl, "I figured I'd take you all to Bell Rock. It's close by."

"Is this Bell Rock another vortex?" said Amanda with breathless anticipation.

"Yup, and the added attraction is that it's shaped like a bell," he told her. "It's a great spot, but really noisy. They've got a road running through it now."

"Noisy? So what?" Amanda said. "As long as it has those energy fields, who cares?"

We hopped into the Jeep for the ride to Bell Rock, which turned out to be another magnificent red rock formation. But Terry was right; it *was* noisy. Never mind the major thoroughfare that wound its way around the cliff. There was also a bustling motel bearing its name, an accompanying restaurant, and several really tacky souvenir shops, all called Bell Rock This or Bell Rock That. The scene reminded me of that old TV commercial where the Indian looks out over land that's been trashed and cries.

Terry guided us up the cliff, delivering another history lesson as we climbed, but we could hardly hear him, what with the loud traffic, made even louder because sound rises. We ended up spending only about a half-hour total at Bell Rock—I think Terry felt obligated to show it to us but didn't especially want to be there. On our way down, Amanda saw something that interested her and called us all over to look.

"It's one of those crystals!" she said excitedly. She was on her hands and knees, scratching and clawing at the shiny piece of quartz embedded in the rock, desperate to pick it out of the ground. "They're supposed to give off special powers. Isn't that so, driver?"

The question was directed at Terry, who responded by grabbing Amanda by the elbow and pulling her up.

"You can't just *take* something that belongs to the land," he said politely but firmly. Then he added, in a more playful tone, "The ancient ones don't look kindly on that."

"The ancient ones?" Amanda's eyes widened.

"That's right," said Terry. "Legend has it that if you're caught stealing from their sacred land, they get angry. And if they get angry—well, we wouldn't want anything to happen to someone as nice as you, would we?"

She stood there, her mouth agape, a guilty child whose hand had been caught in the cookie jar.

I glanced at Terry, once again trying to determine if he was jerking us around or if he believed what he was saying. I couldn't tell.

"But lots of people have crystals," Amanda whined, not quite willing to give up. "I hear that Donna Karan keeps one on her desk in her office. That's why *her* clothing line makes so much money. Because of that friggin' crystal."

Michael nudged me and whispered, "Nutcase."

"Sedona has dozens of stores where you can buy crystals," Terry told Amanda, trying to appease her.

"I know that," she snapped, "but the crystal I was digging up wasn't mass-produced like the ones they sell in those stores. It would make a much better souvenir."

"The crystal you were digging up isn't a souvenir, any more than these mountains are," he said evenly, motioning toward the red rocks that enveloped us.

Amanda heaved a disappointed sigh. "Oh, all right. I broke a nail anyway," she said, then barked at Tina to arrange for a manicure the minute they got back to the hotel.

We were standing by the car, waiting while Amanda grilled Michael on whether the story he was writing about her would make the cover of *Personal Life*, when another car drove up—a beat-up blue Pontiac from about 1968. A man waved at Terry, then got out of the car to talk to him. He was tall and thin and wearing the same wide-brimmed black hat that Terry wore, his skin a darker, richer hue than Terry's deeply tanned face; his hair was coffee brown, glossy and straight, his features reminiscent of that Indian in the commercial.

"Everybody, meet Will Singleton," Terry said, introducing us to the man and patting him on the back. "Will used to be one of our Sacred Earth Jeep Tour drivers, didn't you, buddy? Before you went out on your own, huh?"

Will nodded, offering us a reserved "Hello." He spoke softly and carried a big totem, which is another way of saying he was the strong, silent type. "How come you are driving today?" he asked Terry. "Joe out sick?"

"With the flu," said Terry. "Want your old job back?"

Will shook his head. "Thanks anyway."

"You have your own tour company now. Is that it?" I asked, assuming that while Terry had the concession at Tranquility, there was competition for the other hotels in town.

"Not a tour company," Will said, his speech pattern flat, emotionless, yet not unfriendly.

"Will is Lakota Sioux," said Terry. "He's the authority in town when it comes to Native American tribal rites and rituals. I can show you the vortex sites and other sacred places here, but Will is the man if you're looking for the ultimate spiritual experience."

"The ultimate spiritual experience?" Amanda said, eyeing Will with new respect.

"I specialize in the teachings of my forefathers," he volunteered.

"What do these teachings involve and how much do they cost?" Amanda inquired. "I've come here to *learn.*"

"I think you will be fine with Terry," he said.

"Yes, but *you're* an actual Indian," Amanda said, standing back and observing Will as one would observe a Martian.

"It is true that I am a full-blooded Lakota Sioux. And my wife is full-blooded Navajo," he said proudly.

Amanda shrugged. "Lakota Sioux. Navajo. Whatever. You know, I've always wondered—can you people tell each other apart, looks-wise?"

I was so embarrassed by Amanda's question that I literally hid behind Marie, who was guzzling something from a flask and didn't notice.

Will seemed unperturbed. He was probably used to such indignities. "Each tribe has its own set of customs," he explained, not bothering to address the they-all-look-alike slur. "What I do as a teacher is to give my students an intensive course in spirituality."

"An intensive course. That's perfect, because I'm only in town for a few days," said Amanda. "When I'm through with this Jeep tour at four o'clock, there would certainly be time for—''

"Will conducts Vision Quests," Terry cut her off. "I don't think you came to Sedona for anything that heavy."

"Heavy?" She arched an eyebrow. "That's for me to decide, isn't it?" She turned to Will. "Now. What is a Vision Quest?"

"A true Vision Quest, in Native American terms, is a journey, both of the mind and spirit," Will replied. "For us, it is the traditional rite of passage, the threshold we must cross to prove our strong character, and it is quite involved, quite serious. The Vision Quests I perform for tourists are a scaled-down type of journey, sort of the *Cliff Notes* version, you might say."

"Go on," Amanda urged, becoming intrigued.

"If you sign up for a Vision Quest, I take you to an isolated place, way up into one of the cliffs, meditate with you, chant with you, and then depart."

"Depart? You mean, leave without me?" she asked.

"Yes," Will confirmed. "You would remain at the site by yourself."

"Goodness! For how long?" said Amanda.

"Twenty-four hours," he said.

"An entire day by myself! What would happen to me during that time?" she said.

"I could not say for sure, because each person's experience is different. But I do know that you would be alone at the site, without food or water or comforts of any kind, alone with nature, alone with the elements, alone with the land and the animals and your own thoughts."

"Good Lord. I don't think I've been alone for twenty-four hours in my entire life," Amanda laughed. "You see, I've had a rather large staff since the day I was born."

"Whenever *that* was," Michael whispered to me, referring to Amanda's well-documented tendency to slice years off her age.

"In a Vision Quest, it is the aloneness that brings about self-awareness," Will continued. "When you are stripped of everything you have come to depend on, you are likely to experience visions, and these visions lead you to new understanding of yourself and your connection to our Creator. After you have become one with your aloneness, your life takes directions you never expected."

"Directions I never expected!" Amanda squealed. "That could mean my own clothing line after all. Or, at the very least, a line of costume jewelry."

"If that is what Spirit intends," said Will.

"Well, count me in, sign me up, book me," she told him. "I'm ready."

"You're not serious?" said Billy, amazed. "You're gonna let this guy take you up some mountain and leave you there? Overnight?"

"Why not?" Amanda challenged.

"Because you're scared stiff of the dark, for one thing," Billy countered, causing me to wonder how and when he had come upon that information.

"And this gentleman mentioned going without food and water," Marie pointed out. "How will you manage, Madame, without a good meal and a nice bottle of wine?"

"He also mentioned you'd be out there with animals— and you despise animals," Tina muttered, "judging by all those fur coats in your closet."

"Animals do roam the cliff dwellings at night," Will conceded. "There are the coyotes as well as the javalinas."

"Javalinas? What are they, snakes?" I asked, thinking I would definitely skip the Vision Quest, self-awareness or no self-awareness.

"No. They're wild pigs," said Terry. "They travel in

packs, and since they can't see, they detect each other by their smell."

"Which isn't Chanel No. 5, I'll bet," I said.

"No," Terry laughed.

"Forget about the pigs. This Vision Quest would make a fabulous jumping-off point for the New Age book I'm planning to write," Amanda maintained. "In fact, I can envision a tie-in television documentary based on the experience. Perhaps even a feature film—a *Gorillas in the Mist* sort of picture."

"Mrs. Reid has an incredible knack for marketing, as well as a yearning to enrich the lives of others," Jennifer prattled to Michael. "Her mind is so fertile."

Maybe because of all the manure she shovels, I thought.

"Yes, I'm bound and determined to take this Vision Quest," Amanda announced, nodding her head. "The only question is when. I'll have my assistant telephone you to make an appointment when I'm ready to go forward, Mister—"

"Singleton," said Will.

"Singleton," Amanda mused. "You don't have one of those other names, too, do you? The way the Indians had in that movie *Dances with Wolves?* You know, like 'Hikes with Tourists' or something?"

I hid behind Marie again. She took another swig of her magic potion.

"Will Singleton is my name," he told Amanda. "As for calling me to book the Vision Quest, I do not have a telephone at the cabin where I live."

"No telephone?" said a startled Amanda. "How do you function?"

"Will has chosen to live simply, the way his ancestors did," Terry interjected. "His cabin is very primitive, very rustic. No phone. No TV."

"You could call my wife at her job and leave a message," Will offered.

"I'll have Tina do it. Where does your wife work?" asked Amanda.

"At the Sacred Earth Jeep Tour office," he said. "She's a secretary there. Terry is her boss."

My former husband flashed me a see?-I-told-you-so grin. God, you'd think he was the CEO of a Fortune 500 company.

"Listen, Will," he said. "After lunch, I'll be driving everybody over to Cathedral Rock. Why don't you meet us there, if you're not busy? You can lead the group, just like the old days. It'll be fun if my friends here could see you in action. I'll even pay you twice what I used to."

"I do not care about the money, you know that," said Will. "I care about enlightening people. And some people need enlightening more than others." He looked at our sorry bunch. "I'll be there in an hour or so."

We ate lunch on picnic tables in an area the locals call Indian Gardens Vortex. Set along Sedona's Oak Creek, the narrow body of water that meanders throughout the town, Indian Gardens was the geographical opposite of the cliffs we'd just visited—lush, verdant, relatively flat land. Over our chicken salad sandwiches and Evian water, Terry told us that the spirits of famous Indians—from Sitting Bull to Cochise—were said to show up in the Gardens from time to time. "Since this is a vortex, you get interesting energy here," he explained. His comment prompted Amanda to abandon her sandwich, which she had termed "pedestrian" anyway, and announce that she was going exploring. She dragged the other members of her group along with her, most of whom were still in the middle of their meal.

Once they had all scampered off, Terry and I were left alone. Neither of us said anything for a minute or two. I tried to chew my sandwich, which had suddenly turned to cardboard; Terry stared at the ant that was feasting on what was left of his. The situation was awkward, not unlike the Sundays I spent with my father.

"Tell me—how's Howard?" Terry asked, breaking the ice.

I laughed. Maybe everybody in Sedona *was* psychic. "Dad is his same warm, demonstrative self," I said.

Terry nodded knowingly. He had witnessed the way my father had treated me. He had seen the detachment, the disinterest, the apathy. And he had seen my anguish over it, how personally I took it, how, instead of saying, "Buzz off, Dad. I'm not coming to visit you anymore if that's the way you're going to act," I worked even harder to win his love. Yes, Terry had seen it all and had tried to get me to separate my father's opinion of me from my opinion of myself. And I had always told *him* to buzz off.

"His health is okay?" Terry asked. "He must be getting up there. Eighty-something, right?"

"Eighty-two, and he's in perfect health," I said. "Unless you count his disposition."

"It still bothers you, obviously."

"What does?"

"Your father's attitude toward you."

"Well, sure it bothers me. Wouldn't it bother you?"

"Look, Crystal. What bothers me is that you sound like you're stuck in the same rut you were in twenty years ago."

"Excuse me?" I couldn't believe this. Terry Hollenbeck, the former boy wonder who had turned out to be the world's most disappointing husband, was psychoanalyzing me?

"You and your father. *That* rut," he explained. "You used to keep chasing after his approval and not getting it and then feeling like you could never do enough, never measure up, never prove yourself to him. I hated watching that."

"Gee, I'm sorry I put you through such a terrible ordeal," I said dryly.

"I meant that I didn't like seeing you hurt, okay? Besides, I knew how you felt. I'd been in the same position."

"You?"

"Yeah. It's no fun turning yourself inside out chasing after someone's approval. In the end, it's your own life you've got to live, your own personal satisfaction that really matters."

"And I always thought you had such a good relationship with your father."

"I did. But I wasn't talking about my father."

"Then who were you—"

"Never mind. Let's talk about your job instead," he cut in. "You loved talking about work, as I remember. It was your favorite subject."

"Work didn't let me down, unlike other aspects of my life."

"It didn't keep you warm at night, either."

"Actually, it did. It kept the heat on. The electricity, too."

Terry smiled. "I see you're stuck in *that* rut, too, huh?"

"Some things stay with you."

"Only if you hold onto them. Personally, I think it's a good idea to let them go after a while."

"Oh, really?"

"Really. I say, hang onto the good parts and let go of the rest."

Another sermon. "I'm getting the feeling that you've decided—after spending literally three hours in my company—that I still resent you."

"Don't you?"

"Yes."

He smiled again, this time holding his hands up in surrender. "I don't blame you, Crystal. I was an irresponsible kid when we were married. It's a wonder you put up with me for twelve whole months."

Twelve whole months. His tone was sarcastic, as if he were implying that I had pulled the plug on our marriage too soon; that I should have given him more of a chance; that I should have loved him enough to let him find himself, no matter how long it took.

"I'm teasing you, sport. I *was* an irresponsible kid. I understand why you dumped me. I would have dumped me, too. But people change. Some do, anyway."

I looked at him, studied him, made sure I wasn't conjuring him up. It was so odd, our trading remarks at that picnic table in Sedona, so thoroughly improbable. In the dark of my bedroom, in the privacy of my car, in the quiet of my office after everyone else had gone home at the end of the day, I had traded plenty of imaginary remarks with him. But now that we were face-to-face, *living* the conversations, the experience was very disorienting. On one hand, Terry was my old pal, the guy who knew me when, the guy who'd seen me through the best and the worst of times. On the other hand, he was a complete unknown; I had no idea what his life had been like up to that point, what events had shaped his views of the world, what perspective, if any, he had gained about me, about our marriage. Maybe he *had* changed over the years. Maybe I was the one who hadn't.

"Hey. Why the long face?" Terry asked.

"No reason," I said, shaking off my doubts. "I was just trying to guess what it was that finally made you settle down here in Sedona, start a business, and stay with it."

"As I said, people change."

"Yes, but why did *you* change? What provoked the change?"

Terry was about to answer the question when we heard Amanda and her troop heading in our direction.

"It's a long story and there isn't time for it now," he said as he rose from the picnic table and began stacking the paper plates and cups and throwing them into the garbage.

"Wait a minute, mister. You're not getting off the hook that easily," I said. "You can at least tell me what—" I stopped, wondering if it was a woman who had reined Terry in, a woman he was willing to change for, a woman he loved more than he'd loved me. I felt a pang of jealousy and tried to mask it with a playful, casual tone. "I get it now," I said, nodding. "I'll bet this long story of yours boils down to a female. An extremely fetching female. Am I right?"

Terry glanced up at me. "Extremely fetching."

CHAPTER TWELVE

♥

Cathedral Rock, which was about midway between Airport Mesa and Bell Rock, was yet another vortex site, according to Terry, but unlike the other red rock formations he'd taken us to, this one cost money to climb. It was a tourist attraction of major proportions—a mind-boggling cluster of towering peaks which, when viewed together, did resemble a cathedral or sacred monument.

"See the rocks in the shape of a man and a woman?" Terry said, after we had marched behind him, out of the parking lot, through a grassy field and up toward the cliffs. "They're right in between those peaks there." He pointed into the sun. We squinted.

"I don't see anything," Tina grumbled.

"Neither do I," Billy echoed.

"Mon Dieu! I see them!" Marie exclaimed. "They're standing back to back, like statues, no?"

"Yes, I see them," Amanda said. "It's almost as if someone carved them out of stone."

"People say they resemble the kachina dolls that the Hopi Indians carve out of wood," Terry remarked.

"Dolls? The Indians have a line of toys now?" Amanda scowled, irritated that she hadn't thought of the idea.

"Kachina dolls aren't toys. They're religious folk art," he explained. "A lot of tribes make them now, but the Hopi have always produced the greatest variety."

"How do the dolls figure into their religious beliefs?" I asked Terry. I was still obsessing over the "fetching female" who had changed my ex-husband's life but I was trying to distract myself.

"Hopi men dress in specific costumes for tribal ceremonies, and the kachinas replicate them, right down to the masks and feathers," he said. "One doll symbolizes rain to fertilize the crops, another cures diseases, another makes children laugh. At some point during our tour, I'll drive you all to a place that sells really beautiful kachinas. In the meantime, grab a last look at the man and woman up there before we move on." He pointed again to the figures up on Cathedral Rock. "Will Singleton says they ward off evil spirits."

No sooner had Terry uttered Will's name than he appeared on a plateau just below us. Terry called out to him and waved him over. As Will ambled closer, I noticed that he was carrying a small black bag, like a doctor making a house call.

"Hey. You found us," Terry said when Will had reached us. "Now I can relax and let you take over."

Will did take over as our leader, guiding us further up the cliff and stopping when we came upon a shaded area beside the creek, where he asked us to sit near the water.

"If you're about to try the experiment with the divining rods, we've already done that," Amanda informed Will as he was opening the black bag.

"No divining rods," Will said. "I am going to heal with

crystal." He retrieved a long, rectangular-shaped crystal out of the bag. "Since Cathedral Rock is one of Sedona's most sacred places, I like to come here and use the crystal for what is called 'third eye work.'"

Third eye work, I thought. This ought to be good.

"Our third eye is located right here," Will said, pointing to the center of his forehead. "The Asians call it the spiritual chakra. It sees what our other two eyes cannot."

"That's it!" Amanda said excitedly. "I'll launch a line of New Age sunglasses that protect all *three* eyes from UVA rays."

"Just another example of Mrs. Reid's determination to help people," Jennifer reminded Michael.

"What I am going to do with each one of you is to place the crystal as close as possible to your third eye without actually touching your skin," said Will. "And then I will pull it away, very slowly, and as I do, there will be an expansion of your aura, an opening of consciousness, a greater clarity of sight. This will allow your karma to merge with the power of the land, with the power of oneness, with the power of Spirit."

I glanced at the others, wondering if they were buying this, wondering if they were *understanding* this. *What was the guy talking about?*

I looked at Terry, wondering if *he* was buying it or merely staging Will's little show as expensive but harmless entertainment for the gringos. It was hard to figure out what to believe in Sedona. Who was crazy and who was compassionate? Who was a huckster and who was a healer? How were you supposed to tell the difference, especially if you were as needy and confused as I was? For instance, how likely was it that crystals really did have restorative powers? How likely was it that the world's most complex problems could be solved by expanding our auras? For all I knew, the New Age Movement was a crock, a fraud, the placebo of all placebos. On the other hand, who was I to mock, to discount, to put down New Agers when *I* didn't have a clue how to solve the world's problems? No, I was going to try to keep an open mind, try to get into the mood, try to get my money's worth.

"I'd like to go first," I spoke up.

"Excellent," said Will, seeming pleased. He kneeled down next to me and asked me to close my eyes. "I am going to place the crystal as close as I can to your forehead without actually touching it, okay?"

"Sure."

"Do you feel this?" he asked.

"No," I said. The only thing I felt was mortified.

"How about this?" asked Will. "I am moving the crystal closer."

"No. I still don't feel it."

"How about now?" he said.

"Well, actually there is a slight tingling sensation on my forehead," I conceded.

"Good. That is your third eye communicating with us," Will said with authority. "You are ready for expansion. Keep your eyes closed and let the crystal draw the aura out."

I did as I was told, and as he moved the quartz away from my forehead I felt a sudden pressure—as if my forehead, eyes, and nose were on a string, being pulled toward Will in the opposite direction from the rest of my body. It was weird—like having part of your face sucked off. "I think my aura has been expanded," I said. "Either that or my sinuses are acting up again."

"Expansion of the aura has been achieved," said Will proudly. "You will notice a definite increase in your ability to focus and concentrate over the next few days."

I opened my eyes, focusing and concentrating on Terry, who was applauding.

"What's that for?" I asked him as Amanda and the others took their turn with Will.

"I was just having a good time watching you," he said, looking bemused. "You know, I thought about you a lot over the years, Crystal, and whenever I did, I pictured you sitting behind a desk, doing something practical. I never once pictured you here at Cathedral Rock, connecting with your third eye." He laughed out loud.

"Speaking of which," I said, "tell me the truth, Terry. Is this whole thing a goof?"

"Is what whole thing a goof?"

"Third eyes. Vortexes. Will. All of it. I realize that you've made a business out of the Jeep tour, but do you really believe in this stuff?"

"Do I believe these red rocks are sacred land? You bet. Do I believe people feel an intense sort of energy when they come to Sedona? Absolutely. Do I go along with every wacko who sets up shop here, hangs out his shingle, and claims he can save the world through numerology? No. But Will is no wacko and he's not trying to save the world. He's a sweet, gentle soul who lives his beliefs. No phony baloney."

"But Terry," I said, "do you honestly think that crystals and divining rods and all the other New Age paraphernalia work?"

"That depends on what you mean by 'work.'"

"Do they make people feel better or are they just gimmicks?"

He smiled. "You're spending five hundred big ones on my Jeep tour. You tell me."

I shrugged. "I don't know. I really don't."

"Crystal, I'm surprised at you." He shook his head. "You were always so sure of all the answers. There was nothing that the old Crystal didn't know—or think she did."

"Well, there's a lot that the new Crystal doesn't know. Take holotropic breathing, for instance."

He laughed again. "Where did you hear about that?"

"At The Clearing House over on 89A. Zola gave me the impression that when it comes to breathing, there simply isn't any other kind."

"Oh, that place," he groaned. "A complete rip-off. There's plenty about the so-called New Age Movement that's total crap, but there's also a part of it that has given us back our myths and legends. A lot of what Will Singleton does is based on the myths he was raised with, the legends his ancestors handed down from generation to generation. You don't have to take them as gospel. You don't even have to call them 'New Age' if it sounds too trendy. Just listen and enjoy the experience and see how you feel when your trip is over." He paused, removing his sunglasses as if to get a pure, unadulterated look at me, his deeply set blue eyes serious, sober. "Okay?"

"I don't remember you being so sensible."

"I don't remember you being so beautiful."

His compliment and the suddenness of it stopped me cold. No one had told me I was beautiful in a very long time. His remark catapulted me back to the past, but the way he was looking at me held me very much in the present. There was a yearning in his expression and I didn't know how to interpret it.

"My compliment made you uncomfortable, didn't it?" he said, putting his sunglasses back on.

"Not at all," I lied. "I was just thinking that you look pretty good yourself—for an old geezer."

He smiled. "I feel pretty good. Life is going well for me these days." That makes one of us, I thought. "I'd really like to tell you about it, Crystal, about how things turned around for me—without your new best buddies listening in." He nodded at Amanda and company. "Why don't you come to the house for dinner tonight? We live in a little place overlooking the Creek, about ten minutes from your hotel. I'm dying for you to meet Annie."

Annie. I had forgotten about the fetching female, temporarily. *Annie.* How homespun.

I could see her now, baking bread, sewing curtains, tending to the animals. I envisioned two or three cats, a couple of large, unruly dogs, and a parrot that had been taught to say "vortex". She was one of those radiant, full-bodied ex-hippies, I decided, a woman who never bothered about makeup or clothes or hair—she wore her natural blond locks either long and straight or in braids—a woman who was content to ramble around the house barefoot in a T-shirt and jeans, her melon-shaped breasts bouncing braless under her shirt, her skin smelling faintly of vanilla.

Annie, I thought. How sweet. At least he hadn't picked someone with one of those soap opera names like Tiffany or Ashley or, well, Crystal.

"What do you say, huh?" Terry was asking. "Dinner tonight at our house?"

I stalled, pretending my sneakers needed relacing. I wasn't ready to spend an evening with my ex-husband and his wife or girlfriend. I had only just gotten over the shock of running into him again, of having to confront why and how he had changed. Maybe in another day or so I'd go over there. Maybe in another day or so Steven would be in town and we'd go over there together. Yes, that was it: a lively foursome. Steven and I would drive over to the Hollenbecks' little love nest, ring their wind chimes, and, when they opened the door, present them with a bottle of wine or some after-dinner mints—the perfect guests. Then we would be ushered inside, introduced to the pets, given a tour of the house, and invited to sit down to eat whatever Annie had whipped up. Banana bread, probably, and something consisting mostly of tofu. It would be a very civilized evening—former spouses rehashing the old days while our significant others looked on. A delightful double date.

Who was I kidding? I didn't want to meet Annie any more than I'd wanted to meet Stephanie. Wait, let me amend that. I didn't want to meet Annie even *less* than I'd wanted to meet Stephanie.

"I'm sorry, Terry. I already told Amanda I'd join her and the others for dinner tonight," I said, winging it. "She has a very large casita at Tranquility that comes with kitchen facilities. I think Marie is cooking everybody a special meal."

"It'll be special, all right," Terry said, "if Marie stays on her feet long enough to cook it. Have you noticed the flask?"

I nodded. "She hasn't really tried to hide it. Amanda must know there's a problem, but she hasn't fired Marie, which puzzles me. According to Michael, Mrs. Reid fired several members of her staff just last week. He says she's hard on her help."

"Maybe Marie's got some dirt on Amanda," Terry said with a mischievous grin. "Aren't heiresses always being blackmailed by their unscrupulous servants?"

"Well, there was that scandal involving Doris Duke and her butler," I said. "And I think I read somewhere that—"

"I was kidding," Terry laughed. "Isn't it possible that Marie is a terrific cook in spite of her drinking, that she and Amanda go back a long way, and that Amanda is very attached to her?" He was being sensible again. The nerve.

"I find it hard to picture Amanda Reid 'very attached' to anyone," I said. "She's so superficial."

"Then why are you having dinner with her?" Terry asked. "Especially when you just got a better offer?"

He had me there. "Actually, I want to hang around the

hotel tonight anyway," I said. "In case my fiancé checks in."

"Steven. The lawyer."

"Right. He'll be looking for me."

"And he won't be able to find you at my house? We'll leave my phone number with the front desk and he can call you the minute he gets in. Oh, come on, Crystal. It'll be great to catch up. I really want to tell you what's happened to me over the last few years. And, obviously, I want to hear all about your life—how you've gotten everything you always wanted."

That clinched it. "I can't," I said. "Sorry."

I hadn't gotten everything I always wanted. Or I *had* gotten everything I always wanted but didn't want it anymore. I wasn't sure which.

CHAPTER THIRTEEN

♥

Our final stop that first day took us back in the direction of Tranquility, to Boynton Canyon, another vortex site, this one prized not only for its energy fields but for its Indian ruins. Terry and Will led us up the red rocks to one of the dwellings where, legend has it, the Sinaguan tribe lived hundreds of years ago before abandoning the area suddenly.

"No one knows why they left," Will explained as we chugged up the canyon. "Maybe they ran out of water. Maybe they were under attack. It is difficult to say. But they definitely lived here and you will get to see exactly *how* they lived once we are inside one of their dwellings. By inhabiting their space, you will feel that you actually knew them."

"Mr. Singleton," Amanda said breathlessly as she climbed. "That very same thing happened with the dwelling my husband and I purchased in the Hamptons. The former owners were a nouveau riche couple—there was

marble everywhere, even in the garage!—and all we had
to do was spend one night in that house and we felt as if
we knew those people. I had my decorator redo the place,
of course. Marble is so cold, don't you agree?''

The question wasn't directed at anyone in particular, so
nobody responded. I think we were too busy trying to avoid
all the cactus bushes in our path. I know Marie was. She
had already fallen into one and we'd spent several minutes
pulling those prickly things out of her left arm.

After about a forty-five-minute climb, we arrived at one
of the Sinaguan dwellings. It was literally a cave carved
out of the side of the canyon—primitive but amazingly
practical, particularly the separate little living spaces within
the cave that were, according to Will, allocated for different
domestic activities.

''This was their kitchen,'' he said, indicating the area
where we were standing.

''How on earth can you tell?'' Amanda asked. She was
probably mystified by the absence of a butler's pantry.

''Look at this wall,'' he said, pointing up at the rock
behind us. ''It's black, from where they burned their fires
and grilled their corn and their meat.''

''That's it!'' Amanda exclaimed. ''I'll open a New Age
restaurant called the Sinaguan Cave.''

''Mrs. Reid makes great copy, doesn't she?'' Jennifer
elbowed Michael.

''Better than you know,'' he replied, feverishly taking
notes.

''I will create a complete menu for this restaurant, no?''
Marie said eagerly.

''No,'' Amanda said dismissively. ''I'm going to import
a chef from Sedona. Perhaps Mr. Singleton has a relative
who can cook.''

''Hey, Amanda. What do you say we let Mr. Singleton

get on with the tour?'' Terry suggested. "You can ask him about his relatives later, huh?''

"Well, I suppose I could," she said with a dramatic toss of her head, which caused her cowboy hat to slip down over her nose. She righted it, then said to Will, "We can discuss the matter when we're making plans for that Vision Quest of yours."

"You're not spending the night on some mountain without *me*," Billy said in his manly-man voice, throwing a possessive arm around Amanda. "If you go, I go."

My, what chivalry, I thought. Or was it more than that? It would be such a cliché if Billy and Amanda were sleeping together, so miniseries-ish—the rich older woman cavorting with her muscular boy toy while her famous novelist-husband was off gallivanting with God knows who. But Amanda *was* straight out of a prime-time extravaganza, one of those lavishly produced Aaron Spelling-type shows from the eighties. She very likely was having an affair with her personal trainer because it was such a "yesterday" thing to do. Nowadays, people take their workouts far too seriously to have sex with the professional who is guiding them on their path to fitness. In the nineties, personal trainers are held in higher esteem than accountants, trust me.

"Billy, dear," Amanda said, patting his forearm, which was the size of a tree trunk. "Those who embark on a Vision Quest go all by themselves. You heard Mr. Singleton earlier. He explained that *one* must be *one* to achieve *one-ness*."

I laughed out loud. I couldn't help it.

"It was in this part of the dwelling that the family slept," Will said, motioning for us to move to another part of the cave, an area bordered by a wall of red rocks. "They could be close to the fire, for warmth at night, and look out through these openings"—he pointed to little spaces between the rocks—"and watch for their enemies. As you can see, the dwelling was a fortress."

"But a few minutes ago you said it could have been the Sinaguas' enemies that forced them to leave Sedona so abruptly," I recalled. "If that's true, their fortress failed them."

Will nodded. "When your enemy wants you dead, he finds a way to kill you, no matter how mighty your fortress."

Will had a very solemn way of speaking, which made everything he said seem terribly portentous. How portentous I had no idea.

Before trekking back down Boynton Canyon, Will had us sit cross-legged on the ground of the dwelling's "kitchen," told us to close our eyes, and explained that he was going to lead us in a group meditation.

We sat in a semicircle, Terry to my right, Amanda to my left. I was grateful that Will did not ask us to join hands, as I wasn't especially keen on joining hands with either Terry or Amanda.

He instructed us to concentrate on our senses, telling us to focus on specific parts of our bodies. First our toes. Then up to our feet, our ankles, our calves, and so on. By the time he reached our hips and buttocks, I was feeling quite relaxed. And when he began to chant in his native language, I became downright drowsy, drifting off into what I guessed was a meditative state, having never meditated before. I found myself thinking of absolutely nothing; there was only a blank, a rest, a stillness of my mind, and it was a relief, to tell you the truth, a little vacation for my head. Nice.

It didn't last long, though. Once Will stopped chanting and told us to get in touch with our feelings, I was forced to think about my job, my father, Steven, Terry.

Terry. Wouldn't you know that the second I turned to look at him, he happened to turn to look at me, and we were, therefore, stuck looking at each other. Soulfully. As if the look *meant* something.

My heart did a little dance, which I found extremely unnerving. The last—I mean, the very *last*—thing I needed or wanted or intended at that point in my life was for there to be even the slightest interest or longing between my ex-husband and me. So what if Terry was more appealing now than he'd been twenty years ago, all lean and rangy and cowboy-hippie-New Age-y cool? I was a certified public accountant, not the heroine of some Robert James Waller novel. Marlboro men and horse whisperers and Jeep tour operators weren't my type. Maybe they were hot stuff in bed, but I had a hunch they were losers when it came to the everydayness of life. I ask you: Can you picture the Marlboro Man doing a load of laundry, never mind adding fabric softener during the "Rinse" cycle?

Besides, even though Terry ran a thriving business, owned his own home, and had possibly even metamorphosed into a grown-up, there was no getting away from the matter of Annie, the little woman, his "gal."

"We are all one with each other," Will was saying at the precise moment that I was thinking how I wasn't one with anyone and never had been.

I was exhausted by the time I got back to my casita at 4:30, and so when I walked in the door and saw that the message light on my phone was blinking, I ignored it. Instead, I stretched out on the bed and leafed through the magazine that had been placed on my night table. It was the September issue of a monthly called *Sedona: Journal of Emergence*, and, unlike most of the magazines you find in hotel rooms across the country, it was not a guide to area shops and restaurants. It was a collection of articles with titles such as "Life on Neptune," "Channeling the Archangel Michael," and "How to Protect Children from Possession by Negative Discarnate Entities." Needless to say, I put the magazine down and dialed the hotel operator to find out who had tried to reach me.

"You had three phone calls," said the operator. "One was from Rona Wishnick. That's R-o-n-a W-i-s-h—"

"Thanks, but I know who you're talking about," I interrupted, eager to pass on the spelling bee this time.

"Your second call was from Steven Roth. That's S-t-e—"

"I'm on top of that one, too," I cut her off. "Did Mr. Roth say what he wanted or where he was calling from?"

"No. The message reads: 'Just tell her I miss her and I'm determined to prove how much,'" she replied.

Great. So I still didn't know when or if Steven was flying out to Sedona, only that his ardor for me didn't appear to have cooled.

"The third message came in just a few minutes ago," said the operator. "It was from Tina Barton, a guest in the hotel. She asked that you contact her in Casita 52."

"Tina?" I said, surprised that Amanda's assistant had called.

"Yes. T-i-n-a B-a—"

"—r-t-o-n."

"Exactly."

"Thanks again."

"You're quite welcome. Have a beautiful evening."

"Same to you." I hung up and called Rona at home, since it was after seven o'clock, her time. Unfortunately, she was out of the apartment or communing in the bathtub with Arthur or talking on the other line with Illandra, and I got the answering machine.

"We're sorry we can't take your call right now," her voice announced, "but please leave us a loving, spiritual message and we will get back to you. Now, wait for the beep."

I waited and was about to speak when Rona picked up the phone.

"Hello?" she said.

"It's Crystal, Rona. Did I take you away from something?"

"Not really. I was in the kitchen, putting Otis Tool in the refrigerator."

"You were what?"

"According to Illandra, the best way to chill someone out is to write their name on a piece of paper and stick it in the fridge."

"Between the milk and the orange juice?"

"Whatever. Otis was giving off especially negative vibrations in the office today. I thought I'd try the refrigerator thing and see if he's any less negative tomorrow."

"If not, you can always move him to the freezer," I suggested.

"That's what Illandra said," Rona marveled.

"So. You called me today?"

"I wanted to see if Steven has put in an appearance yet," said Rona. "He hasn't checked in with me since I told him where you were staying."

"He left a message, but he didn't mention his travel plans."

"In a way, it's good that he's not in Sedona yet."

"Is it?"

"Of course. When you're searching for Meaning, you don't need a man around to complicate things."

"No, I don't. Unfortunately there *is* a man around to complicate things."

"Crystal! Don't tell me you met somebody! And so soon!"

"I didn't exactly meet somebody. I was reunited with

somebody. Oh, Rona, you'll never guess who lives in Sedona now—Terry."

"Your ex-husband?"

"In the flesh. He owns the company that operates the Sacred Earth Jeep Tour I signed up for. I nearly died when he showed up this morning to take our group vortexing."

"I can't believe this. How did he act toward you?"

"He told me I was more beautiful than he remembered."

"Crystal. He's sucking you right back in, isn't he? I can hear it in your voice."

"No, of course he's not sucking me right back in. It's just that he seems to have changed, become more stable, less irresponsible. He's a mensch now, a solid citizen."

"A *senior* citizen is more like it. It's about time he got his act together. He looks great, I suppose."

"Why do you assume that?"

"Because if he were fat and bald he wouldn't be complicating things."

"Who said he was complicating things?"

"You did."

"Right."

"So how great *does* he look?"

"I don't want to talk about it."

"That great, huh?"

"What should interest you, Rona, is that he's very spiritual now. I mean, he knows all about vortexes and auras. He invited me to his house for dinner tonight. He said *Annie* would be thrilled to meet me."

"Are you going?"

"No. I told him I was having dinner with Amanda Reid."

"Yeah, like I'm having dinner with Gloria Vanderbilt." Rona laughed. "How'd you come up with that particular excuse?"

"Oh, I forgot to tell you: Amanda Reid is one of the

people taking Terry's Sacred Earth Jeep Tour. She's part of my group."

"You're kidding." Rona sighed. "When Arthur and I take trips, the only people we meet are in the doorbell business."

"That's because the only trips you and Arthur take are to doorbell conventions."

"True. So what's this Amanda Reid like? Fancy schmancy?"

"No. Ditsy schmitzy. Look, Rona. I'd love to chat, but Amanda's assistant left a message for me to call her and I'm dying to find out what she wants."

"Fine. Just promise me something."

"Anything."

"You said Terry is a very spiritual person now."

"From the little I've seen of him so far, yes, he is."

"Well, you're a very *vulnerable* person now. You're out there in Sedona all by yourself, your relationship with Steven is totally up in the air, and you haven't had decent sex in . . . what is it? Weeks? Months? Years even?"

"What was it you wanted me to promise you, Rona?"

"That if Terry offers you a little 'hands-on healing,' you'll say no."

"I promise."

CHAPTER FOURTEEN

♥

"Mrs. Reid wants to know if you'd like to have dinner with all of us tonight," said Tina Barton, her words friendly, her tone mirthless. "That's what I was calling you about."

"Oh, how thoughtful. But I'd hate to intrude," I said, wanting very much to intrude, given that I'd used the I'm-having-dinner-with-Amanda-Reid excuse to wriggle out of Terry's dinner invitation and if I intruded I wouldn't be a liar.

"Believe me, you wouldn't be intruding," said Tina. "Mrs. Reid enjoys taking in strays."

"I see," I said, feeling like a dog about to be rescued from the pound.

"Marie's making a traditional Thanksgiving dinner."

"A Thanksgiving dinner?" It was only September.

"Yes, roast turkey and all the trimmings, something reasonable for a change."

"Why? What does Marie usually cook?"

"Organ meats. You know the French."

"Well, I'd love to join you," I said, delighted not to have to dine alone.

"I'll tell Mrs. Reid," said Tina. "Dinner's at eight. Casita 2."

"Should I dress?" I asked. Not that I'd packed any ball gowns.

"Only if you want to incur Mrs. Reid's wrath," Tina said wryly. "She may enjoy taking in strays, but she doesn't enjoy being one-upped by them."

There was no chance I would be one-upping anybody, fashionwise. The only evening wear I'd brought with me was a four-year-old linen dress in a shade I like to describe as "accountant gray."

"I'll see you at eight," I said. "And please thank Mrs. Reid for including me."

"You can thank her yourself when you see her," Tina muttered and hung up. What a charmer.

I showered, threw on the gray dress, and hurried over to Amanda's place. Sure, the woman was a dim bulb, but how many times do you get to dine with a millionaire heiress? It was true that I had come to Sedona searching for Meaning, not clients, but bagging Amanda Reid for Duboff Spector would be the best job security in the world. With all that money, she had to have unspeakably thorny tax issues which would require hours and hours of work and, therefore, stimulate hours and hours of billings. Of course, if I became Amanda Reid's accountant, I'd also become one of her minions, like Tina, Marie, and the others, setting myself up for the same abuse that they took.

Everything happens for a reason.

Suddenly, I remembered Jazeem's words from the atunement.

Okay, Jazeem, I thought. What's the reason Amanda Wells Reid was thrown in my path, other than to scare me off cosmetic surgery forever? Was she destined to become a client? Or was she supposed to play a role in my personal life?

I didn't have a clue, but if Jazeem was right, there was some preordained purpose for Amanda's signing up for Tranquility's Sacred Earth Jeep Tour the same week I had. *Terry's* Sacred Earth Jeep Tour.

It was all a mystery.

Either that, or it was all bullshit.

Amanda's casita was an enormous, two-story version of the adobe building in which I was staying. Perched grandly on a hill, with staggeringly beautiful views of Boynton Canyon, her villa was at least two thousand square feet, with a living room, dining room and kitchen downstairs, two very large bedroom suites upstairs, plus its own swimming pool and hot tub outside.

"It's $10,000 a day," Michael whispered as I entered the casita. "I asked the reservations clerk."

"It looks it," I said, thinking how the rich really were different. Amanda didn't *need* two thousand square feet all to herself. She could have made do with the same accommodations I had. It was just that she was used to having the biggest, the best, the most expensive; used to spending money as if there were an endless supply of it; used to having whatever she wanted whenever she wanted it. For the second time, I wondered what it was like to be married to all that wealth, particularly if your own net worth had dwindled to next to nothing. Did Harrison Reid love his wife's money or resent it? Had he married her because of it or in spite of it? And why hadn't he come with her to Sedona? Why didn't he accompany her on any of her highly publicized jaunts?

"Crystal. There you are," said Amanda as she descended the staircase slowly and dramatically, pausing at each step as if to allow a battalion of photographers ample time to snap her picture. She was wearing clinging, extremely sheer purple silk pajamas—duds that were probably all the rage with society hostesses a decade ago but looked just plain silly now. On the other hand, who was I to talk? I felt ridiculous in my gray dress. The others were still in their jeans.

"Good evening, Amanda. Thanks for inviting me," I said. She had made it to the bottom of the stairs by then and we shook hands, another one of those dead-fish deals.

"I should have thought of asking you to dinner sooner," she said, "seeing that you're traveling alone." She glared at Tina. "Or rather, my assistant should have thought of it. It's her job to take care of the little things I simply cannot concern myself with."

Obviously, I was one of those "little things," but I smiled anyway.

Amanda ushered me into the living room, where Billy was tending bar, Tina was standing next to him, smoking a cigarette, and Michael was heading for the sofa, Jennifer in tow. I assumed Marie was in the kitchen, cooking, because I heard the crash of a plate and then a loud "Mon Dieu!"

"What can I get for you, honey?" Billy asked me in that lecherous way he had. "Something wet and hard, I'll bet."

You're disgusting, I thought, assuming he meant . . . well, you know.

"I was talking about hard *liquor*," he claimed with a wink. "You want a real drink or some wine?"

"Wine would be fine," I said primly. "White, if you have it."

"Oh, I've got it, all right," he leered at me. "I wouldn't be here if I didn't."

"No, I suppose not." He *had* to be sleeping with Amanda, I thought. He was so in-your-face about it.

He handed me the glass of wine.

"So how did you come to work for Amanda?" I asked him after Tina had disappeared into the kitchen, probably to make sure Marie didn't break the rest of the dishes.

"Tina," he said, pouring himself a tall glass of carrot juice.

"What about her?" I said.

"She's the one who got me an interview with Mrs. Reid," he explained.

"Tina? You and she knew each other before you took the job with Amanda?"

"Yeah, we met a couple of times through my girlfriend, who lived in Tina's building. When Mrs. Reid decided to hire a personal trainer, Tina got my number from my girlfriend and called me. Now, here I am, weight training with Mrs. Reid, traveling with her, whatever. You name it, I do it."

"I sensed that somehow," I said. "Were you always a personal trainer? Or did you used to do something else for a living?" Like trolling for rich widows on cruise ships.

"No, I wasn't always a personal trainer. Were you always so nosy?"

"Oh. Sorry. I was just making chitchat. You know, cocktail conversation."

He wrapped his massive arm around my shoulder and put his face too close to mine. "Hey, I know you didn't mean anything, honey. Ask me whatever you want."

I shook his arm off and moved away. "I just have one more question," I said, hoping he'd at least hint at his real relationship with Amanda. "You mentioned that you were dating a friend of Tina's before you came to work for Mrs. Reid. Are you still?"

Billy Braddick smiled. "I get it now," he said. "You're not nosy. You're hot for me."

God, the guy was a jerk. "Okay, I admit it," I said,

holding up my hands in surrender. "But I'll try to keep my feelings in check, I really will."

Billy nodded, as if this sort of problem presented itself on a daily basis, and took himself and his carrot juice into the kitchen. As Jennifer Sibley approached the bar, I realized that he never did answer my question.

"Crystal! It's great to see you!" Jennifer greeted me, her blond ponytail wagging as she pumped my hand.

"Thanks. How's Michael's article coming along? Everything going well?"

"Absolutely," she enthused, opening a can of Coke. "And to tell you the truth, I feel vindicated because I really had to coax Michael into doing the story. *Personal Life* was pretty lukewarm to the idea at first, but I pitched and pitched and pitched and they finally said yes."

"You must be a very good publicist," I said. "You obviously worked hard to land this piece."

"Sure, but Harrison's worth it." She paused, coloring slightly. "What I meant to say is that both Mr. *and* Mrs. Reid are worth it."

Well, well. What did we have here? I mused. A little crush on the famous writer? An actual involvement with him? Or just a publicist's gushing? "So you do publicity for both of the Reids?" I asked. I had assumed that Jennifer was strictly Amanda's lackey.

"Technically, I work for Mrs. Reid," she explained, "but since Mr. Reid has been between books for some time and hasn't had a publisher to promote him, he's needed someone to keep his name out there."

"And you've been the someone."

"Yes. And it's been a joy."

"Harrison Reid must be pretty special," I said, curious about the legendary novelist with the legendary writer's block.

"Oh, gosh. Where do I begin?" Jennifer sighed after

taking a sip of her soda. "He's a genius, for one thing." And a womanizer, for another, I thought. "His ideas aren't just profound, they're completely original, fresh, innovative. And yet he doesn't pontificate or force them down your throat. He's ... well ... he's a man of greatness. When you're in his presence you *feel* his greatness."

I stifled a laugh as I pictured the adoring Jennifer Sibley in bed with the legendary Harrison Reid, feeling his greatness.

God, I had to get my mind out of the gutter. Maybe Rona was right: the fact that I hadn't had a good *shtup* in a while was warping my perceptions.

"Is Mr. Reid ever going to write another novel?" I asked Jennifer.

"As a matter of fact, he's just started one," she said, as proudly as if she were the book's author. "I'm not supposed to say anything, but Mr. Reid confided to me that he's thinking of making the heroine a publicist named Jennifer."

Ah, so that's his line, I thought. He promises them he's going to put them in a novel and *then* he gets them to feel his greatness.

After Jennifer went to powder her nose, I ambled over to the sofa and sat down next to Michael Mandell.

"How's the accountant?" he asked, putting aside his notes.

"Pretty good. You?" I said.

He leaned closer so he could whisper: "I'd like to catch the first plane out of this nuthouse. That's how I am."

I laughed. "It can't be that bad, can it?"

He nodded. "I don't know what the hell I'm doing here, writing about Amanda Reid and her New Age clothes line. I'd like to wrap a clothesline around the woman's neck. She's a joke. The story is a joke."

"Then why *are* you here?"

"Because *Personal Life* wanted a story on Harrison Reid, but he wouldn't talk to us unless we did a little gem about Mrs. Reid. She wears the balls in the family, obviously."

I didn't comment.

"So here I am," he went on, "stuck in this one-horse town where everybody's on some kind of screwball head trip."

I must have looked wounded because Michael clarified his position. "Well, not everybody." He smiled at me. "You seem dangerously normal."

"Looks can be deceiving," I replied.

"Not when it comes to Amanda Reid. I mean, come on. Do I care if she wants to take that Indian guy's Vision Quest and commune with coyotes on some mountaintop? Does anybody care?"

"I don't know. You're the journalist."

"*Was* the journalist. When I started in this business, I did investigative reporting, wrote stories with depth, stories I was proud of. But investigative reporting went out with Woodward and Bernstein and now, if you don't do the celebrity fluff, you don't pay your bills. It's the way things are, but I'd give anything to cover a *real* story, something readers can sink their teeth into, something that will get me out of this rut I'm in."

"I really relate to your rut," I said. "I came to Sedona hoping to pull myself out of mine."

"Any luck so far?"

I shrugged. "It's too soon to tell."

Michael sank back onto the sofa. "I think it's too late for me. My fate is sealed. For the rest of my life, I'll be writing about pampered, self-absorbed, empty-headed celebrities like Amanda Reid, people whose idea of a 'cause' is doing anything they can to get their names in print. God, I make myself sick when I have to dig up dirt on these space cadets."

"What sort of dirt?" I asked.

"How about the fact that the millionaire heiress told me she's changed her will for the zillionth time and is now giving half her estate to The Clearing House."

"That place on 89A?"

"That's the one."

"But why on earth would she do that?"

"So they'll have the money to hire more ear coning specialists or something. God only knows." He shook his head. "Last year, she said she was leaving a pile of money to the researchers who came up with that fat substitute that gives people diarrhea."

"Swell."

"And the year before that, she was supposedly bequeathing a tidy sum to WAM."

"Which group is that?"

"Women And Men. You know, it's that organization that promotes better communication between the sexes, even though women are from Venus and men are from Mars. Personally, I think Amanda Reid is from another solar system."

"So she actually changes her will every year?"

"Just about. The woman has the convictions of Jell-O."

"How does her husband feel about this?" I asked, thinking of Harrison Reid, of how he had to be counting on inheriting Amanda's money, all of her money.

Michael grinned. "That's one of the questions I intend to ask him during our interview."

"Dinner is served," Amanda said, appearing in the living room. "At long last. It seems Marie had a run-in with nearly every piece of china in the place."

"Whatever she's prepared, it certainly smells wonderful," I said. "Thanks again for inviting me, Amanda."

"You're quite welcome," she said. "I thought it might

be a treat for someone like you to dine with someone like me."

Michael elbowed me, but I kept a straight face.

"It is a treat," I assured her. "One I'll never forget."

Marie's roast turkey was very tasty, despite the plastic bag of giblets she'd forgotten to remove from inside the carcass. The mashed potatoes and stuffing were good, too, and since I was sitting next to Marie, I had the opportunity to tell her so.

"They *are* good, no?" she said.

"No. I mean, yes," I said.

"No," Amanda snapped.

"Yes," Tina said. I think Tina was disagreeing with Amanda, but who could tell with all the yesses and noes?

"Have you been Mrs. Reid's chef for a very long time?" I asked Marie.

"Two years," she said as she downed a whole glass of wine in one swallow. "But maybe I don't work for her much longer."

"Oh? Why is that?" I asked.

Marie nodded at her employer, who was holding forth at the head of the table, yammering on yet again about Will Singleton's Vision Quest. "I worry she is not satisfied with my work. I make mistakes."

"Don't we all," I said, trying to sound encouraging.

"Yes, but I heard she is interviewing other chefs," Marie revealed. "People talk, no?"

"Yes," I said. Especially this crew. They weren't shy about spilling their guts to a complete stranger.

"The situation concerns me so I get nervous and make even more mistakes," said Marie. "I'm not young anymore, you know? The jobs are not as plentiful as they used to be. Society women like Madame Reid"—she nodded at

Amanda again—"they want handsome young boy chefs now, chefs who think food is paint."

"I'm sorry, Marie. I'm not following you. Paint?"

"These boys don't prepare mashed potatoes, like you see here on this plate. They 'create' mashed potatoes. They pipe mashed potatoes into little swirls. They make tall buildings out of mashed potatoes. They put garlic and cauliflower and—Mon Dieu!—sushi into their mashed potatoes. I have become passé, no?"

"No, Marie. No," I reassured her. "If it doesn't work out with Mrs. Reid, there will be other jobs." If you cut down on the booze.

"Thank you for saying so," said Marie. "But what I am hoping is that *Monsieur* Reid will convince his wife to keep me. He is my only hope."

"Mr. Reid likes your mashed potatoes?" I asked.

"Oh, yes," Marie said, beaming. "He makes butter swimming pools in my mashed potatoes. He pays me compliments on my cooking. It is Madame Reid who is not happy with me. If it were not for her, I could keep my job."

I nodded or shrugged or made some other gesture of sympathy. I felt sorry for Marie, but I had my own employment problems.

At some point during the meal, she announced that she was going back into the kitchen to put the finishing touches on her dessert, a blueberry pie. When she was gone, I turned to Tina, who was seated on my other side, and tried to strike up a conversation. She wasn't a barrel of laughs but she was probably my best shot if I wanted to snare Amanda as a client. She'd certainly been Billy's ticket into the Reid household.

"So," I said to Tina. "Are you looking forward to the second day of our Jeep tour tomorrow?"

"The Jeep tour? Tomorrow?" Suddenly, her eyes darted around the table. She seemed afraid, suspicious, jumpy, the proverbial deer caught in the headlights. "Why are you asking me that?" she demanded in a hoarse whisper.

"No reason. I was just wondering, that's all."

"Because you think I'm *not* looking forward to the Jeep tour? Because you think I don't believe in this whole vortex thing? Because you've decided that I'm angry and resentful that I was dragged along on this trip in the first place?"

I was stunned by Tina's outburst. "Actually, none of that even occurred to me," I said. "It was an innocent question. I wasn't insinuating anything. Honest."

Jesus. Talk about a woman who needs her aura cleansed, I thought. I've never met such a defensive person. And jittery. All through dinner, she bites her nails and plays with her hair and fidgets in her chair. And now I merely mention our plans for the next day and she freaks out. Maybe Michael was right about working for Amanda; it does take its toll. I realized that now was not the time to even broach the subject of Amanda becoming a client of Duboff Spector. Not with Tina, anyway.

During dessert and coffee, the phone rang in the casita. Tina made a move to answer it, but Amanda insisted on taking the call herself. She was gone ten minutes or so— I assumed it was her husband on the line, calling to say: How are you? Having fun? Sweet dreams, darling—but when she returned to the table she was rather coy, giving us no hint as to the person she'd been speaking to.

"I hope y'all don't think I'm terribly rude, but I think I'll say goodnight and go upstairs to bed," she said instead. "The hiking has done me in. Just done me in."

"What is it, your left hamstring again?" Billy asked. Amanda's left hamstring, as well as her other body parts, were his responsibility, after all.

"I hurt everywhere" said Amanda. "I'm not as young as I used to be."

My, I thought. That's quite an admission, considering

that Amanda *was* younger than she used to be, if you believed the various ages she attributed to herself in the media.

"Tina, you see to it that everybody has a nice time, while I toddle off to sleep," she said.

"Thanks again for dinner," I called out to her as she ascended the staircase in her purple jammies.

"No thanks necessary," she called back. "As Mr. Singleton would say, I was simply being one with the universe." There was a pause. "Or would he say that the universe was simply being one with me?"

Oblivious to how idiotic she sounded, Amanda Wells Reid waltzed down the hall to her bedroom.

CHAPTER FIFTEEN

♥

I awoke early on Thursday morning after sleeping fitfully. When I'd returned to my casita after dinner, there'd been another message from Steven, this one announcing that he was definitely headed for Sedona but not until Saturday, due to complications concerning a case he was working on. The hotel operator had reported all this to me with her usual remarkable attention to detail, not only spelling Steven's first and last names but offering to have the bellboy deliver a written transcript of the message, which I'd declined. I fell asleep soon after and dreamed that Steven had arrived in Sedona, but instead of heading straight for Tranquility when he hit town, he'd driven over to The Clearing House and said, "I'd like my aura cleansed, no starch." That's when Jazeem entered the dream, and the two of them proceeded to have sex on a bed of burning sage leaves.

As it was another warm, sunny day, I ate breakfast on my patio, washed and dressed, and walked over to the courtyard adjacent to the lobby. There was a little spring in my step as I walked, which is another way of saying that I was excited by the prospect of seeing Terry again, which is another way of saying that I was feeling hostile toward Steven because of the dream, which is another way of saying that I was as confused about my place in the cosmos as I'd been before I left New York.

When I made it to the courtyard at about five minutes of nine, I discovered that Terry and his Jeep were already there, waiting. His glossy brown hair glistened in the morning sun as he leaned against the Jeep, reading a magazine, his long, jeans-clad legs crossed at the ankles. He looked as self-confident as he'd appeared back in college, but more relaxed now, less restless, definitely "comfortable in his own skin," as that dopey but nevertheless apt expression goes. Was it just the passage of time that had matured him? I wondered yet again. Was it living in a laid-back place like Sedona that had calmed his antsy-ness? Or was it his precious Annie?

Of course, the bigger questions were: Had he changed? Did people change? Were people really, in the final analysis, capable of change?

It's so odd, I thought, as I continued to observe him from my vantage point under a tree. I still feel something for this man. In spite of the fact that I am not a stupid person, in spite of the fact that I have firsthand knowledge of his shortcomings, in spite of the fact that he and I lead different lives on different coasts, he still matters to me.

"Hey there! Are you hiding from me?" he called out suddenly, before I had a chance to make my presence known.

"Hiding? Not me," I said casually, ambling toward him. "When I didn't see you or Amanda or anybody, I decided to wait in the shade instead of out here in the hot sun."

He nodded with a little grin, as if he didn't believe me for a second.

"How was dinner last night?" he asked, tossing his magazine into the Jeep. I had assumed it was *Sedona: Journal of Emergence,* the one about life on Nepture, but when I caught a glimpse of the publication, I saw it was *Business Week.*

"Entertaining but a little disconcerting," I said. "I kept feeling as if everybody was in the cast of a bad play and I was the only one without the script. They all seemed to have an agenda, a Big Secret. It was one of the strangest evenings I've ever spent. But then, I don't get out much."

"You? Don't tell me your fiancé doesn't wine and dine you."

I laughed. Steven *whined* and dined me. The last time we went to his favorite Pakistani restaurant, he spent the entire meal complaining about his mother. "He doesn't have a lot of time for wining and dining," I said. "We both work late. Our jobs are incredibly demanding."

"So you've said. You two sound very compatible."

"Oh, we are." A lot more compatible than you and I ever were.

"So where is the guy? You said he was flying out to Sedona yesterday."

"There have been problems with a client. He's coming on Saturday."

Terry looked heartened. "Perfect. Then you'll be free for dinner tonight. My house. Seven o'clock. Done."

"But what about Annie?" I protested, groping for a new excuse. "Won't she need advance notice that you're bringing someone home for dinner?"

"Crystal," Terry said tolerantly. "You're not 'someone.' You're the woman I was married to."

"All the more reason why Annie wouldn't want you to spring me on her. Ex-wives aren't people you want to spring on anybody."

"Annie can't wait to meet you. When I told her you were here in Sedona, she was jumping up and down."

"Was she on a trampoline?"

Terry laughed. "Actually, she was. We have one in our backyard. But I meant that she was very enthusiastic."

Boy, I thought. She's fetching and she jumps up and down on a trampoline. This Annie must be beautiful *and* athletic. I was about to succumb to Terry's invitation when Amanda's troop appeared, minus the millionaire heiress.

"Morning, everybody," Terry said to Tina, Billy, Marie, Jennifer, and Michael. He checked his watch. "It's a few minutes after nine now. Is Amanda on her way?"

Tina looked surprised. "Mrs. Reid isn't around?"

Terry shook his head. "I've been standing right by this Jeep since 8:45 and I haven't seen her."

"Neither have I," I volunteered.

"That's weird, because she wasn't in her casita when we all stopped by to pick her up," said Tina.

"I'll bet she's in the gift shop, buying souvenirs," Jennifer suggested.

"I guess I should go and see," Tina said resignedly and wandered off inside the lobby.

"Perhaps Madame Reid decided to take her breakfast in the hotel restaurant this morning," Marie offered. "She did not telephone me to come and fix it for her. But after the problem with the turkey last night—"

"They have a fitness center at this place," Billy interrupted. "She could have gone there to work out, but I doubt it. She doesn't flex her pinky without talking to me about it first."

"Did anyone speak to her this morning?" Michael asked our group.

Nobody had.

"She went to bed early, I know that," I said. "She could

have gotten up early, too, taken a walk, done a little exploring on her own."

Michael waved me off. "That doesn't explain why she hasn't shown up for the Jeep Tour. She's so gung-ho on this Sacred Earth business, let us not forget."

"Maybe one of you should call her room now," Terry advised. "She could be there, changing into her cowboy outfit, on her way out the door."

"I'll do it," said Jennifer, who bounced into the lobby to call Amanda.

"Personally, I think the lady flew back to New York without telling anybody," Michael said. "Or am I projecting?"

I laughed. I knew Michael was dying to hop a plane out of town.

"She'll turn up," Terry said. "I'm just sorry we're getting a late start today. We have a heavy schedule so I wanted to shove off nice and early."

"What's on our itinerary?" I asked. "More vortexes?"

"Yup," Terry replied. "And a trip to Flagstaff by way of the famous Schnebly Hill Road."

"Is your friend Will Singleton meeting us again?" I said.

"I doubt it," said Terry. "He has his Vision Quests, remember. We were just lucky to run into him yesterday, lucky that he had some time on his hands."

"Are you saying people really sign up for those glorified camping trips of his?" Michael asked skeptically. "Enough people for the guy to make his mortgage payments on his cabin?"

"Will isn't in it for the money," said Terry. "He's in it because he believes in it. And because he loves it. How many people can say that about their jobs?"

None of us raised our hands.

"Amanda's not in her casita," Jennifer reported when

she and Tina returned. "I had the operator ring her extension twice."

"And she's not in the gift shop," said Tina.

"How about the restaurant?" asked Marie.

"Or the fitness center?" Billy inquired.

"We checked the whole building," said Jennifer. "Mrs. Reid isn't anywhere."

"She has to be somewhere," Tina snapped. "Nobody vanishes into thin air."

"The air *is* thin in Arizona, no?" said Marie.

Terry smiled. "She does have to be somewhere," he said. "Do you folks have a rental car in the parking lot?"

"Are you kidding?" said Tina. "Mrs. Reid had me get a stretch limousine to drive us here from Phoenix. I don't think she's set foot in a rental car in her entire life."

"Okay. Let me ask you something else," said Terry. "You were all with Amanda at dinner last night. Was she feeling sick? Was she upset about anything? Did she act strangely?"

"Did Amanda Reid act strangely last night? How would we be able to tell?" Michael smirked.

"She was just fine," Jennifer said protectively.

"Not quite," I pointed out. "She said she was 'done in,' that her body was sore from the hiking we did. That's why she went to bed right after she took that phone call from her husband."

"Harrison called her?" Jennifer said, the veins in her neck popping out.

"Well, I just assumed that's who it was," I conceded. "But now that I think about it, Amanda never said who the caller was. It could have been anyone."

"Yes. Anyone," Jennifer agreed, calming down.

"Let's wait another few minutes and then try her casita again," Terry said. "Crystal might be right—Amanda could have taken a walk and lost track of the time."

We waited. And waited. And waited. It was nearly ten

o'clock when Billy insisted on getting someone from the hotel to let him into Amanda's suite. He returned twenty minutes later—alone—and informed us that there was no sign of her.

"I only took a quick look, but the place seemed okay," he reported. "Nothing was stolen that I could tell. Her handbag was sitting right there on her bed, stuffed with cash."

"It is time to worry, no?" said Marie. "It is possible that Madame Reid was kidnapped."

"Kidnapped?" I gasped.

"For the wealthy, kidnapping is always a real threat," Michael confirmed. "You didn't find a ransom note in her casita, did you, Billy?"

"No, but I wasn't looking for one," said Billy. "What I found was her handbag, like I told you. I don't think a kidnapper would take *her* and leave her *money.*"

"I say we get hotel security to search the grounds," Terry suggested. "If she doesn't turn up after that, they'll bring the police in."

"Does Sedona even have a police force?" I asked, picturing cops brandishing crystals instead of pistols.

Terry nodded. "I think we've got twenty officers in the department now, two of them detectives."

"Only two detectives?" Tina said scornfully. "How in the world do they solve murders around here?"

"First of all, there hasn't been a murder in Sedona since 1995, and that case is still in court," said Terry. "Second of all, what makes you think there's a murder that needs solving, Tina?"

Tina stuck her fingers in her hair and began to braid it nervously. "I'm Mrs. Reid's personal assistant," she said defensively. "It's my job to make sure that no detail is overlooked where she's concerned. All I meant was that in the event that the worst has happened and Mrs. Reid has

been kidnapped or abducted or"—she swallowed hard—
"murdered, a two-detective police force isn't going to solve
diddly-squat."

"No, but Harrison Reid may want to call in the FBI,"
said Michael, who had shed his jaded, who-gives-a-rat's-
ass attitude the minute there was talk of kidnapping and
murder.

"I really think we're getting way ahead of ourselves,"
said Terry. "Let's start with hotel security and go from
there."

Hotel security was as clueless as the two patrolmen who
arrived at Tranquility to file the initial report on the "missing heiress," as Amanda was now being referred to. They
asked us dozens of inane questions and after two hours
came to the brilliant conclusion that Amanda had disappeared. It wasn't until the two detectives took over, discovered three drops of blood in Amanda's bathroom, and
pronounced her casita a "crime scene," that things got
serious. Tina tracked down Harrison Reid, who knew someone who knew someone who had a private jet and would
fly him out to Sedona immediately. I called Rona, who was
adamant that I switch hotels. "If it could happen to her,
it could happen to you," she warned, even though we
still had no idea what the "it" was that had happened to
Amanda. And, despite Jennifer's pleas not to, Michael got
on the phone to his editor at *Personal Life* in New York,
explaining that the article he had planned to write on the
Reids had ballooned into a much meatier, newsier story.
He also called the wire services, the network news organiza-
tions, and the tabloid TV shows, quickly establishing himself as the Dominick Dunne of the Amanda Reid case,
the journalist who was actually on the scene and could,
therefore, feed the nation with first-hand, up-to-the-minute

information. Within a few hours, Tranquility was anything but, the hotel swarming with media and other usurpers of people's privacy. So much for inner peace.

"I want to go home," I told Terry. It was three o'clock that Thursday afternoon. We were sitting in his Jeep in the hotel parking lot, hiding from all the curiosity seekers and scarfing down the sandwiches that were supposed to be our lunch on what was supposed to be the second day of our Sacred Earth Jeep Tour. I was rattled by what had occurred that morning. Amanda Reid and I were far from bosom buddies, but I'd spent an entire day with her, I'd had lunch and dinner with her, I'd meditated with her. And now she was gone.

"I don't blame you for wanting to go back to New York, Crystal, but you heard what the detectives said," Terry reminded me. "You and the rest of Amanda's pals can't leave town until they finish questioning you. You guys were the last people to see Amanda alive."

"We don't know that she isn't alive," I pointed out. "We only know that she's not in plain sight."

"Right, but you've got to stay in Sedona regardless," he said. "And since that's the case, I want you to check out of this circus and move your things over to my house."

"You want me to stay at your house?"

"For as long as they make you hang around."

I regarded Terry. His khaki shirt very nearly matched the color of his hair, a lock of which had fallen across his right eye. I had to fight the temptation to reach out and comb it back. I did not want to make contact with his forehead. God forbid I should poke him in his Third Eye.

"That's very thoughtful of you, Terry. Really. But how can I move into your house?" I said, thinking of Rona and her admonitions. "And how can I check out of this hotel? I booked the casita for ten days. They'll probably charge me for the rest of the week whether I'm here or not."

"I bet they won't charge you, under the circumstances," he said, then smiled, which created little creases around his mouth that were not the least bit unattractive. "Look, Crystal. You're shaken up about Amanda's disappearance. You're afraid it's not safe here at the hotel. You're dying to escape the media madness. My house is your best option. It's not fancy but it's tucked away in the woods. It's got a guest room that looks out over Oak Creek. And the media doesn't know it exists. Besides, if you come and stay with me, it'll give us some time to catch up, talk, get to know each other again. And if you're a good girl, I'll take you on your own, personal Sacred Earth Jeep Tour, gratis. It'll be fun showing you *my* Sedona."

Oh, why not? I thought. It really was the perfect solution. I couldn't leave town. I *was* terrified of staying alone at Tranquility. Steven wasn't coming to Sedona for another couple of days. What was the big deal? So Terry was a lousy husband. He wasn't asking me to marry him; he was just offering me a roof over my head.

"You're sure it would be okay with Annie?" I said, warming to the idea of meeting her. For all I knew, bouncing on trampolines was the "in" thing in Sedona—more New Age than having your ears coned—and she would turn out to be even more enlightened than Rona.

"I'm sure," said Terry. "What do you say I give her a call, tell her you'll be staying with us for a while, and then you and I go back to your room and pack your stuff?"

I shrugged. "I'm game if you are."

Terry was the perfect gentleman, waiting outside my casita while I packed my bags. Yes, we were married once, but it was a long time ago so I was self-conscious about him watching me fold my intimate apparel. When I was finished, he drove me over to the lobby and I checked out of Tranquility, which was quite a task. The place was jammed with reporters and photographers and TV crews, and I was lucky to make it up to the front desk without getting crushed.

"Thank you for choosing Tranquility," said Kara, the sweet young woman who had checked me in when I'd arrived. "We hope you've enjoyed your visit with us."

I stared at her in disbelief. Enjoyed my visit? I was leaving a week early, thanks to the bodily harm that had come to the hotel's most famous guest. Fortunately, Terry was right: They weren't charging me for abandoning my casita on such short notice.

"I'd like to give you a forwarding address and phone number for me here in Sedona," I told Kara. "My fiancé will be trying to contact me when he arrives on Saturday— he'll be wondering where I am."

I know, I know. If Steven was my fiancé, my man, my true love, why hadn't I called him and told him what had happened and where I was going? Why? Because I still hadn't decided if I would marry him, because I wasn't absolutely sure he'd even show up in Sedona, given his devotion to his work, and because I wasn't ready to advise him that I was leaving the hotel so I could move in with my ex-husband. Not after all the shit I'd given him about Stephanie.

Terry gave Kara his address and phone number, I paid my bill, and off we went.

Everything happens for a reason, Jazeem had said.

Jazeem's little slogan was really starting to resonate with me now, even though I was slightly resentful of her for sleeping with Steven in that dream.

I followed Terry's Jeep in my rental car. After a ten-minute drive, we pulled up to a small, white, two-story clapboard house with red shutters. It was nestled in the woods, along the banks of Sedona's picturesque Oak Creek, just as Terry had said it would be; even from my car I could hear the trickling of the creek—soothing, like a gentle waterfall.

So this is where my ex lives, I thought, still pinching myself that I was in his company again, let alone sharing his home and hearth.

He carried my bags up to the front door, put them down on the stone threshold, and hesitated before inserting the key in the lock. He turned to me and shook his head.

"I just had a flashback to the day we moved into our apartment in the city," he said. "I carried your bags to the door that day, too, remember?"

I sighed. "Seems like a century ago," I said, lying through my teeth. It seemed like ten minutes ago.

He smiled, knowing me better than my words, and opened the door.

"Honey, I'm home!" he called out as we walked inside. "Come meet Crystal!"

I heard what sounded like a high-pitched squeal and then an immediate clompity-clomp of footsteps hurrying down the stairs.

I inhaled and exhaled slowly and deeply, just as Jazeem had taught me during our session, hoping I was sufficiently attuned, not to mention attired, for my first face-to-face with Terry's special gal.

"Crystal, meet Annie," he said proudly when she raced to his side to embrace him.

CHAPTER SIXTEEN

♥

Annie *was* fetching, just as advertised. She had silky long brown hair that cascaded luxuriantly down her back, inquisitive brown eyes that held a hint of mischief as well as intelligence, a turned-up nose worthy of at least one of Amanda Reid's plastic surgeons, skin so clear and creamy it would have been a crime against nature to cover it with makeup, and a lithe little figure more in keeping with a ballet dancer than a trampoline jumper.

I said lithe *little* figure because Annie was ten years old. That's right. The lady was a kid.

"She's pretty special, isn't she?" said Terry after Annie had volunteered her age, along with her thoughts on affirmative action, welfare reform, and the balanced budget amendment. Annie wasn't just a callow youth; she was a policy wonk.

I didn't want to be rude to the child, of course, but all I could manage in the way of a response was an idiotic smile, so stunned was I that the female I'd been hearing about wasn't the melon-breasted, banana-bread-baking earth mother I'd envisioned but a very precocious ten-year-old who watched more C-Span than she did MTV, apparently.

I had assumed—Terry had led me to assume—that he lived with a grown-up person, after all, not a minor. Or had I misunderstood him, the way I seemed to misunderstand everyone in Sedona? And where was the Mrs.? The only adult female around was the housekeeper, Mrs. Peebles, who, it was explained to me later, cleaned once a week and often doubled as Annie's after-school baby-sitter.

"Dad said you two used to be married," Annie remarked as she gave me the once-over.

"Yes, dear, we were married," I confirmed. "When we were in our twenties. I hadn't seen or spoken to your father in a long, long time until yesterday."

"That's what he told me. Do you think you two will marry each other again?" she asked with the bluntness only a kid can get away with.

"Hey, you," Terry mock-scolded her, wrapping his arms around her and then tickling her stomach until she begged him to stop. When he did, he turned to me and said, with a wink, "Annie's been on a marriage kick. Ever since Alan Greenspan and Andrea Mitchell tied the knot."

I smiled. "Boy, Annie, you're really knowledgeable about life in Washington," I said to her, wondering what a little girl from Sedona found so intriguing about the goings-on in our nation's capital.

"I'm interested in government," she said proudly. "I'll probably run for President when I'm old enough."

Terry hugged his daughter. "You've got my vote, honey, but in the meantime, why don't I show Crystal the guest room and let her get settled, huh?"

"Is it okay if *I* show her?" Annie asked eagerly. When her father nodded, she lifted one of my suitcases, pretending it didn't weigh more than she did, and motioned for me to follow her up the stairs. "You can bring up the rest of her stuff, Dad."

"Yes, ma'am," he said with a little salute.

I followed Annie up to the second floor, past what I assumed was the master bedroom, past Annie's bedroom— the walls were plastered with posters of politicians, of puppies, of Brad Pitt—past a hall bath, to a small but cozy room with a double bed, a dresser, and, as Terry had promised, a restful view of Oak Creek. As I peeked out the window, I could also see Sedona's ubiquitous red rocks as well as the Hollenbecks' grassy backyard, complete with trampoline.

"My parents stay in this room when they come to visit," Terry said, setting my bags on the floor.

"How *are* Peg and Ron?" I asked.

"Great," said Terry. "My father's had two hip replacements but nothing keeps him off the slopes in the winter."

I was about to ask if Peg still skied, too, when the phone rang.

"I'll get it. You two must have so much to talk about," Annie said, tearing down the hall.

After she had vanished, I shook my head in amazement. "She *is* special, Terry. Really adorable. But why didn't you tell me you had a daughter?"

"I wanted to surprise you." He paused, his expression thoughtful, pensive. "Actually, what I wanted to do was impress you," he said, amending his first answer. "When we were married, you never thought I'd amount to anything, not that I can blame you. Well, Annie is proof that I amounted to something."

"Terry, you've done very well, from what I can see," I said, observing my surroundings, which weren't lavish but seemed comfortable. "There's your tour business and the real estate investments you were telling me—"

"It's Annie who made it all happen for me," he cut me off. "If it weren't for her, there wouldn't be a tour business or real estate investments or anything else, including this house. I'd be exactly the way you remember me: lost, adrift, hopping from job to job, waiting to grow up. Annie didn't just change me. She reinvented me."

"How?" I said. Middle-aged parents were always going on and on about how having kids later in life changed them, forced them to rethink their priorities, put them in touch with the child inside them, yada yada yada. But I had a feeling there was more to Terry's relationship with his daughter. "And where's her mother, if you don't mind my asking?"

"Somewhere. Anywhere. Gone." He shrugged.

"You don't know where she is?"

"Not a clue. She left town when Annie was a week old."

"You're not serious."

"Oh, I'm very serious. If you thought I was irresponsible, you should have met Gwen. She wins the prize."

"She left her own daughter when she was an infant?" I asked, incredulous. "That beautiful little girl downstairs?"

"Yup. Annie doesn't remember her at all, obviously."

"But why, Terry? What happened to make her leave?"

He hesitated for a moment before responding. "Gwen was a quote-unquote Free Spirit," he said finally, "always up for something new and different. We met when I was knocking around in Boulder, about four years after you and I split up. She and I were in the same 'space,' as they say here in Sedona. We were both immature and restless and looking for ways to ignore the fact that we didn't know what the hell to do with our lives. So we traveled together, taking jobs wherever we landed. We had a lot of laughs, a lot of adventures. Gwen was a wild one, the just-do-it type."

"My polar opposite, you mean."

"Your polar opposite."

"Was that on purpose? I mean, did you deliberately set out to find the anti-Crystal?"

He smiled. "Sure, I did. You were—you *are*—very focused, very directed, Crystal. You've always known exactly where you were going, what you wanted to do. But when we were married, I couldn't get it together fast enough to keep up with you, to keep from disappointing you. After we broke up I figured that the next woman I hooked up with should be as undependable as I was. That way, there wouldn't be any disappointments. Timing is everything, you know?"

"Everything," I agreed, still marveling at the change in my ex-husband. In the old days, he was completely unself-exploring, never analyzing or even discussing his actions except to joke about them. "Were you happy with Gwen?" I asked him.

"For a while. We came to Sedona and fell in love with the place. It was as gorgeous then as it is now but minus the casinos, the golf courses, and the astrologers on every corner. We stayed. Gwen got pregnant. We both said, 'Cool. Another new experience.'"

"But it wasn't cool?"

Terry shook his head. "Gwen gave birth only six and a half months into the pregnancy. Annie was a preemie— three pounds, six ounces when she was delivered. The doctors told us she might not make it."

"Oh, Terry. That must have been awful."

"It *was* awful. Annie had a million things wrong with her, not the least of which were her undeveloped lungs. She had to be rigged up to a ventilator until she could breathe on her own. She didn't come home from the hospital for three months."

"But you said that Gwen left town after a week."

"That's what I said. The minute it dawned on her that she couldn't just drop a kid out of her womb and move on to the next Life Event, that she had actually brought another *person* into the world, a child who would need love and support and, possibly, long-term medical care, she couldn't handle it, couldn't deal with the responsibility. Within days after being discharged from the hospital, she was out of here. Gone. So long, Terry. So long, baby daughter. She didn't even wait around long enough to name Annie. I named her the day Gwen took off, and I haven't seen or heard from the lady since. Will Singleton said at the time that it must be my karma—I flaked out on you, so Gwen turned around and flaked out on me."

"Listen, Terry. You can't keep beating yourself up about us," I consoled him. "You've got to let go of the past."

"Oh, you mean the way *you* have?" he said wryly.

He had me there. I decided to change the subject. "You and Will have known each other since Annie was born?" I asked.

"Since I came to Sedona," said Terry. "Will and his wife, Jean, were our first friends here. He's like an uncle to Annie." He smiled. "He explains Native American traditions to her and she explains campaign-finance reform to him."

I laughed. "Before we get off *that* subject, how did Annie become so interested in political issues? It's pretty unusual for someone her age, isn't it?"

"I don't have any idea," Terry said. "She didn't get it from me. I majored in political science in college, as you may remember, but I've forgotten most of what they taught me. I think Annie just likes the idea of good citizenship, of public service. I told you, she's a special kid, and I'm not saying that because I'm her father."

I sighed, thinking of my own father, who was probably planted in his BarcaLounger right that very minute, deeply involved in an episode of "The Rockford Files."

"So tell me what happened after Gwen left," I urged

Terry. "You were all alone with a critically ill newborn in the hospital. How on earth did you manage?"

"I didn't have any choice," he said. "I suddenly had someone depending on me, someone who couldn't survive without me. I suddenly had a *reason* to change."

"*I* wasn't reason enough?" I asked before I could stop myself. "I was your wife. I was depending on you, too." So much for letting go of the past.

"I never viewed you that way, Crystal, I really didn't. You always struck me as someone who would survive just fine without me. And I was right."

He was right. I had survived just fine without him. It was only my chakras that weren't in such hot shape.

"I interrupted you," I said. "You were telling me how having Annie depending on you changed you."

"It changed me and my lifestyle. After she was born, I couldn't live minute to minute anymore. I couldn't think about pleasing myself twenty-four hours a day. There was another mouth to feed and I was the one who was left to feed it. I had to create a stable environment for her to come home to. I was in charge of getting her well, sending her to school, making it possible for her to lead a normal life. How did I do that? During the three months she was in the hospital, I came up with the idea for the Jeep Tour business. My father lent me money to get the company off the ground. When they let Annie out of the hospital, my mother came and helped me take care of her. Jean Singleton helped, too. I bought this house. The business did well. I paid my father back. Along the way I learned how to be a parent—and in learning how to be a parent, I learned how to be a man."

Swell, I thought. He's not only better looking now than he was twenty years ago; he's Mr. Sensitive *and* Mr. Responsible, an impossible combination to resist. It may have taken a while, but he's become the person I'd always hoped he'd become, the person I'd always dreamed he'd become. And I? Well, I had *accomplished* a lot in twenty years, too. I hadn't raised a child all by myself or created a business from the ground up, but I'd made the big bucks and found a man who wanted to marry me and—

Oh, come off it, Crystal, I chided myself. Timing *is* everything, just as Terry said. Twenty years ago, he was the one who was searching for an identity and you were the one who knew what you wanted out of life. And now, your roles are reversed. Face it: He's the one who's found inner peace and you're the one who's out here trolling for it.

I was wracking my brains for something appropriately pithy to say—something involving Beauty, Truth, etc.—when Annie bounded into the room.

"Who's on the phone, honey?" Terry asked, gazing at her with utter devotion.

"A friend of Crystal's named Rona," Annie said excitedly. "She's calling long distance. From New York."

Rona. Obviously, she had tried me at Tranquility and the ever-efficient operator had forwarded the call to Terry's number. I could just picture her face when she found out I had moved in with the very man she'd warned me to stay away from.

"Would you two excuse me?" I said.

"Sure," said Terry. "Go ahead. The phone's in the kitchen."

I thanked him and went downstairs to speak to Rona, who cross-examined me about Terry's house—how many bedrooms he had, whether my room was adjacent to his, things like that.

"Just say it," I challenged her. "You want to know if Terry and I will be sleeping in the same room."

"I want to know if you and Terry will be sleeping in the same room."

I laughed. "No. I'll be ensconced in the guest room.

Down the hall from the master. It's an *arrangement*, Rona. Strictly platonic. Terry's helping me out of a tough situation."

"And I'm the Queen of Sheba."

"Sheba, too? I thought it was Siam."

"Don't make fun."

We chatted for a few more minutes. After we hung up, I went back upstairs to Terry and Annie.

"Your friend told me she worries about you a lot," Annie commented. "It probably gets on your nerves sometimes, but it only means that she cares."

I smiled at her, at her wisdom, at the old soul inside the girlish body. I had never spent much time around children—I had always found them repetitive, not to mention messy—but within minutes, this child had managed to win me over.

"I'm lucky to have Rona for a friend," I told her. "Do you have a best friend, Annie?"

She was pondering the question when the phone rang a second time.

"I'm sorry," I said. "It's probably Rona again, calling to remind me to wash behind my ears."

"I'll get it," Annie said, jumping up from the bed and sprinting down the stairs.

"She's got a lot of energy, your daughter," I said to Terry. "It must be all the vortexes around here."

Terry smiled. "It's either the vortexes or the fact that she's only ten years old. Ten-year-olds have a lot of energy, as you'll see."

Terry and I talked for another minute or two, then he went to get me an extra blanket and some fresh towels. Only seconds after he returned, Annie came flying back into the room, this time her face flushed with fear. She may have possessed a wisdom beyond her years, but at that moment she looked every bit the scared little girl.

"What is it, honey?" Terry asked with concern. "Who was on the phone?"

"It was Aunt Jean," she said breathlessly, referring to Jean Singleton, I guessed.

"Is there a problem at the office?" he said. I remembered then that Will Singleton's wife worked for Terry's Sacred Earth Jeep Tour company.

"No. It's about Uncle Will," Annie told her father, her lower lip beginning to quiver. "Aunt Jean said the police took him down to the station, to question him."

"Question Will? What the hell for?" Terry said with a mixture of confusion and indignation. "He's never even had a parking ticket."

"Aunt Jean said they think he killed that lady. The one who was missing from Crystal's hotel. The one who signed up for your Jeep Tour, Dad," Annie managed before dissolving into tears.

PART
T•H•R•E•E

CHAPTER SEVENTEEN

♥

There was good news and bad news for Will Singleton. The bad news was that the police were convinced that he murdered Amanda. The good news was that, since they couldn't find her body, they couldn't arrest him. Without a corpse, without lab test results, without definitive proof that there actually was a murder, they weren't about to throw Will in jail. Yet.

"But why you, Will?" Terry asked his friend when we had all gathered on Terry's screened porch at about eight o'clock that Thursday evening. "You'd never hurt anybody."

"That's right, Dad. Uncle Will doesn't hurt people. He heals them," said Annie, who was sitting next to me, acting brave in spite of the situation.

She was so cute that I was forced to grab her hand and squeeze it. I couldn't remember the last time I'd grabbed anyone's hand and squeezed it, much less a child's. Annie responded by giving me a quick peck on the cheek. Boy, were we bonding.

"The County Attorney, Dennis Cooley, believes Will had the means, the opportunity, and the motive," said Jean Singleton, a plump, plain-looking woman who seemed to be parroting the legalese she'd been hearing in an effort to make sense of it.

"Let me tell you all what happened and maybe you can figure it out," said Will. "Yesterday afternoon, after Terry brought Mrs. Reid and the other passengers back to the hotel, she called Jean at the office and said she wanted to leave a message for me. I had told her I have no phone at the cabin."

Jean nodded, confirming that Amanda had indeed telephoned the Jeep Tour office.

"You mean the woman was serious about wanting you to take her out on a Vision Quest?" Terry asked in amazement.

"Very serious. I did not have time to call her back until later that night," said Will. "She was in the middle of dinner and she was unhappy that she did not hear from me sooner."

"That's no surprise," I said. "It isn't nice to speak ill of the Disappeared, but Amanda didn't strike me as the most patient person on the planet."

"She was definitely in a big, big hurry," Will agreed. "She said that the Jeep Tour was not giving her the spiritual awakening she was seeking in Sedona. She told me she wanted to speed up her growth. She said she was being written about in a famous magazine, that the magazine had a deadline, and that the reporter needed something 'dramatic' to say about her."

"He's got something dramatic now," I said, remembering how desperately Michael had wanted a *real* story to cover.

"So you said you'd take her on a Vision Quest?" Terry asked Will.

He nodded regretfully. "Mrs. Reid was determined to go, no matter what I said."

"You know, it's odd that Amanda went to you directly to make the arrangements," I told Will. "She usually had Tina, her assistant, handle all her appointments."

"She said it was nobody's business if she did the Vision Quest," Will explained. "She didn't want any of the others to know about it."

"She probably figured they'd try and talk her out of it," I offered.

"That could be," said Will. "Anyway, I went along with her wishes. I thought I could help her."

"And now they think you killed her," Jean Singleton said, shaking her head with the irony of it all. "It isn't fair, is it?"

"No, it isn't. Tell us what happened next, Will," Terry urged.

Will sighed before continuing with the story. He was slumped in his chair, his eyelids heavy with exhaustion. "At four o'clock this morning, I drove to Tranquility to pick up Mrs. Reid," he said.

"Four a.m. That explains why she wanted to go to bed early," I said.

"When I arrived at the hotel's front gate, I stopped and told the guard I was picking up Mrs. Reid," Will went on. "He called her room. She must have said everything was okay because he waved me through without a problem."

"Without a problem?" Jean said, becoming more agitated. "It was that hotel guard who told the police about you, Will."

"He did what he thought was best, Jean. Besides, why should I deny that I was with Mrs. Reid this morning? I have nothing to hide. I did nothing wrong."

"You did nothing wrong," everybody echoed in unison, like a Greek chorus.

I regarded Will then, regarded all of them, and was suddenly struck by how weird the whole scene was, totally surreal. I mean, there I was, an accountant from New York—a CPA whose idea of a big night was taking work home instead of staying late at the office. What in the world was I doing in Sedona, Arizona, the mecca of *meshuggenehs*, sitting around the house of the ex-husband I hadn't seen in twenty years, holding hands with his daughter, discussing the possible murder of the millionaire wife of a famous novelist, attempting to show my support for the Lakota Sioux guide whom the police had dragged from his primitive cabin and fingered as their prime suspect? Talk about a change of scenery.

"After I picked up Mrs. Reid at Tranquility, I drove her out to Cathedral Rock," said Will. "We hiked up the cliffs to an isolated corner where I like to take people for Vision Quests. It was still dark at that hour of the morning and Mrs. Reid was afraid."

"Afraid that she would slip and fall?" I asked.

"Afraid that she would break a nail," said Will.

There were jeers all around.

"It sounds unbelievable but it is the truth," Will maintained. "Mrs. Reid was upset that someone might see her with two bad nails. She told me she broke a nail yesterday, when she tried to dig up a crystal at Bell Rock."

"I remember," Terry groaned.

"The finger was bleeding when I picked her up at the hotel," Will added. "She said she did not know how to fix it."

Gee, she must have been out of Krazy Glue, I thought uncharitably.

"The bleeding finger probably accounts for the three drops of blood the police found in her bathroom," said

Terry. "But three drops of blood from a broken nail are hardly signs of a struggle. They've got to have more on Will than that."

Will shook his head wearily. However innocent he was, he sensed that circumstantial evidence was mounting against him and that even innocent men could be found guilty. "Once we got all the way up the canyon, to the spot I had chosen, I spread a blanket down on the rock and Mrs. Reid sat on it. I told her the Vision Quest was now beginning. I used crystals to activate her chakra centers, I smudged her with burning sage to cleanse her aura, I fanned her with hawk feathers to draw out any illness inside her, I chanted to the Creator and asked him to watch over her, and then I left."

"And she was perfectly fine when you left?" I asked.

"Except for the fingernail, yes," said Will. "I told her that I would be back for her tomorrow morning at four o'clock and that when I did come back for her, we would discuss her journey. I assured her that within twenty-four hours, she would feel one with nature, one with Spirit, one with herself."

"Then you were just doing your job, Uncle Will," said Annie. "I don't understand why the police think you killed the lady. She's not dead, she's meditating. She's up there on Cathedral Rock right now."

"She isn't. That's the trouble," Jean said, wringing her hands. "After the hotel guard told the police about Will driving off with Mrs. Reid this morning, they brought him in for questioning. He explained about the Vision Quest. One of the detectives said, 'Okay, Sitting Bull.' That's how he spoke to Will, with disrespect. 'If you know where she is, take us to her. Show us where she is and you'll be off the hook.' Will took them up to his spot on Cathedral Rock. Mrs. Reid wasn't there. Mrs. Reid wasn't anywhere."

"Maybe she wandered off in the dark and couldn't find

her way back," said Terry. "The woman probably got bored, picked up the blanket Will had given her to sit on, and parked herself somewhere else on Cathedral Rock."

"They organized a search party," said Will. "They even flew over Cathedral Rock in a police helicopter. They could not locate her. They think I hid her body, threw it off a cliff or something."

"Cathedral Rock is one giant rock formation after another," Terry pointed out. "A person could be up there for months and you'd never find him. Or her."

"No matter," said Jean. "The police are sure Will is a murderer. To them, the simple fact is that he took her from the hotel and now she's gone."

"What about the blanket?" I asked suddenly. "Was that gone, too, when the police came to look for Amanda?"

"You know, I do not remember," Will admitted. "I was so surprised not to find Mrs. Reid where I left her that I forgot all about the blanket."

"Jean, a few minutes ago you mentioned that the police think Will had the means, the opportunity, and the motive to murder Amanda," I said. "Opportunity, I understand. He *was* alone with her. But means? Isn't that another way of saying he had the murder weapon?"

Jean shrugged. "Maybe they believe he killed her with his crystals or his totems or his deck of Tarot cards," she said with disgust. "Hit her over the head with them."

"Yeah, right," said Terry. "And what about motive? What reason was Will supposed to have had for killing her?"

"Money," Jean said. "Amanda Reid has it. Will Singleton doesn't."

"Will doesn't give a damn about money and he never has," Terry said angrily.

"*We* know that but the police don't," Jean reminded him, her tone tinged with bitterness. "To the cops in this sleepy little town, Will Singleton is just another redskin who got loose from the reservation."

"Did Amanda pay you, Will?" I asked. "For the Vision Quest?"

"She did, yes," he said. "In cash. I charge one hundred sixty-five dollars for the twenty-four-hour quest."

"Now I really don't get this. Do the police think you wanted more than that?" Terry said. "Do they think you demanded more, she wouldn't give it to you, so you killed her and disposed of the body? Give me a break!"

"We should call up the President," Annie suggested. "I bet he could help Uncle Will."

"Nice thought, honey, but the President's a pretty busy guy," said Terry. "I don't think he has time to help."

"What *are* we going to do?" Jean Singleton asked. "How are we going to keep Will from going to prison?"

Before I could stop myself, before I realized what I was saying, before it dawned on me that I might be biting off more than I could chew, I announced resolutely: "I, for one, am going to find out what *really* happened to Amanda Reid. That's what."

Everybody looked relieved then, as if it were a given that I would save the day. Sure, I was tenacious when it came to solving my clients' tax problems, but tracking down disappearing heiresses wasn't exactly in my line of work. What's more, I still couldn't find my way around Sedona without the map that the rental car lady had given me at the airport. And, of course, I had only just met Will Singleton and his wife; I had no particular allegiance to them other than that they were important to Terry and Annie. For all I knew, Will *had* murdered Amanda, stolen all her money, and stashed her body in one of those Indian ruins.

"It's nice of you to offer to help me, Crystal," Will said. He walked over to me and shook my hand. Then he chanted something at me—something in his native language. It could have been: "Sure, I killed her, you gullible tourist." But since I didn't understand Lakota Sioux, I simply nodded.

"Crystal is a kind woman, Terry," Jean Singleton told my ex-husband. She smiled for the first time all evening. "You always spoke of her great drive and determination, but now I see her caring nature, too. I will never forget the fact that she has taken up our cause—and after spending only a short time in our company." She faced me, pressed her hands together, and said, "Bless you, dear."

Yikes, I thought. What have I gotten myself into?

The Singletons said they were going home and that they would be sure to include me in their nightly prayers to "Spirit." I thanked them and said they shouldn't worry about the police investigation.

"Sleep well and don't let the bedbugs bite," I chuckled, then realized that I wasn't sure if the Singletons slept on a bed; that it was entirely possible that their primitive cabin didn't have a phone, a TV set, or a bed. Not only that, for all I knew, people in Sedona considered bedbugs to be sacred and getting bitten by one was an honor.

"Crystal and I will do some poking around tomorrow," Terry promised his friends. "I'll talk to people, ask if anybody knows anything. And she'll go and see the folks Amanda was traveling with. She's on a friendly basis with them, right, Crystal?"

"Well, 'friendly' might be overstating the—"

"She had dinner with them last night," Terry told the Singletons. "She came away from the evening thinking they each had some kind of hidden agenda."

He glanced at me for confirmation. I smiled weakly, feeling the pressure building.

"Maybe she can wear them down," he went on. "Get one of them to take responsibility for this mess."

He glanced at me again.

"What do you say, Crystal?" he asked expectantly.

I straightened my posture. "Sure I can," I said, wondering how.

CHAPTER EIGHTEEN

♥

It was nine o'clock by the time the Singletons left, closer to Annie's bedtime than her dinnertime, but Terry was reluctant to let her go to sleep without a decent meal.

"What kind of a father would I be if I sent you to bed without your supper?" he said, tussling her hair.

"I'll be in bed by ten," she promised. "First, you and I can make scrambled eggs and bacon for everybody."

"That's breakfast stuff, honey. Maybe Crystal wants real food," Terry said.

"I'd love some scrambled eggs and bacon," I said, thinking they should only know that what I usually ate for dinner came in a can.

"Then eggs and bacon it is," said Terry. "Let's go."

Within seconds, he and his daughter were at work together in their yellow-and-red country kitchen, Annie whipping up the eggs, Terry frying up the bacon, each one knowing just what to do—no standing around waiting for instructions. It was as if they were performing a well-choreographed dance, each sliding effortlessly into his part. They were obviously a very close father and daughter, a father and daughter who were in sync with each other, who interacted seamlessly, who enjoyed a relationship entirely different from the one I "shared" with my own father.

I felt envious, of course, and a bit left out. But then I reminded myself that, as perfect as the Hollenbecks' home life appeared, Annie didn't have a mother, had never laid eyes on her mother, had no idea whether her mother might ring the doorbell someday and say, "Guess what? I'm back!" That had to be rough for a kid: the abandonment, the uncertainty, the it-must-have-been-my-fault. And what of *my* sudden appearance, I wondered, *my* sudden "Guess what? I'm back!" Was it confusing to Annie to have her father's ex-wife waltz into her world? Did she have fantasies that I would stay, step right into the role of her mother, and make us a real family, whatever *that* was?

"Hey, Crystal. Do you still like your bacon extra crispy?" Terry asked, interrupting my fantasies.

"I do," I said. "I'm surprised that you remember."

"I remember a lot of things," he said as the bacon sizzled in the pan, filling the kitchen with a wonderfully smoky aroma.

"For instance?" I prodded.

"He remembers that you sleep with the window open, even in the winter," Annie giggled, "and that you keep a glass of water next to your bed but never drink any of it."

So Terry really had told her about me. Even the silly little details.

"Your father has a good memory," I said. "But *I* remember a few things about him, too, Annie."

"Like what?" she asked, fascinated.

"Well, have you noticed that when you try to wake him

up in the morning, he'll say, 'I'm already awake,' and then go right back to sleep?"

She giggled again. "Sometimes it takes me six tries to get him out of bed. Especially on Mondays."

"You see? And I'll bet he still talks about wanting to learn how to play the saxophone."

"Nope." Annie shook her head. "He knows how to play it now. Cynthia taught him. She can play just about any musical instrument there is."

"Who's Cynthia?" I asked.

"My friend Laura's Mom. She and Dad go out."

"They go out. How about that?" I said cheerfully, my face frozen into a smile, my appetite suddenly gone.

"Don't worry, Crystal. They're just friends," said Annie, who, I decided, was not a ten-year-old; she was a forty-year-old in a ten-year-old's body.

While she went on about Cynthia and her musical talents, I realized that there were probably lots of Cynthias, lots of women to amuse Terry. However devoted he was to raising his daughter, he couldn't have been living like a monk since Gwen skipped town. He was an attractive man. He liked women. Women liked him.

Some things about a person don't change, I thought, imagining Terry making slow, sensual love to the sirens of Sedona, even as I ordered myself to cut it out.

"She's not worried," Terry assured his daughter. "Crystal has a rich, full life of her own. Now, how are those eggs coming, honey?"

"Done," she said, lifting the pan off the gas stove and dividing the spoils among the three plates she had laid out. Once we all sat down to eat at one end of the Hollenbecks' long, pine kitchen table, there was no further talk of Terry and his saxophone teacher. There was talk of some of the people he and I had gone to college with: He had heard that Dick Pelton was a cardiologist in Chicago now and I had heard that Beth Valk was a housewife in La Jolla and both of us had heard that Chip Gilbert was a golf pro knocking around on the senior circuit. It was interesting that neither of us had kept in touch with any of our friends from school—I, because I'd been so focused on my career; Terry, because his life had been so nomadic until he'd settled in Sedona. Still, it was fun invoking the names of those we'd known once upon a time, fun summoning up the old faces, the old feelings, fun remembering what it was like to be nineteen, twenty, twenty-one years old.

"Bedtime," Terry told his daughter eventually, after we had finished dinner and dissected the lives of practically everybody in our graduating class.

Annie, who had enjoyed our reminiscing at first, was tired now and offered little resistance. She got up from the table and kissed him good night. She hesitated as she stood next to my chair.

"Are you going back to New York as soon as the police say you can?" she asked, rubbing her eyes.

I wasn't sure if she was hoping for a yes or a no.

"Yes," I said. "New York is where I work, Annie. It's where I live."

"Crystal is getting married, sport," Terry told her. "Her fiancé is coming to Sedona on Saturday so they can be together. When their trip is over, they'll be going home for the wedding."

Annie pondered the information for a second or two before leaning over and kissing my cheek. After she pulled away, she sashayed out of the kitchen, wagging her finger at Terry and flashing him a mischievous grin.

"Crystal is marrying that man like I'm marrying Trent Lott," she said and bounded up the stairs.

When she was gone, Terry shrugged. "Don't blame me. I'm just her father."

I smiled, but Annie's words had stunned me. Did she know something I didn't? Did she know me better than I knew myself?

"You okay?" Terry asked as we sipped coffee. "Annie was being Annie. She likes having fun with people, likes being the smarty-pants. She didn't mean anything, honest."

"Terry, I have a confession to make," I blurted out before I could stop myself. "Steven isn't exactly my fiancé."

"He isn't?"

I shook my head. "We'd been seeing each other for three years when I found out his ex-wife was back in his life. I threatened to break up with him. He panicked and asked me to marry him. That's the long and short of it."

"So you haven't said yes?"

"No. There's no wedding date. We're not engaged. I don't even know if I'm going to marry Steven. Ever."

"Then why did you let me think the marriage was a foregone conclusion?"

"The same reason you let me think Annie was your wife." My eyes met his. "I wanted to impress you."

"Is that right," he mused, looking surprised and delighted. He reached out and tugged playfully on the ends of my hair, another reminder of the past. "Why did you want to impress me, Crystal? I thought you resented me."

"I thought I did, too."

"I see." He continued to play with my hair. I was glad I had washed it that morning with Tranquility's Spiritually Herbal Shampoo and Conditioner. "Should we talk about this?" he asked.

"Talk about what?"

"About the fact that you don't resent me anymore. About the fact that I'm so happy to see you again that I don't know what to do with myself." As he posed the questions, he let my hair slip through his fingers and moved his hand over to the cleft in my chin, inserting his thumb there and rubbing the tiny crevice gently, back and forth, until I was practically purring. "One of my favorite places on your body," he murmured.

I didn't ask what his other favorites were. I removed his hand from my chin so I could speak. But no words came out.

"Look, Crystal. I'm not going to pretend I'm sorry you showed up in Sedona," he said, his hand on my knee now. "Running into you was one of the nicest things that's happened to me in a long, long time—a miracle, if you really want to know. I always felt there was unfinished business between us. I always hoped I'd see you again so I could show you I turned out okay. I always hoped I'd see you again—just, well, so I could see you again. So this is a big deal for me, having you here. There's no downside to it. Sure, I wish your lawyer friend wasn't coming the day after tomorrow, because I'd rather have more time alone with you. But I'll take these few days. I'll take them because I never expected to have them. I'll take them and make the best of them."

Oy vey, I thought, as Terry's fingers traced little circles on my kneecap. Rona was right: I *am* getting sucked back in. I still find this man achingly appealing. I still—what? Still want him? Love him? Want him to love me? Did I? Or was it all a cruel case of déjà vu? Was my heart beating for him now because it used to beat for him then, the way people who lose a leg can still feel the limb? Were my feelings real or were they Memorex?

"I'm confused," I told him. "At a fork in the road, so to speak. That's why I came to Sedona, Terry. To reevaluate everything—Steven, my work, my relationship with my father, the whole mess." I paused. "And I came to have my aura cleansed, of course."

"Of course." He smiled.

"So, given all my confusion, I don't think it's a good idea for you to run your fingers through my hair or rub your favorite places on my body or anything of that nature."

"No physical contact of any kind?" he teased.

"No."

"No discussion of how good you still feel to me?"

"Please."

"What if I can't hold myself back?"

"Try."

He laughed.

"Listen, I want you to know that I'm happy to see you, too, Terry," I admitted. "It just makes me nervous to talk about it."

"What's safe to talk about then?"

"Amanda. I told Will Singleton I would find out what happened to her. That takes precedence over whether or not you and I find each other irresistible, doesn't it?"

"For now," he agreed. "But only because Will's such a good friend." He leaned back in his chair. "So. Talk."

I removed Terry's hand from my knee and placed it in his lap. "Okay," I said, trying to refocus. "Amanda." I took a deep breath. "It's certainly possible that one of her traveling companions is responsible for her disappearance. Take Michael, for example."

"The magazine reporter?"

"Yes. He kept complaining about what an airhead Amanda was, about how he was dying to cover a real news story, about how he wanted to be an investigative journalist again like the good old days."

"You're not suggesting he killed her so he'd be a media star, are you? I can't believe reporters have gone that crazy."

I shrugged. "It's just a theory."

"Tell me about Tina. She's the one who gives me the creeps."

"Me, too. There's a lot of pent-up rage there," I said, "but conflicting feelings, too. On one hand, she acted as if she despised Amanda. On the other hand, she's stayed with her for so many years. If she's the murderer, then what set her off? Why kill her boss now? What was the trigger?"

"And how would she have known where to find Amanda in order to kill her?" Terry pointed out. "Will left Her Highness on a blanket at some remote spot on Cathedral Rock at four o'clock this morning. Could Tina have followed them up the canyon in the dark, waited for Will to beat it, killed Amanda when she was alone and defenseless, and then chucked the body over the cliffs? Tina's efficient but she's not Superwoman."

"Maybe she had help," I said. "Maybe Amanda's murder was a team effort. Maybe Billy or Jennifer or Marie pitched in."

"I can't picture Marie going along with something like that. Not that lovable old girl. Mon Dieu!"

"Marie told me last night that she was sure Amanda was about to fire her. She said if Amanda canned her, she'd never get another job, because she was passé. Or rather, her style of cooking was passé. There was an anecdote involving mashed potatoes, as I remember."

"You must have been riveted."

"Transfixed. Marie said that if it weren't for Harrison Reid, she would have been jobless a long time ago. She said Harrison liked her cooking but that Amanda was the one who hired and fired the help. In other words, if Amanda were to disappear, Marie could keep her job in the Reid household. How's that for a motive?"

"Great, but can you really see poor, shit-faced Marie staggering up Cathedral Rock in pursuit of Amanda at four o'clock in the morning, whiskey bottle in one hand, murder weapon in the other? It would be a stretch, Crystal."

"I suppose. Then let's take Billy. It wouldn't be a stretch for him to hike up those cliffs at four a.m. He's in terrific shape."

"What's his motive?"

"God, who knows? Unrequited love, maybe? I think he and Amanda were having an affair. It's possible that she threw him out of her bed when she got to Sedona because she decided he wasn't spiritual enough."

Terry smiled. "I only spent one day with the guy, but he struck me as the type who would go out and find himself some other rich bitch to latch onto if Amanda dumped him. He's not a killer, he's an opportunist."

"Okay. That leaves Jennifer, the publicist."

"No motive there, right? She was getting paid to make Mrs. Reid look *good,* not *dead.*"

"True, but she's sweet on Harrison Reid, which complicates things."

"How do you know that?"

"Because he told her he was naming his next heroine after her and she believed him. She's nuts about the man, trust me."

"Nuts enough to murder his wife?"

"Why not? Maybe she deluded herself into thinking he'd marry her if anything ever happened to Amanda. Maybe she killed Amanda so she could become the next Mrs. Harrison Reid. Think of all the publicity!"

"Speaking of Harrison Reid, isn't it possible that *he's* the murderer?"

"I doubt it. He wasn't even in Sedona when Amanda disappeared. Although he certainly had a motive for killing her. Michael told me she changed her will as often as most people change their underwear. Maybe Harrison figured he'd better bump her off before she pissed away all her money."

"Sounds plausible."

"But then again, maybe it wasn't Harrison or Billy or any of them. We can't overlook the possibility that Amanda may not have known her murderer. Some deranged stranger could have found her out there on Cathedral Rock and slit her throat. Maybe there's a serial killer on the loose in Sedona."

"If there is, then Amanda Reid was his first victim. I told you this morning—we haven't had a homicide here since '95."

"All right then. Try this—a coyote got her. Will said that when you go on one of his Vision Quests, you commune with animals. Maybe one of the animals was rabid."

"Then why wasn't there any blood at Cathedral Rock? If a coyote had his way with Amanda, those red rocks would be a lot redder."

I sipped my coffee. "I'm out of ideas," I said. "I need some sleep."

"*That* I have a solution for," said Terry. He quickly got up from his chair and helped me up from mine. "To the guest room with you."

"What about all our dishes?" I said, glancing at the dirty plates and cups and pots and pans.

"If we're very good, the dish fairy will take care of them," Terry said.

"And if we're not?" I asked.

"The dish fairy will still take care of them," he laughed, pointing to himself. "In the morning."

He walked over to the sink, reached for a tall glass from inside one of the cabinets, and filled it with tap water. And then he took my arm and walked me upstairs. When we got to the guest room, he set the glass of water on the night table next to the bed and opened the nearby window just a crack. The air had turned cool, and the light breeze that whistled in through the window was fragrant and soothing.

"That's how you like it, right?" Terry whispered, not wanting to wake Annie.

"That's how I like it," I said softly. "Thank you."

We were standing at the foot of the bed now, only a few inches away from each other, too far apart to touch, too close together not to. The next order of business was to say good night and move on. But neither of us was going anywhere.

My God, I've been married to this man, I thought, as the sexual tension crackled between us. I know what it feels like to make love to him, to feel his hands on me, to feel his body on mine. It would be so easy for us to fall into each other's arms and slip under the bed covers, like slipping into a favorite old pair of shoes. So what if twenty years had intervened? What would be the harm in being together again? For old times' sake? For just one night? It didn't have to *mean* anything. I wouldn't have to *do* anything about it or because of it. I'd still go home with Steven and Terry would still have his life in Sedona. And that would be that.

Or would it?

"Crystal?" said Terry as he took a step toward me, closing the gap between us.

"I don't think so," I said, answering the question he hadn't needed to ask.

He nodded, his expression disappointed yet understanding. He started toward the guest room door.

"Terry?" I called out.

He turned.

"The other day I found out I had a brother who died before I was born," I said. "My father told me during one of our famous Sunday visits."

"That's very sad," he replied, his eyes compassionate, his tone tender. "You lost three family members then."

He was speaking of my mother who died, my brother who died, and my father who might as well have.

"Four, actually," I said. "I lost my husband, too."

He shook his head. "He's right down the hall if you need him," he said and wished me another good night.

CHAPTER NINETEEN

♥

On Friday morning, as Terry and I were finishing up our Frosted Flakes and Annie was winding up her discourse on America's diplomatic relations with China, the phone rang. The caller was Detective Whitehead, the detective who had referred to Will Singleton as "Sitting Bull."

"He wants both of us to come down to the station and answer more questions," Terry told me. "I guess the whole gang will be there—Amanda's entourage, her husband, Will, everybody."

"Can I go along?" Annie asked her father.

"Today's a school day, sport, and you know it," he said.

"Today's a work day, Dad, and *you* know it," she reminded him.

"When you're old enough to own a business, then you can take a day off if you want to," he said. "Until then, it's school, okay?" He checked his watch. "And you're running late."

Annie looked at me and shrugged. "I tried, right?"

I laughed.

While she hustled upstairs to get ready, Terry explained that it was only fairly recently that Sedona had built the West Sedona Elementary School for grades kindergarten through six, complete with classrooms, ball fields, swimming pool, and park; that in prior years, Sedona's kids had to be bused all the way to either Cottonwood or Flagstaff. "In some ways, progress has been good for our little town," he conceded. "Of course, before progress, people hardly ever got themselves murdered."

"Well, if Amanda's pals are at the police station, I'll have a chance to chat with them, see if they'll tell me anything," I said, attempting to sound optimistic.

"Good. And when we're done with all that, we'll do some hunting around by ourselves."

"Where?"

"I'm taking you to a couple of stops that aren't on the Sacred Earth Jeep Tour," said Terry. "There are some real characters around here, folks who don't talk to the police—or hobnob with tourists."

"Then how would they know anything about Amanda's disappearance?" I asked.

He smiled. "They have a way of knowing lots of things." He picked up the phone, dialed, and waited for someone to answer.

"Cynthia. Hi. It's Terry," he said.

Beautiful. He's calling Sedona's answer to Kenny G., I thought, hoping he wasn't going to invite her along.

"I'm great. How about you?" he was saying. "Yeah, she was part of my tour group. Very rich, yeah. I don't have a clue. I got to the hotel to pick her up yesterday morning and nobody knew where she was. No, but I'm talking to the police this morning and doing a little digging on my own after that." On his own, huh? "Actually, that's why I'm calling, Cynthia. I might not be home until late, and

I was wondering if Annie could play with Laura after school today, then spend the night. Right. Right. Oh, that's terrific. I'll tell her. Hey, I owe you one, babe." Owed her one *what?* "I'll see you, Cynthia. Yeah, we'll have to do that soon. Thanks."

Terry hung up. I acted very busy scrubbing the breakfast dishes, so he wouldn't think I'd been hanging on every word of their conversation.

"Cynthia's gonna take care of Annie for the rest of today," he informed me. "That'll give you and me the time we need."

"To help Will, you mean."

"To help Will," he agreed. "And to be alone together in that big Jeep of mine. It'll be nice having you as my only passenger."

I smiled. "It won't cost me extra, will it?"

"We'll see," he said.

The Sedona Police Department was housed in a dinky, beige-colored structure that looked more like a mobile home than a government building. Still, its dinkyness didn't keep the satellite trucks, camera crews, and reporters from jamming its parking lot.

The first person Terry and I stumbled on as we made our way through the crowd and up the steps of the building was Michael Mandell. He had just given an interview to a local television station and was breathless from all the attention he was getting.

"Have you heard the latest?" he asked, pulling us into a little huddle. When we said we hadn't, he seemed overjoyed that he would be the one to impart the breaking news. "First of all, Harrison Reid is inside." He nodded at the building. "And he's not alone."

"Who's he with?" Terry asked.

"His literary agent, I'll bet," I said.

"Nope. His lawyer," said Michael. "His criminal *defense* lawyer. Jerry Jantz, as a matter of fact." Jantz was a New York-based attorney who represented mobsters, professional athletes, and other high-profile clients. His services weren't cheap. I wondered where Harrison was getting the money to pay him.

"If Harrison Reid needs a lawyer, maybe Will isn't the police's prime suspect after all," Terry theorized.

"I wouldn't get my hopes up," I said. "Just because he's got a lawyer with him doesn't mean he *needs* a lawyer. Nobody goes to the bathroom anymore without his criminal defense lawyer present. It's a post-O.J. thing. Your wife is murdered, you call your lawyer. Bam bam. It has nothing to do with your guilt or innocence."

"Speaking of guilt, listen to *this*," said Michael. "My editor in New York got a call from somebody named Dee Caparelli."

"Sounds like pasta," I mused.

"Want to see her?" Michael asked.

"Sure," we said.

He reached inside his briefcase and flashed us a photograph of Ms. Caparelli. She was a curvaceous redhead with two or three inches of black roots.

"Does she have some connection to Amanda Reid?" Terry asked, just before being jostled by a cameraman.

"You know how it is when a celebrity is murdered," said Michael. "Everybody who's even remotely connected to the person crawls out from under a rock."

"So this woman *is* connected to Amanda," I confirmed.

"No. This woman is connected to Tina, Amanda's assistant," Michael said, "and to Billy, the personal trainer."

"I still don't see why she would call your editor at—" I stopped. I had a hunch. I suddenly knew exactly who Dee

Caparelli was. "Billy's girlfriend, right?" I said. "The one who used to live in Tina's building."

Michael looked disappointed. "How did you know?"

"Just a guess," I said. "At Amanda's dinner party the other night, I asked Billy how he'd gotten the job as her personal trainer. He told me it was thanks to Tina, that he'd met her through his girlfriend."

"Dee Caparelli," Michael said, nodding his head.

"I also asked Billy if he and this woman were still dating," I went on, "since I assumed that he and Amanda were doing more than lifting weights together. But he never gave me a straight answer."

"That's because he didn't want anybody to know that he'd broken up with Dee a couple of months after he went to work for Amanda," Michael said.

"Why in the world would anybody care if the guy broke up with his girlfriend?" Terry asked.

"Because he dumped her for Tina," Michael said, getting to the point, finally.

"Billy and *Tina* are an item?" I said, having trouble picturing Tina being an item with anybody, much less a big dope like Billy.

"A major item," said Michael. "They've been keeping their relationship a secret for quite a while."

"Why would they do that?" I asked.

"Because Amanda had a strict rule," said Michael. "No hanky panky among her employees. Billy and Tina were afraid she'd fire them if she found out about their little romance. But that's not all. Not nearly all."

"Go on," I urged, the image of Billy and Tina as lovers still boggling my mind.

Michael moved closer. "Get a load of *this,*" he whispered. "There was another reason Billy and Tina didn't want to be linked as a couple." He paused to wipe away the spittle that had accumulated in the corners of his mouth. "They were planning to kidnap Amanda, demand a huge ransom, and disappear with the money," he said. "And they were planning to do the job during this trip!"

"You're not serious," I said. "Billy and Tina actually kidnapped Amanda?"

"I didn't say they kidnapped her," Michael corrected me. "I said they were planning to."

"Oh, come on," Terry groaned. "You expect us to believe that this Dee Caparelli was telling the truth when she called your editor at *Personal Life* magazine and announced: 'I happen to know that my old friends were planning to kidnap the millionaire heiress?' No way. You said it yourself, Michael. People come out of the woodwork with these celebrity murder cases. She's probably some bimbo looking for her fifteen minutes of fame."

"No doubt about that," Michael conceded, "but she didn't know a thing about the kidnapping plot. As a rusty-but-nevertheless-experienced investigative reporter, *I* was able to squeeze that information out of my sources at the police department. Caparelli only told my editor that Billy and Tina were romantically involved—and that Billy had a record."

"He was in a band?" I said.

"No, he was in a prison, Crystal," Michael said tolerantly. "Billy Braddick served five years at Riker's Island for conning a seventy-year-old woman into ordering bogus exercise equipment. After Caparelli told my editor, my editor told me, and I told Detective Whitehead, who thought the fact that Billy had done time warranted a search of his hotel room. Guess what he found?"

"Not the bogus exercise equipment," I ventured.

"No," said Michael. "He found a whole pad of *practice* ransom notes—Billy and Tina's dry runs—in which they suggested swapping a cool two million dollars for Amanda's safe return. The notes were crumpled up in the trash can in the bathroom, but they were legible enough to provide the police with some interesting reading material, wouldn't you agree?"

"I would," I said, amazed. The only criminal activity I'd ever come in contact with involved tax evasion. "But I'm confused, Michael. You just told us that Billy and Tina *didn't* kidnap Amanda."

"Right," he said. "When Detective Whitehead confronted them with the evidence, they admitted that they *had* planned to kidnap Amanda while she was in Sedona and that the job had been in the works for months. But they also admitted that they were as shocked as everybody else when Amanda disappeared yesterday morning, because it meant that somebody had beaten them to the punch, so to speak. I think they were pissed off about it."

"Wait a second," Terry said. "If those two could lie about their romantic relationship, not to mention concoct a plan to kidnap their boss, how do we know they're not lying about *not* kidnapping their boss?"

"Because, according to my sources, they have an ironclad alibi for yesterday morning."

"Yeah? Like what?" said Terry.

Michael snickered. "Apparently, they made so much noise while they were having sex in Billy's casita that the people next door called hotel security. Three times." He patted Terry on the shoulder. "I know you're trying to help your Indian buddy, but Tina and her boyfriend aren't his ticket out of trouble. They didn't lay a hand on Amanda. They were too busy laying hands on each other."

I couldn't get over this. Billy and Amanda weren't having an affair. Billy and *Tina* were having an affair. What's more, they were planning to kidnap Amanda while they were all in Sedona, but they never got around to it because someone else got around to it first! "Did they ever tell the police *why* they were planning to kidnap Amanda?" I asked Michael.

"They wanted bigger bucks than what she was paying them," he said. "So the motive was money—and the fact that they hated her."

"Wouldn't finding other, higher-paying jobs have solved both problems?" I asked.

Terry took my arm. "Let's go inside and get our interviews over with," he suggested. "And then let's get the hell out of here."

Among those waiting outside Detective Whitehead's office when Terry and I arrived were Marie and Jennifer. Marie was sitting on a bench—her hair tangled, her dress rumpled, her eyes the color of Bloody Marys, what else was new? Jennifer, on the other hand, was standing near the closed door to the detective's office, looking bright and perky, her gleaming white teeth providing the only illumination in the otherwise dimly lit waiting area.

"Is someone in there with him?" I asked her, referring to Detective Whitehead.

She nodded. "Mr. Reid is in there."

I should have known. I should have *felt* his greatness. "He must be terribly upset," I said. "First his wife disappears. Then he finds out that two of her closest associates had actually planned to kidnap her."

"Oh, he's devastated," she confided, "so devastated that he's asked me to cancel all promotional appearances for his new book."

"You know, it's an amazing coincidence," I observed. "Harrison Reid comes out with a collection of humorous essays about death, and, what do you know, he's looking at the very real possibility of his own wife's death. Go figure."

"What are you implying?" Jennifer asked, her smile fading.

"She's implying that Harrison Reid may have had something to do with his wife's disappearance," Terry said, cutting to the heart of the matter.

"That's ridiculous!" Jennifer said huffily. "He was speaking at the 92nd Street Y in Manhattan the night before last. He didn't know Amanda was missing until I called him yesterday morning."

"*You* called him?" I asked.

"That's right," said Jennifer.

"I thought it was customary for the police to contact the next of kin," I said, having spent many a Sunday trapped in my father's den, watching a cavalcade of "B" cop shows.

"Oh. Well. I guess I misspoke," she said, backpedaling. "I meant that I called Harrison—Mr. Reid—moments *after* the police phoned him. To offer my sympathies."

"And then he hopped on a friend's private plane and flew out here," Terry said. "With his lawyer."

"Yes," said Jennifer. "Mr. Reid and Mr. Jantz are dear friends."

I was about to ask if the great and legendary Mr. Reid knew that his wife had changed her will yet again, when the door to Detective Whitehead's office opened and out walked the novelist himself.

I had seen photographs of Harrison Reid over the years—in newspapers, in magazines, on book jackets—but when he appeared before me, only a few feet away, I was taken aback by his size and stature, by how formidable a figure he was.

He was well over six feet tall and weighed at least two hundred and fifty pounds. But it was his scruffy gray beard and wild green eyes, as well as his heft, that made him seem larger than life. And, of course, there was his trademark white suit. Winter, spring, summer, fall, the man wore that goddam white suit no matter what the occasion. I shuddered when I thought of his dry cleaning bills.

And then there was the aristocratic, upper crust-y way he spoke—a sort of George Plimpton-esque, WASP lockjaw that made you feel as if you were violating some immigration law.

"Harrison," Jennifer said, rushing to his side. "Was it terribly difficult for you in there?"

He patted her head as if she were a small child, insignificant, a bother. "They're still searching for her," he said, dropping his r's. "They haven't given up hope, but they're not optimistic about finding her alive. They think the Indian guide who took her up to that canyon could have—"

"He not only couldn't have, he didn't," Terry interrupted. "The only thing Will Singleton is guilty of is wanting to help your wife achieve her goals."

Harrison Reid peered down at Terry. "Do we know each other, sir?" he asked through pursed lips.

Jennifer inserted herself. "This is Terry Hollenbeck, Harrison. He owns the Jeep Tour company. He's the one who introduced Amanda to Will Singleton."

I cleared my throat.

"And this is Crystal Goldstein," Jennifer added. "She was a passenger on the tour with all of us. She's an accountant from New York."

He nodded, then leaned over and whispered something to his lawyer, a heavily toupéed creature. They conferred for a minute or two. Then Harrison said, "I understand you both believe that Mr. Singleton is blameless in this matter."

"That's what we believe, yeah," said Terry. "Will Singleton took your wife up to Cathedral Rock and left her there because she asked him to, because she paid him to."

"Then where is she now?" Harrison asked. "He was the

last person to see her alive. That doesn't bode well for him, does it?"

Before either Terry or I could reply, Marie rose from her bench and zigzagged over to Harrison.

"Monsieur," she said, grabbing his arm to steady herself. "You must be tired and hungry, no?"

"I had a bite of breakfast at my hotel, Marie," he said, then smiled at her. His teeth were yellow compared to Jennifer's, although practically anyone's would be. "It's a French country inn, you know. I felt right at home with the cuisine, as if you had prepared the meal yourself, my dear."

"You must be staying at L'Auberge," said Terry, referring to Sedona's most exclusive lodgings.

"Yes," said Harrison. "Jennifer here made the arrangements for me." He patted her head a second time.

Just then, Detective Whitehead stuck his white head—he could have been Phil Donahue's double—out of his office and asked Terry to step inside.

"Mr. Jantz and I will be back at my hotel if there's any new information," Harrison told the detective, who promised to call him the moment there was a break in the case.

"I'll go with you, Harrison," Jennifer said eagerly. "I've already spoken to Detective Whitehead this morning."

"That's very thoughtful," he said and allowed his publicist and his lawyer to escort him out of the building.

While Terry took his turn with Detective Whitehead, I sat with Marie.

"You haven't been interviewed yet this morning?" I asked her.

"Yes, I was interviewed over an hour ago," she said.

"Then what are you still doing here?" I said.

"I did not know where else to go," she said, then threw her head into my lap and began to sob.

"Back to the hotel maybe?" I suggested. "You have your room at Tranquility, don't you?"

Her head bobbed up and down. She said something but I couldn't make out what it was.

"I can't hear you, Marie," I said, trying to pull her head out of my lap without yanking her by the hair.

She sat up. "I am at the hotel but I am the only one of our little group left to confront all those reporters," she said. "Tina and Billy are gone, Mon Dieu. Jennifer has been working with Monsieur Reid at his hotel. And Madame Reid—" Her head fell back into my lap. There was more sobbing.

"Madame Reid what, Marie?" I urged. "You were going to make an observation, I think."

Up went her head. "Madame Reid is dead, no?"

"No. I mean, not necessarily."

She shook her head. "She is dead. And I am responsible."

I stared at her. Was it a confession that was about to fall into my lap this time?

"I killed her," she said. "I did."

"Okay, Marie. Okay. Let's take this nice and slowly," I said, afraid she'd realize what she was saying and clam up.

"I killed Madame Reid as certainly as if I had stabbed her in the heart," she said, wiping her tears with the back of her hand.

"So you stabbed her somewhere else, is that it?" I said as gently as possible under the circumstances. "In the back? The abdomen? The carotid artery maybe?"

She shook her head again. "I wanted to stab her. I dreamed about stabbing her. She threatened to put me out on the street, no?"

"Yes, Marie. You told me that the other night. You said you were hanging onto your job for dear life."

"Exactement. I was so desperate to keep my job with

Monsieur Reid that I wished to kill Madame Reid. I am guilty, no?"

"No. Not if you *didn't* kill her. Wishing someone would die isn't very spiritual but it's not a crime."

My words elicited more tears. Buckets of them.

"What, Marie? What is it now?"

"I did more than *wish* Madame Reid dead," she said between sobs. "I had a plan to *make* her dead."

Jesus. Another botched murder plot. "Go on," I said. "How were you planning to make her dead?"

She looked to her left, then to her right, checking to see whether anyone was listening. When she thought the coast was clear, she said, "Madame Reid used to tell me my food tasted like rat poison. I decided to return the favor."

"And put rat poison in her food, you mean?"

She nodded. "I carried the plastic bag all the way from New York. It made the clothes in my suitcase smell, no?"

"Yes," I said, finally placing the foul odor that always seemed to accompany Marie.

"I never had the opportunity to use the poison, with Madame Reid dead now, but I will always blame myself for the crime I almost committed. I am ashamed."

"Have you told the police any of this?" I asked, suddenly homesick for the lunatics at Duboff Spector, even Otis Tool.

"No," she said. "I told Monsieur Reid. I had to unburden myself to him, to apologize to him for my bad thoughts."

"How did he react?"

"He was understanding."

"Really?" Your chef tells you she was planning to murder your wife and you're understanding?

"He said he did not believe I would have gone through with my plan. He said he felt it was time for me to retire.

He said he would give me some money so I could go back to France to live. He is a gentleman, you see."

A rich gentleman, if he gets his hands on Amanda's estate, I thought.

Marie spoke about France for a while, how she was looking forward to returning to her native country but would carry her guilt wherever she went. I suggested she see a therapist.

Eventually, Terry emerged from Detective Whitehead's office and I had my turn with Sedona's Finest. I told the cop virtually everything I knew about everyone in Sedona. He took notes and raised his eyebrows and said: "Is that right?" But in the end he stood firm in his belief that Will Singleton murdered Amanda Reid.

"Will didn't have a motive for killing her," I protested vehemently. "In *fact* he's the only one who didn't."

"He was at the scene," the detective countered. "In *fact* he's the only one who was."

CHAPTER TWENTY

♥

"What's our next stop?" I asked Terry as he hustled me through the reporters, into his Jeep, and out of the parking lot.

"We're taking 89A south to Cottonwood," he said, steering us back onto Sedona's main drag.

"I passed through there on my way into town," I recalled. "I didn't see much except a few dozen billboards for a swanky new golf resort."

"Funny, isn't it?" he mused. "Some genius sticks a golf course where grass doesn't grow and where there's no water to water it even if it did. But we're not going to Cottonwood for the golf course."

"No?"

"No. We're going for the casino."

"I knew it," I said, slapping my leg. "You were starting to seem just a little too stable, Terry. You have a gambling problem, is that it?"

He laughed. "No, I don't have a gambling problem,

Crystal. The Yavapai-Apaches run a casino in Cottonwood, and the guy who works one of the blackjack tables is a buddy of mine."

"And?"

"And there isn't a whole lot that gets by him. I'm hoping he's heard something about Amanda, about who might have killed her." He patted the newspaper resting on his lap. It was the latest issue of the *Red Rock News*. The entire front page of Friday's paper was devoted to "The Disappearance of the Millionaire Heiress," complete with a flattering—i.e., ten-year-old—photograph of Amanda. Of course, the article wasn't your basic news story. Not in Sedona. It was a veritable Ripley's Believe It Or Not, filled with wacky theories of what could have happened to Mrs. Reid. One person quoted in the article swore that Amanda had been abducted by Martians. Another person suggested that she'd been swallowed up by an enormous sink hole. Still a third person was convinced that she'd been kidnapped by rabid movie fans who mistook her for Tippi Hedren, to whom, I had to admit, she did bear a striking resemblance.

"What's the name of this buddy of yours?" I asked.

"Buddy," said Terry, who wasn't kidding.

The Cliff Castle Lodge & Casino is actually a Best Western motel, a gambling casino, and an Indian reservation, all in one. Now, I realize that Indian tribes all over America are getting into the casino business these days, but the Yavapai-Apaches have gotten into it in a rather colorless, unglitzy way. In other words, their casino is more trailer park than Las Vegas.

"How do we know Buddy is here at this hour of the morning?" I said when we drove up to the complex. It was only 10:30.

"He's always here," said Terry. "This place is his life, his Command Central. Everybody comes in to talk to him, ask his advice, pick up a little information. He's the Liz Smith of the reservation."

"I can't wait to meet him," I said as Terry parked the Jeep.

I didn't have to wait long, as it turned out. Buddy—I'm not sure he had a last name because no one seemed to know it—was standing by the door, deep in conversation with another man, when we walked in.

What did Buddy look like? Picture a tall fifty-year-old wearing a leisure suit, cowboy boots, and a huge headdress. I hadn't seen so many feathers since my down comforter sprang a leak.

"Hey, Terry. What's the good word?" he said after he finished up with the fellow he'd been chatting with. "Business good?"

"Business is fine," Terry said, shaking Buddy's hand. "What's with all the feathers?"

Buddy chuckled as he patted the headdress. "For the tourists," he said. "They love this stuff. Gotta make a living, right?"

Terry smiled knowingly. "I'd like you to meet an old friend of mine, Crystal Goldstein."

Buddy swung quickly around to face me, his headdress nearly decapitating Terry. "A pleasure," he said, shaking my hand, too. "You here to play a little blackjack, Crystal?"

"Actually, we came to talk to you, Buddy," Terry answered for me. "To pick your brain about something. Could you come outside with us for a couple of minutes?"

If Buddy was surprised by Terry's request, he certainly didn't let on. He simply nodded, as if people sought his counsel on a regular basis.

We stepped outside the casino and stood together in

the parking lot. A dry, dusty breeze had kicked up; I hoped the headdress wouldn't land on somebody's car antenna.

"You wanted to talk, my friend? Be my guest," said Buddy.

Terry showed him the front page of the *Red Rock News,* which he'd brought with him from the Jeep. "You've heard about this?"

"I've heard about it, sure," said Buddy.

"She was on my tour, was one of the passengers," Terry said, pointing to Amanda's photograph. "I introduced her to Will Singleton, too. You've met Will?"

"I've met him, sure," Buddy said.

"The police think he killed her and buried the body somewhere, but if you know Will, you know that's not possible," said Terry. "There has to be another explanation."

"There's another explanation, sure," said Buddy.

"Any idea what it might be?" I said, wondering if there was anything Buddy wasn't *sure* about.

He took another look at Amanda's picture, stroked his chin, and said, "Now that you mention it, I had a guy come in here the night before last, bragging that he knew the woman."

"Bragging?" I asked. "What did he say?"

"He said he sold her a talking stick a few days ago," said Buddy.

"He sold her a what?" I said.

Buddy looked at Terry. "Your friend Crystal is not from around here, right?"

"No, but she's a quick study," Terry smiled.

"A talking stick is part of Native American tradition," said Buddy. "The one who is in possession of the stick is the one who gets to talk—everyone else must listen."

"I see," I said, doubting that this talking stick had anything to do with Amanda's nonstop chatter about her New

Age clothing line. "So the guy who sold her the talking stick works at a store in Sedona?"

"He owns the store, opened it up recently," said Buddy. "He sells crystals, incense, souvenir red rocks, you know. Just what Sedona needs, huh? Another store like that?"

Terry agreed.

"Anyway, this guy was in the casino the night before last telling people how much he overcharged the woman for the talking stick," Buddy went on. "He said she had plenty of money and didn't notice."

"She had plenty of money," Terry concurred. "Let me ask you something else, Buddy. Do you remember how late this guy stayed at the casino the other night?"

"I remember, sure," said Buddy. "He played blackjack until six o'clock the next morning, that's how late. He's a drinker, that guy. He got so loaded we had to put him to bed at the motel. He didn't get up until noon, I hear."

"Then he couldn't have killed Amanda," I said to Terry, reviewing the police's time line. "Not unless he slept through it."

Terry sighed. "Has anybody else come into the casino talking about Amanda Reid?" he asked Buddy.

"Not yet, but after they read the newspaper and watch the news, they'll be in here talking about her, sure," he said. "It's not every day that somebody gets murdered in Sedona. Especially a famous rich lady."

"Buddy, do me a favor, would you? If you find out something that could help Will, give me a call, okay?" Terry asked.

"I'll give you a call, sure," he said. "Will Singleton's a decent guy. It's the cops who are evil. They don't understand that an Indian would never kill on sacred land. Except in self-defense."

Self-defense? It hadn't occurred to me that Amanda might have provoked her killer into killing her at Cathedral

Rock; that *she* could have turned a chance encounter up there on that canyon into justifiable homicide.

"Where to now, O Tour Guide?" I asked when we had strapped ourselves back inside the Jeep and were heading southwest on 89A.

"Jerome," said Terry.

"Another buddy of yours?" I said wryly.

"Jerome is a town," he explained. "A remarkable town, actually."

"How so?"

"Its geography, for one thing. Unlike Cottonwood, which is essentially flat and desertlike, Jerome literally hangs over the side of Mingus Mountain, about five thousand feet above sea level. It's not for the phobically inclined. It defies gravity."

I thought of Arthur, Rona's husband. He probably wouldn't even look at *photographs* of the place.

"How else is Jerome remarkable?" I asked, feeling my ears pop as we climbed higher and higher up the winding road.

"It used to be a ghost town," said Terry. "Well, no. It used to be a prosperous town that *became* a ghost town. It was founded in the late 1800s, when people were willing to brave the steep hills so they could mine for copper and silver and gold. I think the population was close to fifteen thousand back then."

"What happened?"

"A fire destroyed the mines and they started strip-mining with dynamite. Before they knew it, the buildings crumbled and slid down the mountain. The place went bust. In the fifties, there weren't more than fifty people living in Jerome."

"Obviously, things have changed or we wouldn't be going there."

"Things have changed, all right. In the sixties, a lot of artists and writers discovered the town. The housing was cheap, the attitude was laid back, and the view! Wow. To the north, you can see the twelve-thousand-foot summits of the San Francisco Peaks. It's spectacular."

"So Jerome has made a comeback."

"Big time. The buildings are beautifully renovated, the galleries showcase local artists, and the copper and silver have been replaced by espresso and cappuccino. Jerome is trendy now. Sort of."

"So what is our mission in Jerome?"

"We're about to have a chat with a blues singer," said Terry.

"Why am I not surprised?" I remarked.

"Her name's Laverne Altamont," he said. "She sings at a local hangout called The Spirit Room."

The *Spirit* Room. Only in Sedona and its environs, I thought.

"Does Laverne have the power to channel Amanda's spirit?" I asked. "Is that why we're going to see her?"

"No. She's a singer, not a psychic," said Terry. "But aside from having a voice that'll knock you out, she has a lot of friends who do Vision Quests. At Cathedral Rock, for example. I'm hoping one of them may have run into Amanda up there, witnessed the murder maybe, and then told Laverne. It's a long shot, but even if she can't help us, the trip won't be a total loss."

"Because I'll get to hear her sing."

"And because I'm gonna buy you lunch at a picturesque little café on the side of a mountain."

"Sounds romantic."

"That's the general idea."

* * *

Since Laverne didn't begin her set at The Spirit Room until two o'clock each afternoon, Terry and I decided to have lunch first.

The Flatiron Café more than lived up to its description. Perched a few thousand feet above sea level, it's a tiny restaurant, wedged into the crook of the "Y" where Jerome's Main and Hull streets meet, affording its patrons a truly breathtaking view of Sedona's red rocks, Cottonwood's cactus-dotted landscape, and, off in the distance, the extraordinary San Francisco Peaks. Outside the building, which also houses a popcorn and candy store, a green sign that reads "Espresso Bar * Breakfast & Lunch * Fresh Squeezed Lemonade" announces the café; inside are just three tables plus a counter at which you place your order. Across the narrow street, there are a few additional tables for dining al fresco. Across the neighboring street, in the basement of an art gallery, is the café's rest room. Obviously, we're not talking opulence here; we're talking funky. The Flatiron is basically a sandwich shop with atmosphere.

We both ordered what was billed as a house specialty: artichoke hearts, mozzarella, and fresh basil on focaccia, and two tall, frosty glasses of homemade lemonade. We brought the food across the street on trays so we could sit outside and enjoy the fresh mountain breezes. I realized, as I popped an errant artichoke heart into my mouth, that despite the fact that a woman I had just met was missing and presumed dead, I was happy.

Terry noticed. "You like it," he said, nodding.

"By 'it,' do you mean my sandwich, this restaurant, or Jerome?"

"Being here with me," he said, his blue eyes mischievous. "That's what I mean."

"Well, now," I chuckled. "You're putting me on the spot, aren't you, Terry?"

"Yeah, that's exactly what I'm doing," he said.

"All right. Then, yes. I like it. Satisfied?"

"I'm beginning to be." He bit into his sandwich and moaned with pleasure. "Jesus, I forgot how good this place is. As good as you've got in New York, huh?"

"Better," I said, after sampling my meal. "There aren't any rude waiters here."

He smiled. "So what *do* you like about being here with me, Crystal?"

"Terry."

"Come on. Humor me."

I took a long swallow of lemonade. It was so tart I couldn't speak for several seconds; my tongue had shriveled up. "I like that you're committed to helping your friend Will," I said when I had recovered. "Your loyalty is admirable. And contagious. I hardly know the man and yet I want to help him, too."

He shrugged. "He and Jean were there for me when I needed help. Why shouldn't I help them when they need it?"

"Because you used to avoid tough situations," I said. "You preferred the easy route."

"I was a kid then, Crystal. And now I'm not."

I nodded. "And now you're not."

"Any other reasons you like being with me?" he asked, intent on this fishing expedition.

"Yes," I said. "Yes, there are other reasons." Oh, why not, I thought. Tell him the truth. By this time tomorrow, Steven will be in Sedona and you'll be too busy answering *his* questions to answer Terry's. "I like the fact that when I'm with you, you're very attentive, very present," I told him. "I never feel as if you'd rather be doing something else."

"That's because I wouldn't rather be doing something else," he said. "Simple."

Simple. Nothing in my life had ever been simple, except my career. And even that wasn't simple anymore.

"I like the fact that you say personal things to me," I went on, warming to Terry's little exercise, becoming very warm, actually, given the way he was looking at me. "You don't make me guess what you're thinking."

"I'm thinking how lovely you are," he said, causing both of us to abandon our sandwiches. Who concentrates on food at a time like this? *My* appetite was directed elsewhere, I can tell you that.

"I like the fact that you not only flood me with feelings, you force me to face my feelings," I continued, my face flushed with the intimate turn the conversation had taken. "You don't let me get away with my usual 'I'm fine—mind your own business'."

"Everybody else lets you get away with that?"

"Everybody except my friend Rona. She's the one who accuses me of being in denial about virtually every facet of my life. She's the one who encourages me to find balance, meaning, inner peace. She's the one who badgered me into coming to Sedona. I wouldn't be here if it weren't for her."

"I like her already," Terry said with a grin. "Tell her she's got my undying gratitude."

"I will, but I'm not sure how thrilled she'll be. She warned me to keep away from you," I said. "She's worried that you're 'sucking me back in,' as she puts it."

"Is she right, Crystal? Am I sucking you back in?"

While he waited for me to answer him, he reached across the table to hold my hand. I did not pull away. Not even when a light breeze blew my paper napkin onto the ground, into the street. I did not chase after it. I did not move a muscle. I was welded to Terry's touch.

"*Am* I sucking you back in?" he asked again, his question heavy with expectations.

"Is that your intention?" I said softly.

"It is," he said. "If at all possible."

CHAPTER
TWENTY-ONE

♥

We lingered over lunch—lingered over each other, more accurately—until we reminded ourselves why we'd come to Jerome in the first place: to pay Laverne Altamont a visit. Since The Spirit Room was just around the corner from the Flatiron Café, we walked over, chattering merrily all the way, Terry's arm around my shoulder, my arm around his waist. I was enjoying myself immensely.

The Spirit Room, where Laverne sang during what were billed as "Live Afternoon Jams," occupied the first floor of an historic, two-story brick building. I had an inkling of the kind of crowd I would find inside when I saw the kind of vehicles that were lined up outside: motorcycles.

"This Laverne must be a biker chick," I said, judging by all the Harleys.

"Laverne defies description," Terry promised. "She's an original. You'll see."

I couldn't see Laverne or anybody else when we first stepped inside The Spirit Room. The place was so dark—

one of those bar/restaurants where the red neon "Bud-weiser—On Tap" sign in the window provides the only illumination—that my eyes had trouble adjusting, and near-blindness set in momentarily. Then Terry took my hand, a waitress led us to an empty table not far from the small stage, and, just as we were being seated, my sight returned; I was able to get a good look at the fabled La-verne Altamont.

Terry was right. She defied description, but I'll do my best.

For openers, she was bald—an absolute cue ball without a single patch of growth on her forty-something-year-old head. For another thing, her eyebrows seemed to have been tattooed onto her pasty white face in an upside-down "V" position, giving her the appearance of someone who was perpetually surprised. What's more, she was shape-less—a heavy, lumpy woman with breasts so saggy, you couldn't tell where they began or ended. And then there was the chain smoking, the black leather outfit, and the voice. Especially the voice. When we first entered The Spirit Room, Laverne was belting out B.B. King's "The Thrill Is Gone," and it had taken me a few seconds to realize that she *wasn't* B.B. King, that we *weren't* listening to recorded music, that the bald, middle-aged, white woman standing among a trio of ponytailed young dudes—a guitarist, a drummer, and a keyboard player—*wasn't* the great black rhythm and blues singer. Her voice was so low, her delivery so smooth and soulful, that I kept shaking my head and wondering why someone with such talent hadn't been "dis-covered."

"She's not interested in being a star," Terry replied after I'd asked the question. "She's happy doing what she's doing."

She certainly looked happy. Beatific, almost. Her eyes were closed as she sang, her arms outstretched, her black-leather-clad body a veritable metronome swaying back and forth in time with the music. After each song, she beamed, clapping for herself, her band, her audience. Here, I thought, is a woman who likes her job.

"She used to work in a bank in Phoenix," Terry said after we'd ordered a couple of beers.

"You're kidding."

"Nope. She was a teller for years. Then all her hair fell out—it was that stress-related disease you hear about—and the big shots at the bank thought she'd scare the customers away. They told her to wear a wig and she told them to find another teller. She decided her hair loss was a spiritual omen, tipping her off that she should leave Phoenix, move to a place where her uniqueness would be appreciated, and do what she loved."

"So she settled in Sedona and started singing."

Terry nodded. "She came to town the same year Gwen and I did. She sang in area clubs and we'd go and listen to her."

"Oh, so she knows Gwen," I said.

"She knew Gwen. Gwen took off, remember?"

"I remember," I said and wondered not for the first time if Gwen might reappear someday, the way Stephanie had, the way I had. It suddenly occurred to me that yet another downside of middle age is that there are more and more former partners lurking out there, more and more exes with the potential to show up, throw you off course, complicate your life. It's something your parents never tell you about getting older—that the world becomes littered with people you're convinced you'll never see again but inevitably do.

"Anyhow, Laverne developed a loyal following," Terry went on. "Especially with the less 'mainstream' crowd, if there is such a thing in Sedona. The bikers love her. The gays love her. And the New Agers really love her, maybe because she's sort of 'out there' herself—and so they talk to her in a way they'd never talk to the police."

"You don't honestly think one of these people trusts her enough to confess to murdering Amanda, do you?"

"No, but one of them might trust her enough to confess to *witnessing* Amanda's murder. Like I said, the spiritualists around here don't like the cops, and the feeling is mutual. Laverne may have access to information Detective Whitehead will never get his hands on."

"Let's hope so," I said, thinking of Will Singleton, feeling more and more that it was unlikely he had killed anybody.

When Laverne finished her set, Terry waved her over, and she came and sat down at our table.

Her appearance was even more startling at close range, but when she spoke to us, there was a sweetness, if not a girl-next-door way about her, that put me at ease.

"So you're the one he was married to all those years ago," she said, lighting up the first of several Marlboros. "It's real nice to meet you, cookie." She called everyone cookie, it turned out, even herself, as in: "I'm one smart cookie."

"It's nice to meet you, too, Laverne," I said. "You have an incredible voice."

"It's just the one Spirit gave me," she said, shrugging off the compliment. "Whatever flows through me flows from Him."

I nodded. Who was I to argue with a large bald woman?

"Crystal came to Sedona on a little vacation and, coincidentally, signed up for my Jeep Tour," Terry explained. "Now we're taking advantage of our dumb luck and getting to know each other again."

Laverne smiled. "Coincidentally? You know better than

that, cookie. There are no coincidences. Everything happens for a reason."

Gee, I thought. It really is a small world. Laverne has probably had an attunement with Jazeem.

"Whatever the reason, I'm glad she's here," said Terry, referring to me, "but there is something I'm not so glad about."

"Your friend Will Singleton," Laverne guessed. "You're worried because the police think he killed that woman. I've been reading about the case in the newspaper, cookie."

"Yeah, I'm worried," said Terry. "Listen, Laverne. You've got friends who spend a lot of time up on Cathedral Rock. Maybe one of them saw something yesterday morning after Will left Amanda Reid there. Maybe one of them came to *you* with the information instead of going to the police. Is that possible?"

Laverne sat back in her chair and motioned for a waitress to bring her a beer. When the bottle arrived, she curled her stubby fingers around it and brought it to her lips. She took a few swallows, then addressed Terry's question.

"I'm about to disappoint you, cookie," she said. "I'm gonna put a damper on your nice day with your long-lost sweetheart."

"How?" said Terry.

"Because I do have friends who were up at Cathedral Rock yesterday morning—four of them—and they all saw Amanda Reid," Laverne said. "They didn't know that's who she was at first—then they saw her picture in the paper and figured it out."

"Was she alone when they saw her?" Terry asked.

"No, and there's your problem. She was with Will," said Laverne, who took a drag on her cigarette, then exhaled the smoke in a long, thin stream. "My friends swear he was yelling at her—he and Miss Socialite were having an argument, maybe—and he was holding something over her head."

"Yeah, his hands, probably," Terry said, growing exasperated. "And he wasn't yelling at her, he was chanting at her. You know these Vision Quest rituals, Laverne. There's a lot of praying and chanting that goes on. Will was only doing his thing. When he finished, he left Amanda at Cathedral Rock and went back down the canyon. End of story."

"Hey, I'm sure Will's as innocent as they come," said Laverne. "I'm just telling you what my friends told me."

"So you believe he didn't kill Amanda," said Terry.

"I believe this, I believe that. It doesn't matter what *I* believe. Only Spirit knows what really happened up at Cathedral Rock," she said. "Only Spirit knows where Amanda Reid is now and why nobody has been able to find her. If I were you two, I wouldn't waste my time talking to me. I'd go talk to someone who talks to Spirit."

"For instance?" Terry asked.

Laverne laughed. "Take your pick. Sedona's full of people who talk to Him on a regular basis—or think they do."

"I was hoping you'd be that person," said Terry.

"Spirit tells me to sing, cookie," she said. "He doesn't tell me to meddle in murder. Now I've gotta go back to work, huh?" She winked at me as she took a final swig from the beer bottle, then rose from the table, stuffing her matches and pack of cigarettes into the front pocket of her black leather jacket. "Maybe it'll cheer you lovebirds up if I sing you a special number."

Before we could respond, she waddled over to the stage, had a few words with her band members, and stepped up to the microphone for a bluesy rendition of Peter Gabriel's rock ballad, "Don't Give Up."

"Let's not," Terry said as Laverne crooned. "Give up, I mean."

"Are we still talking about Will?" I asked.

"Yeah," he said. "Among other things."

And so we didn't give up. We got back into the Jeep, drove the forty-five minutes or so to Sedona, and headed up the ultra-windy, not-for-the-faint-of-heart Schnebly Hill Road, the alternate "historic" route north to Flagstaff. With much of it unpaved as well as terrifyingly steep, Schnebly Hill Road provides some of the best lookout points for tourists wanting to view Sedona's incredible red rock formations. As the saying goes, if your car makes it up and back, you'll get some great photographs.

According to Terry, Schnebly Hill Road is also a popular camping ground, albeit an illegal one, for those among Sedona's New Age residents who love communing with nature and hate paying real estate taxes. As a result, the flatter, more wooded spots are dotted with tents and sleeping bags.

"They're relatively safe up here, because the cops have no desire to patrol the area, especially at night," he said as we made our way uphill. "The road is rough enough during the day, when you can actually see all the potholes."

"Is there someone in particular we're looking for?" I asked, wondering if anybody could top Buddy and Laverne.

"Yeah," he said. "I thought we'd try a guy named Keith. I've never met him, but he's supposed to have a pipeline to 'Spirit.'"

"Really? How does he accomplish that?" I said.

"He *channels* Spirit," said Terry. "Or so he claims on his business card. He channels Him through an entity he calls Sergei."

"Ah, a Russian entity. How global."

"Very. Sergei is said to be an ancient cossack warrior who speaks for Spirit through Keith."

"Sort of like a conference call. Does Sergei have a last name?"

"Not that I can pronounce."

"How about Keith? Does *he* have a last name?"

"It's Love. Keith Love. He changed it when he moved to Sedona from Buffalo. It used to be Lutz, I hear."

"Smart career move. So we're hoping Keith will communicate with Sergei, who will communicate with Spirit, and that one of them will communicate with us about what really happened to Amanda."

"Exactly."

I shook my head. And people think communicating with the IRS is convoluted.

We reached Keith's tent just before sundown. How did we know it was Keith's tent, since all tents look pretty much alike? Keith's had a sign in front of his. It read: "Spirit by Sergei" and it reminded me of the beauty salon I went to in New York, which was called "Styling by Suzanne."

Encouraged that Keith was home, since his car was parked next to the tent, we got out of the Jeep and proceeded toward the campsite.

"How do we make our presence known?" I asked. "Tents don't have doorbells. Or even doors."

"Like this," said Terry, who lifted the front flap of the tent, stuck his head inside, and called out Keith's name.

"Come on in," a voice answered. *"Mi casa es su casa."*

"A Soviet entity that speaks Spanish?" I giggled as Terry pulled me into the tent, a rather modest dwelling furnished mostly with air mattresses.

Terry introduced himself and me to Keith, who was a tall, thin, jeans-clad man with wire-rimmed glasses, a dark beard and mustache, and a Jewish Afro, also known as a Jew'fro. He looked like a seventies version of a psychotherapist from Manhattan's Upper West Side.

"Good to meet you both," he said. "Have a seat."

Terry and I sat together on one of the mattresses.

"Want some nacho chips?" Keith asked. "I've got salsa, too. Extra spicy."

We passed on the chips and salsa, explaining that we'd had a big lunch.

"So. What can I do for you folks?" he said. "Or is it Sergei you're looking for?"

Gosh, I thought. How do we answer that without hurting one of their feelings?

"We have questions to ask Spirit," Terry said, not committing us either way. "Very important questions. Spirit's answers could save someone's life." I wasn't sure if he meant Will's or Amanda's, but I felt he handled the matter brilliantly.

"Then you've come to the right place," said Keith. "I book by the hour and the half-hour. It's $65.00 for the hour, $32.50 for the half-hour. And, if you don't mind, I like people to fill out this Comments Card after their first session. You can mail it to my P.O. box."

Keith handed Terry a little postcard that asked a series of questions, like: Where did you hear about "Spirit by Sergei?" Advertisement? Friend or relative? Travel agent? I tried to squelch a laugh and couldn't. Keith asked me what was so funny. I said it was just a nervous laugh. He told me there was nothing to be nervous about because Sergei was a very nice guy, for a cossack warrior.

"We'll take the half-hour," Terry told Keith.

"Cool," said our host, glancing at his watch so he could time our session. "Before we begin, I'll turn on the music." He walked over to the boom box in the corner of the tent and pushed the "Play" button on the tape deck. I assumed that he had selected the sort of mellow, nondescript, New Age music you hear all over Sedona, but on came a sudden crash of drums and cymbals and horns.

"Russian marching music," Keith explained. "Sergei likes it."

"It's lovely," I said, compelled to say something.

Keith sat down on a nearby mattress, adjusting his position until he was comfortable. "It'll be just a minute while I tune in to Sergei," he said, closing his eyes and breathing deeply.

I grabbed Terry's hand. I had never been in the company of a channeler, unless you counted my father, the channel surfer.

"Greetings! Greetings! Greetings!" boomed a voice I hadn't heard before, a voice that came from Keith but didn't sound like Keith. It was low, a deep baritone, and its accent was heavy on the Slavic. Think: Boris Badenov from Rocky and Bullwinkle. "I am Entity Sergei," said the voice, "and I speak to you through Keith Love."

Boy, I thought. Channeling is a lot like ventriloquism. Or multiple personality disorder.

"Before you ask your questions of Spirit," Sergei went on, speaking loudly in order to compete with the clanging and banging of all the percussive instruments in the background, "I wish to bring several issues to your attention."

"By all means," said Terry.

"I am here to tell you that there is a dimensional shift in the energies of human bodies," said Sergei. "Your residual self resides inside this dimensional shift and your frequency must be measured and corrected so that your souls will be ready to make the trip. Be the light that you are and become aware of your DNA molecules."

Sergei paused, so I took the opportunity to lean over and whisper to Terry, "Okay. So the guy's a kook. He was worth a try, wasn't he?"

Terry looked terribly discouraged.

"Conjecture regarding the overlap projection of souls originates from the energy fields that crop up in the universe," said Sergei, resuming his nonsensical pronounce-ments, "and if there is spatial displacement, there will be chaos in the cosmos."

Chaos in the cosmos. The perfect title for Amanda Reid's book, I thought, wondering if she'd live to write it.

"And now, peaceful travelers," said warrior Sergei. "What is it you wish to know from Spirit?"

"What do you think?" I asked Terry. "Should we bother?"

"We're here," he said resignedly.

"You go first," I said.

He nodded. "Entity Sergei," he began. "A woman vis-iting Sedona from New York asked my friend Will to take her on a Vision Quest."

"This woman is Amanda Reid," said Sergei. Obviously, Keith had read the newspaper.

"Yeah," said Terry. "The police think Will murdered her. I know that isn't true."

"Because you trust your friend," said Sergei.

"That's right," said Terry. "I believe in his innocence and I'd like you to help me *prove* his innocence. I'd like you to contact Spirit and ask Him what really happened to Amanda Reid, where she is now, whether she's dead or alive."

"Entity Sergei has processed your request," said Sergei. "Now, if you will give me a moment or two?"

While we waited, the Russian marching song crescen-doed with a tumultuous crash of a cymbal, which made my eardrums throb.

"Spirit has three things to say to you, peaceful travelers," Sergei said eventually. "The first is: Amanda Reid is alive."

Terry and I clasped hands. Who cared if Keith was a wacko? At least *somebody* was going on record that Will wasn't a killer.

"What's the second thing Spirit wants to tell us?" I asked Entity Sergei.

"That Amanda Reid is very close by, yet somehow hidden from view," he said.

"If she's hidden from view, how are we supposed to find her?" I asked.

"That is the third thing Spirit has to say to you," reported Sergei, as Keith smiled and wagged his finger at me. "*You,* peaceful traveler, hold the key to finding her."

"*I* do?" I said. "I'm an accountant, not a detective."

"Spirit is very clear about this," he said. "You hold the key to finding Amanda right there on that . . . on that . . . on that . . ."

"On that what?" I urged.

"Sorry. I am losing my connection with Spirit," Sergei said apologetically. "I cannot seem to—"

"Look, our half-hour isn't up yet," I interrupted. "So try again, would you, Sergei? You were saying that I hold the key to finding Amanda right there on *what?*"

"Right there on that . . . that . . . piece of paper you have," he said, blinking rapidly.

"What piece of paper?" I demanded.

"Spirit is not giving me . . . He is only indicating . . . Da. Da. Good. He is telling me that there is a piece of paper in your possession. A piece of paper that has writing on it, important writing, in connection with Amanda Reid's disappearance. A piece of paper that will point you in her direction, that will lead you straight to her door."

I threw up my hands in frustration. "Do you have any idea how many pieces of paper I have in my possession?" I told Sergei. "Can't Spirit be a little more specific?"

"It's okay, Crystal," Terry said, trying to calm me down. "Maybe we should go now."

"Maybe we should," I said, not knowing what to believe about Keith Love, in particular, and channelers, in general.

Terry helped me up from the mattress. "I think we're all set, Entity Sergei," he said. "You can bring Keith back now."

Keith closed his eyes and breathed deeply. Before we knew it, he had returned. "How'd everything go?" he asked us. "Did you folks get what you came for?"

Terry reached into his jeans pocket, pulled out exactly $32.50, and handed the bills and quarters to Keith. "We're not sure," he said. "But thanks for your time, just the same."

"No problem," said Keith. "Stop by whenever."

Terry and I were on our way out of the tent when we heard Keith speak in Sergei's voice.

"How about offering *me* some of those nacho chips and salsa," he said. "I haven't eaten since the czars were in power."

CHAPTER TWENTY-TWO

♥

It was dark by the time Terry and I made it back down Schnebly Hill Road, and while neither of us was especially hungry, we agreed that we could both use a drink.

"The Hideaway's close to my house," he said, his voice weary. "It's an Italian restaurant right on the Creek. We could start with a bottle of wine and go from there."

"You're the tour guide," I said. "The Hideaway it is."

The restaurant, a cozy, rustic, red-and-white-checked tablecloth kind of place, was crowded when we got there, but we cajoled the hostess into seating us on the patio, which was set high above the banks of Oak Creek—yet another of Sedona's many atmospheric spots.

Terry ordered us a bottle of Pinot Grigio.

"Well, what should we drink to?" I said, holding up my glass after the waiter had poured the wine.

"To your last night before old what's-his-name rides into town," Terry replied with a wry smile.

We clinked glasses and drank.

"You looking forward to seeing him?" he asked.

"To tell you the truth, I forgot he was coming," I admitted. "I spent fifty percent of the drive back from our session with Keith taking a mental inventory of all the pieces of paper in my possession, wondering which of them could possibly lead us to Amanda."

"And the other fifty percent?"

"I spent that trying to decide if it was *worth* taking a mental inventory of all the pieces of paper in my possession. I mean, we're assuming that Keith is a fraud, but what if he really has special powers? What if these special powers somehow give him an instinct or intuition or perception about where Amanda is and that he's right—I *do* have a clue written down on a piece of paper? I guess the question I'm asking is: Should we discount what he told us or not?"

Terry shrugged. "Will maintains that there are spiritualists around here who are genuinely gifted, totally on the level. He says that even the most talented sometimes resort to wearing crazy costumes and speaking in foreign tongues and making outrageous statements, mostly because people *expect* them to. He says that the tourists want a little theatre with their channeling, that they want to feel they're getting their money's worth, that they want to be able to go back to Ohio or Oregon—or New York, for that matter—with amusing cocktail party material. Now, whether Keith Love falls into this category, who knows? My suggestion is that when we're finished with dinner, we go back to my house, you take a quick look through the papers you've got in your suitcase or handbag, and if a clue screams out at us, we run with it. If not, we chalk Keith up to an entertaining afternoon."

"As I said the other day, I don't remember you being so sensible."

He reached across the table and stroked my cheek. "And

as *I* said the other day, I don't remember you being so beautiful."

I flushed from the compliment, as much as from the slow, sensual way the tips of his fingers were caressing my face.

"I have another suggestion," he said after pulling his hand away to take another sip of wine. "I think we ought to shelve all talk of Amanda Reid, Will Singleton, Steven Moth—"

"Roth."

"Steven Roth, and everybody else. I propose that, for the duration of this evening, we talk exclusively about you."

"Me? Please. My life is hopelessly dull compared to yours, Terry. Everybody you know is either a blues singer or a blackjack dealer."

"Not everybody. Take Cynthia, the woman Annie's staying with tonight. She's a soccer mom."

I laughed. "I thought she was a musician."

"No, she just plays a few instruments in her spare time. She's divorced, devoted to her kids, and a very nice person—someone you'd enjoy meeting. But we were talking about you, Crystal. Stop changing the subject."

"Fine. What do you want to talk about? Or, should I say, what about *me* do you want to talk about?"

"How about your work? You're a partner at Duboff Spector. What's that like?"

I sighed. "You really want to know?"

"I wouldn't have asked if I didn't."

I sighed again. "It stinks. I hate it. That's what it's like." I drank some wine. "Surprised?"

"Sure. I thought your career was going great, that it meant everything to you."

"It did. That's what stinks. It meant everything to me and now it's over."

"Over? Come on, Crystal."

"All right. So it's not over, exactly. The story is, I've worked my ass off at Duboff Spector and now, all of a sudden, they want to make the firm leaner and meaner, which means eliminating a partner or two, one of whom is me. I'm not out on the street yet or anything—they haven't even started to negotiate a contract settlement with me—but I'm history at Duboff Spector, there's no doubt about it. They're into hiring younger people who'll work for less money. It's a very upsetting situation, believe me."

"I believe you. But were you *ever* happy at Duboff Spector? Before this recent trouble?"

"Happy? Who's happy? Life isn't about happiness anymore. It's about finding a half-hour in the day to read a magazine or call a friend or just put your feet up and do absolutely nothing. I'm so busy being busy, so consumed with getting everything done and crossing everything off the list, that I don't have time to be happy. I'm too *tired* to be happy."

Terry shook his head. "If you haven't been happy at Duboff Spector, why haven't you left? You're a good accountant. Be a good accountant somewhere else."

"Ha! You act as if it's a snap to leave a job and get another one."

"That's because it is. There are plenty of jobs. I ought to know. I've had three-quarters of them."

I smiled, thinking he probably had. Still, I found the conversation ironic, to say the least. There I was, receiving career counseling from a man I'd written off as a deadbeat.

"So take it from me, Crystal. If Duboff Spector isn't treating you right, go do what you do someplace else, someplace where they'll appreciate you." He leaned forward, as if he wanted to emphasize the point he was about to make. "You know," he said, "for all your ambition and directedness and sense of purpose, you're afraid of change, aren't you?"

"Afraid? Oh, I don't—"

"You've spent so many years zeroing in on a single goal that you can't let go of that goal and take a different path. It's true, isn't it?"

"No. It's not that I can't ..." I stopped, hearing the denial in my voice, hearing how phony I sounded. "Look, I'm not you, Terry. I can't just try this job or that job and say, 'Hey, if it doesn't come together, what the hell.'"

"Why not? What are you waiting for? You've worked hard, made money, supported yourself and your father. Now it's okay to be flexible, to experiment, to change course. Otherwise, you'll always wonder, 'Could I have? Should I have?'"

I didn't say anything.

"You told me at lunch today how much you respect the changes I've made in my life," he went on. "So? If I could change, what about you?"

"You don't like me the way I am?"

"No, Crystal. *You* don't like you the way you are. That's what you said—that you haven't been happy."

I nodded.

Terry sat back in his chair. "I'm giving you a lecture, aren't I?"

"That's okay. It's your turn. I gave the last lecture—the day I divorced you."

"I remember."

"Do you?"

"Every word."

I saw the pain in his eyes then, the years of "Could I have? Should I have?"

"Why didn't you ever call me or write to me, Terry? Why didn't we stay in touch?"

"I told you—I remember that last lecture. You said you didn't want to see me again. I assumed you meant it."

"I did mean it. At the time."

God, it was awful to have to explain yourself after twenty years. It was so much easier to stick your head in the sand—or in someone's tax return, as it were. I refilled my wineglass.

"Tell you what," said Terry, sensing my discomfort. "Why don't we lighten up and eat dinner?"

I was relieved. "Why don't we?"

We looked around for our waiter. I didn't spot him, but I did spot my blond pal with the blue jeans and the "Om" T-shirt. He wasn't wearing the turquoise-and-silver cross around his neck, but he was making a nuisance of himself, as usual. On this occasion, he was hovering over an older man who was sitting two tables away from ours, puffing on a cigarette.

"You're in a bad space, a bad state, and a bad *seat*," he told the man.

"Darn. They didn't put me in the nonsmoking section by mistake, did they?" asked the man, who was, obviously, as dense about this stuff as I was.

The Reiki healer shook his head, explained that he was referring to the "seat" of the man's anxiety, and handed his latest sucker his business card.

Minutes later, our waiter appeared. Terry and I ordered shrimp scampi, Caesar salads, and a basket of garlic bread.

"Whew! That's a lot of garlic," the waiter laughed. "You two must like each other."

"We do like each other," Terry told him. "We just don't know what we're going to do about it."

When we got back to Terry's house, reeking of garlic, fuzzy from the wine, giddy with our reunion, we ambled hand in hand into the kitchen and noticed that the light on Terry's answering machine was blinking.

"You've got a message," I said, sinking down onto one of the kitchen chairs.

He came over to me and stood behind me, parting my hair to one side so he could massage my shoulders.

"I should play the message in case it's from Annie," he said as he continued to knead my muscles.

"You're a good father and an even better massage therapist," I praised him, turning my head slightly so I could see his face. He responded by bending down and kissing my mouth.

His action was not a surprise—I had been expecting, anticipating, hoping that we would kiss, probably since the first moment I saw him again but certainly since the previous evening, when we'd come awfully close up there in that guest room. And when his lips finally did meet mine, it was as if nearly two decades hadn't passed, as if we had kissed this way only yesterday, as if it were perfectly natural for us to kiss so passionately, so wantonly, so avidly.

I reached up and wrapped my arms around Terry's neck, drawing him further into the kiss, pulling him down, down, down until he was nearly squatting next to me as I sat on that chair.

We kissed for what seemed like a very long time, neither of us questioning the appropriateness of our behavior, neither of us trying to wriggle out of the embrace, neither of us bothering to breathe. The sensations were too sweet, too powerful, too many years in coming.

At some point, Terry did remind himself of the message on the answering machine, but after instructing me not to move and promising me he'd only be away from me for a second, he stayed right where he was and started kissing me all over again.

"Check the message," I whispered. "I'm not going anywhere."

He nodded and walked toward the answering machine.

He kept his eyes on me as he pushed the "Play" button, as he listened to the message, as he realized that it was Steven's voice on the tape, not Annie's.

"Hello. This is Steven Roth for Crystal Goldstein," said the voice. "Her hotel gave me this number, but I have no idea where I'm calling. In any case, I'd like her to know that I'll be arriving in Sedona about noon tomorrow, but I won't be staying at Tranquility, due to the media frenzy there. I've arranged to stay at a place named L'Auberge. The phone number there is—"

Terry pushed the "Erase" button before the message had fully played out. "I have the phone number at L'Auberge," he said to me. "If you want it."

"Thanks. I guess Steven and Harrison Reid will be neighbors."

"Bully for both of them," Terry said, walking back toward me. "I've got other things on my mind."

I didn't have to ask, "What things?" Terry's lips were on mine before I could even pose the question.

"I was planning to look through all my papers tonight, to see if I had anything that would lead us to Amanda," I reminded him during a brief lull in the kissing.

"Tomorrow," he said softly, nuzzling my ear. "Tonight's booked."

"Is it?"

"Yeah." He went to the sink, reached inside the nearby cabinet for a tall glass, and filled it with tap water. And then he came for me.

"Ready?" he asked, handing me the glass.

Oh, I was ready all right. But, I must admit, it did cross my mind in that instant that sleeping with Terry could complicate my life, particularly where Steven was concerned. Despite his marriage proposal, despite his imminent arrival in Sedona, I no longer felt bound to Steven Roth in the way I once did, no longer considered our relationship a "given." Still, would I be cheating on him if I slept with Terry, betraying him with my former spouse just as he had betrayed me with his? Would I be making a big, fat, irrevocable mistake?

"Our being together doesn't have to affect anything or anyone," Terry said, picking up on my hesitation. "You can see it as a tiny blip on the radar screen or a quick trip down memory lane or two people who've loved each other indulging in a night of pleasure. How you look at it is up to you. But don't—whatever you do—*don't* deny yourself this. You want it as much as I do, Crystal."

"Yes," I said, tired of denying myself things, tired of servicing everybody else, tired of settling. "I want this as much as you do, Terry. Maybe more."

CHAPTER
TWENTY-THREE

♥

At my insistence, we spent the night in the guest room. Sleeping in Terry's bedroom, in Terry's bed, would have made a statement I wasn't prepared to make.

"You've still got those freezing cold feet," he said after we'd slid between the sheets and pressed our naked bodies up against each other.

"I'm afraid so," I laughed. "And *you've* still got that tremendous—"

He silenced me with another of those wondrous, stirring kisses, the kind that bring about both an exquisite rush of excitement and a profound sense of well-being.

"Terry," I murmured, repeating his name over and over as he reacquainted himself with my body, revisited his "favorite places," remembered where I liked to be touched and how.

"Who would have guessed this would happen?" he said softly when I took my turn exploring his body, the body that had once been almost as familiar to me as my own.

We reveled in our lovemaking, marveled at the very fact of it, lost ourselves in the sheer pleasure of it. It didn't matter that we were divorced, that we hadn't seen each other since Gerald Ford was President, that we were trying to determine the whereabouts of a woman lots of people wanted dead. All that mattered was that Crystal Goldstein and Terry Hollenbeck were up there in that little bedroom creating a miracle—a miracle that lasted most of the night and into Saturday morning. It wasn't what I had in mind when I came to Sedona searching for Meaning, but it wasn't chopped liver, either.

"We've gotta get up, Terry," I said at about nine a.m., recalling that he'd told me his friend Cynthia was bringing Annie home at nine-thirty. "Wake up, okay?"

"I'm awake," he mumbled, his eyes shut, his body paralyzed, the same Terry that Annie and I had joked about.

I shook him. "Annie will be home soon," I tried again. "I wouldn't want her to see us—"

"Relax," he said, coming alive. "Your secret's safe with me."

"Thanks, but we do have to get up," I said, starting to climb out of bed.

Terry pulled me back down next to him and kissed the tip of my nose. "Look, before everybody starts piling in here—my daughter, your boyfriend, whoever—I'd like you to know that I think you're the best."

I smiled lasciviously. "The best at what, may I ask?"

"The best at whatever you want to be the best at," he said, his tone turning serious. "You can do anything you put your mind to, Crystal, whether it's making it work with Steven or finding a job at another accounting firm or even staying at Duboff Spector. You have it all, right there inside you. If you need to make changes in your life, there's no reason why you can't."

"Boy, you have more confidence in me than I have in myself."

"I love you. That's probably why."

"Terry."

"It's true. I love you."

I stared at him. "Let me get this straight. Are you saying that you love me *still*, as in: you never stopped loving me? Or are you saying that you love me *now*, as in: you didn't really love me the first time around?"

"Neither. I'm saying that I love you *differently*, as in: I have a capacity for loving you now that I didn't have the first time around, that I'm in a better position to love you now than I was then."

"But how can you tell that *this* love is different?" I asked. "We hurt each other once. It would be crazy to have another go at it, wouldn't it?"

"Not crazy. Just a little risky, maybe."

"Risky. My specialty," I said dryly.

"Look, this subject is too important for us to talk about on the run. We can pick it up again later. Like this afternoon."

"I can't. Steven will be here. I'll be going over to L'Auberge this afternoon."

"Right. Sorry."

"I've got to see him, Terry. He's coming all this way."

"I know." He kissed me again. "Better get up then."

I nodded. Better get up.

Terry had predicted that I would like Cynthia Kavner the minute I met her and he was right. She was a delight— warm, friendly, and down-to-earth. A short woman with frizzy auburn hair, she was about my age and had two children: Laura, Annie's friend from school, and Karen, who was four years older. She was a Phoenix native who had spent summers in Sedona, then moved to town permanently after her divorce.

"So you're the famous Crystal," she said with a hearty laugh. "Annie's been talking about you nonstop."

"I guess it was a little strange for her to find me on her doorstep yesterday," I said. "She was great to me though."

"She's a great kid. She's very excited that you've decided to move to Sedona."

"That I've what?" I said, stunned.

"Uh-oh. I'm getting the sense that Annie's been doing a little wishful thinking here. You're *not* moving to Sedona?"

"No. As a matter of fact, I told Annie yesterday that I'll be going back to New York when the detective who's investigating the Amanda Reid case gives me the okay. I can't imagine why she'd tell you I was staying."

"She wants you to stay, obviously. She's been without a mother her entire life. She probably envisions you stepping into that role, because you and Terry used to be married to each other."

"Maybe, but she and Terry are incredibly close, a real twosome. Most girls would have at least *some* resentment toward a woman who shows up and changes the dynamic."

"Annie isn't 'most girls,'" Cynthia pointed out.

"I'm beginning to see that," I said.

After Cynthia left, Terry announced that he was going over to the office to change cars. We'd been driving around in the tour company's big Jeep while his own four-seat Jeep Wrangler was still in the lot. He said he'd be home in a couple of hours and that Annie should play hostess while he was gone.

"I'll bring us back the fixings for a cookout on the Creek," he promised. "A good old-fashioned burger barbecue."

"My dad loves burgers," Annie whispered to me.

"I remember," I whispered back. "Medium rare."

She giggled, seeming pleased that she had someone with whom she could share tidbits about her father.

"I've got a great idea," she said. "We'll go outside and I'll show you how to jump on my trampoline!"

I smiled at her, combing back the lock of hair that had fallen into her face. She was a little sprite, that Annie, a charmer with an amazing ability to sound like a grownup one minute and a kid the next. I wasn't fooling myself or idealizing her—she had to have her bratty days, just like other children her age—but from what I'd seen of her, she was swell company.

"I'd love to play on your trampoline," I told her, "but could we do it in a half-hour or so? There are some papers I've got to look through first, upstairs in the guest room."

"Sure," she said. "I'll be outside waiting for you."

She hurried off into the backyard, leaving me to wonder how I'd allowed myself to miss out on the experience of raising a child, of being a mother, of being a caregiver to someone other than my unappreciative, unresponsive father. When I was young and newly married, I had taken it for granted that I'd have kids someday. I had imagined that I would be one of those so-called "superwomen" who would juggle family and career as if there was nothing to it. Then came the quick divorce, the long hours at the office, the single life in New York, and before I knew it, I had forgotten all about ever wanting children, had convinced myself they were more trouble than they were worth. I was out of the loop when it came to the hottest toy at Christmastime, the coolest snack to bring to school, the latest trend in computer games. I didn't even have the vocabulary to *talk* about children, much less have them. And so life went on—without them.

"See you in a little while," I called out to Annie as I heard the screen door bang shut.

I made myself a cup of coffee and took it upstairs to the

guest room. And then I got down to business. I sorted through my suitcase and came upon the following pieces of paper: a copy of *Fortune* magazine, which I'd brought with me to read on the flight to Phoenix; a folder containing my plane tickets and travel itinerary; a second folder containing my rental car information; assorted credit card receipts; and a brochure promoting Tranquility and its many amenities. Nothing there that could point to Amanda's whereabouts, right? Next, I checked inside my carry-on bag, but its only contents were my makeup case and prescription drugs. I didn't even bother to open my purse, since the only pieces of paper in there were traveler's checks and a hundred bucks in small bills. Obviously, Keith/Sergei/Spirit was mistaken about their being any clues in *my* possession.

Disappointed that I couldn't help Will Singleton, that I couldn't save the day after all, I trudged downstairs, through the back door, out onto the lawn.

There was Annie, jumping up and down on that trampoline, up and down, up and down, up and down. I was getting queasy just watching her.

"Come and try it, Crystal!" she said excitedly. "It's easy. I'll teach you how."

I guess she hasn't seen the movie *Accountants Can't Jump*, I thought. Oh, well. She looked so eager for me to join her that there was no way I could refuse.

"I should take off my shoes, right?" I said.

"Yeah. Kick 'em off and climb up."

Here comes the cup of coffee I just drank, I said to myself, wondering if it would have been prudent to pop a Pepcid AC before all the jumping.

I took off my sneakers and approached the trampoline. It seemed more and more intimidating the closer and closer I got.

"Here, Crystal. Grab my hand," the ten-year-old girl said to the forty-three-year-old chicken.

I grabbed her hand and she pulled me up onto the trampoline. I tried to steady myself; it was like steadying yourself on a waterbed.

"Okay. Now jump," she said and did.

I jumped, too, but my feet were like lead. I barely left the canvas.

"It's fun, Crystal. Come on!" she whooped with unmitigated joy.

I jumped again, higher this time. Boing. Boing. Boing.

"Hey! You're doing it!" Annie cried as we bounced together. Our bouncing wasn't in sync, but it wasn't causing either of us bodily harm.

"This *is* fun!" I said, turning to face the Creek as I bounced. The water looked cool, clear, inviting. I shared my observations with Annie.

"Oh, yeah. The Creek is great for swimming," she said between breaths, "especially when you're all sweaty from jumping."

We jumped and sweated and squealed like a couple of kids, and then we ran into the house, put on our bathing suits, and went swimming. The water in the Creek was chillier than I had anticipated but it was invigorating, and it was Annie who tired of it before I did.

By the time Terry got home from the office, I had worked up quite an appetite.

"Well, well. Look at you two," he said, noticing our wet heads.

"Crystal and I played on the trampoline, then went swimming," Annie reported. "Now I'm going to take her to my school."

"Nothing doing. It's lunchtime, sport," said Terry. "Aren't you hungry after all the activity?"

"Sure. Are *you* hungry, Crystal?" Annie asked, gazing up at me.

"Starving. Why not let your Dad and me make lunch for you?"

"Yeah, honey," Terry agreed. "Crystal and I will get the burgers ready for the grill while you relax, read the Declaration of Independence, maybe." He winked at her.

"I've already read the Declaration of Independence," she boasted.

"Then how about the Constitution?" he teased.

"I think I'll just hum a few bars of 'Hail to the Chief,' " she countered.

We all laughed.

"Why don't you come right out and say you want to be alone with Crystal, Dad?" Annie asked.

"I want to be alone with Crystal," Terry said. "For a few minutes."

"I'm gone," she said and took off for her room.

As soon as Terry and I were alone, he came charging over to me and wrapped me in his arms.

"Hello, you," he said after kissing me.

"Hi," I said. "Everything all right at Sacred Earth Jeep Tours?"

He shook his head. "Jean was there and she had about a hundred media people on her heels. I swear, they're all hanging out at the office, wanting to know everything about the tour Amanda was on, where she went, what she wore, what she said, and especially where Will took her before she disappeared."

"My God. Of course they'd show up at your office," I said. "I didn't think about that."

"Neither did I until I got there. But it's not just the media. It's the lawyers."

"The lawyers?"

"Yeah. The bottom fishing types that crawl out when

there's a big case. They're offering to represent Will if he's arrested."

"Please. I think I'm going to be sick."

Terry hugged me. "Be sick *after* lunch, okay? I've got burgers to feed you."

He had a point. "I had a wonderful morning with Annie," I said as we prepared the meat for the grill. "Is she always so . . . so . . . good?"

"She's happy," he replied. "Happy kids are good kids, for the most part."

"But she got off to such a rough start in the world," I said. "It's amazing that she's as well-adjusted as she is, or seems to be."

"She has her moments," he acknowledged, "but they're moments. They pass. We work them out."

They work them out, I thought, remembering the difficult moments Terry and I had during our marriage, how he was never willing to work them out, how he would make a joke when there was a problem or storm out of the apartment in a huff or tell me he didn't know what I was getting all upset about. What a difference a couple of decades make.

We had a picnic lunch out by the Creek, each of us perched on the rock ledge, our feet dangling in the water, our plates on our laps. Terry and I told Annie stories about college and she told us stories about her elementary school. We laughed a lot, particularly when Annie did a priceless imitation of a substitute teacher who had recently taught her class. So kids are still making fun of their substitute teachers, I mused. Some things don't change.

Terry was in the middle of an anecdote about one of his old political science professors when we heard the phone ringing.

"I'll get it!" said Annie as she jumped up and ran inside

the house before Terry could even form the words: Let the answering machine pick it up.

Seconds later, she came back outside, looking very satisfied with herself.

"It was for you, Crystal," she said. "It was Steven."

"Oh," I said, getting up quickly. "Yes, it must be close to one o'clock."

"It's one-thirty," Terry informed me after glancing at his watch.

"Then he must have checked in at L'Auberge," I said. I turned to Annie. "Isn't he still on the phone?"

She shook her head. "I told him you were in the middle of lunch," she said. "Dad doesn't like it when people call here during meal time."

I smiled. Annie was a cagey one.

"Well," I said, "I'll be sure to reprimand Steven when I go inside and call him back. May I be excused?"

I looked at Terry.

"Permission granted," he said.

I looked at Annie.

"Okay, but I wouldn't run up the phone bill if I were you," she said. "Dad doesn't like that either."

CHAPTER
TWENTY-FOUR

♥

L'Auberge de Sedona promoted itself as the area's most romantic hideaway—an exclusive French country inn set along picturesque Oak Creek. Only minutes from Terry's house, the chichi resort was comprised of several individual cottages, all tucked along the banks of the Creek, all equipped with fireplaces, all sumptuously decorated. There was also a gourmet French restaurant, a more casual outdoor eatery, and a lodge housing a gift/home accessories shop called The Armoire. In short, if you were casting about for the perfect backdrop against which to propose marriage, L'Auberge de Sedona would certainly fit the bill.

I arrived at the inn in my burgundy rental car at two o'clock that Saturday afternoon. I did not bring any luggage with me, having decided that I should see how things went between Steven and me before committing to a sleepover date with him. It was bad enough, I thought, that I had cheated on Steven with Terry; I couldn't very well cheat on Terry with Steven. I left my bags in Terry's guest room, telling him and Annie that I intended to return later that evening. They were great sports about the situation.

"Sure. Eat and run," Terry said.

"Yeah. Leave *us* with all the dirty lunch dishes," Annie chimed in.

I knew they were teasing me, but I went off to L'Auberge feeling a tad conflicted.

Steven had given me directions to his cottage when we'd spoken on the phone, so I knew precisely where it was located on the property. Still, before I could get to it, I had to make my way through the hoards of media types who were camped out at L'Auberge's entrance. They were not permitted to roam the grounds, according to the security guard I spoke to, but they were there anyway, hungry for a glimpse and/or comment from Harrison Reid. Eventually, I bypassed everybody and found the cottage.

"Steven!" I said with great enthusiasm as he opened the door. "How are you?"

Not a very original opener, I know, but I had expected that my presence alone would elicit an embrace of some significance, an embrace befitting lovers who had been apart for a period of time.

"I'm fine," Steven said hurriedly as he brushed my cheek with his lips. "Let me just finish this call and I'll be right with you. Okay, Crystal?"

"No problem," I said. "Pretend I'm not here."

Isn't this nice, I thought sourly. The guy flies nearly three thousand miles to convince me to marry him, and he can't get off the fucking phone. Steven was on a business call, even thought it was a weekend. I could tell by the fact that he was saying things like: "Pursuant to Paragraph D in the contract . . ."

While he droned on about settlements and payout schedules and other matters of no possible consequence to me, I checked out his cottage, which was quite spacious—a bedroom complete with a wrought iron canopy bed, a sitting area in front of the fireplace, a large porch overlooking the Creek. The cottage was also, as advertised, quite romantic, but the longer Steven stayed on the phone, the more unromantic I felt.

"Steven," I whispered, tugging on his arm. "Wind it up, can't you?"

He covered the mouthpiece with his hand and whispered back, "I'm really sorry, Crystal. It'll only be another five minutes, I promise."

I sat on the overstuffed love seat by the fireplace and waited. I was about ten minutes into the waiting when it dawned on me that Steven's treatment of me—making me twiddle my thumbs while he conducted business, placing his job ahead of our relationship, acting like an asshole—was exactly the same treatment that I'd been dishing out to him for the past three years.

My God, he's only doing to you what you've always done to him, I realized, thinking back to all the times I'd instructed Rona to put him on "Hold" when he called or to tell him I was too busy to talk or to just get rid of him. He's making it clear that his career comes first, which is the very reason you chose him, Crystal Goldstein. You chose him because he was consumed with his work, which freed you to be equally consumed with yours. You chose him because he left you alone to drown yourself in your clients' lives. You chose him because he didn't require that you love him.

I let these little epiphanies sink in, as painful as they were, sink in, sink in, sink in. I allowed myself to face the fact that if I hadn't walked in on Steven and Stephanie that night in his apartment, hadn't provoked his declaration of love for me, hadn't rocked the boat by leaving New York so abruptly, he and I would still be coasting along just as before, getting together for a meal or a movie now and then, slotting each other in. We would continue to be partners, companions, consorts, probably into our old age, probably for the rest of our lives. We would be the kind of people who are forever maintaining that compatibility is preferable to passion, the kind of people who never argue, the kind of people other people pity.

No, I thought with stunning clarity. Not anymore. Not for me.

Steven concluded his telephone conversation and came and sat down next to me on the love seat. He looked very handsome, I noticed, his pale green eyes matching almost exactly the color of his Ralph Lauren shirt, his dark brown hair newly shorn for the trip. Yes, he was an attractive man, there was no doubt about it. Bright, energetic, successful, too. A "good catch," all things considered. A catch I was about to throw back.

"Now," he said, extending his arm around my shoulders. "Before we talk about us, I want to hear all about Amanda Reid. What an adventure your trip has turned out to be, Crystal!"

You don't know the half of it, I thought, flashing back to my night of sin.

"I'll bet you have as much information about the case as I do," I said. "I'm sure the New York papers were full of the story yesterday."

"Absolutely. It's O.J. all over again. Everybody's debating whether the Indian guy killed her or she had some sort of supernatural experience and disappeared. I guess people equate Sedona with the Bermuda Triangle or something. You come out here and you take your chances."

Steven laughed. I didn't.

"The Indian guy didn't kill her," I said. "I don't think anyone did."

"Ah, so you subscribe to the Bermuda Triangle theory,"

Steven chuckled. "You believe that Amanda Reid just vanished from the radar screen, right?"

"No, but I believe she's still alive." To be more accurate, it was Sergei who believed she was still alive, but I kept that little detail to myself.

Steven asked me a zillion more questions about Amanda—what she was like, what the people in her entourage were like, etc.—and I told him what I knew. I wondered when he would drop the subject and ask me to marry him. That was why he'd come to Sedona, wasn't it?

"Oh. I meant to ask you," he said finally. I braced myself. "Where on earth are you staying now?"

"Staying?" So he wasn't proposing.

"Since you checked out of Tranquility. I think I spoke to a child when I called you earlier." He laughed. "I know we're at that age when everybody sounds young to us, but this person *was* young. Eight or nine, maybe."

"Ten, actually."

"Ten?"

"Listen, Steven. I should have mentioned this before, but it turns out that my ex-husband owns the tour company. He was the one who took Amanda, me, and the rest of the group up to the vortex sites."

"He took you where?"

"He took us sight-seeing," I said, trying to keep things simple.

Steven shook his head disbelievingly. "You're saying that the man who introduced Amanda Reid to the Indian guy—that's what the newspapers indicated, that this Jeep Tour operator put her in touch with the Indian—is *your* ex-husband?"

"That's what I'm saying."

"What an incredible coincidence."

"Incredible."

"Particularly since you haven't seen him in years."

"Or spoken to him. Not since our divorce."

"Incredible," Steven repeated.

"His name is Terry—Terry Hollenbeck—and he and his daughter, Annie, live down the road from here. When the media descended on Tranquility, he was nice enough to invite me to stay in his guest room."

Steven nodded as he processed these unexpected developments. "So it was his little girl who answered the phone when I called."

"Yes. I'm staying with Terry and Annie until the police don't need me to hang around Sedona anymore. After that, I'll fly back to New York."

He nodded again, this time as if he fully understood the situation. "I think I see what's going on," he said. "You're staying with your ex-husband because I had that ill-advised fling with my ex-wife. You're punishing me, paying me back, playing tit for tat. Isn't that what we're dealing with here?"

I smiled. "No, Steven. I'm not playing tit for tat. I'm not playing games, period. The truth is, running into Terry has made me more forgiving of your relationship with Stephanie."

"It has?"

"Sure. You tried to explain that you and Stephanie have a history together. Well, now I've realized that Terry and I have a history together, too, a past that can't be erased."

Steven scowled. "The guy's single, I'm assuming."

"Yes. He's single."

"How do you feel about him? After all these years, I mean."

"I don't know."

"You don't know?"

"No."

He arched an eyebrow. "Should I be worried about this?"

I took a deep breath. "My feelings for Terry—whatever they are—have nothing to do with us, Steven."

He looked relieved. "That's good news. For a minute, I was thinking that there might not be an 'us' anymore."

Okay, I thought. Here it is, Crystal. Your opening. Your chance to bail out. Your opportunity to break it to Steven that you're not going to marry him or even see him anymore. Your moment to explain that you're not about to settle for a man you don't love.

I cleared my throat, intending to speak. Suddenly, the cottage seemed extremely claustrophobic. I had the urge to bolt.

"Steven, there are some lovely paths that meander between the cottages," I said, rising quickly from the love seat. "Could we pick up this conversation outside, while we take a walk together?"

"Why not?" he said, glancing at his watch. "My client won't be calling me for another fifteen minutes. You and I should be all talked out and back at the cottage by then, right?"

"Right," I said. "With any luck."

We strolled along the little paths that wound their way around the rear of the property. The surroundings were breathtaking in their natural beauty—the gardens, the Creek, even the trees, which heralded fall's arrival with their leaves, some of which had turned from green to gold, others from gold to crimson.

"Steven," I began as we ambled past the cottage adjacent to his. "I came to a conclusion today. Just a little while ago, as a matter of fact."

"Did you?" he said hopefully.

"Yes," I said. "I came to the conclusion that we're good people who deserve better."

"Better? How?"

"Well, for starters, we deserve a partner who will pay attention to us. Not all the time. Not every minute. When it counts."

"How do we know when it counts?" Steven looked genuinely baffled at first. Then he nodded. "I get it. You're not angry that I was with Stephanie. You're angry that I was on the phone when you—"

"This isn't about one phone call," I cut him off. "This is about all the phone calls. You and I have had a more meaningful relationship with our long distance carriers than we've had with each other."

"That's not true."

"Yes, it is. Steven, I'm not pointing the finger at you. I'm guilty, too. We've both allowed this charade to go on far longer than it should have. We haven't loved each other. Not really. We've loved the fact that we've left each other alone, that we haven't conflicted with each other's schedules. That was fine for a while. It isn't fine now."

"It isn't?" The man was a shrewd, street-smart lawyer, but he was clueless when it came to his personal life. Just as I had been.

"Not for me," I said. "If you and I got married, it would be more of the same—you'd work, I'd work, and we'd see each other two weeks from Saturday. That's not a life— that's an appointment book."

His face fell. "You're telling me it's over between us."

"I am," I said tenderly.

"I'm disappointed," he said. "I thought we'd get married, you'd move into my apartment, and we'd redecorate."

I patted his arm. "Your paisley's safe now," I soothed.

He was about to cry, I think, but he was distracted, as I was, by the yelling that was coming from the cottage directly behind us. Its windows were open and we couldn't miss a word if we'd tried.

"You said you loved me," a woman's voice wailed. "You said we would be together forever. You said you were naming the heroine of your next book after me."

Jennifer Sibley? Harrison Reid? A lovers' tiff?

Steven made an attempt to speak. I shushed him.

"Don't be a ninny," boomed a voice that was unmistakably Harrison's. "You didn't actually think I would leave Amanda, did you?"

"No!" Jennifer sobbed. "No! I knew you'd never leave her. You're too loyal, too caring, to abandon your wife. *I* had to take charge of the situation. *I* had to eliminate her. She was coming between us, Harrison darling. Always coming between us."

Steven tried again to say something. This time, I clamped my hand over his mouth.

"But you didn't eliminate her," Harrison ho-ho-hoed. "Someone apparently got to her first. That's the irony of this melodrama. You all had plans to murder my wife and you all failed. Tina and Billy had their pathetic little kidnapping scheme. Poor Marie had notions of poisoning Amanda. And you, Jennifer. You were actually going to shoot her and make it look like a suicide. 'Mrs. Reid was distraught over her inability to launch her own clothing line,' you were going to tell the media." Harrison ho-de-hoed some more. Clearly, *he* was not distraught. "To all of your surprise and, very likely, dismay, this local man— this Indian fellow who took Amanda on some sort of jaunt—ended up murdering her and doing away with her body. It's too much, really. If I put it in a novel, my editor would never buy it. 'Unbelievable,' he'd say. 'Doesn't ring true.'"

So Jennifer didn't kill Amanda either, I thought, wondering what would have happened if the millionaire heiress hadn't disappeared when she did. Which of her faithless flock would have beaten out the others and bumped her off? It might have been a fight to the finish.

"You're not going to tell the police, are you?" Jennifer was asking Harrison. "I didn't commit murder. There's no proof that I was even contemplating it. It's only my word against yours."

Harrison really guffawed at that one. "Your word against mine? My dear Jennifer, words are my profession. If I decide to tell the police what you've just confided to me, they will believe me, no matter how passionately you protest. But no. I'm not going to tell anybody. If I told Detective Whitehead that you were plotting to murder my wife because you and I were having a brief dalliance, news of the affair would be leaked to the media, and I'm afraid my readers would find out and think me rather lecherous. I've got a new book due to arrive in stores shortly, as you well know. Now is certainly not the time for me to tarnish my image."

"No, it isn't," said Jennifer, the image consultant.

"Besides," Harrison went on, "what would be the point of telling the police anything? Once they find Amanda's body, we'll all go back to New York and begin anew. You'll find another grasping socialite to publicize and I'll find another young woman with whom to amuse myself."

"Jesus. He's one cool customer, huh?" I whispered to Steven, removing my hand from his mouth.

The moment I let go, he emitted a loud expulsion of air, as if he were a tire going flat.

"Are you all right?" I asked.

"Now I am. I couldn't breathe with your hand on my mouth."

"Why didn't you say so?"

"Because your hand was on my mouth."

"Oh. Then why didn't you breathe through your nose?"

"I must be allergic to all the sage out here," he said. "My sinus passages are completely clogged."

"I'm sorry," I said, hugging Steven. I was going to miss him, I realized. It had been nice having someone to commiserate with when it came to allergies and sinus problems.

"That's okay," he said. "It was worth it. It's not every day you get to eavesdrop on a murdered woman's husband and his girlfriend."

Just then, I heard a noise, a rustling in the trees behind me. I turned and there was Michael Mandell, scribbling fast and furiously in his notebook. And he wasn't alone. He was with another man—a man lugging a camera with one of those lenses that can zoom in on people and take their picture from a quarter of a mile away. Michael waved at me. "Guess we got more than enough for tomorrow's front pages," he said cheerfully, then raced off with his pal. So much for Harrison and his image. So much for Michael and his journalistic integrity.

"Want to go back to the cottage now?" Steven asked. "Relax? Talk? Whatever? Then have dinner at the restaurant here? I remember that when you left New York, you were having problems with the other partners at Duboff Spector. I could help you with that. I could go over your legal options with you. I could structure a negotiating strategy that would allow you to walk away with a very sweet 'Screw them' package." He paused, waiting for my response. "We probably won't be seeing each other after today, Crystal," he pointed out. "So if I were you, I'd take advantage of my offer, you know?"

I smiled and linked my arm through Steven's.

CHAPTER
TWENTY-FIVE

♥

It was close to eleven o'clock when I pulled up to Terry's house. He had left the outside light on for me, I noticed. A beacon in the darkness. I hoped he was still awake. I had a lot to tell him.

I opened the front door and entered the house. I was tiptoeing through the dimly lit living room, on my way into the kitchen, when I tripped over a body.

I gasped as I went down, my feet instantly becoming entangled with the feet belonging to the body, the rest of me falling in a heap across a mound of flesh I could feel but not see.

"Ouch!" came a voice. "Didn't anyone ever tell you that it isn't nice to kick a guy when he's down?"

The voice, I was relieved to discover, was that of the man of the house.

"Yes, but no one ever told me that guys stretch out on their living room floor even when there's a perfectly good sofa available," I retorted.

Terry rubbed his eyes. "I *am* on the living room floor, aren't I?"

"You are. The question is, why?"

"Why," he mused. "Well, the last thing I remember was sitting on the floor, playing cards with Annie—she was beating the heck out of me at gin rummy. I guess I fell asleep. When she couldn't wake me up, she must have turned the light out and gone to bed. And here I am."

"Here we both are." I didn't believe the bit about his falling asleep in the middle of the card game. I had a hunch he'd decided to wait up for me after the card game and nodded out in the process.

We disentangled ourselves.

"So how'd it go with Steven?" Terry asked as we remained on the floor, two lumps in the dark.

"We had a good time together," I replied. "And then we said goodbye."

"I assume you'll be seeing him tomorrow?"

"No, I told you. We said goodbye, farewell, hasta la vista. It's over between Steven and me, Terry. We broke up."

"You broke up?" He sat up very straight. He was wide awake now. "But you said you had a good time."

"We did, once the decision was made and the pressure was off. We had a lovely dinner in the restaurant at L'Auberge. We ate beautifully prepared food, drank expensive French wine. Steven gave me legal advice about dealing with the partners at Duboff Spector. I gave him tax advice to pass along to his mother, a client of mine who will probably take her business elsewhere."

"Sounds very civilized," said Terry. "Not like when you and I split up."

"No, it wasn't like that at all. For the most part, this breakup was surprisingly painless. I don't think Steven wanted to marry me any more than I wanted to marry him. It was just that we'd been together for three years. We had an investment in each other. A minor investment, as it turns out, but an investment nevertheless. I finally persuaded him that the relationship wasn't going anywhere, that we weren't the same people we were when we met, and that I, for one, had to make a change."

"I can't believe what I'm hearing, Crystal. The other day you were convinced that you weren't ready to make changes, but you sure made them today."

"I made one, Terry. That's all."

"Gotta start somewhere, right?" Even in the dark I could see the huge grin on his face. Clearly, the fact that I had ended things with Steven did not upset him. "I'm glad the old boy took it so well."

"There were a few teary moments, but he did take it well. He's a gentleman. Most of all, he's practical. He told me he's got a client in Phoenix. He said he's going to write off his brief visit to Sedona as a business trip. No muss, no fuss."

"From the way you describe your relationship, it *was* a business trip."

"Funny. Now, moving off the subject of Steven for a minute, I have interesting news about Amanda. About her husband and his mistress, to be precise."

I reported word for word the conversation I had overheard between Harrison and Jennifer. "We'll be reading about it tomorrow, courtesy of Michael."

"Amazing," Terry said. "So the publicist was standing in line to kill Amanda, too." He shook his head. "Murdering Mrs. Reid is like going to a deli counter—you've gotta take a number."

"They're all a bunch of ghouls. Especially that husband of hers. He's a louse if ever there was one."

"Look, the real bad news here is that none of these confessions gets Will off the hook," Terry pointed out.

"The police are still hung up on the idea that he was the last one to see Amanda alive."

"It's awful. Everyone's taking his guilt for granted. Even Steven said he thought Will did it, just from what he read in the New York papers."

"Well, I'm not giving up on my pal. He and I are hiking up to Cathedral Rock tomorrow morning. We're going straight to the spot where he deposited Amanda and we're not leaving until we find something, some clue, some piece of evidence that will tell us what really happened."

"Some piece of evidence that the police haven't found? Come on, Terry. They've already searched the area."

"Cathedral Rock's a big place, and Will Singleton knows it better than any cop."

"So you're hoping you'll stumble across something the cops missed?"

"That's what we're hoping."

"I'd like to help. How would you feel about my tagging along?"

"About as good as I'd feel if you kissed me."

"You want me to kiss you? Right here on this living room floor?"

"Exactly."

"Isn't Annie upstairs?"

"Yeah."

"What if she walks in on us?"

"Then she'll *see* you kiss me."

"Terry."

"She's sleeping, Crystal. And even if she weren't, the sight of you kissing me isn't going to scar her for life."

"No, I don't suppose it will."

I reached out with my hands, into the darkness of the room, and made contact with Terry's face, running my fingers along his nose, his cheeks, his chin. When I found his mouth, I drew myself closer, drew my mouth closer.

"Is this what you have in mind?" I asked before pressing my lips to his.

"Yeah. Give it a whirl," he said, and so I did.

It was a kiss that began as a playful extension of our conversation but quickly took on a life of its own—a kiss that kept growing in intensity, forcing us to adjust our positions several times as our excitement heightened.

The kiss went on and on until we realized, to our great amusement, that we were now sprawled on top of each other on the floor of Terry's living room, "making out" like a couple of horny teenagers.

I sat up, straightening my hair and clothes. "We can't do this. Not with Annie right upstairs," I maintained. "Kissing is one thing. What we're doing is—"

"Then we'll move the party somewhere else," Terry cut me off. "To a room with a door that locks."

"To a room with a bed," I suggested. "This floor is hard and I'm not as young as I used to be."

He helped me up. "Your glass of water, madame, before we go up?" he said, motioning toward the kitchen.

"I think I'll skip it tonight," I said, my mouth thirsting for more than water.

Terry smiled and took my hand as we mounted the stairs, treading carefully so as not to wake Annie. When we came to her room, en route to the guest room, we stopped in her doorway for a minute or two and watched her. She was tucked under the covers, completely still, the picture of serenity.

"She's sleeping so soundly," I whispered as we peered at her.

"All that bouncing on the trampoline and swimming in the Creek must have tired her out," Terry whispered back.

"What about me?" I said. "I did all that bouncing and swimming, too, and I've managed to stay awake."

"You're motivated to stay awake," he said, running his

hand along the inside of my right thigh. "At least, I hope
you are."

The first night I'd slept with Terry after our twenty-year
hiatus, I'd been almost too nervous to get the most out
of the experience. Don't misunderstand me—I'd enjoyed
myself tremendously—but part of me had been detached,
overthinking the situation, painfully aware that I wasn't a
nubile young thing anymore. I'd expended entirely too
much energy sucking in my stomach and willing my cellul-
ite to disappear and wondering how I compared to the
women Terry had been with since he'd been with me.

But the second night—ah, that second night—as Annie
slept, as the coyotes howled, as the cool breeze blew, I
didn't overthink any of it. I didn't think at all. I surrendered
completely to the moment, to the sensations, to the plea-
sures I gave as well as received. I made love with my ex-
husband with a spontaneity I hadn't accessed in years, not
since I had all but buried that part of myself in my work.
As I've said before, people are quick to stereotype accountants as plodding, robotic, even asexual, and such stereo-
typing has always infuriated me. But it seemed to me, that
second night I made love with Terry, that perhaps, without
realizing it, I had become the very stereotype I'd been so
defensive about.

No more, I thought as I nuzzled Terry. I've got my juice
back.

"There's something I want to ask you," he said as we
lay together. It was dawn and the sunrise was beginning
to poke through the guest room window.

"Ask away," I said.

"Will you stay here, Crystal? Will you stay in Sedona and
give us another chance?"

The question threw me. It was Terry who'd said, "Our

sleeping together doesn't have to mean anything"; Terry who'd promised we could be intimate with each other and still go on with our lives.

"I've just ended a relationship," I said finally. "I'm not ready to jump into another one. You can see that, can't you?"

"Yeah, but you can't blame me for asking," he said, curling his legs around mine. "Can't blame me for wishing."

I hugged him. "That's the wonderful part of our new friendship," I said. "I don't blame you for anything. All that's behind me now."

Terry said he was glad that my anger and resentment toward him had evaporated, but he urged me to explore the feelings that had replaced them.

"You might love me, Crystal," he said. "Not *still*. Not *more*. But *differently*. The way I love you."

"I might," I conceded, not being coy, just careful. "But I'm not impulsive in my choices, Terry. You know that about me. I don't love often or easily."

"What makes you think I do?" he asked, then covered my lips with his own.

Terry snuck down the hall, into his bedroom, at about six a.m., ten seconds before Annie woke up. She was an early riser, he'd explained, used to getting herself ready for school during the week.

By the time I was out of bed, washed, and dressed that Sunday morning, she and Terry were in the kitchen eating cereal. They had placed an extra bowl on the table for me.

"Well. Good morning, you two," I said, as if I hadn't spent the night in Terry's arms. "How'd everybody sleep?"

"Great. How about you?" he asked, winking as he pulled a chair out for me.

"Like a baby," I said and sat down. "What about you, Annie? Did you sleep well?"

Annie rolled her eyes. "As well as I could with that racket you guys were making. The next time you want to party all night, do it downstairs in the living room, okay?"

Terry nearly choked on his cereal. I nearly choked, period.

During breakfast, Annie asked me if I was still planning to marry Steven and go back to New York. I said I wasn't planning to marry Steven but I was going back to New York. She reminded me that there was a lot of pollution in New York.

"The air's cleaner here," she said. "You'd live longer if you stayed."

I gave her a hug, flattered that, unlike a certain member of my own family, *she* cared how long I lived.

Of course, Sedona's clean air hadn't done much for Amanda Reid, who was either dead or as good as dead by this time. It had been three days since Will had taken her up to Cathedral Rock, three days since anyone had seen or heard from her. How likely was it that she was still alive somewhere? Still in one piece? Still barking orders at people?

Terry told Annie that he and Will and I were hiking to Cathedral Rock. "I know it's a Sunday, honey, and we usually spend Sundays together, but Will's in trouble and we've got to do what we can to help him, right?"

"Sure," she said. "How long will you be gone, Dad?"

"The rest of the morning and part of the afternoon, I guess. I'll call Cynthia, if you want, and see if you can spend some time with Laura."

"How about if I stay here by myself? All the Sunday political shows are on—'Meet the Press,' 'Face the Nation,' 'The McLaughlin Group.' I'll have the time of my life."

Terry shook his head. "I don't leave you alone here,

sport. You know that. Your choices are—stay at a friend's house or stay here with a sitter. Maybe Will can bring Jean over when he comes to pick Crystal and me up. You can watch your shows with her, huh?"

Annie gave that idea the thumbs-up sign.

Terry got on the phone to Jean Singleton, who had been forced to flee the cabin, thanks to the media, and was camping out with her husband at the Jeep Tour office. While Terry chatted with her, Annie and I chatted with each other—about her homework for school, her friend Laura's new puppy, Brad Pitt's new haircut, you name it. I loved talking to her, no matter what the subject. Her enthusiasm was infectious.

At 8:30, Will and Jean arrived. Jean looked thoroughly exhausted; Will looked remarkably composed.

"I believe I will be protected by the truth," he said when I commented on how calm he seemed under the circumstances.

Bless his heart, I thought. If the media had branded *me* a murderer, I'd have fled the country already.

Terry kissed Annie goodbye as he, Will, and I prepared to leave the house. "You'll be okay, honey?" he asked her.

"Sure," she said. "Why wouldn't I be?"

He tweaked her nose. "No reason. Later, dude."

"Later, Dad."

CHAPTER TWENTY-SIX

♥

Unlike my first trip there, when it was a stop on the Sacred Earth Jeep Tour, Cathedral Rock wasn't teeming with adventurers this time, perhaps because it was only nine o'clock on a Sunday morning. In fact, for a major tourist attraction, the canyons felt eerily quiet, as if Amanda's disappearance had cast a spell over the place, an aura of fear.

"Look. There are the kachina dolls, remember?" Terry said to me, pointing to the man and woman carved out of rock, standing back-to-back, perched imposingly atop one of the cliffs.

"I remember," I said, gazing up at them. I also remembered Terry saying they warded off evil spirits. Where were they the day Amanda vanished? I wondered.

We began our climb, letting Will lead us up the canyon to the exact spot where he'd left Amanda. It was slow going. It had rained briefly but heavily during the night and, despite the brilliant morning sun, the hiking trails were still muddy, making for slippery conditions.

"We'll take it nice and easy," Terry advised, positioning himself right behind me in case I stumbled.

I tried to concentrate on my footwork, tried to watch where I was stepping, but I was more focused on solving a mystery, more intent on succeeding where the police had failed. I kept posing theories to myself as I hiked, kept picturing Amanda sitting on that blanket all by herself in the wee hours of the morning, kept wondering if someone had forcibly dragged her off or if she had gone willingly— where and for what reason I couldn't imagine. Nothing added up.

"Tell me, Will," I said to him. "I know it was the crack of dawn when you brought Amanda up here, but Laverne Altamont, a friend of Terry's, told us that three of her friends saw you two that morning. Did you see them—or anyone else?"

"Unfortunately, I saw no one," he said. "When I do my spiritual work, I look inward, as if my mind is a long tunnel. On the morning you are asking about, it was the same way. I was looking inward, meditating on Mrs. Reid so that I would be prepared for the ceremony I would be conducting. Vision Quests are serious business. For serious seekers."

"That's the part that puzzles me most," I said. "Amanda Reid was no serious seeker. She was a superficial socialite whose single goal in life was to one-up Blaine Trump. She didn't come here searching for meaning—she came here searching for media attention. She was dying for a way to promote herself."

"Yeah, but *did* she die to promote herself?" said Terry. "And if she did die, *how* did she die?"

None of us knew the answer to that one, so we continued on our hike. Up, up, up Cathedral Rock. We'd been climbing for forty-five minutes or so when Will pointed to an area not far from where we had stopped to rest. It was relatively flat—a small plateau between the jagged peaks on either side of it. The perfect place for a picnic, a photo op, or, I supposed, a Vision Quest.

"I brought Mrs. Reid there," said Will, his eyes fixed on the spot. "And I left Mrs. Reid there. Alive."

"We know you did, buddy," Terry said. "Now. Let's check it out, huh?"

We all trudged to the scene of the aborted Vision Quest. There was nothing unusual about it, we discovered when we got there. No sign of a struggle. No sign of the blanket. No sign of Amanda.

"Last night's rain washed away any footprints," Will observed as he bent down and ran his fingers over the still-damp ground.

"There'll be other clues," Terry said optimistically. "If not here, then nearby. Things will move a lot faster, though, if the three of us split up to search the area."

Will and I agreed, so I went one way, Will another, Terry another, the idea being that we would each comb our section and yell if we found anything interesting. We were like kids on a scavenger hunt, except for one tiny detail: We didn't know what the hell we were looking for.

My territory was east of the spot where Will had left Amanda, but it could just as well have been west or north or south. Peaks and valleys aside, Cathedral Rock was one giant mass of red rock formations, and, unless you'd spent years mapping out which was which and what was where, it all sort of looked alike.

Nevertheless, I studied the area to which I'd been assigned, checking, for example, for markings Amanda could have carved into the rock or fragments of the blanket Will had given her or even remnants of her broken fingernail. Nothing.

And then something several feet away caught my eye, something half-buried under the earth that had shifted during the rain storm, something shiny. At first, I assumed it was a crystal—the kind Amanda had tried to dig out of the ground at Bell Rock—but as I approached the object and saw how it sparkled in the sunlight, I surmised that it might be a piece of metal. Silver, I thought. Yes. Silver jewelry.

I hurried closer to the glittery article and when I came upon it, I knelt down and inspected it where it lay partially obscured by the rock and dirt and cactus.

All that was visible initially was a sliver of silver—a tip, a point, a sharp end of a larger object. And when I swept away the debris covering it, I saw that I was correct; the silver tip indeed belonged to a larger object—a silver cross inlaid with turquoise in the style commonly associated with jewelry designed in the American Southwest. What's more, the silver-and-turquoise cross hung from a long black cord which, judging by its two ragged ends, had torn and come apart, probably causing the cross to drop off the neck of its wearer. Of course, there was also the possibility that it had been *yanked* off the neck of its wearer. During an argument, maybe. A very physical argument.

"Hey, you guys!" I shouted, my voice echoing across the canyons. "I think I found something!"

Terry and Will abandoned their battle stations and were with me in a flash.

"Look," I said, pointing at the cross. "It could be evidence, couldn't it?"

"If it's evidence, then why didn't the police collect it?" Terry said.

I shrugged. "Maybe they didn't 'sweep' every inch of this place," I said, recalling the term from my father's favorite cop shows. "They sure as hell didn't see the cross from all the way up in their search-and-rescue helicopter.

For all we know, it could have been here for days. Since the morning Amanda disappeared."

"I never saw it here before," Will volunteered.

"But you told us you never see anyone or anything before a Vision Quest," I reminded him. "You're too busy looking inward."

"That is true," Will conceded. He dropped down to his knees to examine the cross more closely, picking it up, rubbing it between his palms, then placing it against his forehead, then laying it across his heart. I assumed he was measuring its energy or testing its vibes or whatever.

"I do not know this cross," he said finally.

That's when it occurred to me: I *did* know this cross— or one that looked just like it.

"Terry," I said anxiously. "Remember when you took our tour group out that first day?"

"How could I forget? It was the day we saw each other again after twenty years."

"Right, but we had just climbed up to Airport Mesa and while you were scouting around for an uncrowded spot, I saw this blond guy talking to some sunbathers, telling them they were in a bad space. He was wearing a T-shirt with the phrase 'There's No Place Like Om' on it. He was also wearing a silver-and-turquoise cross around his neck—a cross that bears a striking resemblance to the one Will's holding. I asked you about the man and you told me he was a local character."

"He is," Terry said. "We all call him the 'Om-bre.' Get it? *Hombre?*"

"Very clever, but the point I'm trying to make is that he was wearing this cross the day I saw him at Airport Mesa," I said. "He was also wearing it the very first time I saw him—in the parking lot at Tranquility, the afternoon I was checking into the hotel."

"It's not a one-of-a-kind piece of jewelry, Crystal," Terry said. "They sell these crosses by the hundreds out here."

"Yes, but when the 'Om-bre,' as you call him, turned up at The Hideaway the other night, he wasn't wearing the cross," I said. "I'm positive of it."

Terry considered my observations. "So you think this cross is his?"

"I do. More to the point, I think it's evidence," I said. "He was wearing the cross the day before Amanda disappeared. He was not wearing the cross the day after she disappeared. And now, lo and behold, here's the cross—only a short distance from where Will says he last saw Amanda. Coincidence? I doubt it."

"For argument's sake, let's say the cross does belong to this guy," Terry agreed. "What would—"

"Sorry to interrupt, but do we know this person's name?" I asked.

Terry glanced at Will. "I don't. You?"

"Not me," said Will.

"I guess we don't," Terry admitted.

"Okay. Go on," I said.

"Let's say the cross is this guy's," he continued. "What possible connection could he have to someone like Amanda Reid? He's a two-bit hustler, a small-time rip-off artist. One year he claims he's a psychic. The next year he tells everyone he's a numerologist. Now he walks around town passing himself off as a Reiki healer. He gets the tourists to spring for a few bucks every now and then, but most people in Sedona ignore him."

"Maybe they shouldn't," I said. "Maybe he's not as harmless as you make him out to be."

"Maybe, but look at the facts," said Terry. "Amanda isn't the first New Age-crazed celebrity to make the pilgrimage to Sedona. If our friend with the cross really intended to rob or kidnap or even murder a rich-and-famous person, he would have had plenty of other opportunities before now."

"Yes, but Amanda isn't just another New Age-crazed celebrity," I said. "She's a ditz, a dim bulb, a dented can. She could have had some sort of encounter with this man and pissed him off. She had a habit of pissing people off."

"There is a way to answer all these questions," Will said in his solemn, unflappable manner. "We can go to this man, confront him with our suspicions, see what he tells us."

Terry shook his head. "How do we find the guy if none of us knows his name? I'm willing to bet he isn't listed in the phone book under 'Om-bre.'"

We all pondered the matter. For some reason my pondering brought me back to Sergei's pronouncements, to the words Terry and I had all but written off as the ramblings of a nutcase.

Amanda Reid is close by, yet somehow hidden from view.

That was the second message we'd been given that afternoon, the first having been that Amanda was alive.

If she's close by, she's somewhere in Sedona, I thought. And if she's hidden from view, maybe it's "Om-bre" who's keeping her hidden. Maybe he's holding her captive because he wants her to change her will and leave him everything. Maybe he's holding her captive because he wants her to hire him as her personal Reiki healer. Maybe he's holding her captive because he finds her irresistible.

Then again, maybe not.

You hold the key to finding her.

That was the third and most startling of Sergei's channeled messages—that *I* had the answer to the mystery of Amanda's disappearance.

There is a piece of paper in your possession. A piece of paper with writing on it. A piece of paper that will lead you straight to Amanda Reid's door.

But I had rummaged through all the pieces of paper in my suitcase and carry-on bag, I thought, and I didn't find a single clue. As for my purse, the reason I didn't bother to fish around in there was that the only pieces of paper to speak of were money—the traveler's checks and the bills in my wallet.

Wait! My wallet! Of course! What could I have been thinking? And I'd called *Amanda* a dim bulb!

Suddenly I remembered that I had dozens of business cards in the zippered section of my wallet—and that one of them belonged to "Om-bre."

"Guess what?" I said excitedly, tugging on Terry's shirt-sleeve. "I know exactly how to get in touch with Mr. Reiki Healer. I've got his business card in my wallet!"

"So? Let's see it!" Terry said, extending his hand toward me, his eyes on the fanny pack strapped around my waist.

"What are you looking at?" I said. "It's not in there. My allergy pills are in there. And a couple of Kleenexes."

"Jesus, Crystal. I thought women cram everything they own into their pocketbooks," he said.

"Don't generalize," I said. "This isn't a pocketbook—it's a thing you wear when you want your arms free. Why would I bring a wallet to go mountain climbing? There aren't any hot dog concessions around here, are there?"

"Okay. Then where *is* your wallet?" Terry asked, attempting to remain calm.

"It's back at your house," I said. "In the guest room."

"Are you sure?" he said. "There's no chance you brought it with you? In that thing?"

I unzipped the fanny pack and exposed its contents. Just as I'd indicated, there was a box of Benadryl and one of those travel packs of tissue. And a couple of Pepcid ACs. Just in case.

I smiled to myself as I suddenly thought of Steven, winging his way back to New York. I hoped his sinuses weren't giving him trouble on the flight. I genuinely wished him the best.

"Crystal," said Terry, bringing me back to the matter at hand. "I believe you about the wallet. I'm sorry. You can close that thing now."

I zipped the fanny pack. "I guess we'd better head back to your house. On the double," I said, then wondered how anyone could climb down Cathedral Rock "on the double." You couldn't exactly take two cliffs at a time.

"We'll save a few minutes if we call Annie from the parking lot instead of stopping at the house," Terry suggested. "Either she or Jean can find the business card and read us the information over the phone."

"How will they know which business card is 'Om-bre's'?" I asked. "In the few days I've been in Sedona, I've been handed dozens of business cards, many of them by people claiming to be Reiki healers."

"I guess they'll have to look through all of them then," he said and started down the canyon.

CHAPTER TWENTY-SEVEN

♥

I placed the call to Terry's house. Annie picked up after two rings.

"Hi, Annie. It's Crystal," I said. "We need you to do us a favor, okay?"

"What kind of a favor?" she asked.

"One that could get your Uncle Will out of trouble," I said.

"Tell me," she said excitedly.

"My wallet is in my purse, which is in the guest room, on the bed," I explained. "Would you mind running upstairs, finding the wallet, and bringing it down to the phone?"

She didn't waste time answering my question. She simply dropped the telephone onto the kitchen counter and hurried off. When she returned within seconds, she was out of breath but sounding extremely pleased that she'd been included in our sleuthing.

"What should I do now?" she asked.

"Open the wallet and you'll see a zippered compartment," I said.

"Got it," she said.

"Good. Unzip it and there'll be a whole bunch of business cards," I said.

"Got 'em," she said.

"Beautiful. Pull out the cards and flip through them until you find one with a man's name on it. He's from here in Sedona, and the card should have the words 'Reiki healer' or 'Reiki expert' or 'Reiki specialist' printed on it, along with this man's address and phone number. Oh, and Reiki is spelled R-e-i-k-i."

"How do you spell the man's name?"

"We don't know his name."

"So you mean I should just look for a card that says 'Reiki' something?"

"Exactly."

There was a brief silence as Annie began to shuffle through the business cards.

"You've got a lot of these, Crystal," she commented, "mostly from New York. There's one for a BMW dealer, one for a beauty shop, one for a gastro . . . entom—"

"Gastroenterologist, honey," I said, helping her with her pronunciation. "That's a doctor you go to for acid reflux."

"Acid what?"

"It's not important. Tell me about the other cards, specifically the ones with Sedona addresses and phone numbers."

"Well, there's one for a guy who does emotional clearings."

"That would be the waiter at Tranquility," I said to Terry and Will, who were huddled next to me around the pay phone, hanging on my every word.

"There's one from somebody named Jazeem," Annie went on.

"From The Clearing House," I told them.

"There's one from somebody named Dan."

"Dan?"

"Yeah. Just Dan. No last name. But the card does say 'Reiki healer.'"

"Fantastic! What else does it say?"

"It says, 'Tune in to the Universal Life Force Through Touch to Harmonize the Mind, Body and Spirit.'"

"What does it say in the way of an address or phone? We're trying to reach this man."

She read me Dan's address and phone number and I scribbled the information down on a five-dollar bill Terry had in his wallet. "Do you think Dan killed Amanda?" she asked.

"We don't know, but he might have been at Cathedral Rock the day she disappeared. We're very interested in talking to him, and, thanks to you, Annie, we'll be able to. Now, your dad wants to say a quick hello."

I turned the phone over to Terry, who told her she did a swell job and said he'd see her later.

"Next project—getting ahold of Danny Boy," he said after he hung up.

"Wait," I said. "Let's think about this for a minute. Are we just going to come right out and tell this guy that we suspect him of killing Amanda?"

"Not immediately," said Terry. "First, we're going to tell him we have something that may belong to him—the silver-and-turquoise cross. Then, depending on how he reacts, we'll hit him with our suspicions."

"But if the cross is evidence that could incriminate him *and* exonerate Will, why not take it to the police?" I said. "Why hand it over to this Dan person, whom we don't know or trust?"

"The police do not want evidence that directs them away from me," Will said. "Detective Whitehead has made up his mind that I am guilty. He does not listen to other ideas, other theories. He hears what he desires to hear. If we bring him the cross, he will disregard it. I know this."

"Will's got a point," said Terry. "Whitehead's never been fond of Indians, and he's never had a case that's generated so much publicity. He's in a big hurry to put somebody away and that 'somebody' is Will. He doesn't want anything to muddy the waters."

"So you both agree that we should forget the police and confront Dan?"

Terry and Will nodded.

"Then I guess we're going for it," I said.

"We're going for it," said Terry, who volunteered to call Dan.

He dialed the number I'd written on the five-dollar bill and we waited. We had anticipated that we'd have to leave a message on an answering machine, since a major part of Dan's shtik was getting out among the tourists and diagnosing the "badness" of their spaces, but, surprisingly, the man himself picked up the phone.

Will and I were practically on top of Terry, straining to hear both sides of the conversation.

"Love and light" was Dan's greeting, as opposed to your basic "Hi."

"Is this Dan?" Terry asked. "The Reiki healer?"

"Yeah," said Dan. "You're in a bad space, man. I can hear it in your voice. A really bad space."

"Actually, Dan, you're the one who's in a really bad space," said Terry. "You lost a piece of jewelry, didn't you? A silver cross on a black cord?"

No response.

"Are you there, Dan?" Terry asked.

"So you're not calling to make an appointment?" Dan said.

"I *am* calling to make an appointment," said Terry. "I don't want you to heal me, though. I want you to identify your cross and tell me how you came to leave it at Cathedral Rock."

Again, a pause.

"Who is this?" asked Dan. "My clairvoyant gift alerts me to the realization that you have toxic thoughts toward me. It is important for me to have information about who you are and what your spiritual goals are."

"No problem," said Terry. "My name is Terry Hollenbeck and I live and work in Sedona. I run Sacred Earth Jeep Tours—you've seen our vehicles around town—and I'm at a public phone right now with my friends Crystal Goldstein and Will Singleton. We have your cross and we want to give it back to you. That's our spiritual goal."

Dan coughed or sneezed. I couldn't tell which from where I was standing. "What makes you think this cross you keep talking about is mine?" he asked before coughing or sneezing again.

"One of my friends remembers seeing you wearing it," said Terry. "She also remembers seeing you not wearing it—after Amanda Reid vanished from Cathedral Rock."

"Amanda who?" Dan said.

Obviously, he was playing dumb. Everybody in Sedona knew who Amanda was. There was no escaping the story of her mysterious disappearance.

"Amanda Reid," said Terry. "Look, Dan, how about we cut to the chase here? My friends and I would like to get together with you, return your cross, ask you about the day you dropped it at Cathedral Rock. We'd like to have this little chat within the hour. At The Coffee Pot on 89A."

"Sorry. I'm tied up," said Dan.

"Now that's a shame," said Terry. "But, hey, if *you* don't

want your cross, I bet the police will be happy to have it.
You get my drift, Dan?''

Wow, I thought. Terry's good at this tough talk. He
should have been a cop.

And then I laughed to myself. Given the numerous jobs
he'd had over the past twenty years, maybe he'd been one.

"We'll see you at The Coffee Pot in an hour," Terry
repeated. "Is it a date, Dan?"

Dan sighed. "How will I know you?" he said, his voice
heavy with resignation.

"Not to worry," said Terry. "We'll know you."

The Coffee Pot was a Sedona institution, Terry
explained—an all-day diner/restaurant set in the shadow
of Coffee Pot Mesa, a red rock formation shaped like a
guess what. Located on Sedona's main road, across the
street from Kentucky Fried Chicken, it was a gathering
place for psychics, who spent hours over coffee swapping
predictions.

"This is it," said Terry as he swung the Jeep into the
parking lot. "Before there was Starbucks, there was The
Coffee Pot."

The antithesis of trendy, the coffee shop was housed
in a low-slung beige building whose most distinguishing
feature was its blue and red sign near the entrance. It read:
"Home of the 101 Omelettes."

"I didn't know there were 101 things you could put in
an omelette," I remarked as we got out of the car.

"If you stay in Sedona, you can find out what they are,"
Terry said, giving my hand a squeeze. "How's that for an
incentive to hang around, huh?"

I smiled at him. He was so sweet, so loving, so appealing.
I was enjoying our time together more than I thought
possible. But stay in Sedona? Uproot myself? Relocate?

How could I? My father was in New York. My best friend was in New York. My business was in New York. Duboff Spector or no Duboff Spector, there weren't any big accounting firms in Sedona. People in Sedona didn't need CPAs; they had their psychics to tell them how much they owed the IRS. And then there was the fact that, as beautiful as red rock country was, as wonderful as Terry was, as endearing as Annie was, I'd experienced them all while I was on vacation, when everything looks rosy and nothing is as it seems. Most of all, no matter how much Terry had changed since we were divorced, no matter how much I had changed since arriving in Sedona, the reality was, he and I had failed as a couple once. Why fail as a couple twice? Why set myself up for more frustration, more disappointment, more hurt? Maybe I did love him—*still* or *more* or *differently,* as he'd put it. Or maybe I was simply stuck in the past, unable to resist the temptation to make things come out right this time.

No. Of course you can't stay, Crystal, I said to myself. There are too many unanswered questions, too many unknowns. Have some fun, find out what happened to Amanda Reid, and go home.

We sat at a table for four, ordered coffee, and waited for Dan to show up. After twenty minutes or so, I spotted him standing at the entrance to the restaurant, looking warily over the sea of faces, trying to guess which of us had made the phone call. I felt a chill of recognition as I recalled the first time I'd seen him at Tranquility. He had seemed so harmless then, just another intense young seeker—seeking to make a fast buck. But on this Sunday morning, he seemed sinister—darker than the "local character" with the shoulder-length blond hair, the faded blue jeans, and the "There's No Place Like Om" T-shirt.

Terry stood up and waved him over to our table. He nodded and walked toward us. When he sat down, he introduced himself.

"Dan Kelly," he said. Nobody shook his hand.

"Coffee, Dan?" I asked, not sure how else to begin. He wasn't as young as I'd thought, now that I was seeing him up close. Late thirties, I supposed. Forty, maybe. And he had a lazy eye, the kind that never lines up with the other one, a defect I hadn't noticed during our initial encounter, as he'd been wearing sunglasses.

He shook his head, declining the java. "You said on the phone that you have my cross," he said. "Let's see it."

Terry produced the cross from the back pocket of his jeans. He held the black cord between his fingers and dangled it right in front of Dan's face. "Look familiar?"

Dan took a swipe at it.

"Uh-uh-uh," Terry taunted, pulling the cross away from Dan. "You don't get it back until you tell us what you were doing at Cathedral Rock the day you misplaced it."

"I was doing what I do," said Dan as he twisted the hair on his left eyebrow. "I was searching for those in need of healing. The cord must have been frayed. I guess it finally broke."

"You guess?" Terry said skeptically. "The cross that was hanging from that cord is silver. When metal falls on top of rock, it makes a sound. A little 'clunk.' You know?"

"I didn't hear anything," Dan maintained. "I was probably deep in meditation when it slipped off my neck."

"But surely you must have realized it was gone," I said. "Why didn't you go back and look for it?"

"Because it's a material possession," said Dan. "I'm not about material possessions."

"Is that it? Or is it that you couldn't take the risk?" said Terry.

"Risk? What are you talking about?" Dan bristled.

"You couldn't risk going back to the scene of the crime," Terry persisted. "Isn't that true?"

Dan rolled his eyes. "You people are in a bad space. A really bad space. Keep the cross. You need it more than I do."

He started to get up to leave, but Will, who had been silent up to that point, placed his hands on Dan's shoulders and pushed him back down into his chair. "We have not finished our meeting," he told Dan. "You have not been truthful with us about Amanda Reid. You saw her at Cathedral Rock the same day you lost your cross."

"I didn't see her at Cathedral Rock," Dan protested. "I saw her picture in the paper like everybody else."

"Oh?" I said. "On the phone, you gave us the impression you'd never heard of her. 'Amanda who?' you asked. Remember?"

"Okay, okay. Listen," said Dan. "I did drop the cross the same day Amanda Reid disappeared. But I didn't admit it because I don't want the cops breathing down my neck the way they're breathing down this guy's." He nodded at Will. "I'm just a small businessman. I can't afford to lose customers, sitting in some detective's office answering questions about a murder I had nothing to do with. So I've kept my mouth shut. So sue me."

Boy, I thought. It's amazing how unspiritual some spiritual people can sound when they're not paying attention.

"What you're telling us—what you expect us to believe—is that you were at Cathedral Rock the day Amanda Reid was there and the cross dropped off your neck only yards from where she was sitting, yet you didn't see or speak to her," Terry summed up.

"That's what I'm telling you," said Dan. "Can I go now?" He glanced at Will, who shook his head.

"I'm not sure we shouldn't give the cross to the police," Terry bluffed. "Why not let them decide if it's relevant to the case? Or, better still, we could give it to our pal Michael Mandell. He's covering the investigation for a national magazine."

"No," Dan said quickly. "No media. No way."

"Then keep talking," said Terry. "We've got plenty of time."

No one spoke for several seconds, a standoff. Eventually, Dan threw in the towel. He seemed eager to get us off his back and beat it.

"Fine," he said. "Here's what happened. I did see the Reid woman that morning. She was sitting on a blanket. I told her she was in a bad space. She said, 'You're not kidding, mister. If I don't get out of here, I'll die of boredom.'"

"And *did* you take her out of there?" I asked. "To someplace more private, perhaps?"

"I didn't take her anywhere," Dan said. "I wished her love and light and went about my business."

"That's funny, Dan," I countered. "Your 'business' is Reiki healing. Why didn't you offer to heal Amanda? Suggest that she schedule an appointment with you? Give her your business card?"

"Because I didn't," he snapped.

"She must have offered you money to help her down the canyon, though, didn't she?" I asked.

"No," he said. "I don't remember."

"You don't remember if she offered you money?" I said, incredulous. The man was a hustler, after all.

"No. Yes. Look, I talked to her, she talked back, and then I split," he said, growing angry at being put on the defensive. "That's the truth."

"You have told us different truths," Will pointed out. "If a person lies once, he lies often."

"Nice speech, but *I'm* not the one the cops are about to arrest," said Dan, flashing Will a little sneer. Clearly, he'd had enough. *"I'm* not the one with a noose tightening around my neck. You want to give them my cross? Go ahead and give it to them."

He rose from his chair. This time, Will made no attempt to stop him.

"You must be some terrific healer," Terry said sarcastically as Dan moved to leave the table.

"Heal this," Dan responded, flipping us all the bird.

CHAPTER TWENTY-EIGHT

♥

"Anybody hungry?" I asked after Dan had bid us such an unceremonious farewell.

"I could go for an omelette," said Terry. "We could each order a different one. Then we'd only have ninety-eight more to try."

Will agreed. He had the ham and spinach, Terry had the ham and swiss, and I had the ham and sage. When in Rome, I figured.

While we ate, we rehashed the meeting with Dan. All three of us were convinced that he was involved in Amanda's disappearance; he had acted too suspicious not to be, changing his story, becoming so belligerent, refusing to tell the police he had not only seen Amanda at Cathedral Rock but had spoken to her there.

"The man is a liar," said Will.

"And a bastard," said Terry.

"And a bad dresser," I said. "I think he wears the same clothes every day."

Between bites of our omelettes and sips of our coffee, we debated whether we should follow our instincts and pursue Dan further.

"He's guilty of something," Terry asserted. "I say we drive over to his house and poke around. Who knows what we'll find?"

"What if he's there?" I said, horrified that we would be trespassing on someone's property—and that we might get caught.

"We'll wait until he isn't," said Terry. "He's not gonna sit home all day, not with so many tourists roaming the vortex sites. Not our Dan."

"Terry is right," said Will. "If we go to Dan's house, we can watch and listen. I believe there will be a sign, some evidence that Mrs. Reid has been there."

Suddenly, I was reminded yet again of the pronouncement that Sergei had made.

You have it in your possession . . . A piece of paper that will lead you straight to Amanda Reid's door.

Dan's address was printed on his business card. Annie had read it to me. I knew where to find him.

"It could be dangerous to go to Dan's house," I pointed out.

"It could," Terry conceded.

"Not only that, it would be a nightmare if we found Amanda lying there, dead," I added. "The victim of some bizarre, ritualistic torture."

"Might be a grisly scene, yeah," said Terry.

"God, I don't think I could handle that," I said.

"Then we'll drop you at my house," Terry suggested. "You could stay with Annie and Jean while Will and I look around."

I considered the idea. Why not let the men handle this? Who needs grisly?

And then I remembered. Sergei had been very definite

about the fact that *I* held the key to finding Amanda, that the piece of paper was in *my* possession, that it would lead *me* straight to her door.

Terry signaled the waitress to bring us the check. Apparently, he was treating.

"It's all set then. We'll swing by my house, drop you off, and drive over to Dan's," he said to me.

I shook my head. "I'm going with you."

"But you said—"

"It's destiny," I interrupted him. "Don't fight it."

Dan Kelly lived in a mobile home park off 89A. And not one of those nice, lushly landscaped mobile home parks, either—the kind where people fuss over their trailers as if they were mansions, charming them up with hanging plants and patio furniture and welcome mats. No, there was nothing remotely "parklike" about Dan's trailer park. It was a trailer slum—a barren, sad-looking junkyard of a place where everything was run down, even the "Enter" and "Exit" signs, each of which was missing its first letter and, therefore, they read: "nter" and "xit." Garbage in, garbage out.

Dan's trailer was particularly unattractive. It was basically a long turd with wheels—a brown rectangle with a door, windows with their curtains drawn, and a broken TV antenna.

"I don't see a car," I said as we rolled past the trailer in the Jeep. "He must not be home."

"I told you. He's probably out hustling," said Terry. He put the Jeep in reverse and backed it up to the front of Dan's mobile home. Then he turned off the engine.

"Now what?" I asked. "We're not going to just barge in there, are we?"

"Not this second," said Terry. "First, we're gonna snoop around outside."

"That's a relief," I said dryly.

The three of us got out of the Jeep and began to prowl around the trailer, constantly looking over our shoulders for inquisitive neighbors, the police, or, God forbid, Dan. We tried the front door, but it was locked. We peered into the windows, but couldn't see a thing, thanks to the dark curtains. We checked the pathetic excuse for a lawn, but there were no signs of Amanda, only a few cigarette butts.

"Any ideas?" Terry asked.

Will shrugged. "It would not be right for us to break in," he said. "*I* would not feel right about it."

"Neither would I," I said. "Maybe we could come back later, when Dan's home. We could ring the bell and invite ourselves in."

"I say we break in," Terry argued. "We know this guy's hiding something."

"I say we come back later," Will countered. "I have had my own home invaded over the last few days. It is not a pleasant experience. It would be wrong to do to another what has been done to me. No matter how guilty he may be."

Terry sighed, patting Will on the back. "I feel sorry for Amanda Reid, wherever she is," he said. "If she'd hung around, she could have learned a lot from you—like what true spirituality is. You're the genuine article, Will. And we'll prove it to Detective Whitehead and whoever else is interested. You'll see."

Will smiled. He was about to respond to Terry's pledge of support when all three of us heard a noise from inside the trailer—a bang, a thump, something.

"Maybe Dan *is* home," I said, my body tensing.

"Or maybe he's got a cat," said Terry. "Cats knock things over."

Then came another thump, followed by a succession of thumps.

"That's no cat," I said.

"No cat," Will concurred. "Time to break in."

Terry laughed. "Don't worry, pal. You're still a paragon of virtue in my eyes."

"Same here," I told Will. Spirituality was one thing; getting the police to believe you didn't commit murder was another.

Will found a rock and smashed one of the windows. Then he and Terry found more rocks and cleared away any jagged-edged pieces of glass that would make our entry into the window more treacherous than it already was, as far as I was concerned.

"See anything?" Terry asked Will, whose head was now inside the window.

"Only a small kitchen," said Will. "Nothing special."

"Then we'd better have a look around the rest of this palace," Terry said.

Will nodded and climbed inside the trailer. Terry went next. He extended a hand to me. "Coming, darling?"

I looked to my left, then to my right. None of the neighbors had rushed from their mobile homes to accuse us of anything. Not yet, anyway. And even if we were caught and word of my felonious behavior got back to the partners at Duboff Spector, what were they going to do, fire me?

I grabbed Terry's hand and let him pull me inside.

The first thing I noticed as I stood in that poor excuse for a kitchen was that Dan was as bad a housekeeper as he was a dresser. There were dirty dishes everywhere—everywhere, that is, where there weren't crumbs or candy wrappers or ants swarming around the crumbs and the candy wrappers. And the dust—God—no wonder Dan was coughing and sneezing when Terry spoke to him on the phone. Ten seconds in that kitchen and my sinus passages were as clogged as the Midtown Tunnel at rush hour. Fortunately, I had some Kleenex in my fanny pack and was able to blow my nose and regain partial use of my olfactory nerve.

Which led to the second thing I noticed: I smelled perfume, one of those heavy scents you can sample on the pages of magazines—the first pages you rip out if you're as allergic to things as I am. Either Dan was a drag queen or there was a woman in his trailer.

I was sharing this thought with Terry and Dan when we heard more thumping. My own heart thumped as I wondered what I'd gotten myself into, what Sergei had gotten me into.

"The sound is coming from that direction," said Will as he pointed to our left.

Without further discussion, he crept through the kitchen, around the corner and into the next room, with Terry right behind him and me bringing up the rear. When they both stopped suddenly, I nearly broke my nose on Terry's back, so abruptly did they halt their movements.

"Hey! What's the big—" I shut up when I saw what they saw.

Yup, it was Amanda. Nope, she wasn't dead. She was lying faceup on what I assumed was a massage table in what I assumed was Dan's "Reiki room," and she was bound and gagged, rope around her designer-clad body, duct tape across her collagen-enhanced lips. The thumping noise we had heard were her gyrations—her attempts to wriggle out of her restraints. When she focused on the fact that we were now in the room with her, she grew so excited that she began flopping around on the table like a just-caught fish.

"I guess we'd better get her out of here before Dan comes home," said Terry. Will nodded, and the two of them hurried over to untie her.

"You can pull off her duct tape, Crystal," Terry instructed me.

"Okay." I hesitated as I stood over the squirming Mrs. Reid, the millionaire heiress with the appeal of a fingernail on a blackboard. Part of me wanted to hear the whole story of how she had ended up in Dan's trailer. The other part wanted to leave the duct tape right where it was.

Terry glanced at me. "Crystal?"

"I'm doing it," I said and ripped the tape off Amanda's mouth in one clean motion—instant electrolysis.

She yelled at me. And then she thanked me, thanked us.

"I never thought I'd be rescued," she said, as Terry and Will set her free. "Never! I must look a fright."

None of us disagreed with her.

"How in the world did you people know where to find me?" she asked.

"We'll go into it later," said Terry. "First, you'd better tell us about Dan. He kidnapped you, obviously."

"Yes," she said. "Well, not in the beginning, he didn't."

"What's that supposed to mean?" asked Terry.

Amanda heaved a heavy sigh, as if it were all too painful to recount. "As you may remember" she said, "I journeyed to Sedona to become more spiritual."

"*I* remember," said Will. "That is why I agreed to take you to Cathedral Rock."

"Yes, and you were sweet to do it, Mr. Singleton," she said. "But after you left me on that mountain all by myself, I was absolutely out of my mind with boredom and hungry beyond words."

"That's the idea, Amanda," Terry said impatiently. "Vision Quests aren't fun and games."

"Don't I know it," she said. "Nevertheless, I was determined to stick it out, in order to become a spiritual person. And then this man, this Dan somebody or other appeared before my eyes. I was so delighted to have company that I invited him to sit down on my blanket. Heavens, what a mistake!''

"What did he do to you?" I asked, wondering if Amanda had been, well, *violated*.

"He looked at me in a rather peculiar manner," she went on. "He has a problem with one of his eyes, you understand. In any case, he looked at me and then he said, 'You're in a bad space. A really bad space.'" She paused to collect herself, as if the memory upset her. "I said to him, 'I'm sitting in a bad space? You mean because it's not a vortex?' Dan said, 'Your bad space is in here.' He placed his hand on my chest! Can you imagine the audacity? He said, 'I can heal you. I do Reiki.' Naturally, I didn't know what he was talking about, so I asked him to explain. He said that he was a Reiki healer, that he had the power to attract energy from the universe and pass it along to me, just by touching me. He said a one-hour Reiki session could do much more for my spirituality than a twenty-four-hour Vision Quest ever could. No disrespect intended, Mr. Singleton."

"So you went off with him," I said. "Of your own free will. He didn't kidnap you after all."

"I'm getting to that," Amanda snapped. "I asked him how much this Reiki business would cost me. I said that even wealthy women such as myself have to watch our pennies."

"You came right out and told him you were wealthy?" Terry asked.

"I assumed he knew," Amanda said huffily. "I take it for granted that people recognize me from my photographs."

"I'm pretty sure Dan isn't an avid reader of *Town and Country*," I said. "But I could be wrong."

"Well, he didn't recognize me, oddly enough, and so

he asked me a lot of questions about myself," said Amanda. "We sat on that blanket and talked and talked and talked."

"About your bad space?" I asked.

"Yes," she replied. "And about my spiritual goals. I confided that my most fervent hopes were to launch my own clothing line, author both a book and a film about my spiritual quest, and have a Web site."

A Web site. I was tempted to reach for the duct tape when Amanda finally got to the part of the story where she ended up in the trailer.

"I poured my heart and soul out to this man," she continued, "and he promised that for sixty-five dollars— that's what he charges for a Reiki session—he could *guarantee* that my goals would be realized. He said all I had to do was come with him, let him practice Reiki on me, and I'd have universal energy. Whatever that is."

"So he drove you here," Terry said.

"Yes," said Amanda. "In a rather dilapidated old Ford, by the way. When he pulled up to this unfortunate trailer— please—you can picture my reaction." She rolled her eyes. "Still, I forged ahead, wanting desperately to achieve my spiritual goals. He brought me into this room, which turned out to be his bedroom as well as his work area, and told me to recline on this massage table. He lit a few candles, put on some of that New Age-y music, and touched me with his hands as he mumbled a few Oriental-sounding words. And then he asked me for the sixty-five dollars, saying the session was over. Over! I was furious! I didn't feel any more spiritual after he was finished than I felt before I met him! And I told him so!"

"An argument ensued?" I said.

"A heated argument," she said. "I accused him of taking advantage of me. He accused me of reneging on our agreement. Eventually, we came to an understanding, though."

"You agreed to pay him half of the sixty-five dollars?" asked Terry.

"No. I agreed to permit him to kidnap me," said Amanda.

Terry, Will, and I exchanged glances.

"It was a business decision," she explained. "A bad business decision, as it happened."

"Go on," I said, thinking of what Rona would say when I told her all this.

"It's quite a tale, but, in a nutshell, Dan said, 'Amanda, Reiki's cool, but if you want the clothing line, the book deal, and all the rest of it, you've got to create some major excitement surrounding your trip to Sedona. You've got to get the media salivating. You've got to be a *happening*. Otherwise, you can forget the whole Martha-Stewart-of-Metaphysics bit.' Needless to say, Dan had my attention."

"Needless to say," I repeated.

"He proposed a deal," Amanda pressed on. "He said that if I were to disappear from that mountain and let the world wonder if I'd been kidnapped or killed, I would ignite a media frenzy and become front-page news. He said everyone would be speculating about what became of me. He said people would feel affection for me, because of the tragedy, including my philandering husband. He said even *I* could never buy the kind of publicity I would get from such a plan. The idea was that I would vanish from that mountain and then, miraculously, I would re-emerge. 'The clothing line will be a piece of cake,' Dan promised."

"So it was a hoax. All of it," said Terry, shaking his head in disbelief. "And you had no problem letting Will take the heat for murdering you, just to get a goddam line of clothes."

"It was not a hoax," Amanda corrected him. "It was a business deal, as I told you. I had planned to give Dan a large sum of money in exchange for keeping me hidden until the time was right. As for Mr. Singleton, I'm truly sorry if he was inconvenienced."

"He's touched beyond words," Terry answered for his friend. "But there's still something I don't get. Why were you bound and gagged when we broke in here? Dan could have kept you hidden without tying you up."

"Yes indeed, he could have," Amanda nodded. "The plan was moving along just fine in the beginning. But look around this dump. Would any of *you* spend more than ten minutes here? When I walked around and inspected the place, I nearly fainted. The decor! The filth! The food! Dan's idea of a meal is canned ravioli! And when I asked for a glass of white wine, do you know what the man said?"

"No," said all three of us.

"He said, 'I don't have any.' I was stunned. 'Not even Chablis?' I asked. 'It's beer or nothing' was his answer. Well. I realized then and there that the arrangement wouldn't work. I said, 'Take me back to my hotel. I'll give you the sixty-five dollars for the Reiki session and we'll forget we ever met.' He became irate. He saw his payday slipping away and he couldn't take it."

"So he decided to go ahead with your plan without your consent," said Terry.

"Exactly," said Amanda. "He tied me to this table, covered my mouth with tape, and let me lie here for days. But now you've rescued me, and to show my gratitude I'll leave you each a nice little treat in my will."

"No wonder they all wanted to kill you," Terry sighed.

"No wonder *who* wanted to kill me?" said Amanda, clueless as usual.

"Never mind," he said. "There are more important things to settle. We've got to get you down to the police station so you can tell Detective Whitehead everything you've just told us and clear Will of this bullshit. As for

Dan, I assume Whitehead will pick him up and arrest him for something. Did he say when he'd be back here or even where he was going?"

Amanda considered the question. "You know, Mr. Hollenbeck, now that I think about it, Dan did say where he was going. I didn't mention this before because I assumed you and he were friends, living in the same town together."

"Mention what, Amanda?" Terry demanded.

"When Dan came back to check on me a couple of hours ago, he mentioned that he intended to pay you a visit. In fact, I actually overheard him telephoning your home to announce that he was on his way over. When he hung up, he marched in here, like the cat that swallowed the canary. He said—and I quote, 'Well, what do you know? The Jeep Tour guy's got a kid.' And then he left."

CHAPTER
TWENTY-NINE

♥

"If he touches Annie he's a dead man," Terry muttered as we raced along 89A, he and Will in the front seat of the Jeep, Amanda and I in the back.

"Annie will be fine," I said, trying to calm him. "The police are on their way over to your house as we speak, right?"

"That's what Whitehead said," Terry acknowledged. He had called the detective from Dan's trailer, the instant he realized his daughter was in jeopardy, and been assured that Sedona's Finest would arrive at the scene as soon as possible.

"You see?" I comforted him. "They'll protect her, not that she needs protecting. She's much too smart to be taken in by a loser like Dan."

"Unlike *me*, you mean?" asked Amanda, arching an eyebrow.

"If the shoe fits," I snapped.

I was long past making polite conversation with the mil-

lionaire heiress; just sitting in the same car with her was a
trial. I still couldn't get over the story of how she came to
meet and be kidnapped by Dan, not even after hearing
her tell it a second time, to Detective Whitehead. Never
mind that she was vain and selfish and oblivious to other
people's feelings. She was a complete dipshit—the Queen
of Dipshits—and I couldn't wait to shed her.

I leaned over, into the front seat, and patted Will's shoulder. "Jean will be fine, too," I said, knowing how worried
he must be about his wife.

"She and I have been married for fifteen years," he said
wistfully. "She is my family—we have no children."

"*I* have no children," said Amanda, insinuating herself
into the conversation yet again. "And from what I've seen
of my friends' children, I consider it a blessing. No children, no trust funds to squander."

"Amanda, you must be exhausted, too exhausted to
talk," I said hopefully. "But before you rest your voice,
there is one thing I'd like to ask you. How did Dan's silver-
and-turquoise cross end up on the ground at Cathedral
Rock? You two weren't arguing at that point. You didn't
rip it off his neck, did you?"

"Of course not," she scoffed. "He ripped it off his own
neck, then threw it down—a little showmanship. He was
making a statement that material possessions were unim-
portant to him, that the sixty-five dollars he charged for
the Reiki session was only a 'love donation.' Love donation,
my buttocks."

Well, that answered that.

Everybody was quiet for the ten more minutes it took
to get to Terry's. When we finally drove up to the house,
there were two cars parked outside: Will's beat-up blue
Pontiac and Dan's dilapidated old Ford.

"No sign of the police," Terry said tightly as he brought
the Jeep to a stop. He reached across the dashboard and

grabbed the kitchen knife he'd swiped from Dan's trailer. "I guess we're on our own here."

The fact that he was brandishing a potentially lethal weapon didn't thrill me, but I understood his instinct to defend his child—a child, who, for all he knew, was at that very moment in the clutches of an extremely loose cannon.

"Wait," Will cautioned as we were all about to bolt out of the Jeep. "I think we should go slow, stay very quiet, try to move inside the house without attracting Dan's attention. I say we surprise him, throw him off balance, make him vulnerable. The more vulnerable he is, the better our chances of getting Jean and Annie away from him."

Terry considered Will's strategy for several seconds. "Okay," he said. "We'll go the sneak-attack route. I'll unlock the front door, and then we'll slip inside, nobody saying a word, nobody making a sound. Not until we figure out what's going on in there. Agreed?"

Will and I nodded. Amanda whispered, "I'll be so quiet you'll forget all about me."

Would that I could, I thought.

We exited the Jeep, followed Terry toward the house, and waited while he let us in through the front door. And then we tiptoed over the threshold and began taking our silent inventory. We moved stealthily from room to room, our dread mounting as we discovered that a coffee table had been overturned, a lamp shattered, a mirror cracked. Trouble.

There was no evidence of Annie or Jean or Dan anywhere; there were only the broken furnishings and the violent behavior that must have led to them. Terry's jaws clenched as we crept deeper into the house, past the living room, into the den, where the TV set was blaring even though no one was there watching it. On screen were ABC's political pundits Cokie Roberts and Sam Donaldson—two of Annie's favorite Sunday commentators, I suspected. The sight of them made me want to cry out, to shout, to yell: "Annie? Where are you, honey?" But Terry placed his forefinger over his lips, reminding me—reminding each of us—to stick to our plan, to hold our emotions in check, to keep absolutely still so as not to tip Dan off that we were in the vicinity.

We were making our way past the television set, en route to the kitchen, when Amanda let out a shriek—a scream loud enough to wake the dead, let alone tip Dan off.

"Good Lord!" she squealed, pointing at the TV screen. "It's my old friend Arianna Huffington! She's being interviewed on that show!"

The three of us were paralyzed by her outburst, completely taken aback. Was the woman so self-absorbed that she could foil our agreed-upon rescue mission without batting a mascara-ed eyelash?

"Arianna and I used to travel in similar social circles," she explained, nodding at Mrs. Huffington's image on the screen. "Now she's too busy for parties—she's promoting the Grand Old Party on network television, of all things." Amanda paused, as if an actual insight had been visited upon her. I could almost see the lightbulb go on. "That's it!" she squealed, louder this time. "I've changed my mind! Why be *spiritual* when you can be *political*?" She clapped her hands, applauding her brilliance. "Yes, that's what I'll do. I'll throw myself into the political arena, just like Arianna did. I'll become a lobbyist of some sort, or maybe a diplomat to one of those darling little countries we're still friendly with. I'll make appearances on 'Crossfire,' I'll sleep in the Lincoln bedroom, the sky's the limit! Who needs an article in *Personal Life* when you can have the cover of *Newsweek!* Oh, think of it. I'll get my own clothing line after all!"

Terry looked as if he wanted to throttle her, but Will persuaded him that there were more pressing issues.

"It is Annie and Jean who matter," Will told him. "Better to save your strength for them."

Terry nodded, shaking his fist at Amanda, who seemed perplexed by his anger.

That was when we heard the ruckus. Apparently, our own little ruckus had brought Dan out of hiding.

"He must be outside!" Terry said, gesturing toward the backyard, tightening his grip on Dan's kitchen knife.

We left Amanda in front of the television set, to plot her political future, and made a mad dash to the rear of the house, afraid of what might have happened before we arrived, afraid of what we might find, afraid that it was taking the police an eternity to show up.

We opened the screened door and rushed outside.

There were Dan and Annie rolling around on the lawn, engaged in a bizarre sort of wrestling match. He must have had her in his grip, I speculated, been distracted by the commotion we were making, and allowed her to wriggle out of his control, momentarily. Now she was fighting to escape from him, kicking him, trying to beat him off. She would get free for an instant, then he would recapture her.

Horrified by what he was witnessing, Terry was poised to attack Dan—only to be stopped in his tracks.

The man had a gun.

"Stay away!" Dan shouted at us as we stood there helplessly. "My first plan went bust but I've got a new plan— with a new victim. How much will you pay me for your cute little girl, Mr. Jeep Tour? Huh?"

Terry was stunned, his face draining of color. "The police will be here any second," he bluffed, undoubtedly praying they would be. "I won't have to pay you a cent."

Dan responded by pointing the gun at Annie's head. "You want me to shoot her? Is that it?" he sneered.

"No!" Terry backed down. "I want you to let her go. I'll pay you whatever I've got."

Dan laughed at Terry's change of heart, then grimaced—Annie had just kicked him in the shins.

Good work, I praised her silently. Just keep kicking the son of a bitch until the police get here. Stall him for a few more minutes and you'll be in the clear. We all will be.

Astoundingly, as if Annie had read my thoughts, she dealt Dan another blow to the shins, wounding him enough to weaken his grasp and provide her with an opening.

"Yeah, I'll stall him!" she cried triumphantly, sprinting not into her father's arms, which, she sensed, would have put *his* life in danger, but onto the nearby trampoline!

What happened next was the stuff of dreams, of miracles.

"Annie! What in the world?" Terry shouted at her. He was about to make another try for Dan's throat when the Reiki huckster waved the gun at him.

"Wait," I whispered to Terry. "Annie's great on that trampoline. It's possible that she knows exactly what she's doing."

"She's only ten years old," he said, nearly choking with fear and frustration.

"Since when was she 'only' anything?" I reminded him, thinking of her specialness, of the precocious, eccentric little girl who had flourished in spite of her rocky beginning, of the sick child Jean Singleton had helped to raise.

Jean!

Suddenly, I realized that we hadn't seen *her* anywhere!

I glanced around and discovered that Will was gone, too! He must have slipped away to search for his wife. I only hoped he'd find her inside the house—alive.

"Shit!" Terry cursed. "Dan's climbing up there after Annie! And he's not letting go of that gun!"

Sure enough, Dan had hoisted himself up onto the trampoline, refusing to let Annie get away. But he was no match for her. As she bounced up and down, up and down, he kept falling down and getting up, falling down and getting up.

"I could shoot the fucking kid if she'd just stop jumping!" he moaned, unable to hold the gun steady.

You can't shoot her *unless* she stops jumping, I thought, admiring Annie's ingenuity. She had made herself a moving target. The perfect stall.

"Come on, jump!" she taunted Dan as she bounced higher and higher, tugging on an overhanging tree branch each time she reached high enough to make contact with it, like a kid on a merry-go-round, grabbing for the brass ring.

As Terry and I watched in absolute awe, she continued to thwart Dan's ability to aim the gun at her, bouncing him around so that he had no control of his own jumps. He had become her puppet, his movements utterly dependent on hers. The higher she jumped, the higher he was catapulted—a passive player in one of the strangest athletic contests I'd ever seen.

"I'll shoot. I swear I will!" Dan yelled as he struggled to take charge of the situation, much less of his own body.

"I don't think so!" Annie shouted at him. It was like observing two people on a seesaw—as one went down, the other flew up—but it was Annie who was running the show.

The longer the trampolining went on, though, the more nervous Terry and I became. Out of control or not, there was always the chance that Dan could simply fire the gun in the midst of one of his jumps and hit Annie on her way up or down.

"Where's Whitehead?" Terry demanded at the precise moment that the detective finally appeared, along with reinforcements.

"Freeze!" Detective Whitehead barked, as he and four

uniformed officers surrounded Dan, their guns drawn. "Did you hear me? I said, 'Freeze!'"

"Freeze?" Dan whined as he continued to jump involuntarily. Boing! Boing! Boing! "How the hell am I supposed to freeze with this kid bouncing me up and down?"

"Annie!" Terry called out to her. "Let the police handle things from here."

"Sure, Dad," she said. "Just one last jump for Dan, okay?"

As her father and I looked on, as Detective Whitehead and his officers looked on, Annie propelled herself as high up off the trampoline as she could, reaching out to touch the tree branch and then coming down onto the mat for a big landing—a landing that shot Dan straight up in the air, boosting him so high that the sleeve of his "There's No Place Like Om" T-shirt got caught on the tree branch and hooked him.

"Look! He's stuck up there!" I shrieked with relief as Dan's gun fell to the ground.

Terry rushed over to Annie, while the police let Dan twist in the wind, literally, his arms and legs flailing in all directions, his face purple with rage, exasperation, and, very likely, exhaustion.

Annie climbed off the trampoline to embrace her father. Wanting to give them a private moment together, I strolled over to the tree from which Dan was hanging and peered at him.

And then, because I couldn't resist, I cupped my hands around my mouth and called up to him. "Hey, Dan. You're in a bad space," I said. "A really bad space."

He muttered something unprintable, but I just laughed. Eventually, the cops untangled him from the tree, handcuffed him, and took him away.

"See what happens when the government is soft on crime?" Annie said, nodding at the departing Dan. "You get repeat offenders back out on the street. This guy told me he's been in and out of jail five times."

I hugged her, stroked her hair, wiped the sweat from her brow. I was so glad she was safe, so glad she had come into my life.

"You're very brave *and* very smart, Annie," I told her.

"Thanks," she said. "It's funny. You don't really know you're brave until you have to be."

I smiled. The kid had a way about her.

Detective Whitehead was in the midst of explaining to us what would happen next in the case when Will emerged from the house, his arm around a healthy but visibly shaken Jean.

"Where was she?" Terry asked his friend.

"In a closet," said Will. "Bound and gagged, just like Mrs. Reid was."

"Are you all right?" I asked Jean Singleton, touching her arm lightly. She was as taciturn and unexpressive as her husband, but, like him, she had a quiet dignity.

"He didn't hurt me," she said of Dan. "Mostly, he made me angry. Especially when I realized that he was the one who had brought Will and me such unhappiness." She glared at Detective Whitehead, who was unapologetic.

"We had a job to do, that's all," he said. "We thought your husband was a guilty man. We pursued our theory. We were wrong. It happens."

"I only hope it does not happen to anyone I care about," said Will, showing his first flash of anger since the ordeal began.

Detective Whitehead shrugged and said he'd better get back to the police station to file his report. As he was leaving, Amanda trudged out of the house, joining us on the lawn.

"I never expected all this to take so long," she complained. "The man who kidnapped me is in police custody, is that correct?"

"Yes, Mrs. Reid," Detective Whitehead replied, slipping effortlessly into his unctuous public servant mode. Amazingly, he was showing respect for a woman who didn't deserve any, while he barely gave Jean Singleton the time of day. "We've apprehended the perpetrator now. He's on his way to the lockup."

"Well then, why hasn't anyone telephoned my husband to pick me up and deliver me to my hotel?" Amanda demanded. "I understand he's in Sedona, awaiting word of my condition."

"We can contact him from my car phone, but I'd be honored to escort you to your hotel," said the detective. "The question is, which hotel? You were staying at Tranquility, Mrs. Reid, but your husband is booked at L'Auberge de Sedona."

"Oh, my," said Amanda. "That *is* a dilemma. Which hotel do *you* think I would prefer, Detective Whitehead, given the trauma I've suffered?"

The detective answered quickly. "I'd go to L'Auberge, since your husband's there," he said. "It's a nice, romantic place—perfect for a reunion."

I thought of Steven, of our reunion at L'Auberge, and wondered if I'd ever run into him when I got back to New York. At a Pakistani restaurant, maybe.

"How's the food at this L'Auberge?" asked Amanda, speaking of restaurants.

"Excellent," said Detective Whitehead, cop-turned-food-critic.

"Is there a manicurist on staff?" she inquired.

"I'm not sure, Mrs. Reid," he admitted.

Amanda pouted. "There was a divine girl at Tranquility," she recalled. "She was so skillful I was ready to bring her home with me." She paused, clearly conflicted. "I've decided that we'll have Mr. Reid move his things over there," she said finally.

"Whatever you want, ma'am," Whitehead bowed.

Amanda turned her attention to us. To Terry, Annie, Will, Jean, and me. To the people who, essentially, put their lives on the line for her.

"Well, now," she said. "It was quite an experience we all shared, wasn't it?"

"Quite an experience," I said.

"Perhaps I'll return to Sedona in the years ahead," she said, "as a visiting politician." She chuckled, visions of Arianna Huffington dancing in her head, no doubt. "Who knows? The next time you see me, I could be the governor of someplace or other!"

"Nope," said Annie. "The next time we see you, you'll be growing organic vegetables or breeding King Charles spaniels or developing property in Vietnam. You'll be playing Follow the Leader, like always."

Out of the mouths of babes, I thought.

Amanda was mortified, of course. She demanded that Terry reprimand his daughter for her "insolent remarks."

"Try and have a nice life, Amanda," he said instead and ushered her and Detective Whitehead off his property.

CHAPTER THIRTY

♥

Later that night, we celebrated with a chicken and ribs barbecue at Terry's. The Singletons were there, and Cynthia Kavner and her two daughters, and everybody had a wonderful time, the sort of time you have after you've survived a harrowing event and the adrenaline's still running. After dinner, the girls scampered up to Annie's room, where she regaled them with tales of her heroics. In the living room, the adults traded opinions of the circus Amanda Reid had so cavalierly set in motion, amazed that the whole sorry episode had happened at all. By eleven o'clock, we were bleary-eyed, our jubilance having been replaced by serious fatigue.

The Singletons were the first to rise from their chairs.

"Time to go," Will said, helping his wife up. "My lids are heavy."

"You'll be here for a few more days, won't you, Crystal?" asked Jean as we said goodnight.

I hesitated. Terry and I hadn't had any further discussions of when I would leave Sedona or if I would leave. As a result, I didn't know how to answer Jean's question, particularly with Terry standing beside me. My flight back to JFK, the return portion of my round-trip ticket, was scheduled for Thursday, four days away. I was fairly sure I'd be on it, but I hadn't come out and said as much, not in so many words.

"A few more days," I replied finally. "I hope we'll see each other again, Jean."

"I'd like that," she said, shaking my hand warmly.

"The same goes for me," Will added. "You supported me through my trouble, Crystal. I am grateful."

I smiled, a lighthearted thought crossing my mind. "How grateful?" I baited him.

"Very grateful," he said.

"Grateful enough to cleanse my aura?" Well, that *was* one of the reasons I'd come to Sedona, wasn't it? Because Rona had told me mine was dirty? I had to have it cleansed before I left town—and I wasn't about to place it in the hands of a shyster like Dan, either. Will Singleton was the only one I could trust with such matters. "If you're not too tired, that is," I said.

I glanced at Terry and Jean and Cynthia, to get a sense of whether my request was kosher under the circumstances. For all I knew, you didn't invite someone over for dinner and then ask the person to cleanse your aura. Maybe it was considered a social gaffe, like asking the doctor you meet at a party for free medical advice. But they indicated that I was on solid ground, etiquette-wise.

"I am not too tired. I am honored to do the cleansing," said Will. "Or, as we Native Americans call it, the 'smudging.' It would be best if you stepped outside with me, Crystal. We will do the smudging there, just the two of us."

I looked at the others again. "Here goes," I said, and

followed Will out of the house, wishing Rona could see me now.

We walked to his car. When we got to the Pontiac, Will opened the door on the driver's side and reached down onto the floor for his black bag. He retrieved it and pulled out what appeared to be a long, cylinder-shaped object.

"It is sage and juniper, rolled together and tied with colorful thread," Will explained. He fished around in the black bag for a matchbook. "Now I will light the ends of the sage."

He lit the match and held it against the leaves, the tips of which quickly blackened and began to smoke. The aroma was pungent and sweet and reminded me of my college years, those wild and crazy days when smoke from a different type of leaf filled the dormitories on a regular basis.

"Stand right here, Crystal," Will instructed me, guiding me to a spot directly in front of him. "Extend your arms straight out, like a bird in flight." I did as I was told. "Close your eyes. The smudging will be more powerful for you that way." I closed my eyes. "I will be chanting in my native language as I wave the smoky sage around your body. You will not understand the words, but you will feel them. They will be expressing our thanks to Heaven, Earth, and Spirit. They will also be asking for light along your path and peace to your journey."

I opened my eyes. "My journey? So I'm taking the flight back to New York on Thursday?"

"I am a spiritualist, Crystal, not a travel agent." Will chuckled at his own joke. Obviously, he had a sense of humor he trotted out on special occasions. "I was speaking of your spiritual journey," he said more seriously. "I cannot advise you about your plans or tell you what to do or not do. My role is to lead you inward, to move you toward your own insights."

I nodded, thinking what a burden it was to have to come up with one's own insights.

But then I closed my eyes and surrendered to the smoky sage, the lyrical chanting, the mild, dry evening. It was such a pleasant experience, having so many senses activated simultaneously. I felt suspended in time, as if I were floating in some never-never land where nothing mattered and everything mattered, where ideas flowed freely, abstractly, randomly, where you could be detached from your own body yet exquisitely aware of it.

So this is what it's like to have your aura cleansed, I mused. Relaxing. Calming. Like having a really good facial.

At some point, a coyote's howl echoed through the darkness, a note that reverberated in perfect harmony with Will's chanting. It was a startling moment, a musical coming-together of man and nature, a stunning example of the "oneness" everybody in Sedona was always talking about.

The aura cleansing lasted about ten minutes. When it was over, Will blew out the burning sage and returned it to his black bag.

"Was it what you expected?" he asked me.

"I don't know what I expected," I admitted. "All I know is that when I first came to Sedona, I was dismissive of auras and vortexes and people who channel ancient entities. I had a blanket skepticism toward anything 'New Age.' But now I'm open to alternative ways of looking at things. My focus used to be so narrow, Will. I filled my life with numbers and calculations and spreadsheets. But this trip has made me more curious about the way other people lead their lives, about rituals and legends, for instance. I've enjoyed just being exposed to them, to you. What I'm trying to say is that meeting you has been a gift, Will. I mean that."

He smiled, reaching for my hand.

"Terry used to speak about you," he said, "about how much he admired you. I see why. You are honest. You do not pretend. You are your own person, a slave to no one."

"That hasn't always been the case," I said. "Before I came here, I was a slave to everyone. And pleasing none of them, by the way."

"You feel differently now?"

"I'm beginning to."

Will nodded, releasing my hand.

"Peace to your journey," he said again.

"And to yours," I said.

After the Singletons left, Cynthia tried to round up her daughters, calling upstairs to them, reminding them that tomorrow was Monday, a school day, and that it was way past their bedtime. They promised they'd be right down but weren't, which gave us a few minutes to ourselves while Terry was in the backyard, sipping the last of the wine.

"I have a confession to make," she said as we stood together in the foyer. "I've always had a soft spot for Terry."

"Have you?" I said, not surprised. A lot of women had a soft spot for Terry, back when we were in college. Why not now?

"Yes," she admitted. "But he's never been interested in me romantically. As a matter of fact, I'd never seen him interested in anybody romantically until you came to Sedona. He's crazy about you, Crystal. You must know that."

"I know he wants me to stay here, to give us another chance."

"And?"

"And I don't see how I can."

She shook her head. "I don't see how you can't."

"You weren't married to Terry, Cynthia. He didn't disappoint you."

"From the look on your face, he isn't disappointing *you* anymore."

"No, but it's one thing to spend a few days with an old flame, another thing to throw yourself into the fire."

"And it's still another thing to douse the fire before it's even gotten started. You haven't spent enough time with Terry to know for sure whether you two could make it work the second time around. You haven't let him show you—"

Cynthia stopped, realizing that she was lecturing me. She broke into a wide grin. "Would you listen to me?" she laughed, "sticking my nose where it doesn't belong?"

"Actually, I *was* about to tell you to mind your own business," I said, laughing with her.

"I wouldn't have blamed you if you had," she said. "I'm sorry if I was badgering you. I like you, Crystal. Aside from wanting to see Terry happy, I have a selfish reason for seeing you stay in town—I think we could be friends."

"I think we are already," I said. "I only let one other person badger me and I've known her a lot longer than I've known you."

"Look," she said. "You sound as if you've made up your mind to leave Sedona. But if you ever feel the need to talk, just call me, okay? We can be telephone friends, if nothing else."

"It's a deal," I said, realizing, suddenly, how many years it had been since I'd made a new friend.

Once Cynthia and her daughters went home and Annie collapsed into bed, Terry and I tackled the dishes. Neither of us said much—there was only an occasional "I'll do that" as he washed and I dried. We were both too worn out for a conversation—or too wary of one, I wasn't sure which.

It wasn't until everything was clean and put away that he finally looked at me and remarked, "Some day this was, huh?"

I walked over to him and wrapped my arms around his waist. "Some day," I agreed. "Some vacation."

"Is the vacation over?" he asked.

"No," I said. "Not yet. In fact, I happen to know that there's a nifty little guest room upstairs. We could ask the guy who owns this place if it's free for the night. How about it?"

"You ask him. He's sweet on you, I hear."

I smiled. "He's sweet, period."

Our lovemaking that night was quiet, silent almost. And not because we were afraid of waking Annie, whose earlier acrobatics, we were certain, would knock her out for at least eight hours. No, it was that we were especially gentle with each other, tender, careful. Terry, who had nearly lost his daughter that afternoon, now seemed resigned to losing me instead and, as a result, held his usual passion in check, barely making a sound when he climaxed in my arms. And I, conflicted about loving him, conflicted about leaving him, was fearful that I would be leading him on if I reveled ostentatiously in the pleasure his lovemaking brought me.

In the morning, it was he who roused me from sleep, kissing the tip of my nose and then slipping out of bed, back to his own room, showering and dressing before Annie came downstairs for breakfast.

"You sure you want to go to school today?" he was asking her when I entered the kitchen. "You're a star now, a big cheese. The media might hound you during recess."

"Then Doug Freehan will protect me," said Annie.

"Who's Doug Freehan?" I asked.

"Yeah. Who's Doug Freehan?" Terry echoed.

"A kid in my class," Annie explained. "Last night, Laura told me he likes me."

Terry and I tried to keep straight faces.

"How do you feel about him?" I asked.

Annie considered the question. "I'm not ready for a serious relationship," she said finally. "I'm too young."

"A wise girl," said Terry, relieved.

"But in a month, I'll be eleven," Annie added. "I might like Doug Freehan better then."

When it was time for her to leave for school, she kissed her father and me goodbye. "See you guys later," she said. "Don't do anything I wouldn't do."

Terry and I laughed and watched her scoot out the door. Just then, the phone rang. He ran back into the kitchen to answer it.

"Hello?" he said. "Who? Oh, it's the famous Rona Wishnick. The one I've heard so much about."

Dear Rona. I wondered how long it would take before news of Amanda's miraculous reappearance would reach her. I assumed she was calling to get the gory details.

"Yup. Crystal's still staying here," Terry said to her. "She's standing right next to me. I'll put her on."

He handed me the telephone.

"Hi, Rona. How are you?" I asked, realizing how much I had missed her, missed her meddling in my life.

"I'm exhaw-sted," she said in her nasal honk. "I haven't been sleeping well."

"Why not?" I asked. Ever since she'd started taking melatonin, she'd been sleeping like a log.

"Because I was worrying about *you*, why else?" she said. "Between the Amanda business, the Steven business, and the ex-husband business, I've been a mess."

"I'm sorry," I said. "Everything's okay now. I promise.

When I get home on Thursday, I'll fill you in on all of the above."

There. I'd uttered the words. In front of Terry. I was leaving Sedona on Thursday as originally planned. No, blurting it out to Rona on the phone wasn't the tactful, sensitive way I'd hoped to break the news to him, but judging by the look on his face, my confirmed date of departure wasn't a total revelation. In fact, he didn't seem the least bit surprised. Just disappointed. He took my hand and brought it to his lips.

"If I were you, I wouldn't wait until Thursday, Crystal," Rona said. "That's why I called."

"Uh-oh. What's going on?" I asked.

She sighed. "Big doings, that's what. Otis stopped by my desk this morning, full of his usual doom and gloom. He told me to tell you that a partners' meeting has been scheduled for Wednesday at nine a.m. He gave me the distinct impression that you're expected to be there. He said it was an extremely important meeting involving key personnel changes."

"Key personnel changes?"

"That's what he said."

Well, this is it, I thought. This is really it. They're getting everybody in one room so they can fire me together. It's the old united-front thing, the old safety-in-numbers thing, the old gang-up-on-her-so-she'll-be-too-intimidated-to-fight-us thing. They're anticipating a lawsuit, just the way Steven warned me they would, so they want to make sure I understand that it's me against the company. The fuckers.

"Crystal? Are you changing your flight or not?" asked Rona.

"Give me a minute."

Today is Monday, I thought. The meeting at Duboff Spector is Wednesday morning. In order to get back in time for the meeting, I'd have to fly out of Phoenix tomorrow afternoon instead of on Thursday afternoon. Which would mean I'd have to leave Sedona tomorrow morning. Which would mean tonight would be my last night with Terry.

Damn. What was I supposed to do? Stay? Go? What?

I was planning to leave Sedona anyway, wasn't I? I reminded myself. What difference did it make if I left a couple of days earlier? Saying goodbye to Terry and Annie was going to tear my heart out, whether I did it tomorrow, the next day, or the day after that. It was going to hurt like hell and I wasn't looking forward to it. So why not get it over with?

Besides, I really had to take care of the situation at Duboff Spector, had to deal with it. Putting in an appearance at the partners' meeting would enable me to look my colleagues in the eye, speak up for myself, control my own destiny. I wouldn't have to be summoned into Otis Tool's office the day I got back like some poor, pathetic shlep, wouldn't have to hear everything after the fact.

Everything happens for a reason.

Sure, Jazeem, sure. But what's the reason this time? Did Rona call me about the meeting so I'd be nudged into leaving Sedona sooner rather than later? So I'd have to pull away from my past once and for all? So I'd be forced to resolve my feelings for Terry quickly and cleanly?

I looked at him then, studied his ruggedly handsome face, his athletic, sinewy body, his blue, blue eyes.

I love you, I thought. Not still. Not more. Not differently. *Always.* I love you always.

But sometimes love isn't enough, my long-lost college sweetheart. It wasn't enough for us before. It won't be enough for us now. I have to leave you, have to go home.

"I'll call the airlines," I told Rona, swallowing the lump that had formed in my throat. "I'll let you know if I have any trouble changing my flight. If you don't hear from me, I'll see you Wednesday morning. Nine o'clock."

"Are you okay, Crystal?" she asked. "You don't sound so great all of a sudden."

"I'm fine," I said. And I was. It was just that making tough decisions is a bitch, whether you've had your aura cleansed or not.

CHAPTER
THIRTY-ONE

♥

"Aren't you going to say anything?" I asked Terry a few minutes after I'd finished speaking to the ticket agent at America West and had changed my flight without a hassle.

"What's there to say?" he replied from across the kitchen. He was leaning against the sink, his legs crossed at the ankles. He seemed distant, suddenly, sullen, as if the actual fact of my leaving had finally sunk in. "I told you the first night we spent together that I was grateful you came back into my life, grateful that I could be with you again after all these years. Do I want you to stay in Sedona? Relocate here? Live with me? Yeah. Do I expect you to? Not a chance. You made it clear right from the get-go that your home is in New York."

"It is," I confirmed.

"Even though the boyfriend's history," he said.

"Yes. My father's in New York," I reminded him.

"You have no relationship with your father, Crystal," he reminded me.

"Well then, there's my career," I pointed out.

"At Duboff Spector," he said sarcastically. "The outfit that's about to can you."

"Look, Terry. If you don't understand why I have to be at that meeting on Wednesday—"

"I understand perfectly," he interrupted. "Your work comes first. It always has."

"It's always *had* to," I shot back. "You can't depend on other people to pay your way in this world. I learned that lesson the hard way."

"Oh, give it a rest," Terry said, waving his hand in the air. "The past is the past. It's over and done with."

"My thoughts exactly," I said hotly.

There were several seconds of awkward silence during which we both stared at the floor. When I couldn't take it anymore, I started things up again.

"The meeting at Duboff Spector has nothing to do with why I'm leaving," I said. "It only has to do with *when* I'm leaving."

"Meaning?"

"Meaning that I was leaving anyway. You predicted that I was leaving. You said so yourself."

"Right. I'm psychic."

Great. He's doing just what he used to do whenever we fought, I thought. He's covering up his feelings with jokes, sarcasm, little digs.

"You expected me to leave," I kept on, "because you knew I'm not the type of person who shirks responsibility."

"And I am?"

"No. Not anymore."

"So?"

"So I can't just pick up the phone, call the partners at Duboff Spector, and announce that I'm not coming back. I can't call my father and tell him I'm not coming back, either. And then there's my apartment. I'm not about to have Rona mail me my clothes, put my furniture in storage, and sell the place."

"I've heard of stranger scenarios."

"I'll bet you have."

"Excuse me?"

"Forget I said that. I was making the point that my leaving has nothing to do with my career. It has to do with us, Terry. We aren't compatible."

He laughed scornfully. "Compatible the way you and Steven Moth were?"

"No. Compatible the way you and I never have been."

"Really? I thought we were pretty compatible upstairs in that guest room."

"I'm not talking about sex."

"Then what the hell are you talking about, Crystal? I'm totally in the dark here."

"I'm talking about our marriage, okay? I'm talking about the fact that it bombed."

"So what? That was almost twenty years ago. We're different people now."

"How do you *know* that, Terry? What if I go back to New York, pack up all my worldly belongings, kiss the Big Apple goodbye, move into this house with you—and the relationship bombs again? Then what?"

"Then you'll do something else."

"Just like that?"

"Just like that."

I shook my head. "You're not facing reality."

"Sure I am. We have different realities, that's all. Yours is that people can't afford to take chances. Mine is that people can't afford not to. If you hadn't flown out here on a whim, we wouldn't even be having this conversation. I might never have seen you again."

"True. But for me to change my life so radically—"

"I'd help you. My friends would help you. Annie would help you."

"Annie. Now there's another factor to consider. What if you and I got together, it didn't work out between us, and I went back to New York? She'd be abandoned yet again. She doesn't deserve that."

"What if it *did* work out between us? Have you considered *that* possibility? Or is happiness too mind-boggling for you to deal with? Yeah, maybe that's the problem. You came to Sedona looking for Happiness with a capital 'H,' you found it, and now you can't handle it. Maybe your idea of a good time is running back to a company that's about to dump you, to a boyfriend who bores you, to a father who ignores you. Maybe you *like* to suffer, Crystal. Maybe, when you get right down to it, you're more comfortable being miserable, and all this Happiness stuff isn't what you're searching for after all."

"Maybe." My eyes flooded with tears, my breathing became labored. I felt stung, didn't know how to respond to Terry's harsh assessment, didn't know whether his words were triggered by hurt or truth. I only knew I had to get away, had to be by myself. I turned to leave the kitchen.

"Where are you going?" he asked, his voice soft now, concerned.

"Got to pack," I managed and rushed out of the room.

I didn't have much packing to do, given that I'd been living out of my suitcase ever since I'd moved into Terry's guest room. So I sat on the bed and sobbed, wishing my trip to Sedona didn't have to end on such a sour note, wishing Terry and I could enjoy our last day together, wishing things could be different between us.

An hour went by and then there was a hesitant knock on my door.

"Come in," I said, dabbing at my eyes with a Kleenex.

Terry opened the door. "This is dumb," he said. "You've gotta be out of here by 8:30 tomorrow morning if you're making the 12:25 out of Phoenix. That only gives us a few more hours. Personally, I don't feel like spending them with you up here crying and me down there sulking."

I smiled through my tears. "I was thinking the same thing. Any ideas?"

He walked toward the bed and sat down next to me. "I'm not going into the office," he said, putting his arm around my shoulders. "And Annie will be at Laura's house after school. We're on our own. We could take a drive, have lunch, come back here for an afternoon nap. Does any of that appeal to you?"

"It all appeals to me," I said. "Thanks." I leaned over and kissed him.

"You taste salty," he said, then stroked my cheek. "I'm sorry about the tears, babe. I never wanted us to—"

"I know," I said. "I'm sorry, too. So very sorry."

We made the best of the day. Terry drove me to Tlaquepaque, a charming, Spanish-style village with courtyards and gardens and, most notably, dozens of art galleries specializing in Southwest and Native American crafts. He drove me to an area known as "Uptown," where there are more galleries and shops, these set along Oak Creek. And he drove me to Garland's, a legendary store that carries authentic kachina dolls—hundreds of them.

"I'd like to buy you one," Terry offered as we browsed through the shop, coming upon display after display of the carved wooden images. "Sort of as a souvenir, you know?"

I knew, but I didn't need a souvenir—some token to spark memories of the trip. My heart was flooded with memories, and I hadn't even left town.

"I'd love to own a kachina," I said. "But how could I ever choose one over the others? They're all beautiful works of art."

"How about him?" he said, lifting a doll up off a table. "The Sun God. He's a cheerful-looking guy, isn't he?"

"He is," interjected a saleswoman. "He's also the work of one of the Hopi tribe's most accomplished artists."

She went on to describe how real kachina dolls are crafted by the Hopis from the root of a cottonwood tree after it has eroded and dried, and she explained the process by which each doll is coated and painted.

"Set the Sun God on a table in your bedroom, where you can see him first thing every morning, and he'll surely brighten your day," she added.

"We'll take it," said Terry, winking at me.

Seeming pleased, the saleswoman jotted down my name and address and promised that the kachina would be carefully wrapped and boxed and shipped to me.

I thanked her and later, when Terry and I were walking toward the car, I thanked him.

"I'm crazy about Mr. Sun God," I said. "I'll have to find a very special place to put him."

"Maybe on your dresser?" he suggested. "If you have one, that is. I've never seen your apartment, so I'm just guessing here." He smiled, trying to act chipper. We both were. But underneath everything we did and said that day, behind every word and gesture, there was a terrible sense of inevitability. I was leaving. We wouldn't see each other anymore. Our brief encounter was coming to an end. And all the kachina dolls in the world weren't going to change that.

"Lunch?" Terry asked as we pulled out of the store's parking lot.

I looked at him and shrugged. "I'm not all that hungry. You?"

"Nope."

"What should we do then?"

"What about the nap? We could go back to the house and conk out. I don't know about you, but after all the excitement yesterday, I'm pretty beat."

"Oh. Well, yes. I'm tired, too. Sometimes there's a real letdown after a big event." Bullshit, I thought. If we go to sleep, we won't have to pretend everything's peachy between us.

We drove back to Terry's. I assumed we'd be "napping" in separate rooms, but he invited me into his bedroom.

I hesitated.

"I know you've had a thing about us sleeping together in my room," he said, "but it's your last day, Crystal. What difference could it make now?"

"None," I agreed and followed him into his bedroom.

It was a well-proportioned room, twice the square feet of the guest room. Terry kicked off his shoes and stretched out on the queen-size bed, his head propped up by a couple of pillows.

"Coming?" he asked.

"In a second." I unlaced my sneakers, walked over to the bed, and lay down next to him. We didn't touch, didn't talk, didn't move—until Terry suddenly rolled over and kissed me.

"I'm gonna miss doing that," he said, after he released me.

"Then you'd better do it again," I said.

He kissed me again, but this time he didn't release me. This time he held me close and kissed me over and over.

At some point it became clear to both of us that napping was no longer on the agenda.

"Just one for the road?" he murmured.

"One for the road," I whispered.

Our lovemaking was fiery and passionate, yet purposeful. We not only craved each other, we meant to leave an indelible impression on each other—as if, with each caress, we were saying: I dare you to forget me; I dare you to find someone who can make you feel this good.

Later, we showered together, each wanting to linger over the other's body, each wanting the moments of intimacy to last, each painfully aware that they would not.

"How will this work now?" Terry asked as he was toweling me dry. "Will we be pen pals? E-mail each other? Have phone sex once in a while?"

I smiled.

"I'm serious, Crystal. Are we going to keep in touch?"

"I've thought about that. We could stay in contact, of course. I know where to reach you now, and I'll give you my number at—"

"Or we could leave it right here," he cut me off, "with this afternoon. I'm not wild about calling you at your place some night and hearing another guy in the background. I'd rather remember the way you are when you're with me. That sound okay with you?"

I nodded. I understood.

Annie came home from Laura's and asked why my luggage was sitting in the foyer. Terry explained that he was about to load it into the trunk of my rental car, because I was flying back to New York first thing in the morning.

She looked at me with surprise. "You're leaving tomorrow?"

"Yes, Annie, I am," I said. "There's an important meeting at the company where I work. It's on Wednesday and I've got to be there."

"Are you coming back here after the meeting?" she said. "We could do stuff together over the weekend."

God, this is brutal, I thought. Worse than I expected.

"I live in New York, honey," I said. "I was only visiting Sedona. Now my vacation's over."

"Oh. Got it," she smirked. "You and Dad had a fight, right?"

"No fight, sport," said Terry. "Crystal's going home. That's all."

Her smirk faded. "So you didn't like it here with us?" she said to me, the little girl in her reemerging.

"Of course I did," I said. "But all good things come to an end eventually."

"They do? Why?" she said.

I had no answer for that one, except that it had been my experience that happiness is elusive, that nothing lasts forever.

"Let's get dinner ready, huh?" said Terry, trying to distract his daughter. "It's spaghetti tonight. I'm cooking the sauce. Crystal's making the pasta."

Annie shook her head, her expression hardening. "Crystal's bailing out," she said and scooted up the stairs.

We ate dinner. Then Annie did her homework while Terry and I cleaned up the kitchen. When we came upstairs to say good night to her, she was fast asleep in her bed—or appeared to be.

Terry and I spent the night in the guest room. We did not make love; we simply held each other until the sun came up.

In the morning, I stuffed the last of my things into my

carry-on bag, threw back some coffee, and prepared to hit the road.

"Say goodbye to Crystal, Annie," Terry urged her. All three of us were standing in the foyer. The front door was open, beckoning.

"I'm really late for school," said Annie as she permitted me to hug her briefly.

"Thanks for being such a wonderful hostess," I told her, in spite of her coolness. "And for teaching me how to jump on the trampoline. It was fun."

"But fun things come to an end. Right, Crystal?" she said.

"Yes, but I want you to know that I'll never forget you, Annie. You'll always be very special to me."

"Yeah. Whatever," she said, sounding more like a typical monosyllabic kid than her usual articulate self. "Hey, gotta run. Have a nice trip."

And off she went, out the door, a knapsack slung over her shoulders, a tear running down her cheek.

I turned to Terry. "She'll be okay, won't she? You'll make sure she's okay, right?"

"I'll take care of it," he assured me, then glanced at his watch. "You really should get a move on. You don't want to miss the flight."

I flung my arms around him. "Terry, I—"

He kissed me. One last time.

"I love you, Crystal," he said.

"I love you, too," I said.

"Better go, huh?"

I nodded, trying desperately to hold myself together, trying as hard as I could to save the sobs for the long ride to Phoenix.

I removed my arms from around Terry's neck and released him. He walked me out to the burgundy rental number and helped me into the car.

"Peace to your journey," he said, his voice choked with emotion.

"And to yours," I said.

I placed the key in the ignition, strapped myself in, and drove away.

E·P·I·L·O·G·U·E

The Christmas season in New York is very festive—unless you have to get somewhere, in which case it's a nightmare. The traffic in midtown Manhattan is such gridlock that you can literally sit in a taxi for twenty minutes and not advance a single block.

Fortunately, I had done my Christmas shopping the day after Thanksgiving, along with millions of similarly compulsive Americans, and had no need to get anywhere this particular holiday season. I wasn't dating, wasn't taking in the theatre or the ballet, wasn't rushing to cocktail parties, not counting the office party Duboff Spector threw for its employees at Tavern on the Green.

Yes, I was still a partner at Duboff Spector, still sorting out my clients' tax problems, still working side by side with my pal Rona. It turned out that the meeting I'd rushed back from Sedona to attend had not been convened in order to squeeze *me* out of the firm; the partner who ended up getting the heave-ho was a rather surly man in his late

fifties named Clyde Hicks whose unpopularity had more
to do with his attitude than his age. But he wasn't the only
one forced out that Wednesday morning. His long-time
secretary was canned, too, along with two people in the
bookkeeping department, two in clerical, and the receptionist, who rarely showed up anyway and was, therefore,
not missed.

"I guess you and I are in the clear," Rona declared
when I'd returned to my office after the meeting.

"For the time being," I responded with a shrug. I'd felt
oddly let down when I found out I wasn't the focus of the
meeting, the focus of Duboff Spector's "key personnel
changes." It was as if I wasn't even important enough to
fire, as if I had worked so hard to serve my clients, had
logged in so many long hours to keep everybody happy,
that, as far as the other partners were concerned, my little
corner of the company practically ran itself. Which meant
that I had, effectively, rendered myself invisible.

"Oh, you know how it is in business today," Rona
attempted to console me. "They only pay attention to you
when you screw up. Nobody takes the time to say, 'Good
job.' It just doesn't happen. Companies aren't very spiritual."

"No, they aren't," I agreed.

"That's why you can't live your life strictly to please
them, Crystal," she lectured. "You have to satisfy yourself,
find your own source of joy. Didn't they teach you that in
Sedona?"

I nodded wistfully. "They gave it their best shot."

As the weeks after the partners' meeting became months,
as the season changed, as the air turned cold, my dissatisfac-
tion with Duboff Spector grew, as did the pain of missing
Terry. I thought about him constantly, replayed our week
together, wondered if he was right when he'd suggested

that I couldn't handle happiness, that I enjoyed being miserable.

And then came a blizzardlike afternoon in mid-December—the day I realized how right he was.

The occasion for this realization was one of my regular Sunday visits with my father, who, despite my absence back in September, was as distant toward me as ever. His cable TV system had added six new channels, which gave him six more reasons to ignore me. As I was nearing the Larchmont exit en route to his house on this particular afternoon, my snow-tire-less BMW skidded off the Hutchison River Parkway, into a guardrail. Thank God, there were no other cars involved in the accident, nor was my own car as badly damaged as it could have been. But *I* was a wreck, totally shaken up. After the police came and wrote a report of the incident, I proceeded cautiously on to my father's, since I was almost there anyway. When I arrived— still trembling, an hour later than expected—he met me at the door with his typical remoteness, told me to deposit my snowy boots outside, and advised me that something terrible had just happened to *him*.

"What was it?" I said.

"The TV's on the fritz," he said bitterly. "The cable's out. Must be the storm, dammit. Now I won't have anything to do today."

"Anything to do?"

I blinked at him. Had I heard him correctly? Had I not driven my car off an icy road so I could keep the old man company? Had I not plowed my way to his doorstep, wet, cold, seeking a little companionship myself? Had the bastard not told me his day was ruined because his television set didn't work? I mean, really. Enough was enough.

"Don't make trouble, Crystal," he sighed, trudging back inside the house after seeing the look on my face.

I did not "make trouble." I did not follow him inside

the house, either. I remained outside, the big chill waking me up at last.

My God! I thought, as the snow covered my eyes and cheeks and lips. I'm as pathetic as he is! I, too, have chosen misery over happiness. I, too, have rejected someone who loves me. I, too, have isolated myself because of a past hurt. How could I not have seen the parallels between his life and my own? How could I have been so dense?

There was still time to remedy the situation, to change things, I told myself. There *had* to be.

"See ya, Dad!" I called out through his open front door and hurried back to my car.

I drove carefully but excitedly back to the city, the car radio blasting with the sound of some opera I didn't understand a word of. The minute I walked into my apartment, I rushed to the phone and called Cynthia Kavner, praying she hadn't forgotten me. After two rings, she answered. I inhaled deeply, my heart thumping in my chest.

"Cynthia," I said. "It's Crystal Goldstein."

"Hey! You were just on my mind, I swear it," she said enthusiastically. "Annie was over here this morning and—"

"And she mentioned me?" I said hopefully.

"No. She mentioned that the magazine writer who was here when you were here—the one who took the Jeep Tour with you—is doing a book on the Amanda Reid case and wants to interview her. She thinks the whole thing's a hoot."

So Michael Mandell's writing a book, I thought wryly. It was Amanda who was desperate for media attention and yet it was Michael who ultimately got it.

"How is Annie?" I asked, wondering if she'd grown, wondering if she was looking forward to Christmas, wondering if she liked Doug Freehan any better than she had in September.

"Great," said Cynthia. "Doing great."

"I'm glad," I said. "And you?"

"Busy. Laura had the chicken pox last month. Karen's the lead in the school play."

Okay, Crystal. Ask her the next question, I dared myself. Go ahead. Ask her.

"And Terry? How's he doing?" I said, then braced myself for "He's met someone" or an equally gruesome answer.

"He's good, too," Cynthia said instead. "But he misses you, if that's what you're asking."

"Does he?"

"Of course he does. He loves you, Crystal."

I didn't say anything.

"How is New York?" she asked, changing the subject.

Tell her, I thought. Tell her how New York is. Tell her how you've lost all interest in the city and its breakneck pace; how you don't feel the same devotion to your father and your job that you once did; how you want to come home . . . to Terry and Annie . . . to Sedona. Tell her.

I cleared my throat. "Do you need an accountant, Cynthia?"

"What?"

"Do you have someone to do your taxes?"

"Sort of. Why?"

"I was considering the possibility of opening a practice in Sedona. I was hoping you'd be my first client."

"Crystal! You're coming back here? Terry never said a word!"

"Terry doesn't know about it," I said. "I didn't know about it myself until an hour ago." I paused, trying to remain calm. "I was thinking of flying out and surprising him, Cynthia—he gets a kick out of spontaneous gestures—but I figured I should call you beforehand, to make sure he still wants me."

"Still wants you?" she laughed. "He'll be ecstatic that

you've had a change of heart. In fact, I've got a terrific idea. Could you be here by Christmas Eve? Terry and Annie are coming for dinner that night. It would be perfect if you could join us. Quite a Christmas present.''

Could I be there by Christmas Eve? I wondered. It was only ten days away. There would be a million loose ends to tie up by then, a million details to take care of. Still, it was doable. I'd *make* it doable.

"I'll be there on Christmas Eve," I told Cynthia. "But it'll be our secret, right? You won't say anything to Terry or Annie?"

"No way! I can't wait to see their faces when you walk in the door. Oh, Crystal. I'm so happy for you."

"I'm happy for me, too."

On December 24, I boarded America West's 12:45 flight out of JFK, which was scheduled to land in Phoenix at 2:51. I was so charged up I could have flown all the way to Arizona without the plane.

Of course, getting a seat on the flight had been tricky. It was Christmas Eve, after all, and the ticket agent had said he only had one seat left.

"I'll take it," I'd told him.

And so there I was, in the middle seat yet again, stuck this time between "Tiger Man" and "Mr. Ferocious," two impossibly muscular professional wrestlers who were continuing on to Las Vegas after the plane made its connection in Phoenix. They were only slightly more talkative than Larry and Dave had been, back in September, but they seemed more tolerant of my frequent trips to the lavatory.

"You guys ever been to Sedona?" I asked them as we were flying somewhere over this great country of ours.

"No. Where's that at?" said Tiger Man.

"It's in Arizona," I said. "Two hours north of Phoenix."

"Whad do they got there?" asked Mr. Ferocious, his voice heavy with an accent I couldn't place.

"They have really good energy," I said. "And a lot of sage."

And that was the extent of our conversation.

When we arrived at the Phoenix airport, I hustled over to the Avis counter and picked up my rental car, another burgundy model. Apparently, rental cars come in either white or burgundy and the white ones get snapped up first. I threw my bags into the trunk, hopped in, and pulled out.

"Here we go," I said out loud as the car and I chugged onto Interstate-17. "No turning back now."

The two-hour drive was a blur. I was so hyper that my mind positively raced. First, I'd picture the look on Terry's face when I showed up at Cynthia's. Then, I'd flash back to my last few days in New York—from my instructions to my cousin Vivian to look in on my father every once in awhile, to my final meeting with Otis, during which I told him exactly where he could stick his tool.

And then there was my poignant exchange with Rona.

"This is the most thrilling thing that's ever happened to me," she exclaimed when we'd said goodbye.

"That's ever happened to *you*?" I laughed.

"Sure. I feel a spiritual connection with you after all these years, Crystal. What happens to *you* happens to *me*."

She hugged me so tightly she nearly cut off the circulation in my arms.

"I love you, Rona. I don't know what I'm going to do without you," I said tearfully.

"What makes you think you'll do anything without me?" she insisted.

"Well, of course, we'll talk on the phone all the time and—"

"Talk on the phone? I'll be two steps away."

"What do you mean?"

"I'm moving to Sedona, too," she announced. "You'll need a secretary when you open your accounting practice."

"You're quitting Duboff Spector?"

"Gave them my notice yesterday," she said. "This place doesn't deserve either of us."

"What about Arthur and his fear of heights? Does he know that Sedona is 4,500 feet above sea level?"

"Illandra suggested I give him special herbs," she said. "To counteract phobias. He'll be sky diving when I'm through with him."

As I headed north on I-17, I beamed, reliving that conversation with Rona. Having her with me was going to be the icing on the cake.

I was forty-five minutes outside of Sedona when I spotted the familiar red rocks in the distance, so majestic, so welcoming.

Almost there, I thought, trying to contain my excitement. Almost there.

Cynthia's directions were easy to follow. I pulled into her driveway at 6:02 and parked right alongside Terry's Jeep. The house was ablaze with Christmas lights, the front lawn dotted with Styrofoam Santas.

I checked my reflection in the rearview mirror, combed my hair, wiped a smudge of lipstick off my teeth.

I was about to get out of the car when I suffered a momentary loss of confidence. Am I doing the right thing? I wondered suddenly, my heart in my throat. Am I?

And then I caught a quick glimpse of Terry, moving across what I assumed was the living room window. The mere sight of him erased all my doubts.

I'm here, my love, I smiled to myself as I approached Cynthia's front door. I'm home.

ROMANCE FROM FERN MICHAELS

DEAR EMILY   (0-8217-4952-8, $5.99)

WISH LIST   (0-8217-5228-6, $6.99)

AND IN HARDCOVER:

VEGAS RICH   (1-57566-057-1, $25.00)

THE MYSTERIES OF MARY ROBERTS RINEHART

THE AFTER HOUSE   (0-8217-4246-6, $3.99/$4.99)

THE CIRCULAR STAIRCASE   (0-8217-3528-4, $3.95/$4.95)

THE DOOR   (0-8217-3526-8, $3.95/$4.95)

THE FRIGHTENED WIFE   (0-8217-3494-6, $3.95/$4.95)

A LIGHT IN THE WINDOW   (0-8217-4021-0, $3.99/$4.99)

THE STATE VS.   (0-8217-2412-6, $3.50/$4.50)
ELINOR NORTON

THE SWIMMING POOL   (0-8217-3679-5, $3.95/$4.95)

THE WALL   (0-8217-4017-2, $3.99/$4.99)

THE WINDOW AT THE WHITE CAT
                             (0-8217-4246-9, $3.99/$4.99)

THREE COMPLETE NOVELS: THE BAT, THE HAUNTED
LADY, THE YELLOW ROOM
                             (0-8217-114-4, $13.00/$16.00)

Available wherever paperbacks are sold, or order direct from the Publisher. Send cover price plus 50¢ per copy for mailing and handling to Kensington Publishing Corp., Consumer Orders, or call (toll free) 888-345-BOOK, to place your order using Mastercard or Visa. Residents of New York and Tennessee must include sales tax. DO NOT SEND CASH.

CELEBRITY BIOGRAPHIES

BARBRA STREISAND   (0-7860-0051-1, $4.99/$5.99)
By Nellie Bly

BURT AND ME   (0-7860-0117-8, $5.99/$6.99)
By Elaine Blake Hall

CAPTAIN QUIRK   (0-7860-0185-2, $4.99/$5.99)
By Dennis William Hauck

ELIZABETH: (0-8217-4269-8, $4.99/$5.99)
   THE LIFE OF ELIZABETH TAYLOR
By Alexander Walker

JIMMY STEWART:
   A WONDERFUL LIFE   (0-7860-0506-8, $5.99/$7.50)
By Frank Sanello

MARLON BRANDO:
   LARGER THAN LIFE   (0-7860-0086-4, $4.99/$5.99)
By Nellie Bly

OPRAH!   (0-8217-4613-8, $4.99/$5.99)
   UP CLOSE AND DOWN HOME
By Nellie Bly

RAINBOW'S END:
   THE JUDY GARLAND SHOW   (0-8217-3708-2, $5.99/$6.99)
By Coyne Steven Sanders

THE KENNEDY MEN: (1-57566-015-6, $22.95/$26.95)
   3 GENERATIONS OF SEX, SCANDAL, & SECRETS
By Nellie Bly

TODAY'S BLACK HOLLYWOOD   (0-7860-0104-6, $4.99/$5.99)
By James Robert Parish

Available wherever paperbacks are sold, or order direct from the Publisher. Send cover price plus 50¢ per copy for mailing and handling to Kensington Publishing Corp., Consumer Orders, or call (toll free) 888-345-BOOK, to place your order using Mastercard or Visa. Residents of New York and Tennessee must include sales tax. DO NOT SEND CASH.